# ROYDEN LEPP
# RUST™
## SECRETS OF THE CELL

Published by
ARCHAIA™

ROYD

# RU

## SECRETS O

N LEPP

S T ™

T THE CELL

ROSS RICHIE.................................................CEO & Founder
MATT GAGNON.........................................Editor-in-Chief
FILIP SABLIK.................President of Publishing & Marketing
STEPHEN CHRISTY.....................President of Development
LANCE KREITER.................VP of Licensing & Merchandising
PHIL BARBARO.............................................VP of Finance
BRYCE CARLSON......................................Managing Editor
MEL CAYLO.............................................Marketing Manager
SCOTT NEWMAN.................Production Design Manager
KATE HENNING....................................Operations Manager
SIERRA HAHN................................................Senior Editor
DAFNA PLEBAN.................Editor, Talent Development
SHANNON WATTERS.......................................Editor
ERIC HARBURN....................................................Editor
WHITNEY LEOPARD..............................Associate Editor
JASMINE AMIRI.......................................Associate Editor
CHRIS ROSA..............................................Associate Editor
ALEX GALER..............................................Associate Editor
CAMERON CHITTOCK...........................Associate Editor
MATTHEW LEVINE...................................Assistant Editor
KELSEY DIETERICH.............................Production Designer
JILLIAN CRAB.......................................Production Designer
MICHELLE ANKLEY...........................Production Designer
GRACE PARK.........................Production Design Assistant
AARON FERRARA......................Operations Coordinator
ELIZABETH LOUGHRIDGE..........Accounting Coordinator
STEPHANIE HOCUTT.................Social Media Coordinator
JOSÉ MEZA...................................................Sales Assistant
JAMES ARRIOLA.................................Mailroom Assistant
HOLLY AITCHISON...........................Operations Assistant
SAM KUSEK...................Direct Market Representative
AMBER PARKER...........................Administrative Assistant

RUST VOLUME TWO: SECRETS OF THE CELL, March
2017. Published by Archaia, a division of Boom
Entertainment, Inc. Rust is ™ and © 2017 Royden Lepp.
All Rights Reserved. "Oswald's Letter" was previously
published in MOUSE GUARD, LABYRINTH, AND OTHER
STORIES, A FREE COMIC BOOK DAY HARDCOVER
ANTHOLOGY 2012. ™ & © 2012 Royden Lepp. All Rights
Reserved. Archaia™ and the Archaia logo are trademarks
of Boom Entertainment, Inc., registered in various
countries and categories. All characters, events, and
institutions depicted herein are fictional. Any similarity
between any of the names, characters, persons, events,
and/or institutions in this publication to actual names,
characters, and persons, whether living or dead,
events, and/or institutions is unintended and purely
coincidental.

BOOM! Studios, 5670 Wilshire Boulevard, Suite 450, Los
Angeles, CA 90036-5679. Printed in China. First Printing.

ISBN: 978-1-60886-895-7, eISBN: 978-1-61398-566-3

Written & Illustrated by
# Royden Lepp

Flatted by
**VShane**
**Joanna Estep**

Logo Designed by
**Fawn Lau**

Designer
**Scott Newman**

Original Series Editor
**Rebecca Taylor**

Collection Associate Editor
**Cameron Chittock**

Collection Editor
**Sierra Hahn**

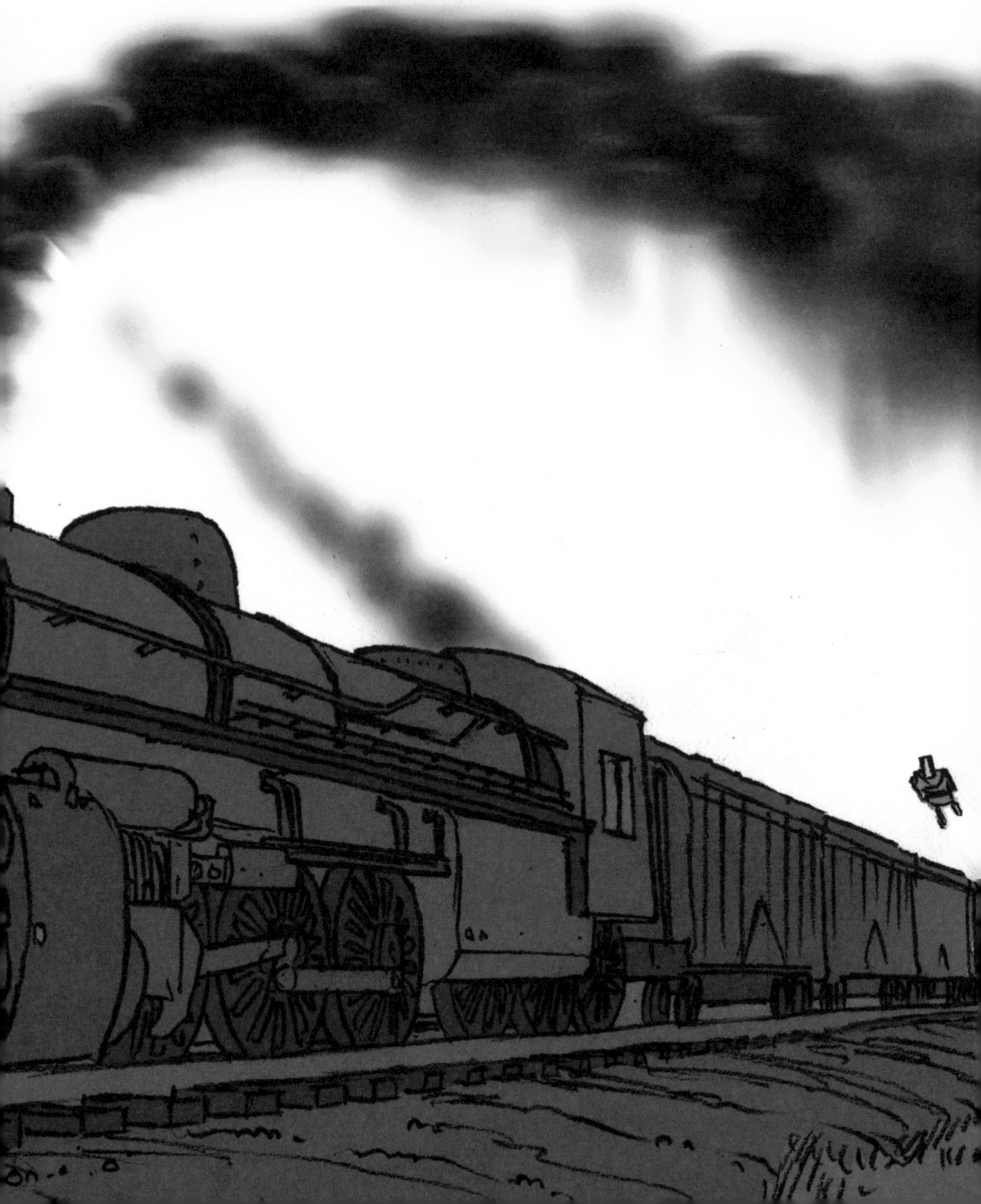

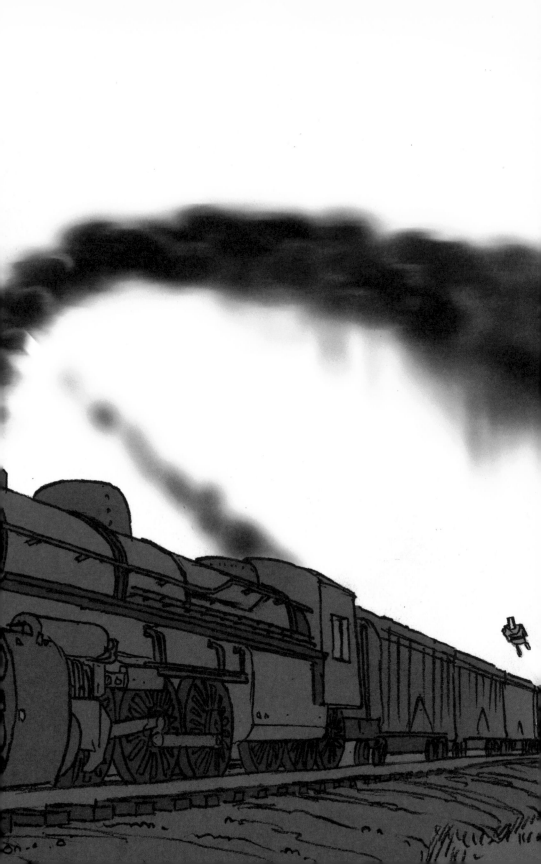

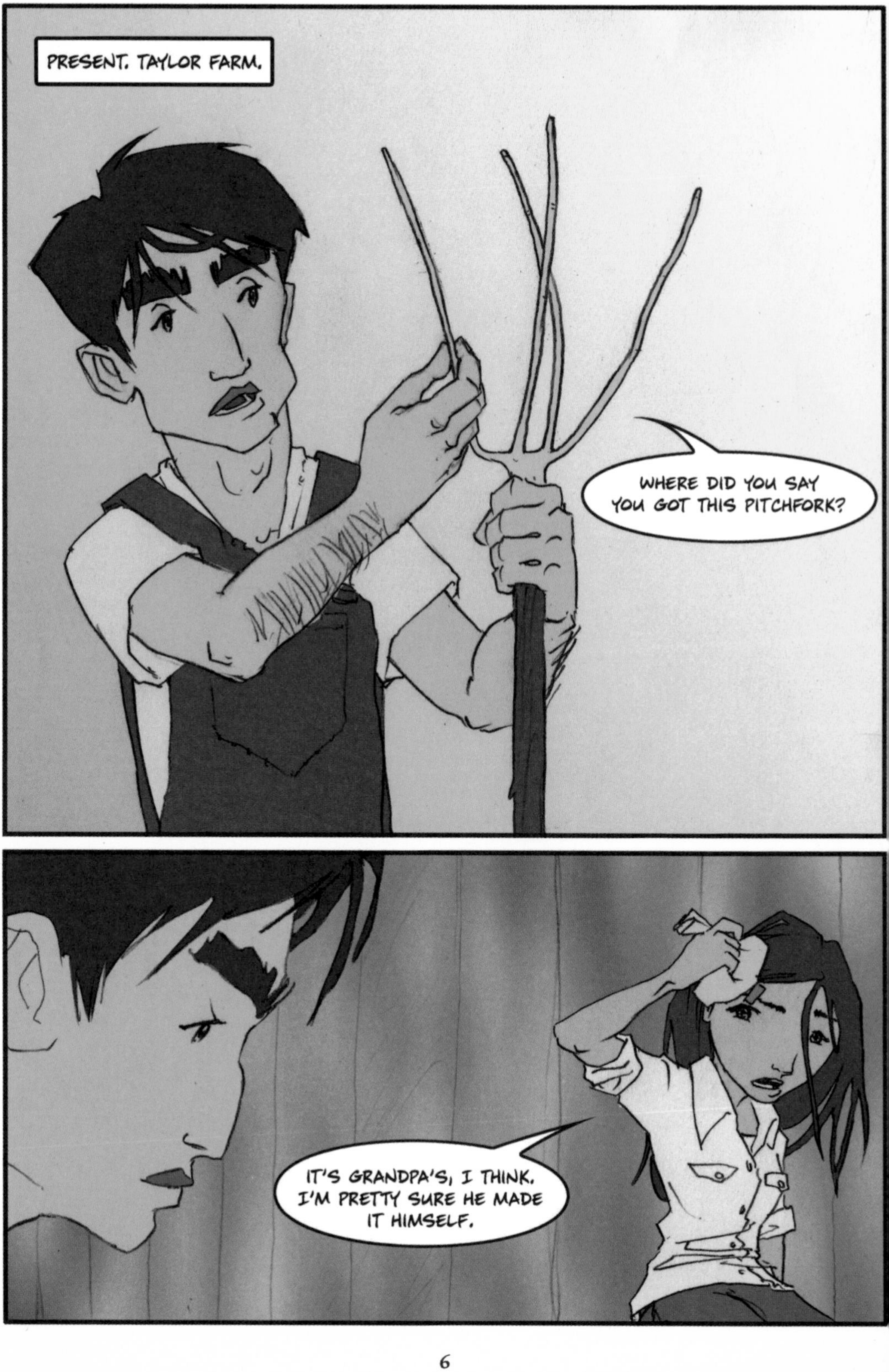
PRESENT. TAYLOR FARM.
WHERE DID YOU SAY YOU GOT THIS PITCHFORK?
IT'S GRANDPA'S, I THINK. I'M PRETTY SURE HE MADE IT HIMSELF.

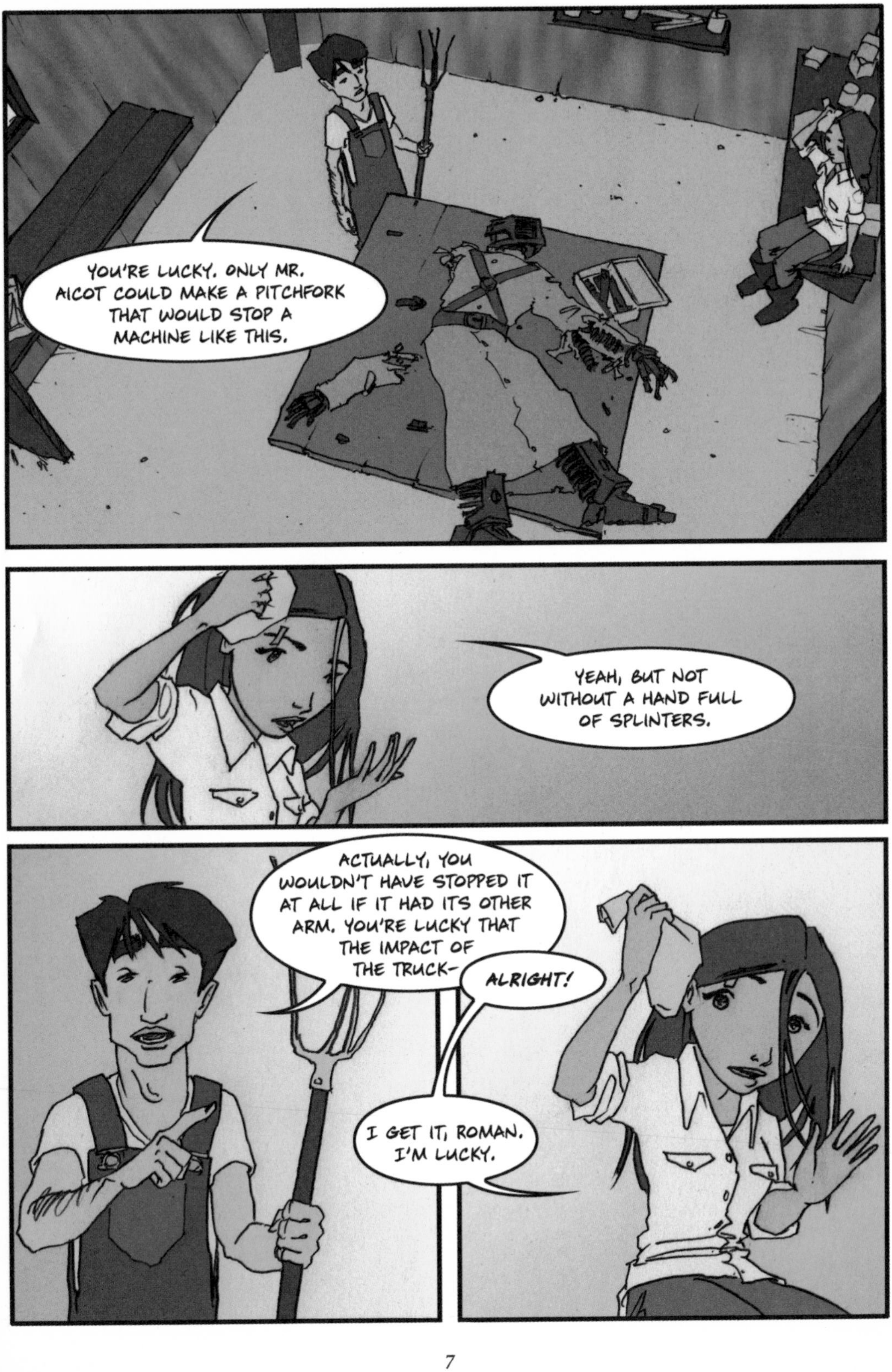
YOU'RE LUCKY. ONLY MR. AICOT COULD MAKE A PITCHFORK THAT WOULD STOP A MACHINE LIKE THIS.
YEAH, BUT NOT WITHOUT A HAND FULL OF SPLINTERS.
ACTUALLY, YOU WOULDN'T HAVE STOPPED IT AT ALL IF IT HAD ITS OTHER ARM. YOU'RE LUCKY THAT THE IMPACT OF THE TRUCK-
ALRIGHT!
I GET IT, ROMAN. I'M LUCKY.

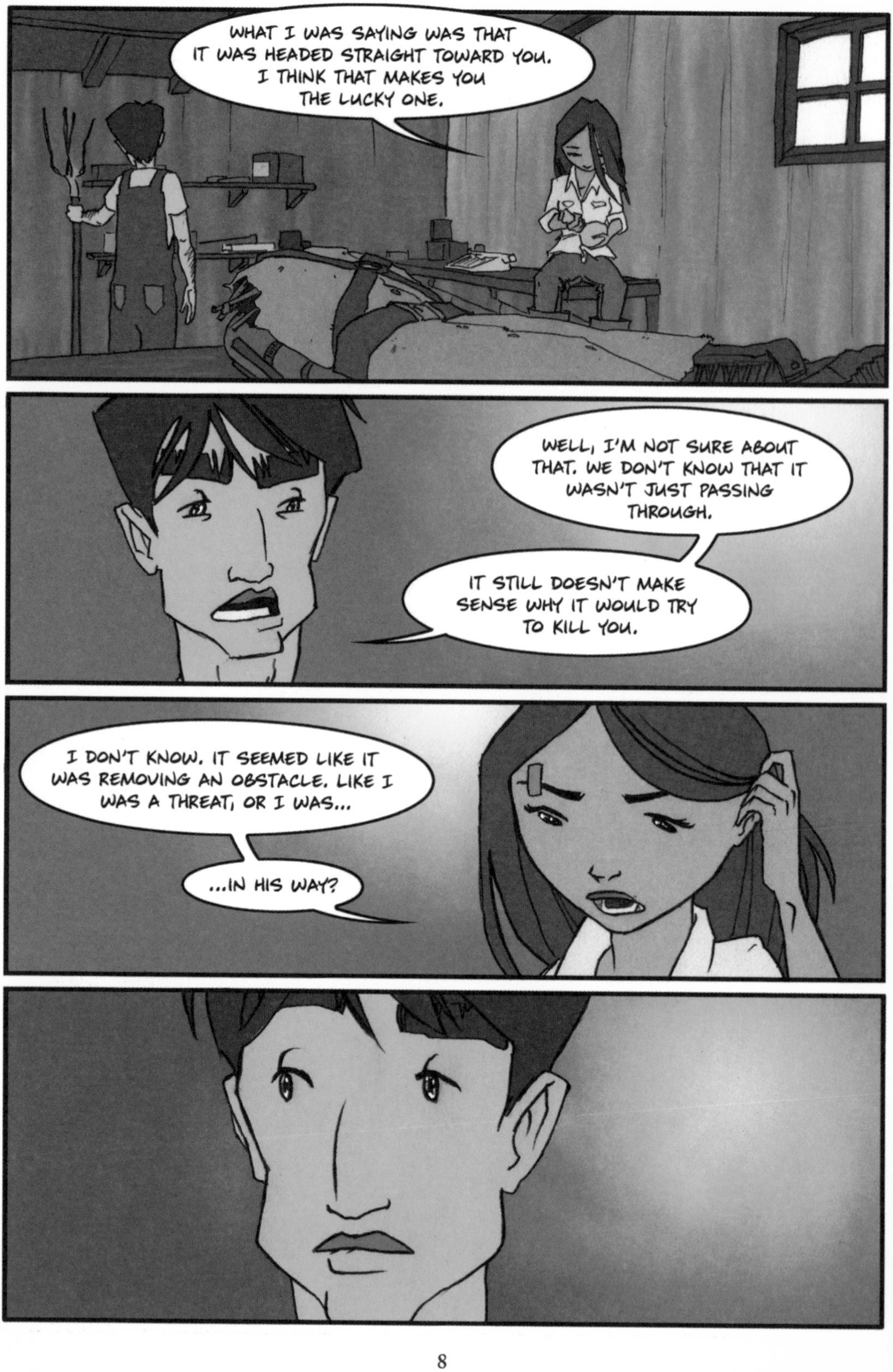
WHAT I WAS SAYING WAS THAT IT WAS HEADED STRAIGHT TOWARD YOU. I THINK THAT MAKES YOU THE LUCKY ONE.
WELL, I'M NOT SURE ABOUT THAT. WE DON'T KNOW THAT IT WASN'T JUST PASSING THROUGH.
IT STILL DOESN'T MAKE SENSE WHY IT WOULD TRY TO KILL YOU.
I DON'T KNOW. IT SEEMED LIKE IT WAS REMOVING AN OBSTACLE. LIKE I WAS A THREAT, OR I WAS...
...IN HIS WAY?

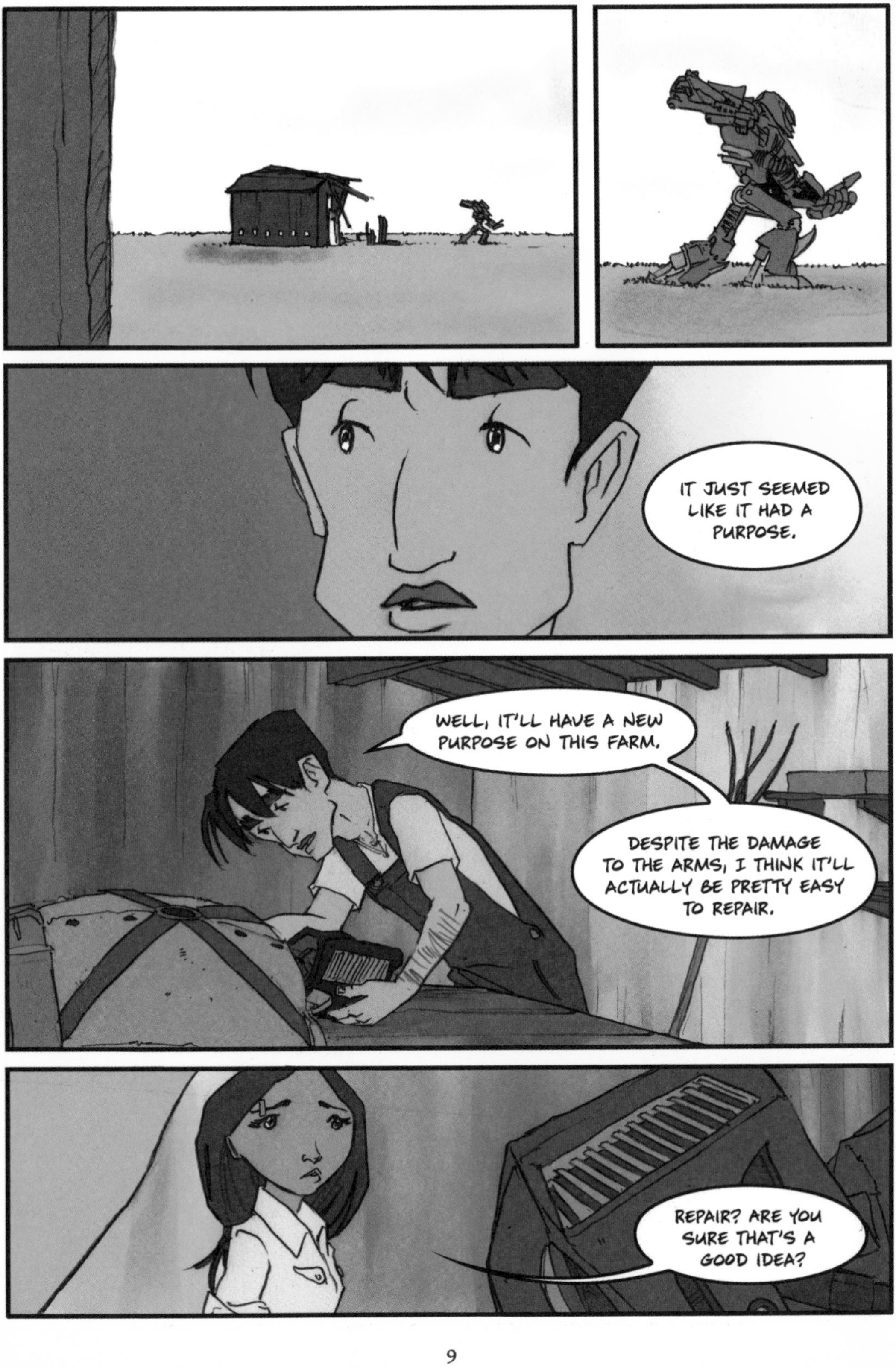
IT JUST SEEMED LIKE IT HAD A PURPOSE.
WELL, IT'LL HAVE A NEW PURPOSE ON THIS FARM.
DESPITE THE DAMAGE TO THE ARMS, I THINK IT'LL ACTUALLY BE PRETTY EASY TO REPAIR.
REPAIR? ARE YOU SURE THAT'S A GOOD IDEA?

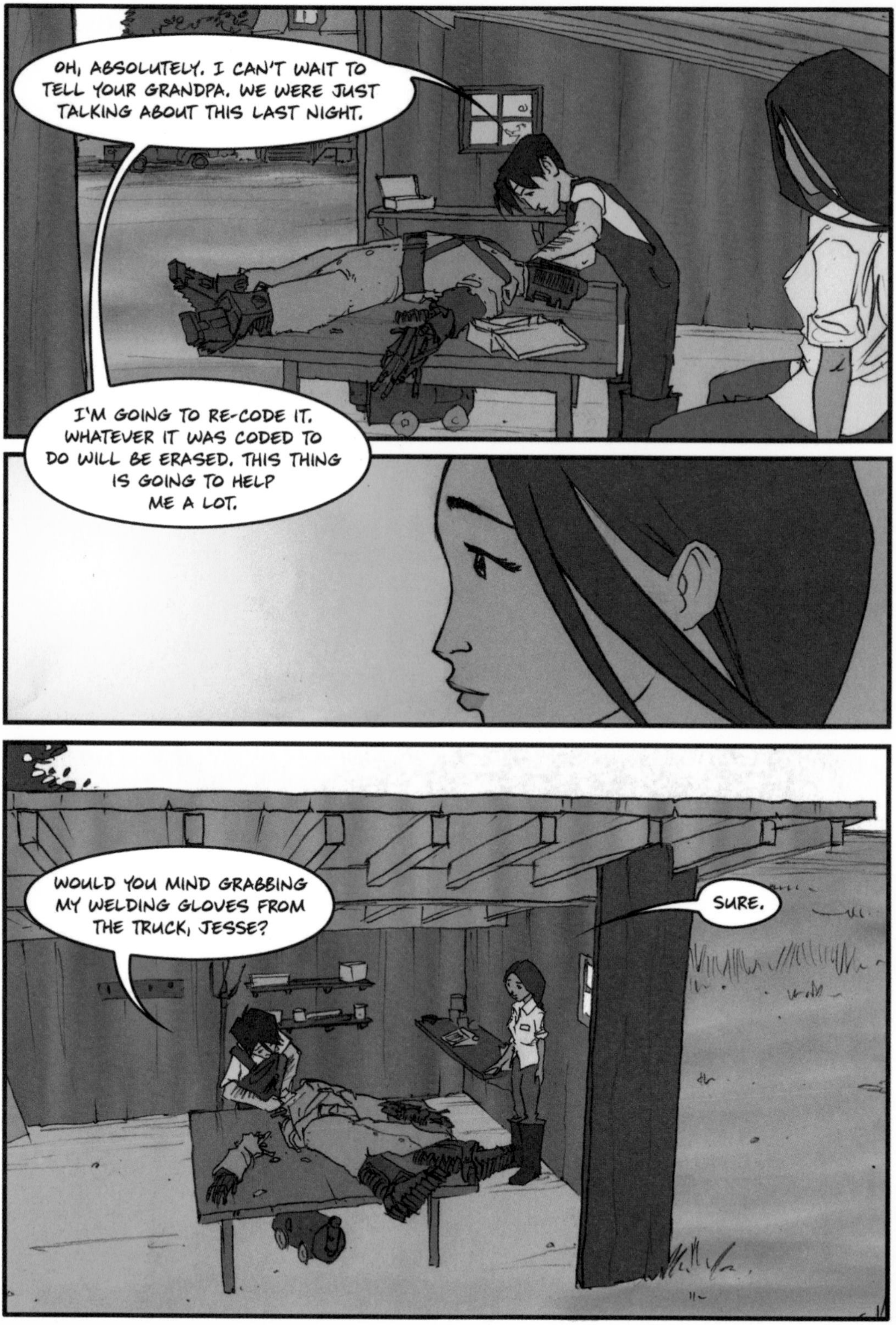
OH, ABSOLUTELY. I CAN'T WAIT TO TELL YOUR GRANDPA. WE WERE JUST TALKING ABOUT THIS LAST NIGHT.
I'M GOING TO RE-CODE IT. WHATEVER IT WAS CODED TO DO WILL BE ERASED. THIS THING IS GOING TO HELP ME A LOT.
WOULD YOU MIND GRABBING MY WELDING GLOVES FROM THE TRUCK, JESSE?
SURE.

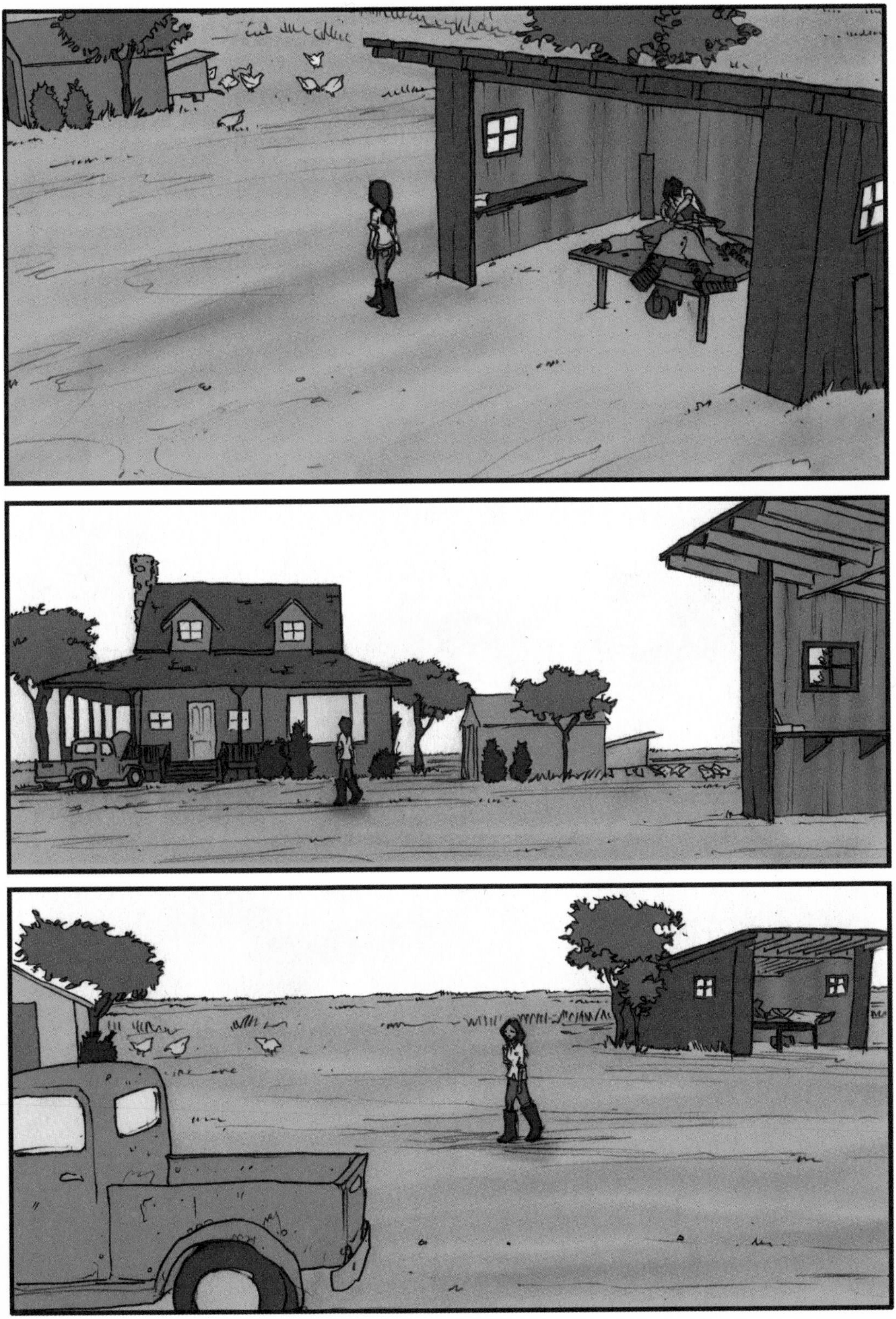

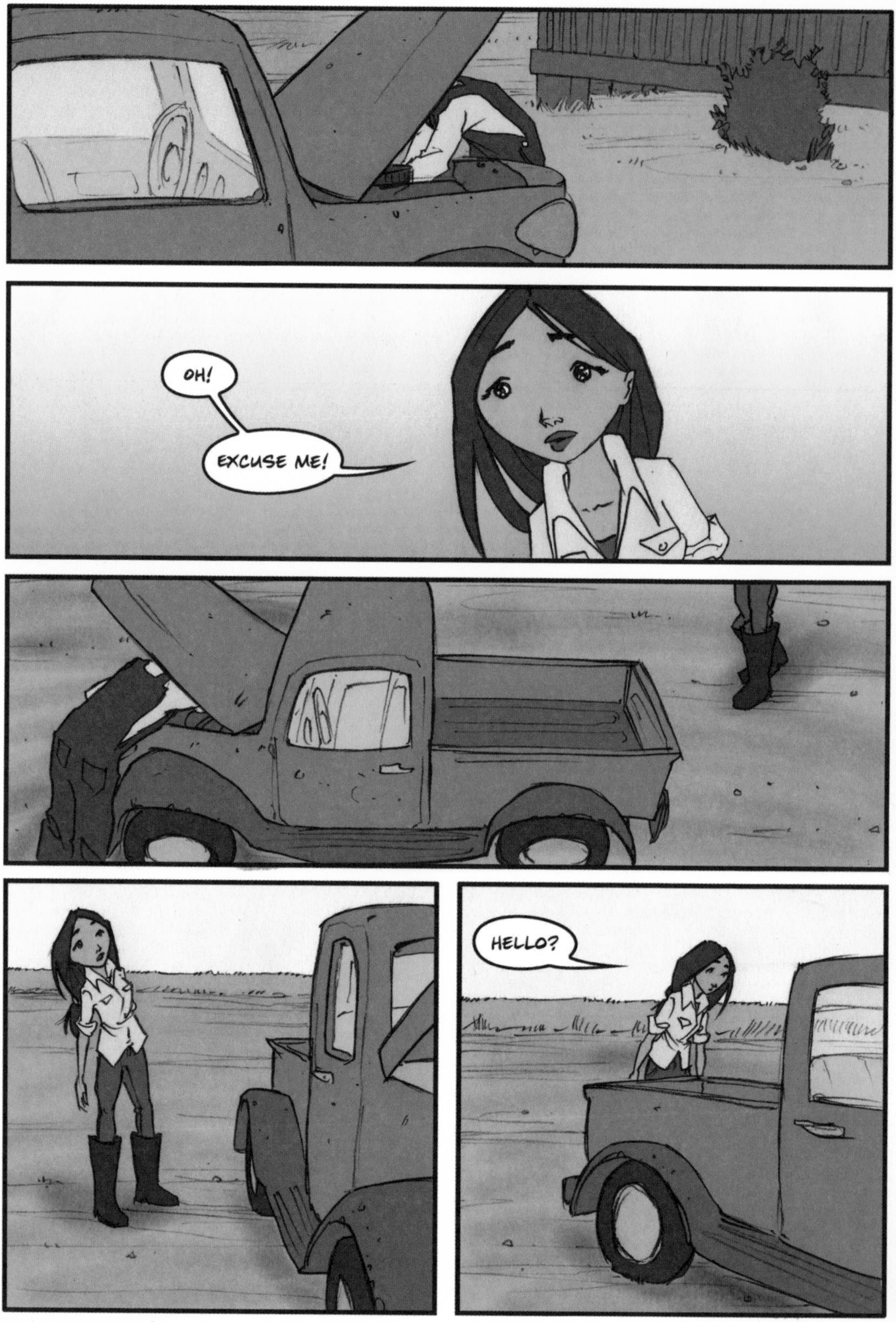
OH!
EXCUSE ME!
HELLO?

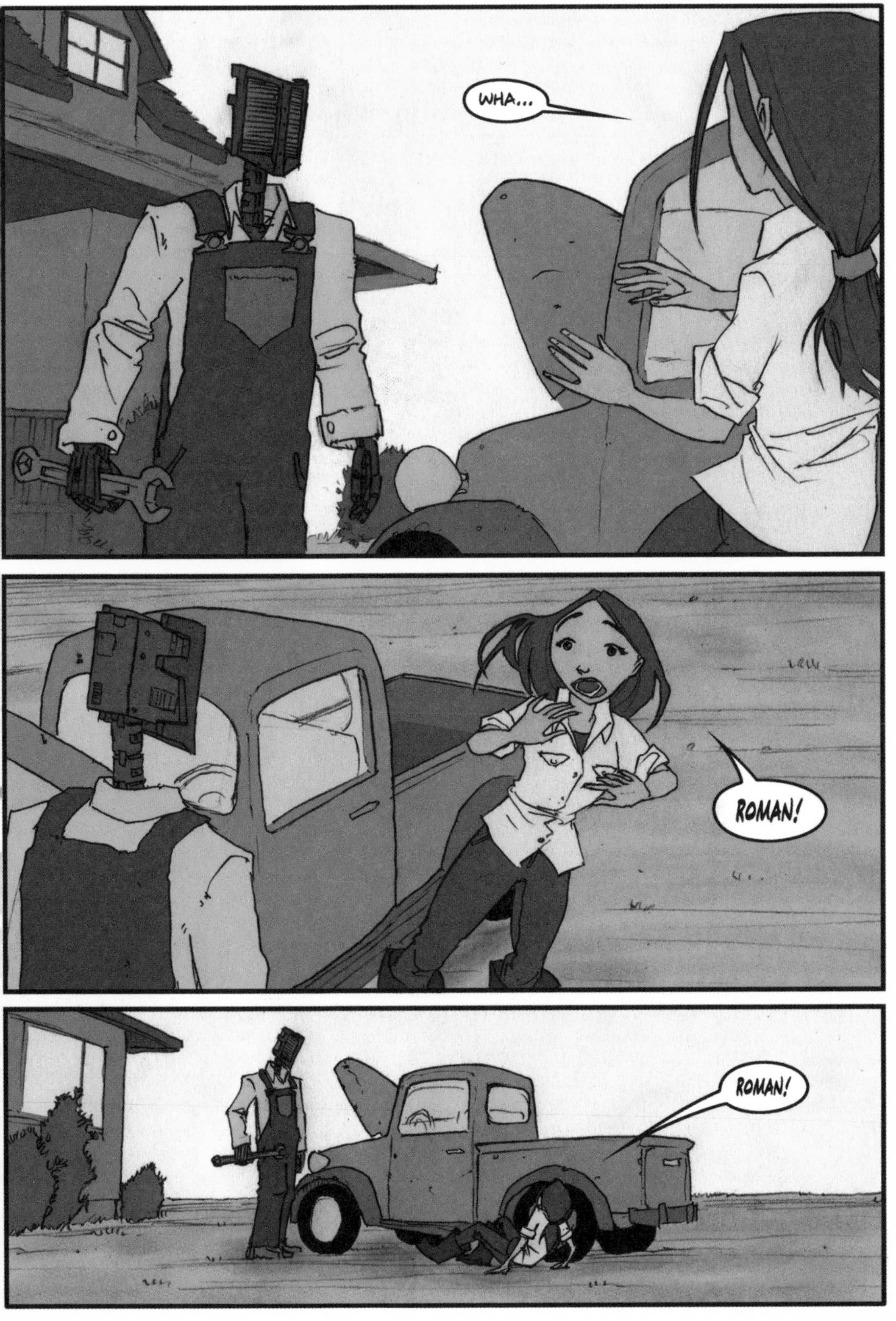
WHA...
ROMAN!
ROMAN!

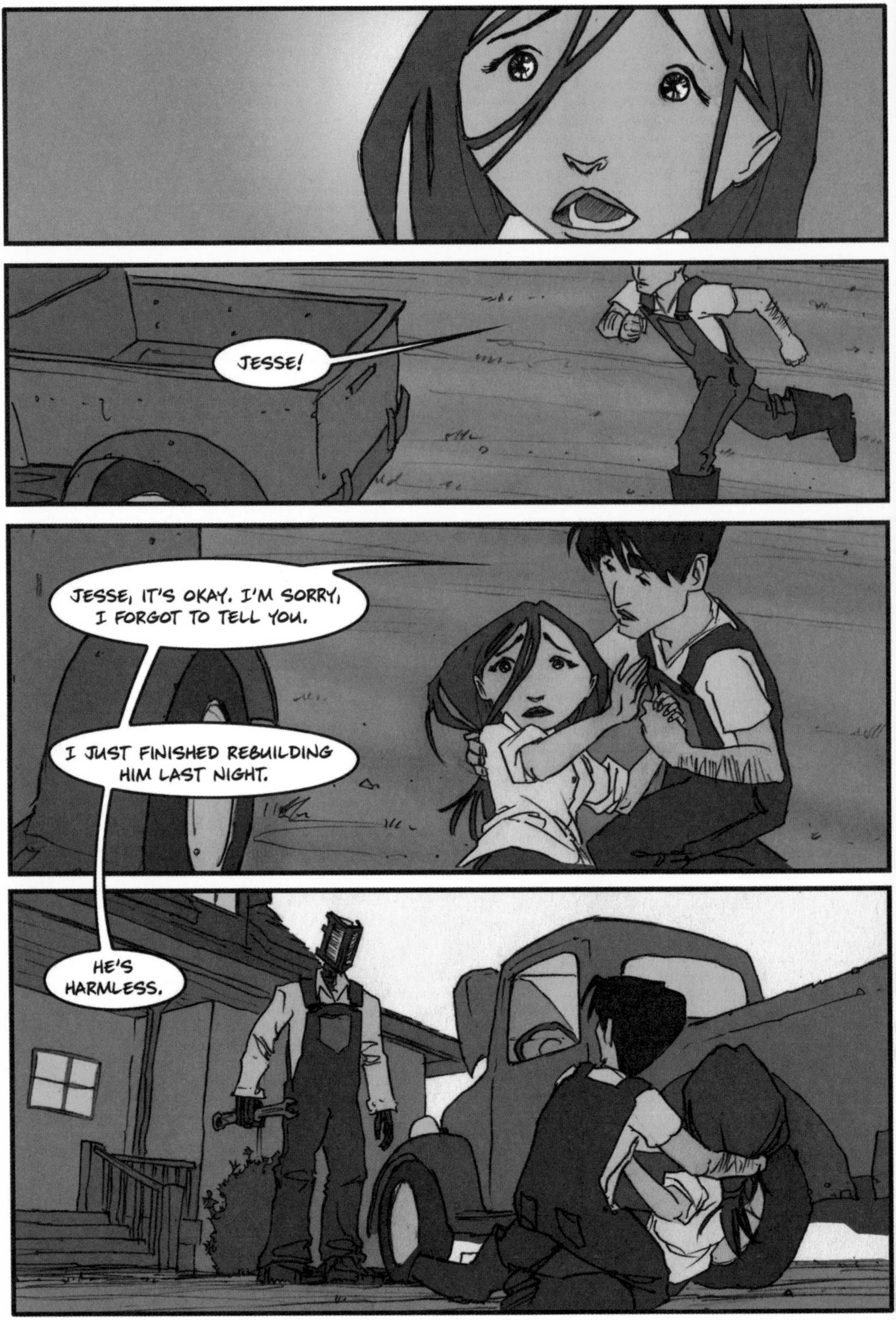
JESSE!
JESSE, IT'S OKAY. I'M SORRY, I FORGOT TO TELL YOU.
I JUST FINISHED REBUILDING HIM LAST NIGHT.
HE'S HARMLESS.

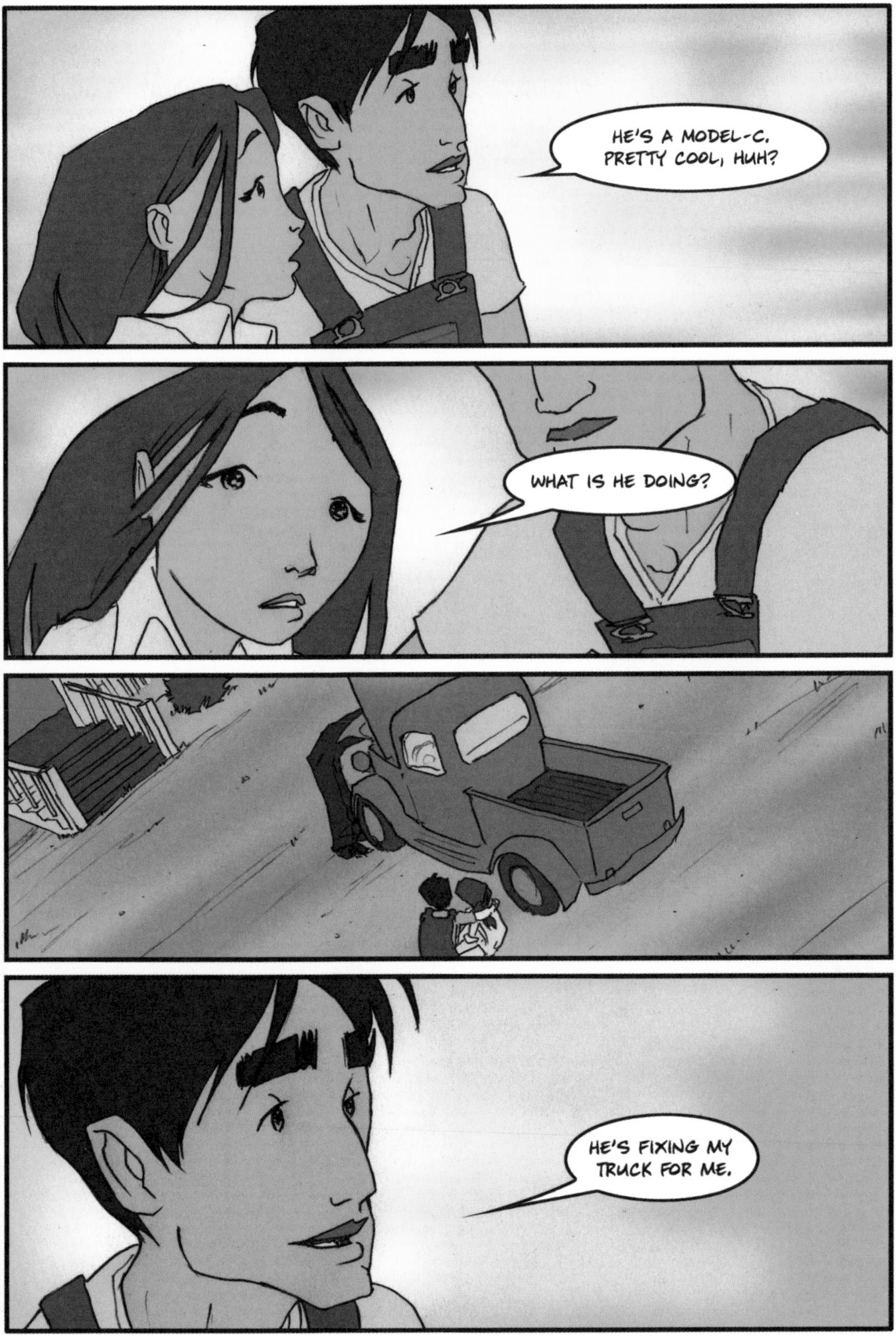
HE'S A MODEL-C. PRETTY COOL, HUH?
WHAT IS HE DOING?
HE'S FIXING MY TRUCK FOR ME.

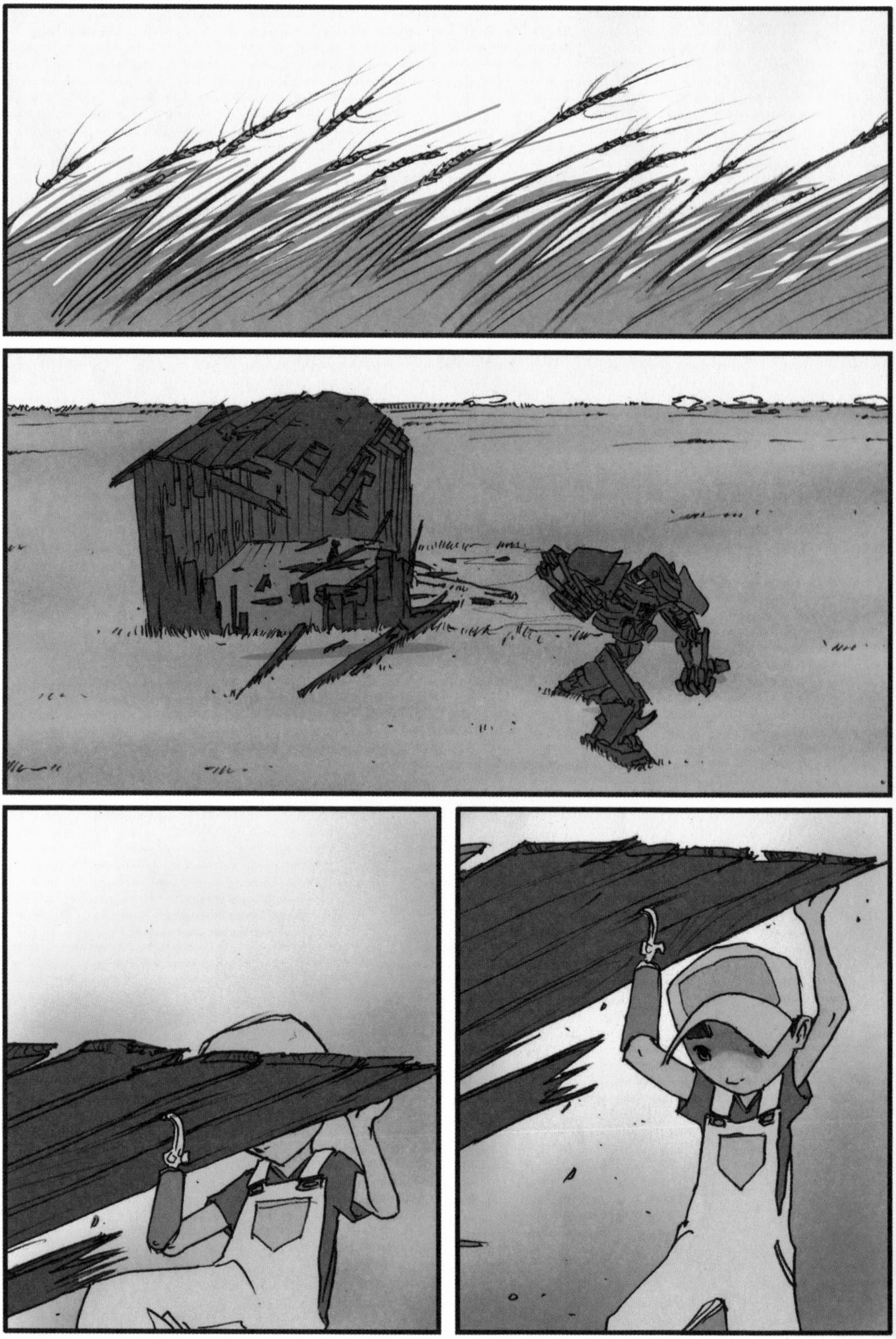

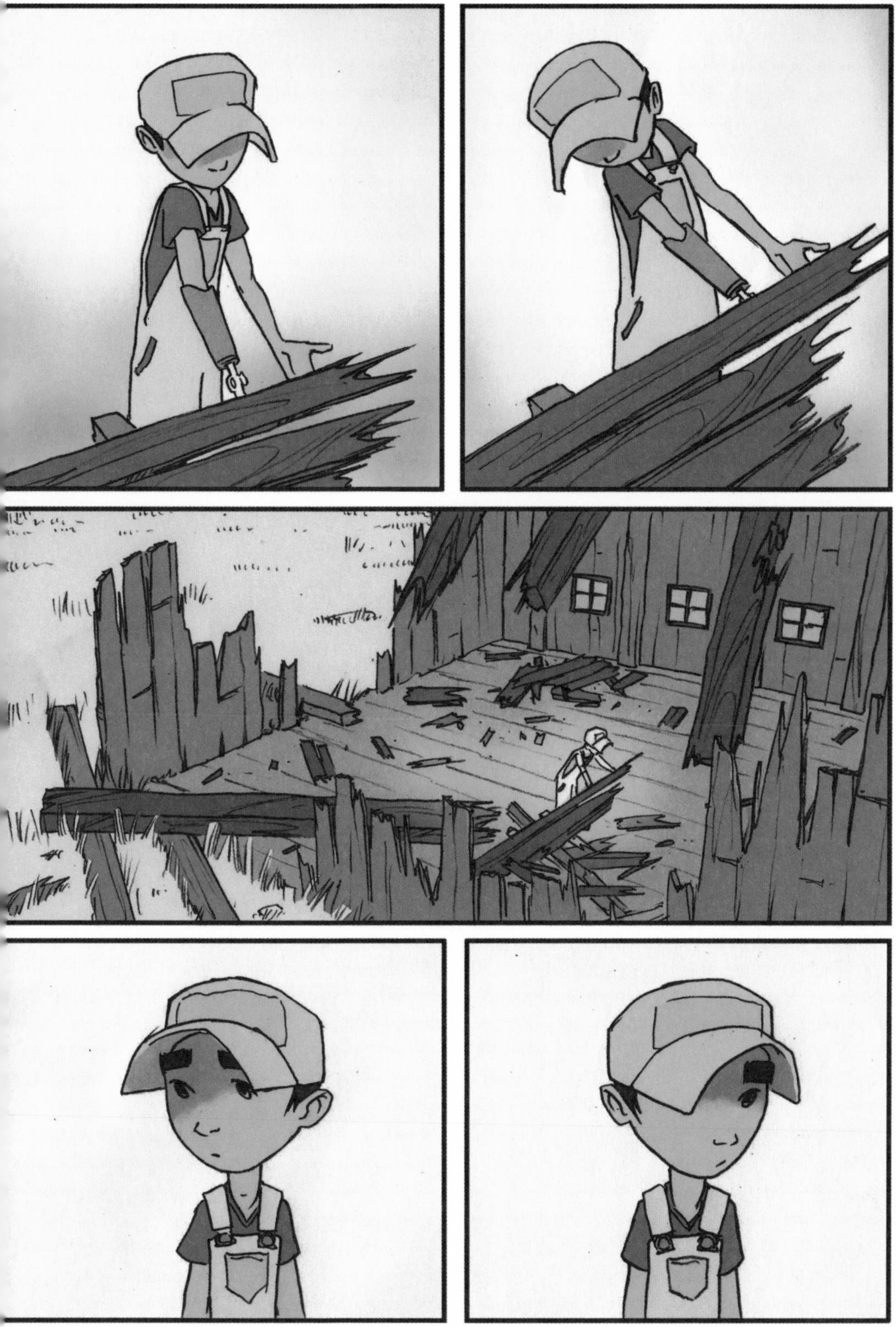

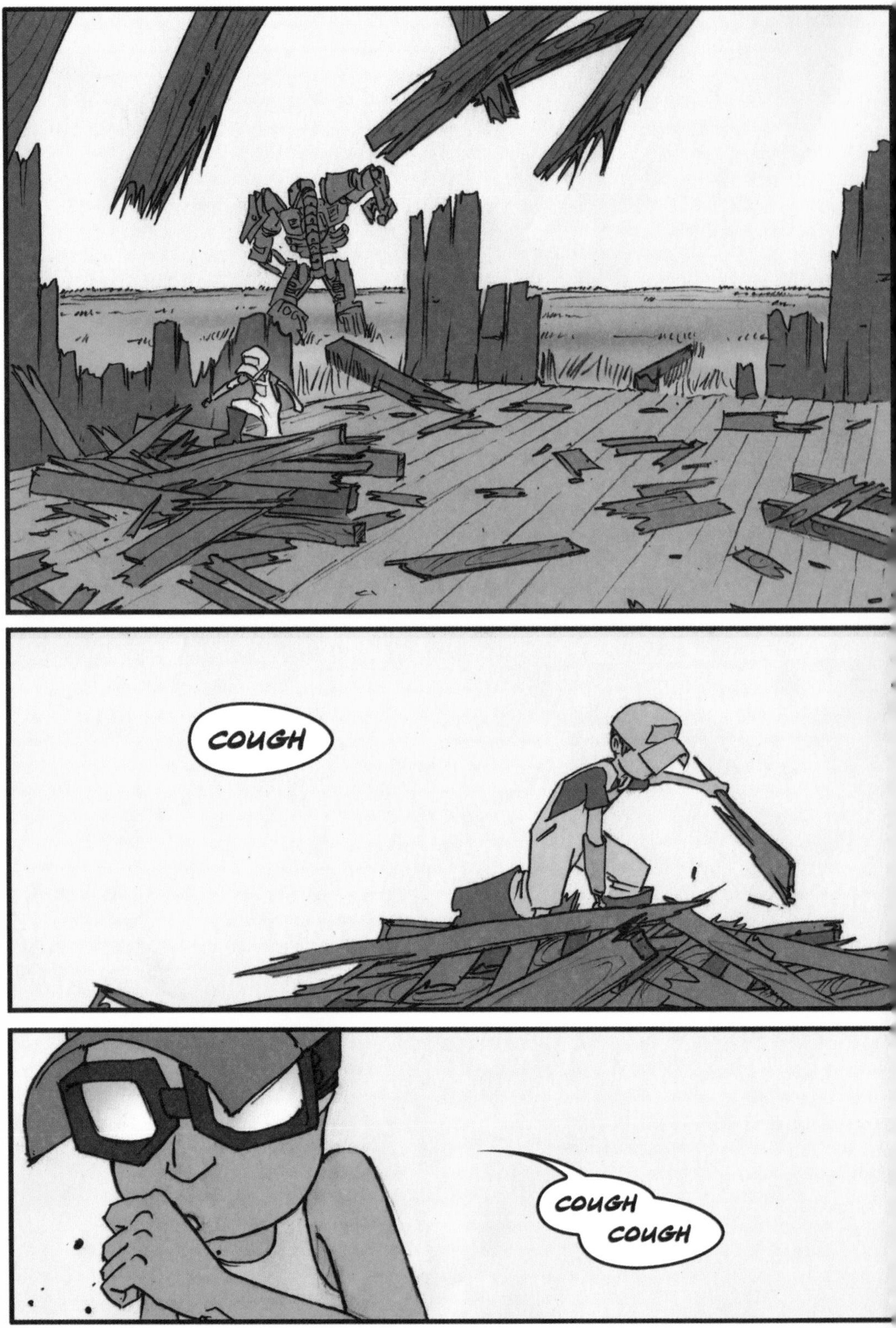
COUGH
COUGH
COUGH
COUGH

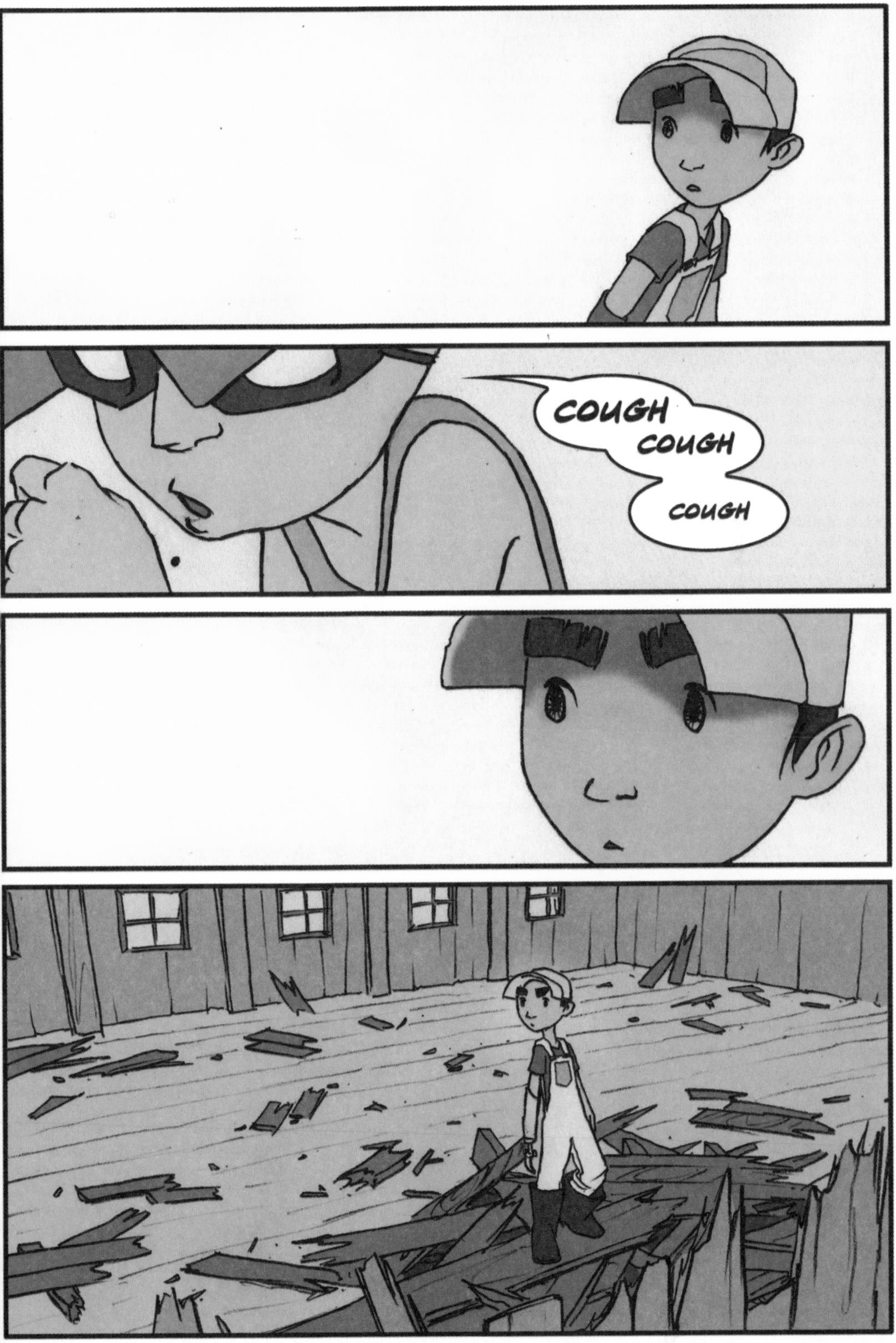
COUGH
COUGH
COUGH

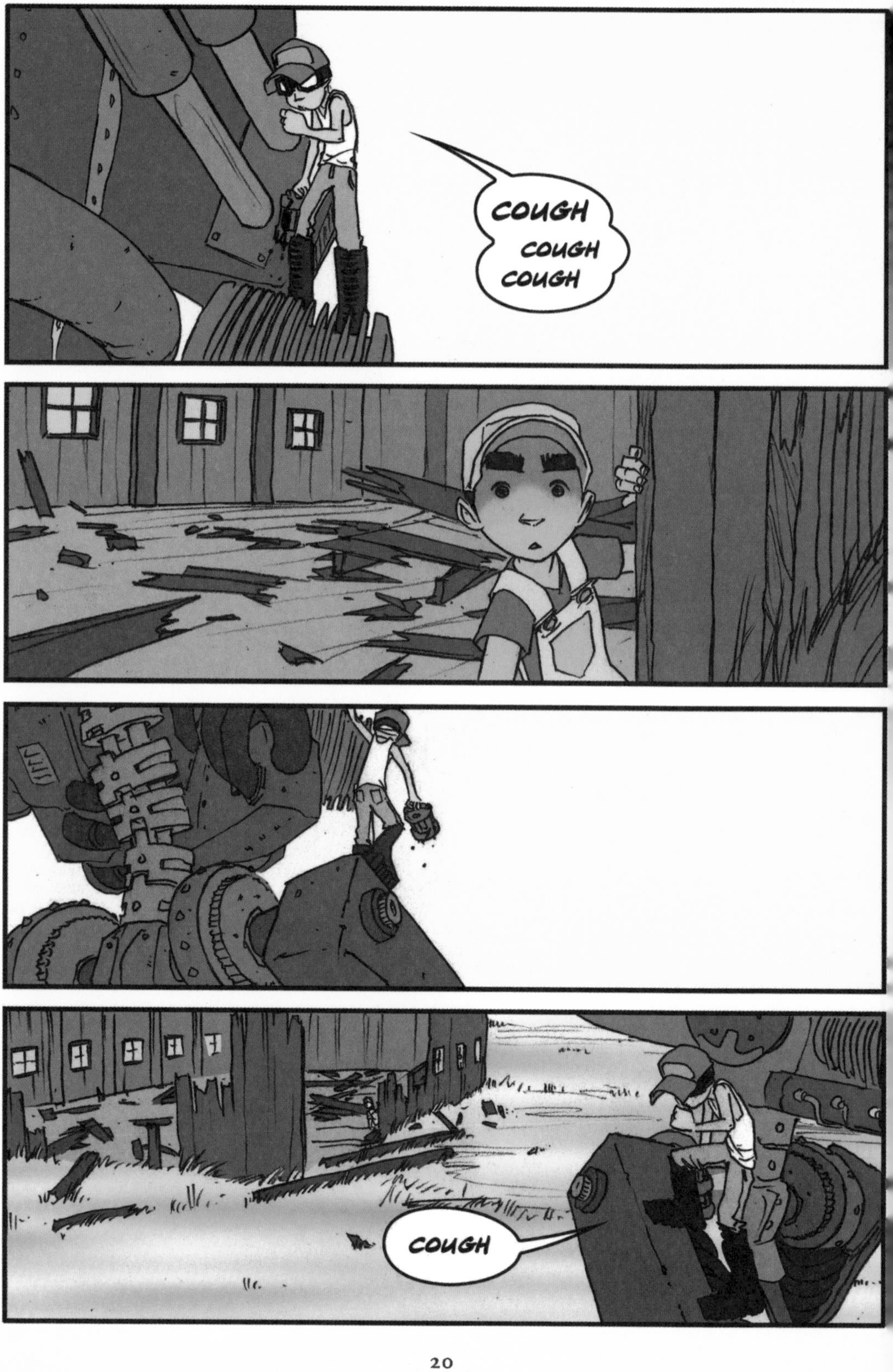
COUGH
COUGH
COUGH
COUGH

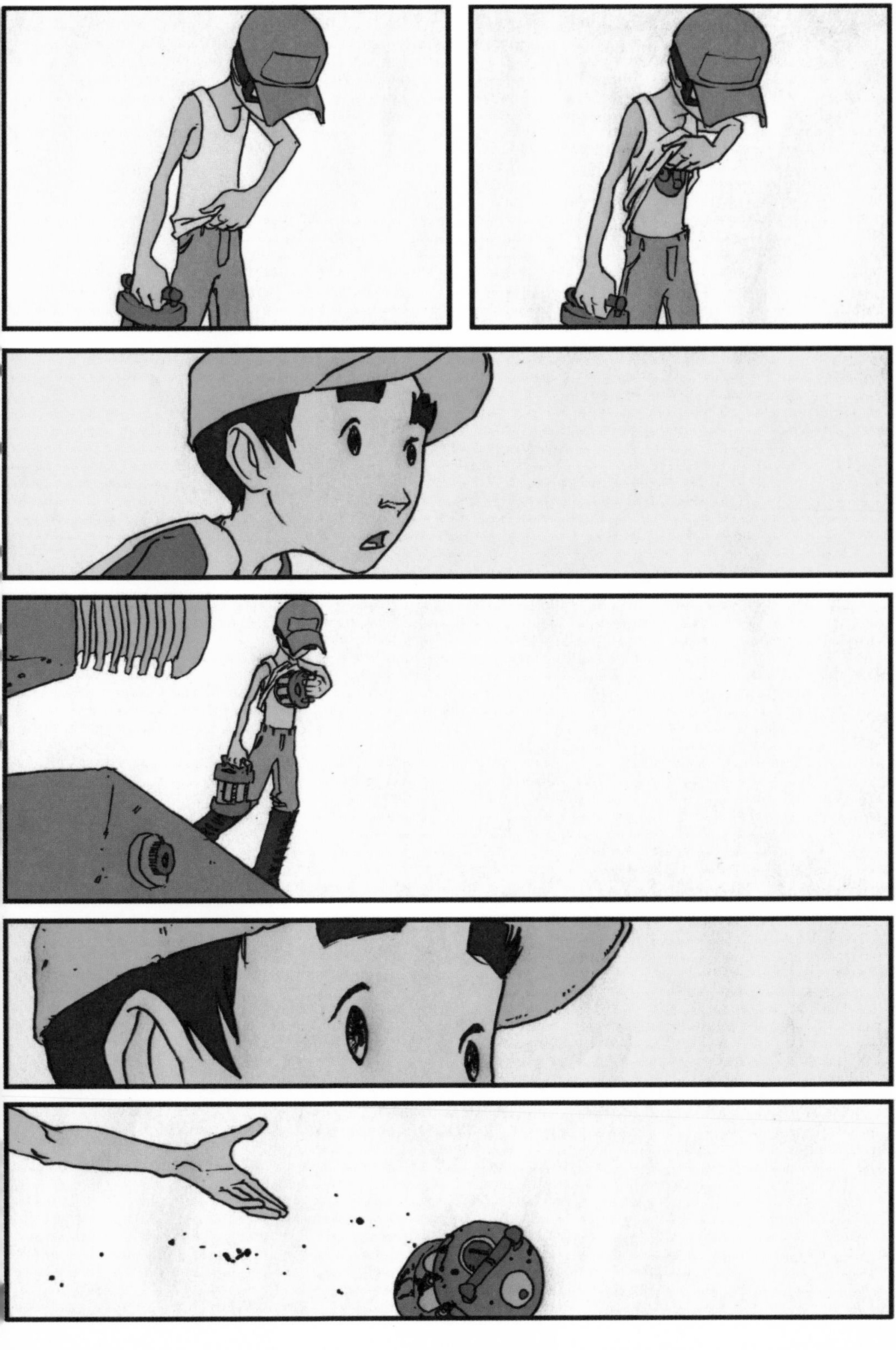

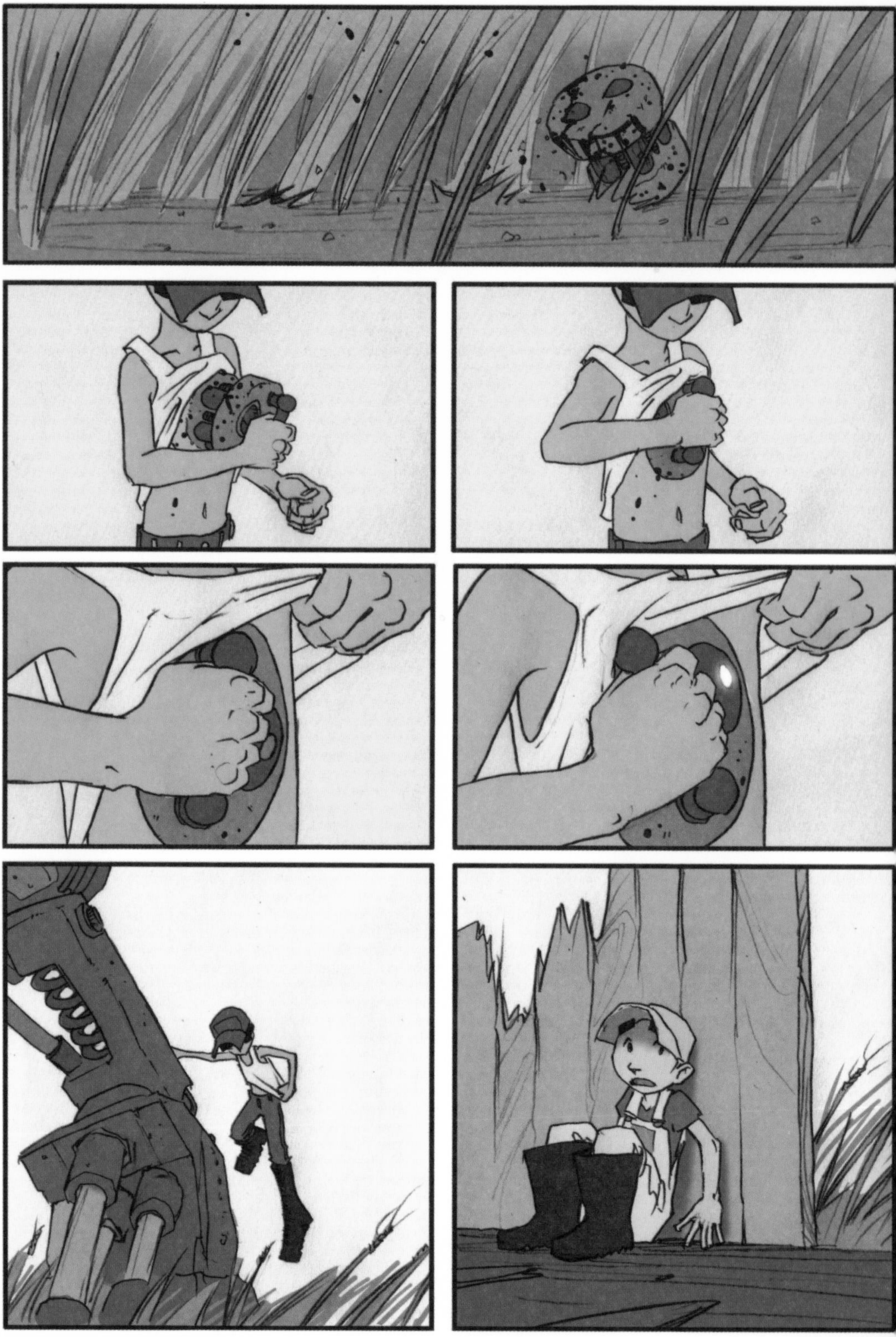

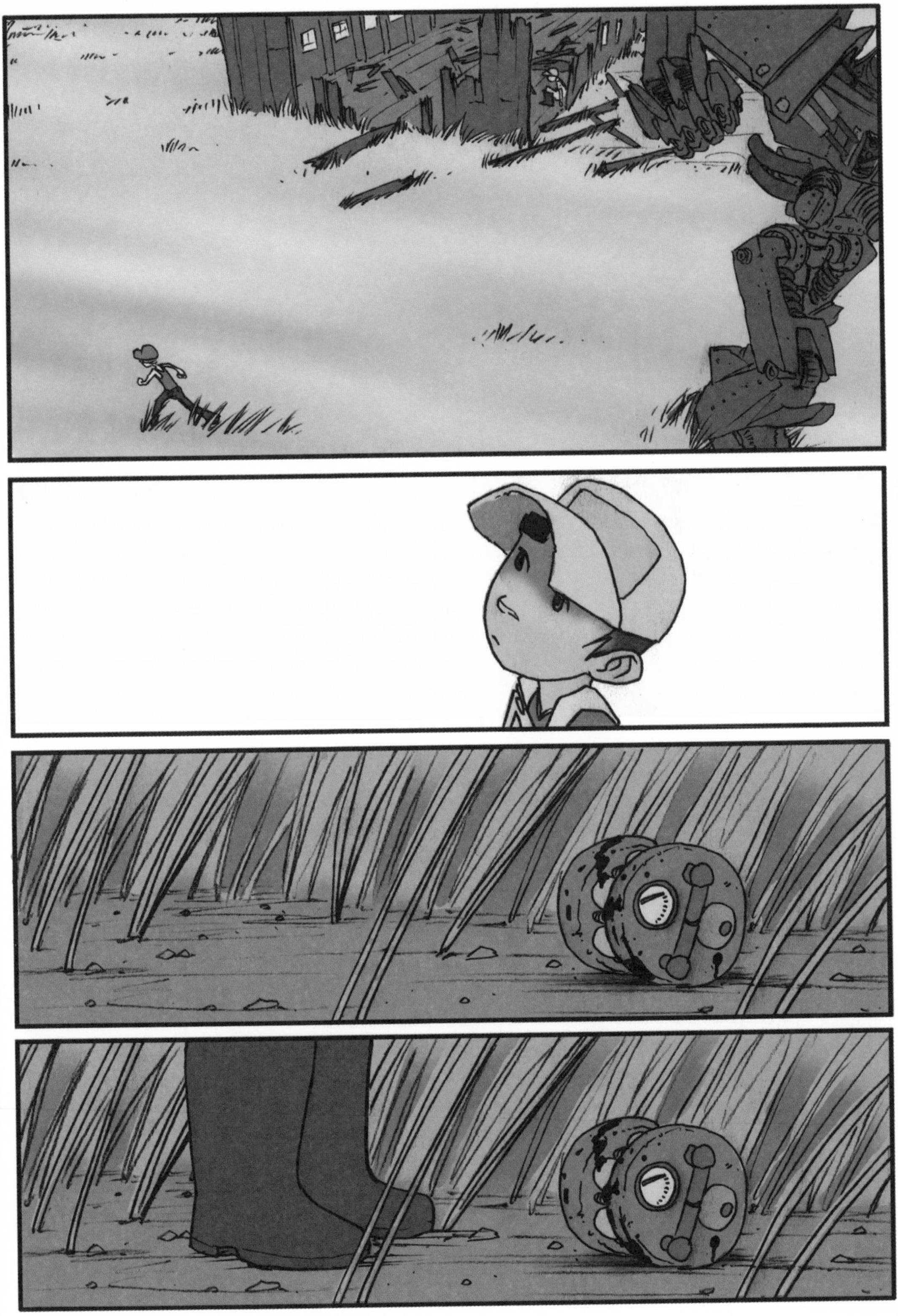

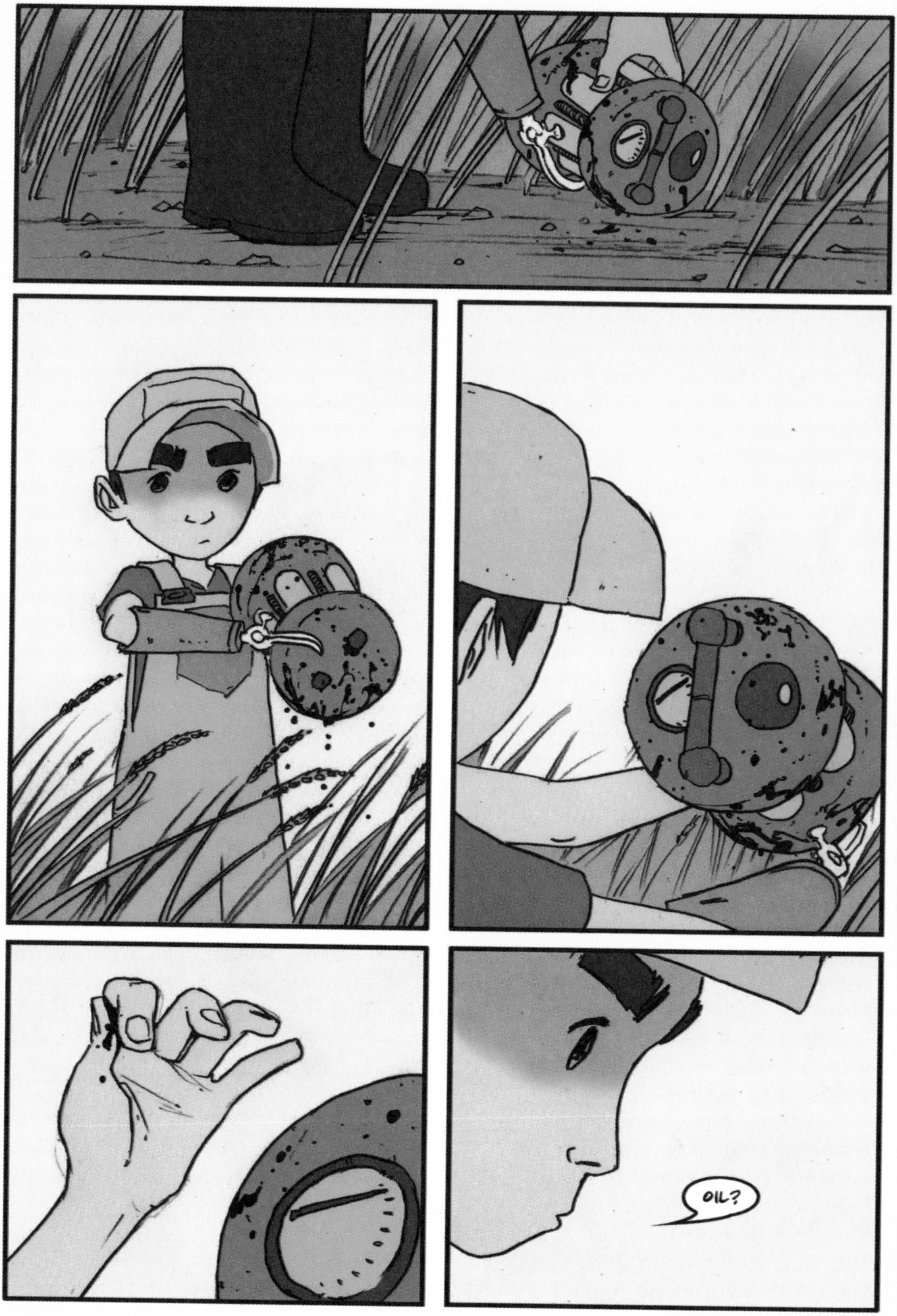
OIL?

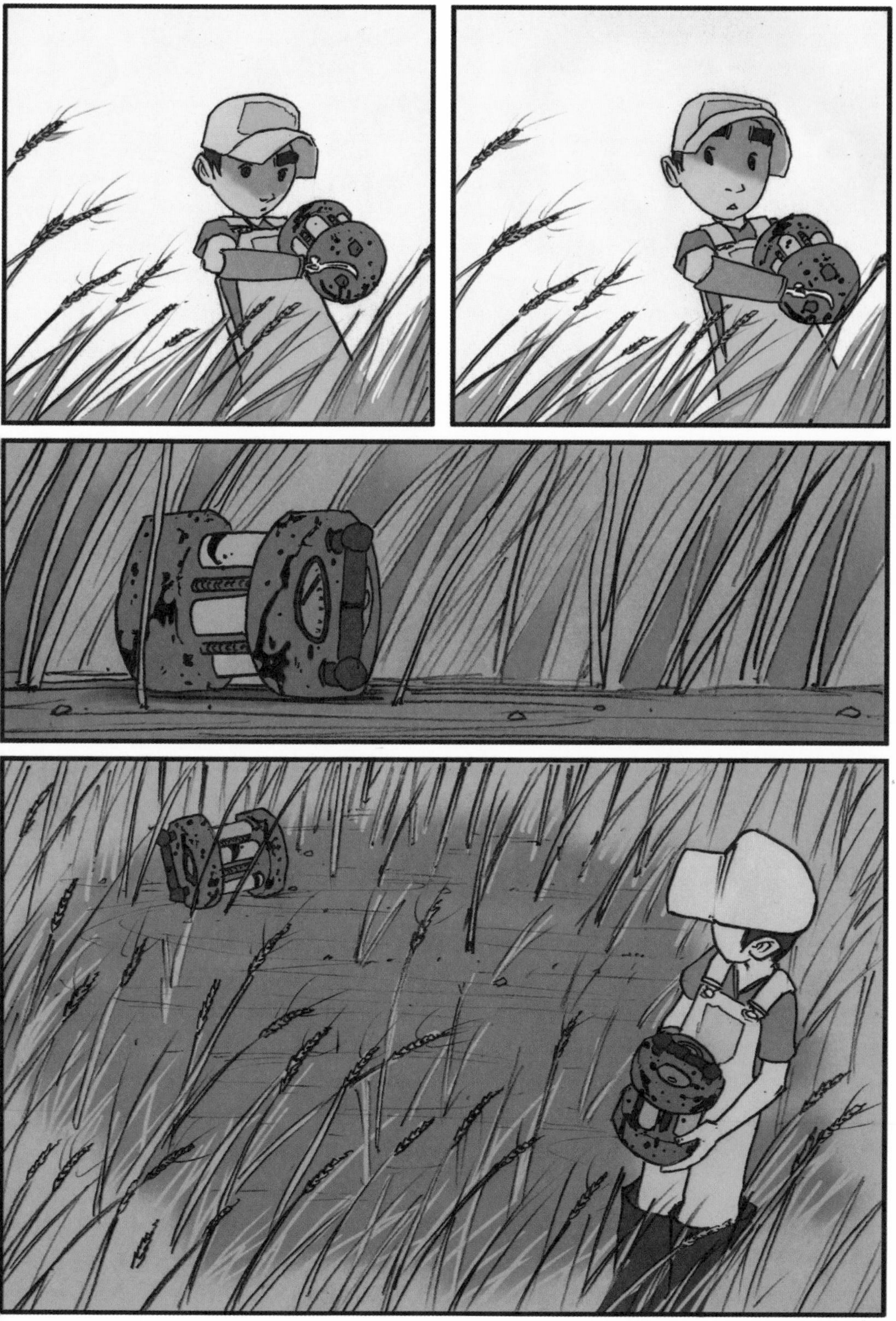

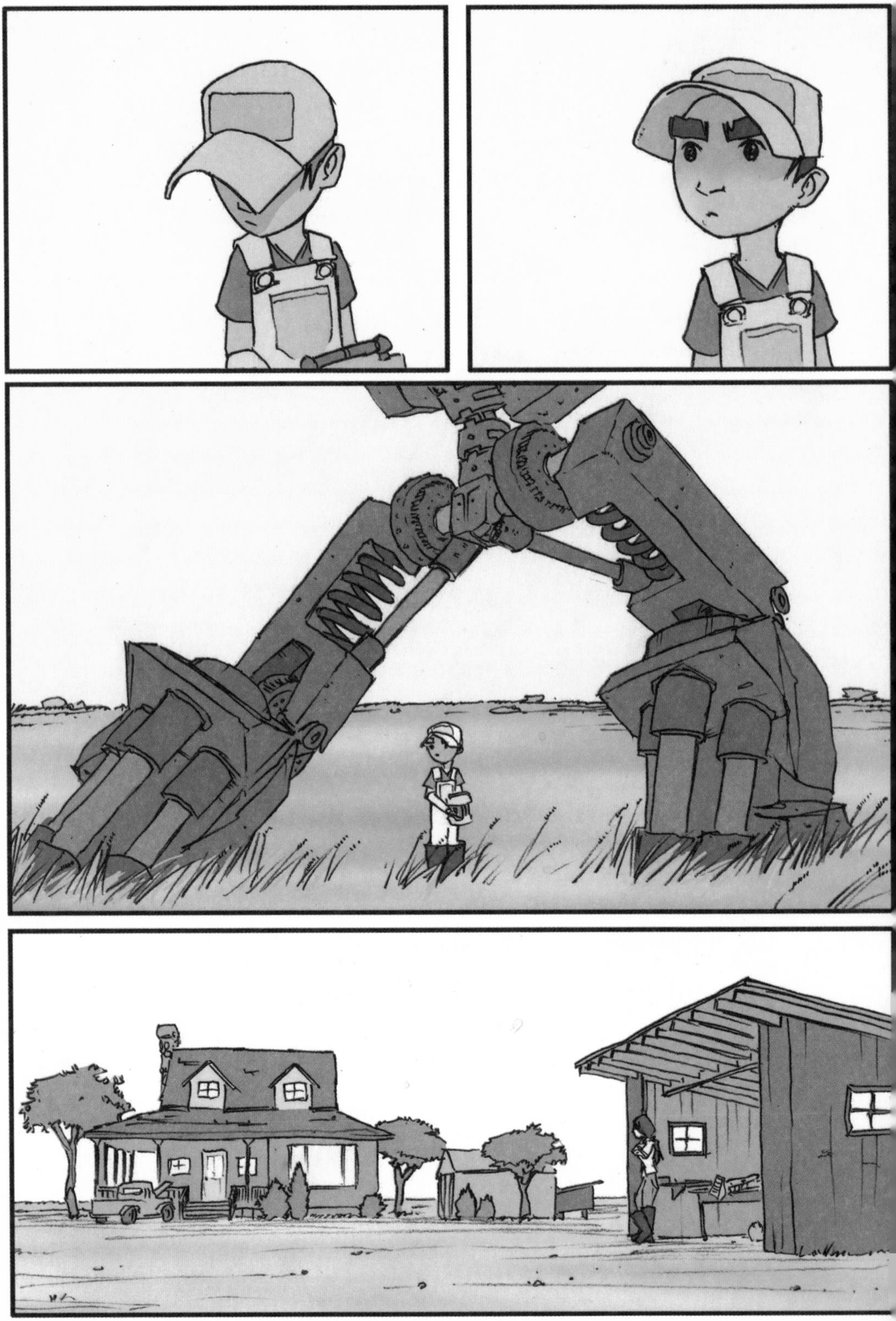

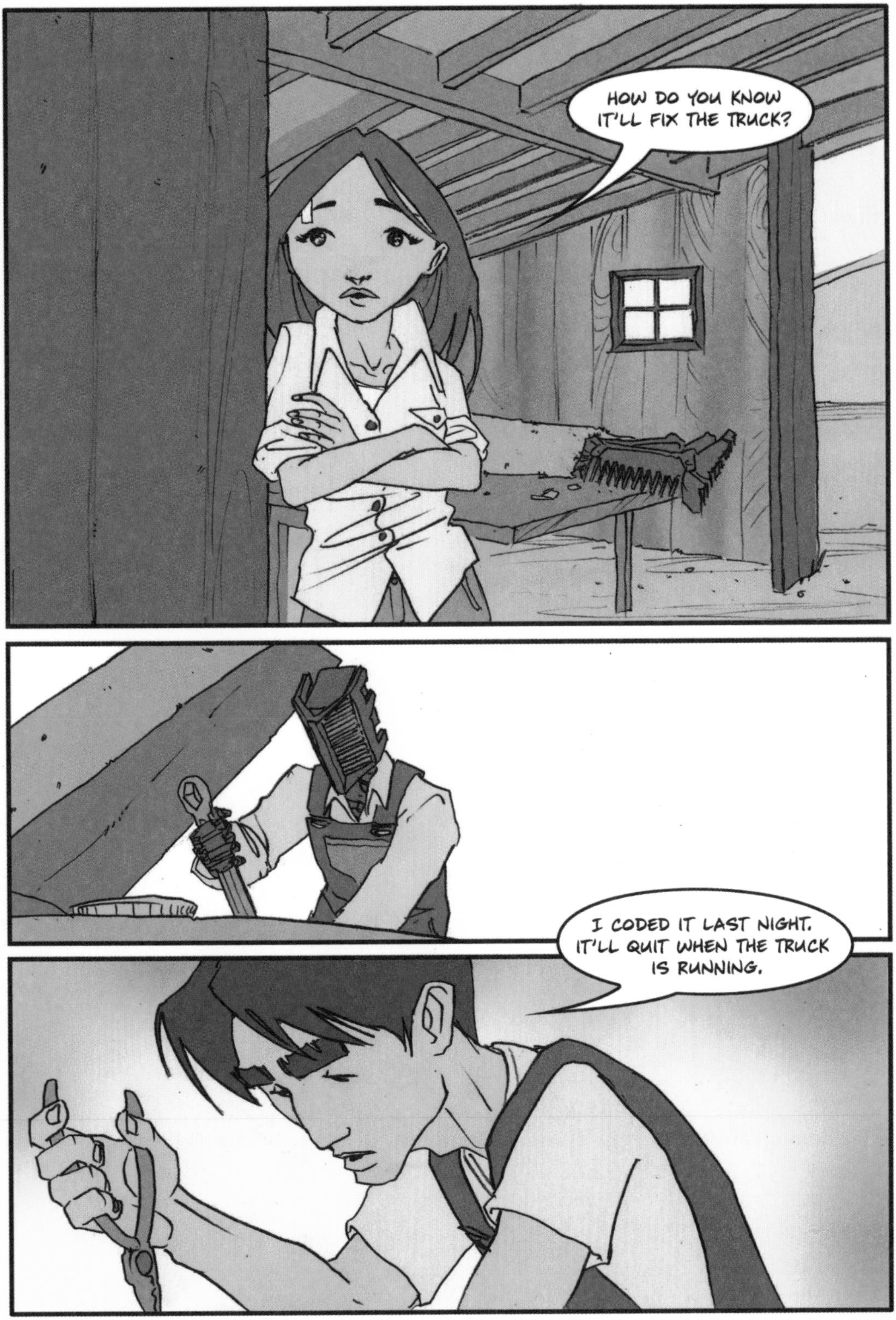
HOW DO YOU KNOW IT'LL FIX THE TRUCK?
I CODED IT LAST NIGHT. IT'LL QUIT WHEN THE TRUCK IS RUNNING.

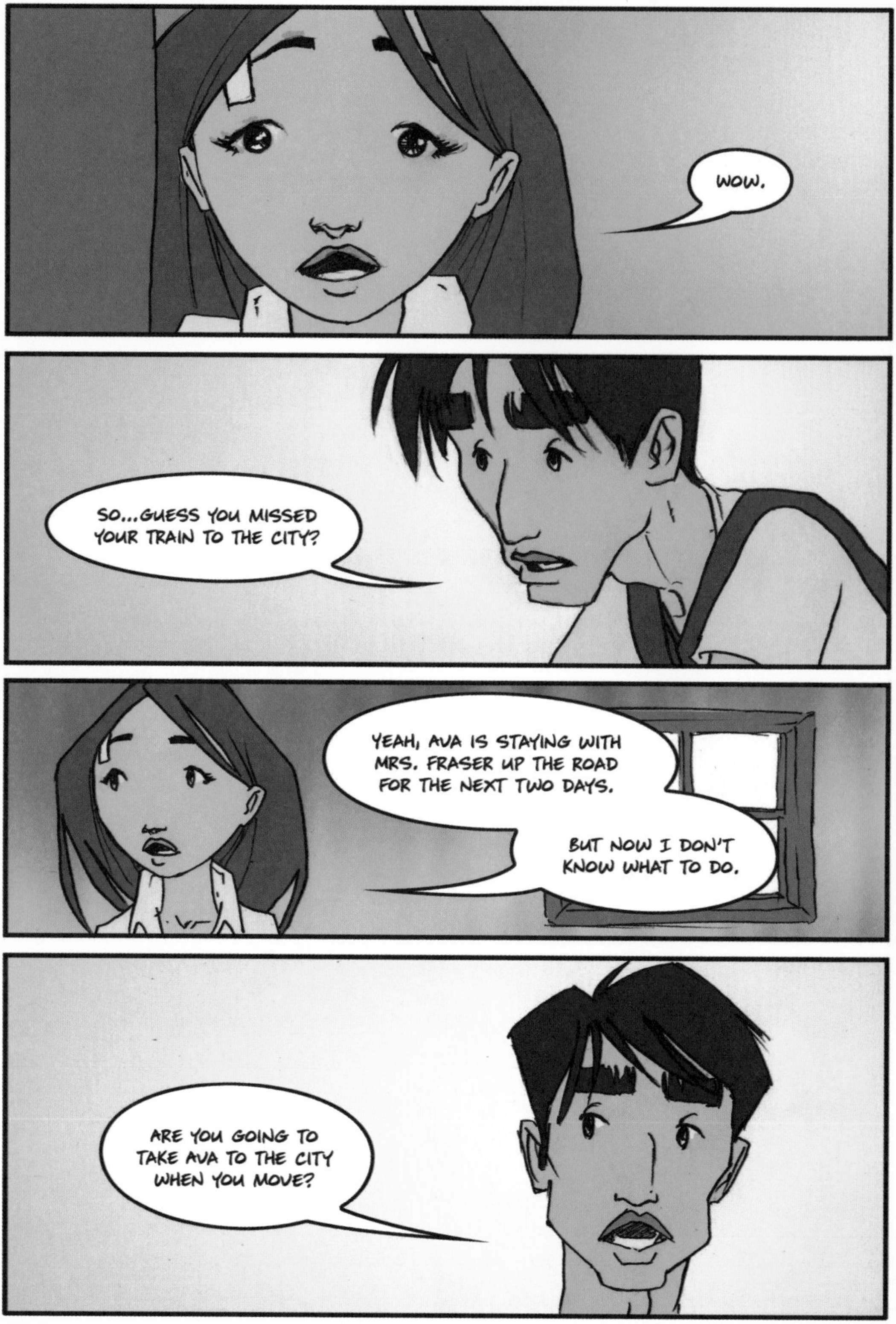
WOW.
SO...GUESS YOU MISSED YOUR TRAIN TO THE CITY?
YEAH, AVA IS STAYING WITH MRS. FRASER UP THE ROAD FOR THE NEXT TWO DAYS.
BUT NOW I DON'T KNOW WHAT TO DO.
ARE YOU GOING TO TAKE AVA TO THE CITY WHEN YOU MOVE?

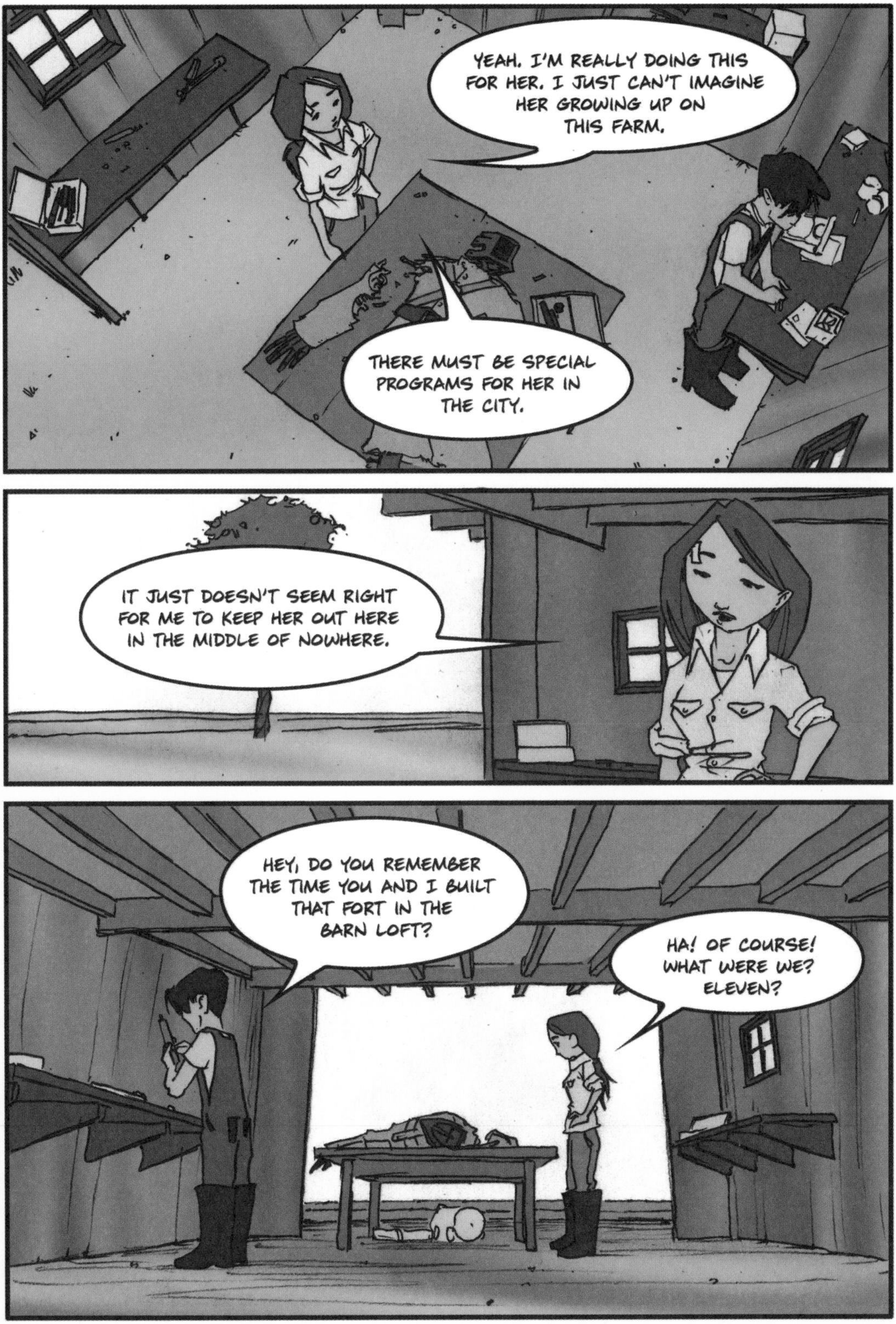
YEAH. I'M REALLY DOING THIS FOR HER. I JUST CAN'T IMAGINE HER GROWING UP ON THIS FARM.
THERE MUST BE SPECIAL PROGRAMS FOR HER IN THE CITY.
IT JUST DOESN'T SEEM RIGHT FOR ME TO KEEP HER OUT HERE IN THE MIDDLE OF NOWHERE.
HEY, DO YOU REMEMBER THE TIME YOU AND I BUILT THAT FORT IN THE BARN LOFT?
HA! OF COURSE! WHAT WERE WE? ELEVEN?

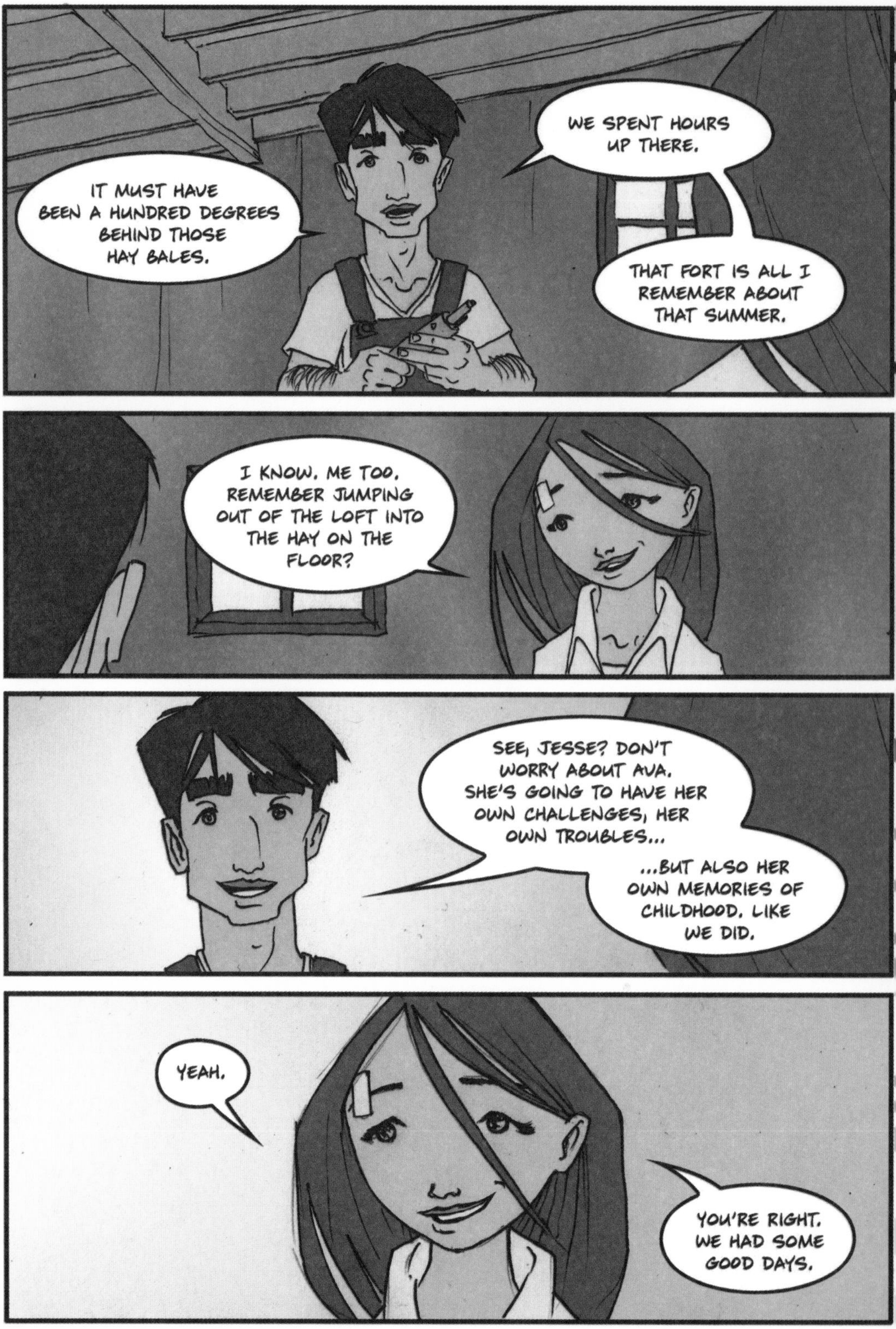
IT MUST HAVE BEEN A HUNDRED DEGREES BEHIND THOSE HAY BALES.
WE SPENT HOURS UP THERE.
THAT FORT IS ALL I REMEMBER ABOUT THAT SUMMER.
I KNOW. ME TOO. REMEMBER JUMPING OUT OF THE LOFT INTO THE HAY ON THE FLOOR?
SEE, JESSE? DON'T WORRY ABOUT AVA. SHE'S GOING TO HAVE HER OWN CHALLENGES, HER OWN TROUBLES...
...BUT ALSO HER OWN MEMORIES OF CHILDHOOD. LIKE WE DID.
YEAH.
YOU'RE RIGHT. WE HAD SOME GOOD DAYS.

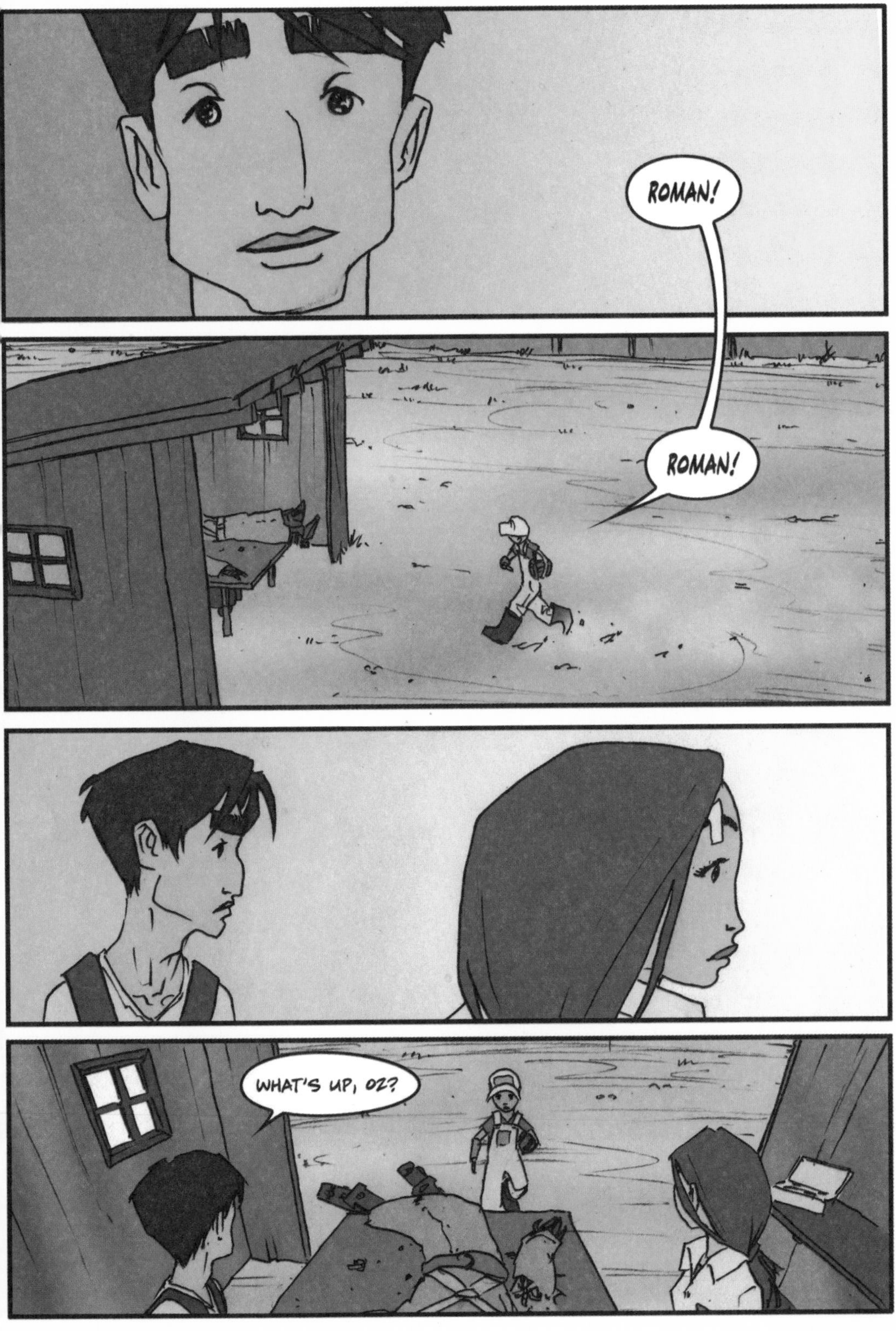
ROMAN!
ROMAN!
WHAT'S UP, OZ?

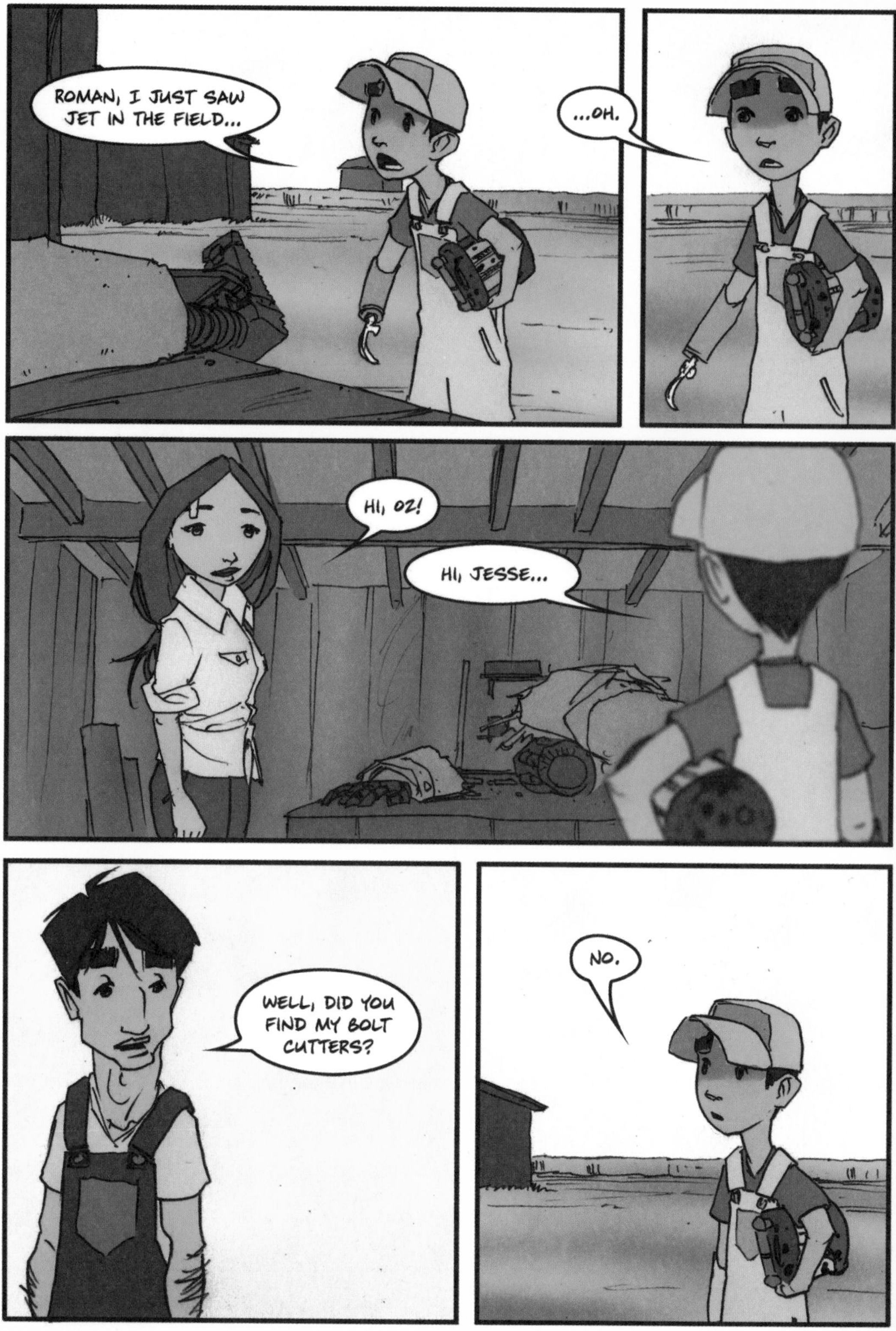
ROMAN, I JUST SAW JET IN THE FIELD...
...OH.
HI, OZ!
HI, JESSE...
WELL, DID YOU FIND MY BOLT CUTTERS?
NO.

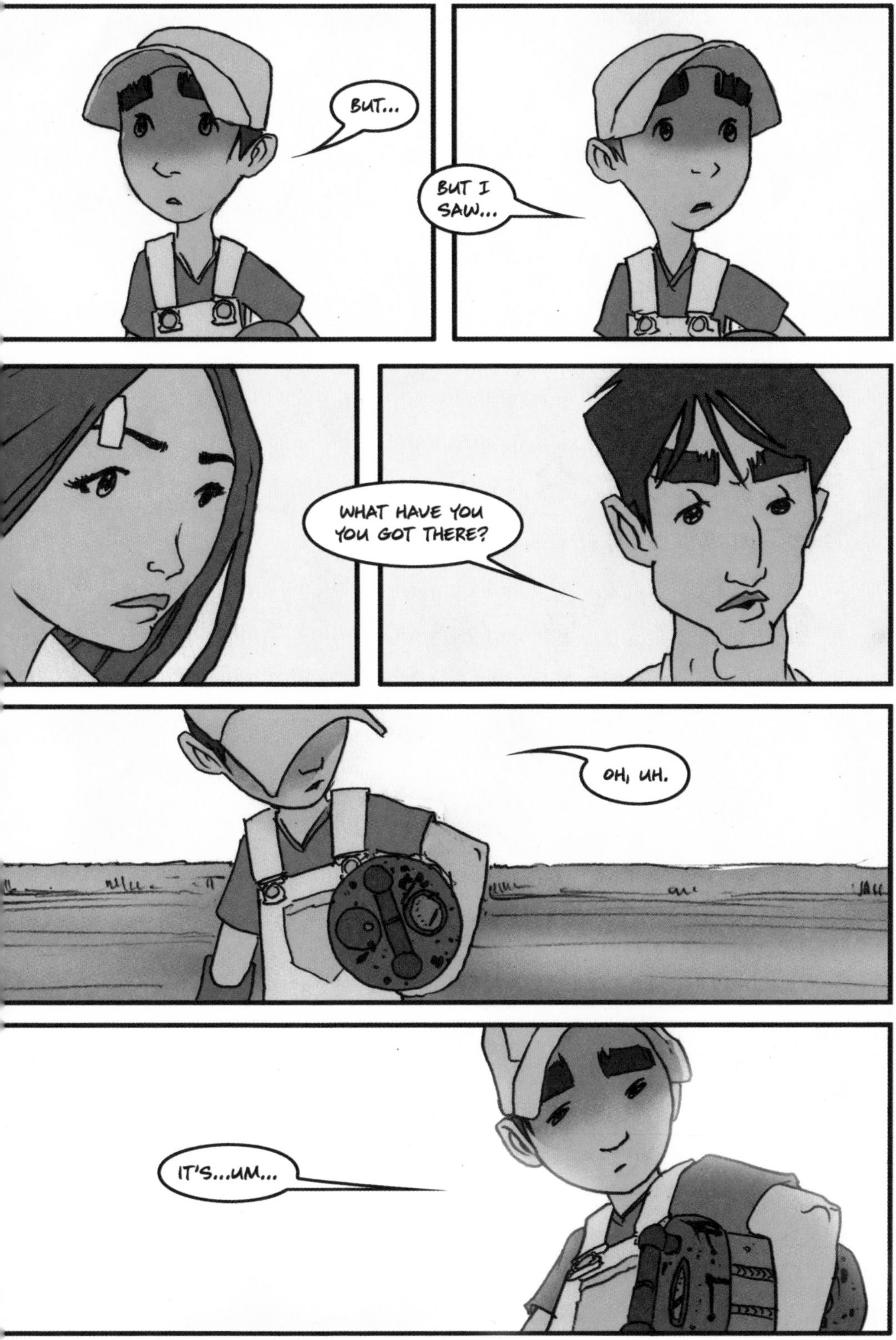
BUT...
BUT I SAW...
WHAT HAVE YOU YOU GOT THERE?
OH, UH.
IT'S...UM...

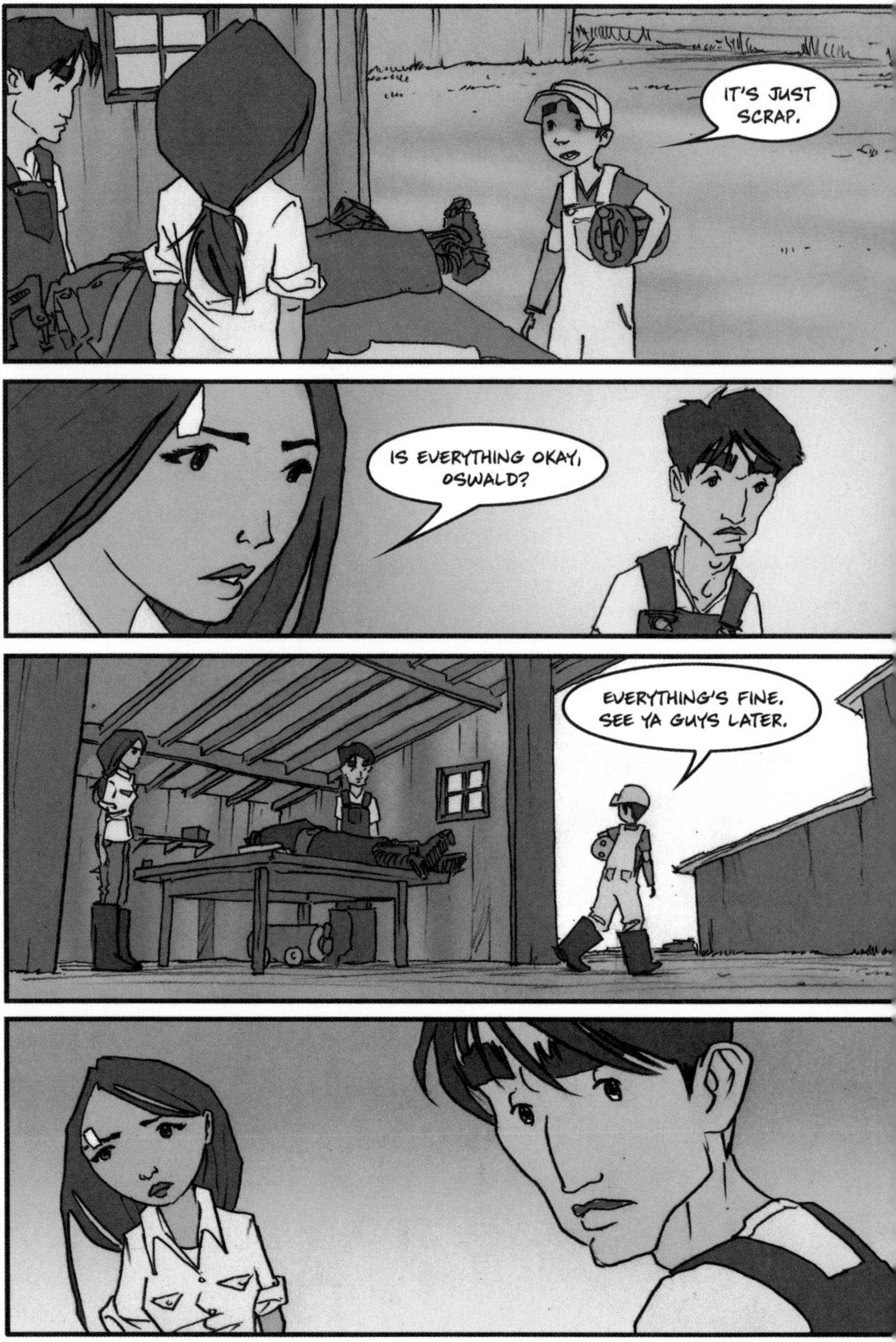
IT'S JUST SCRAP.
IS EVERYTHING OKAY, OSWALD?
EVERYTHING'S FINE. SEE YA GUYS LATER.

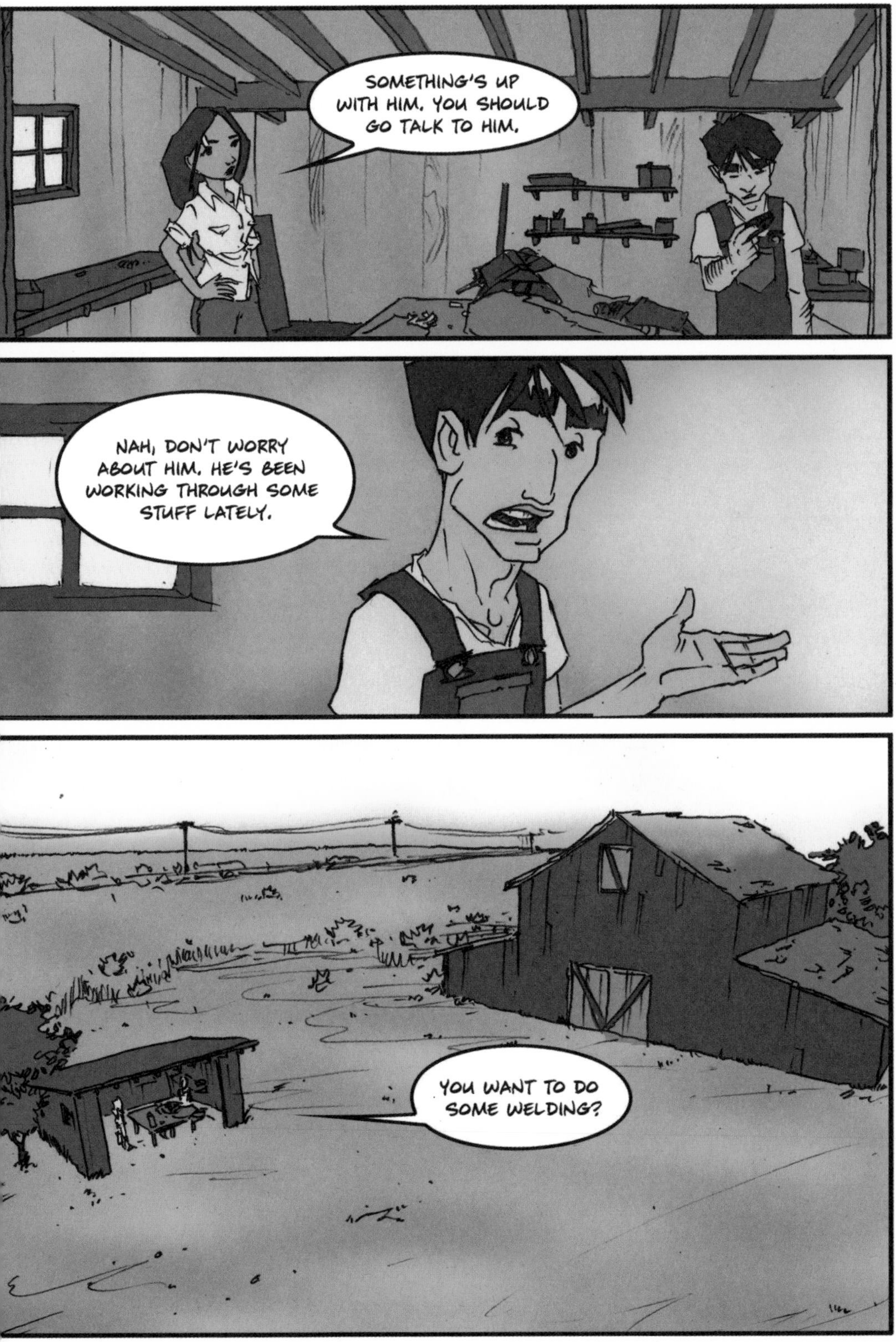
SOMETHING'S UP WITH HIM. YOU SHOULD GO TALK TO HIM.
NAH, DON'T WORRY ABOUT HIM. HE'S BEEN WORKING THROUGH SOME STUFF LATELY.
YOU WANT TO DO SOME WELDING?

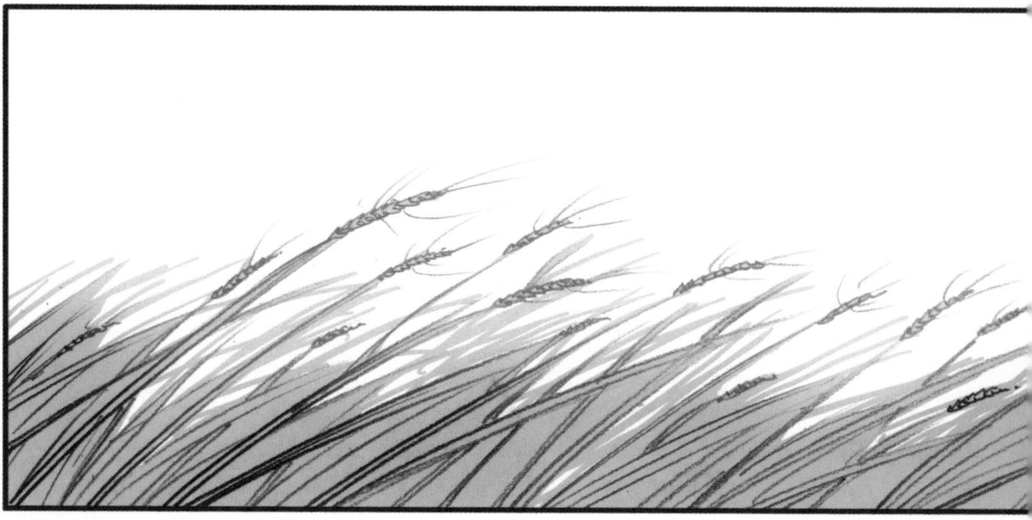

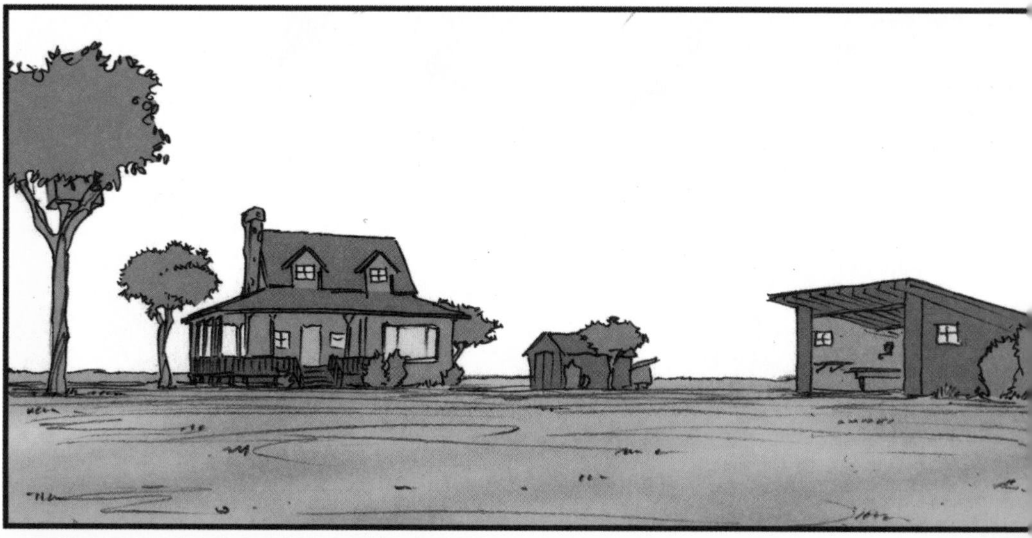

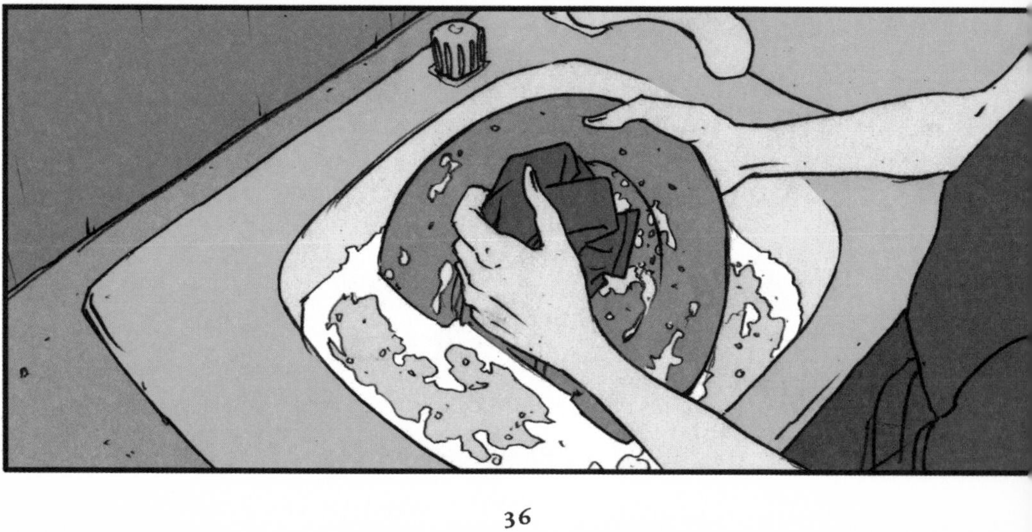

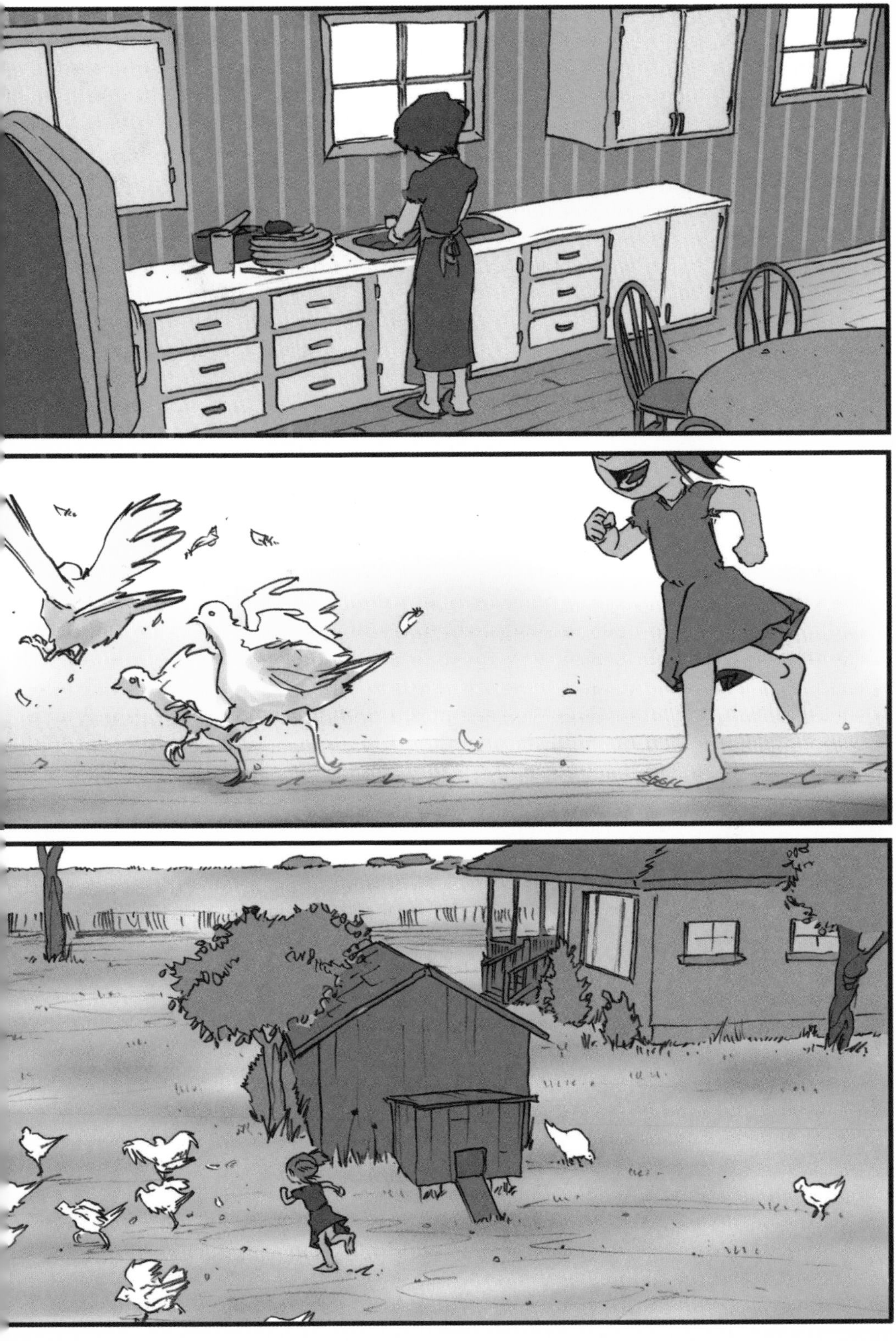

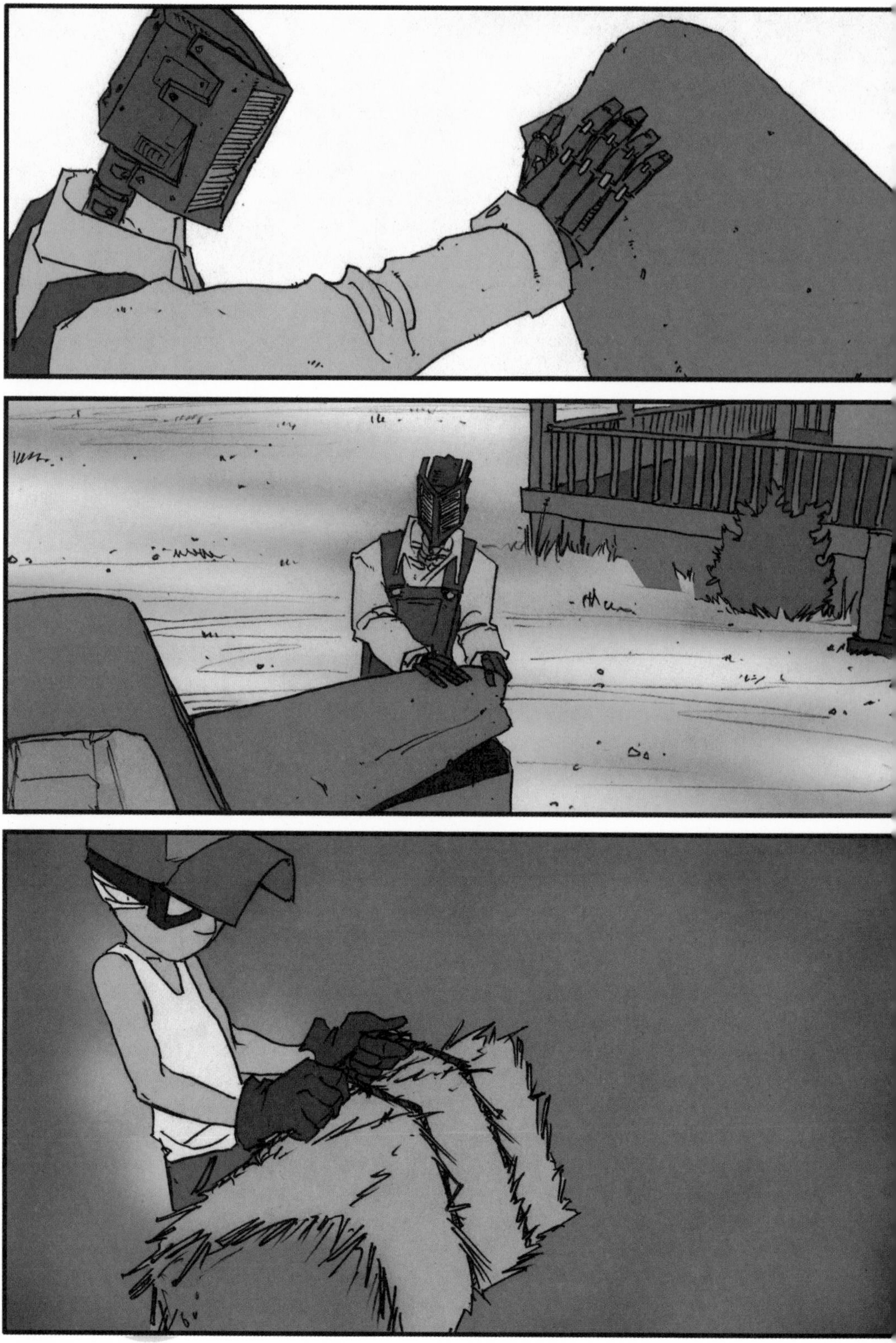

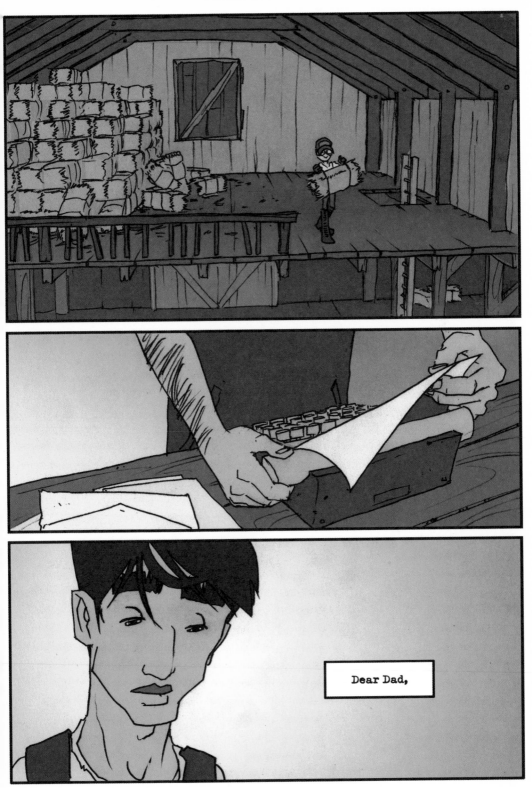

Dear Dad,

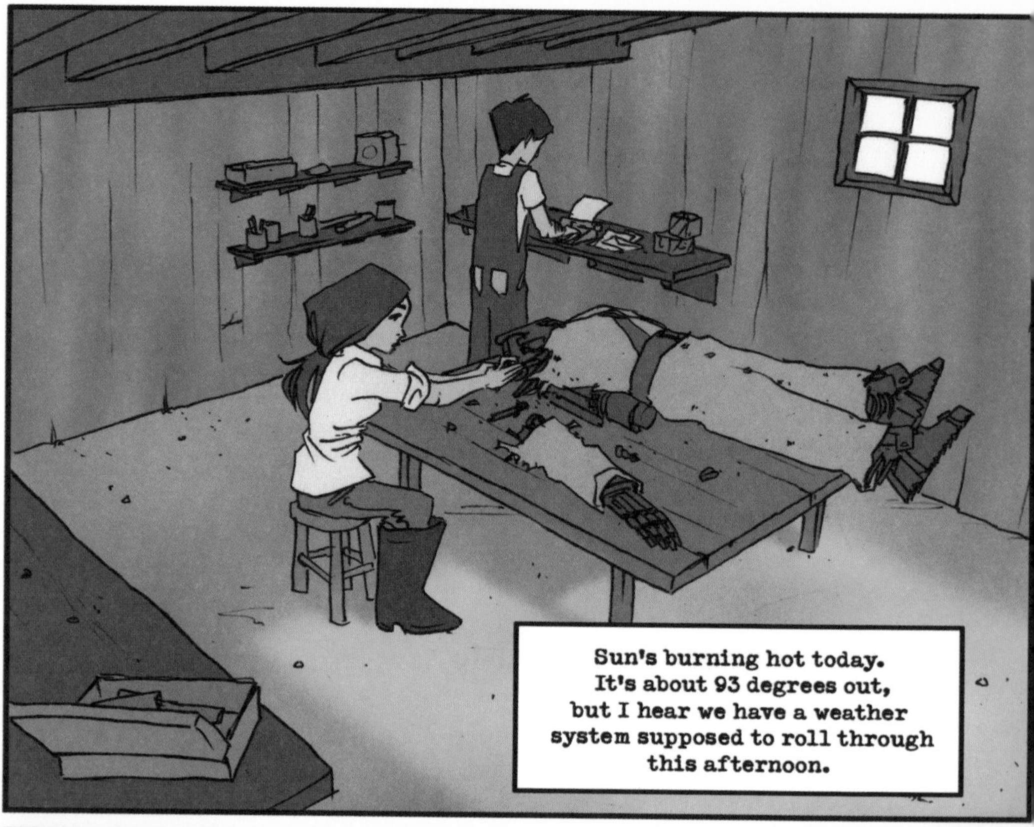
Sun's burning hot today.
It's about 93 degrees out,
but I hear we have a weather
system supposed to roll through
this afternoon.

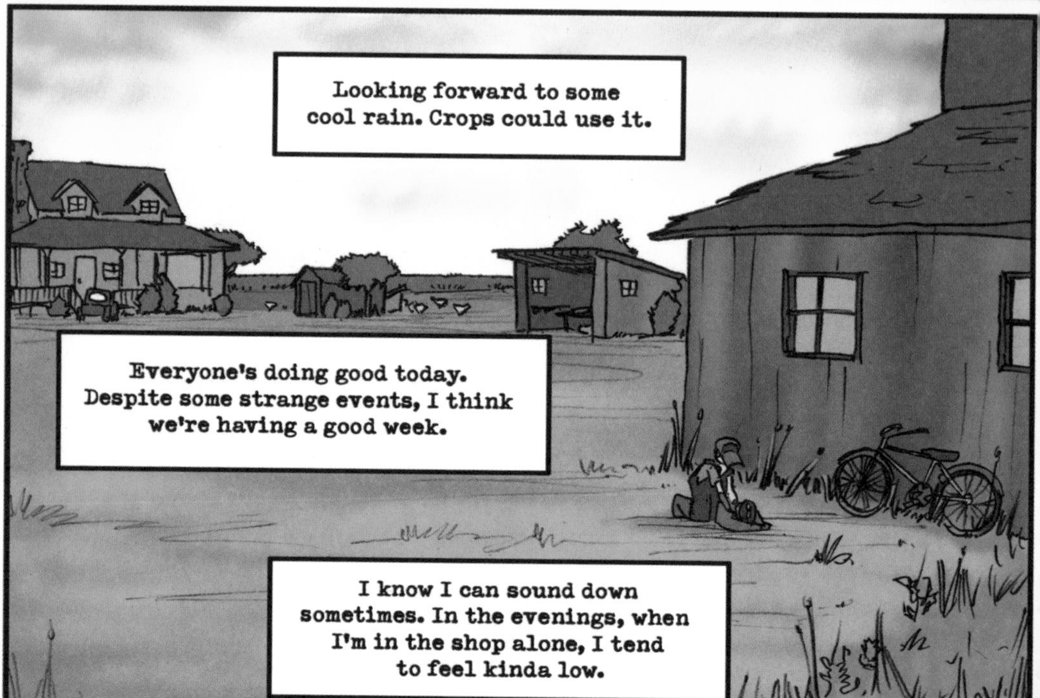
Looking forward to some
cool rain. Crops could use it.
Everyone's doing good today.
Despite some strange events, I think
we're having a good week.
I know I can sound down
sometimes. In the evenings, when
I'm in the shop alone, I tend
to feel kinda low.

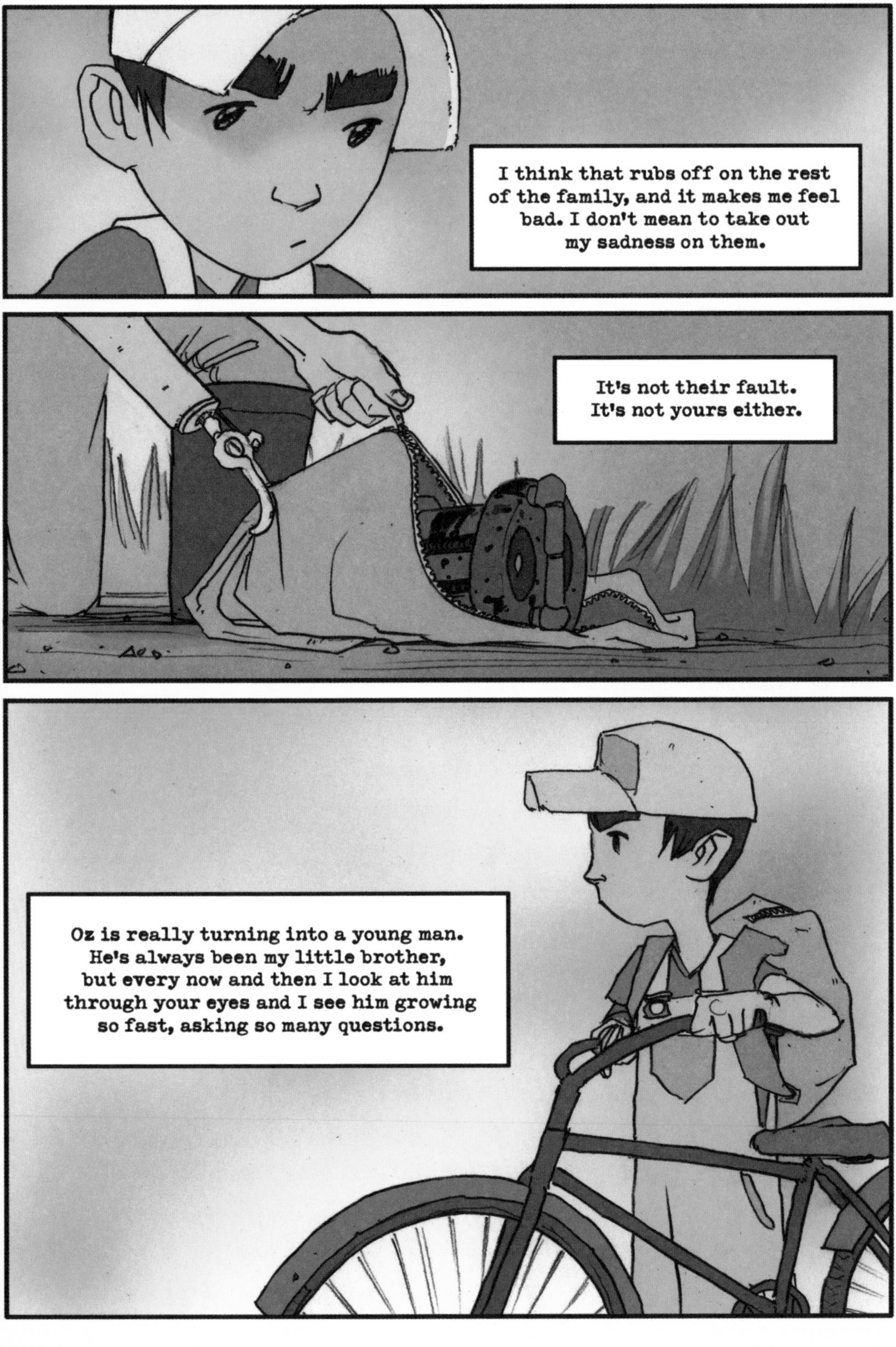
I think that rubs off on the rest of the family, and it makes me feel bad. I don't mean to take out my sadness on them.
It's not their fault. It's not yours either.
Oz is really turning into a young man. He's always been my little brother, but every now and then I look at him through your eyes and I see him growing so fast, asking so many questions.

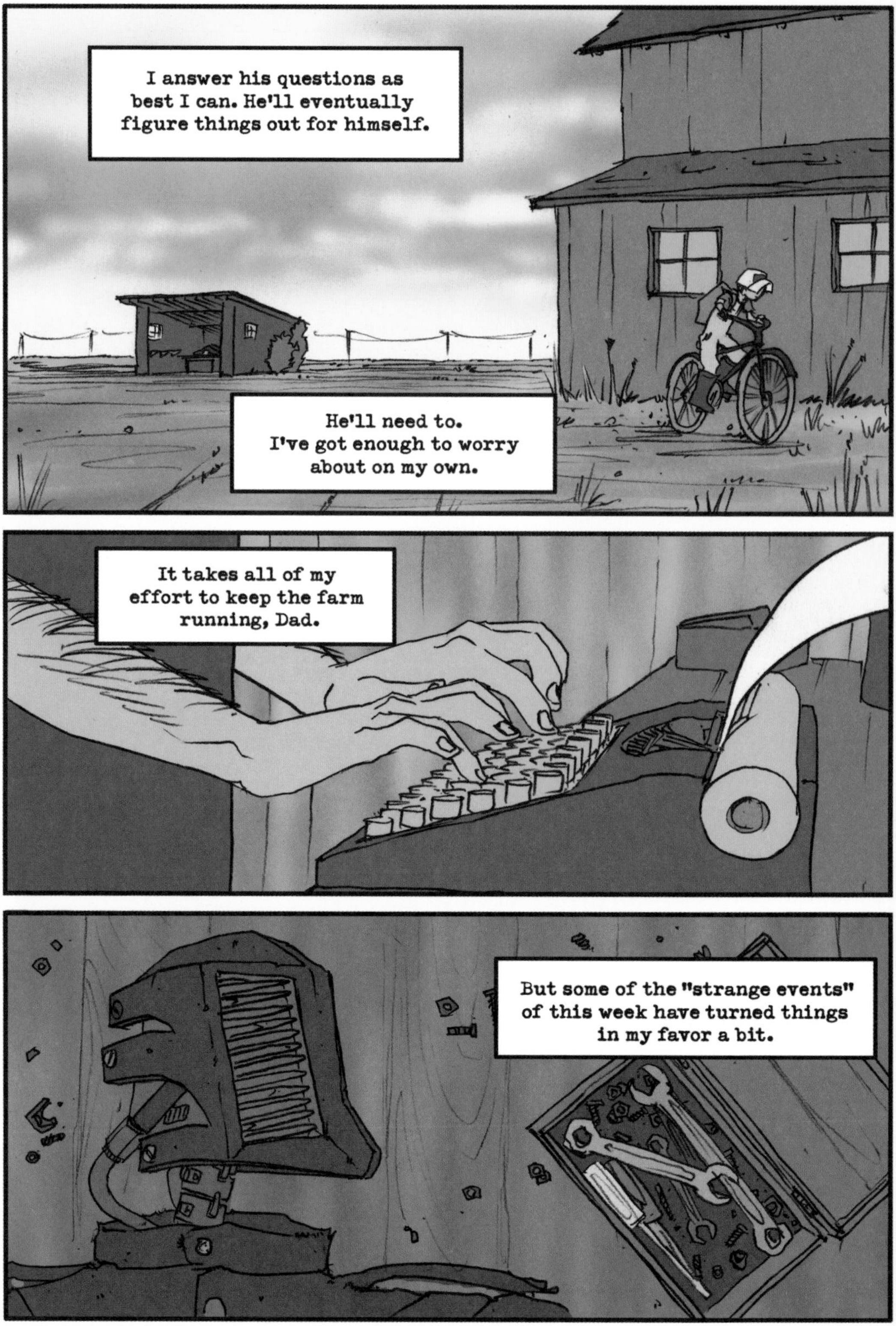
I answer his questions as best I can. He'll eventually figure things out for himself.
He'll need to. I've got enough to worry about on my own.
It takes all of my effort to keep the farm running, Dad.
But some of the "strange events" of this week have turned things in my favor a bit.

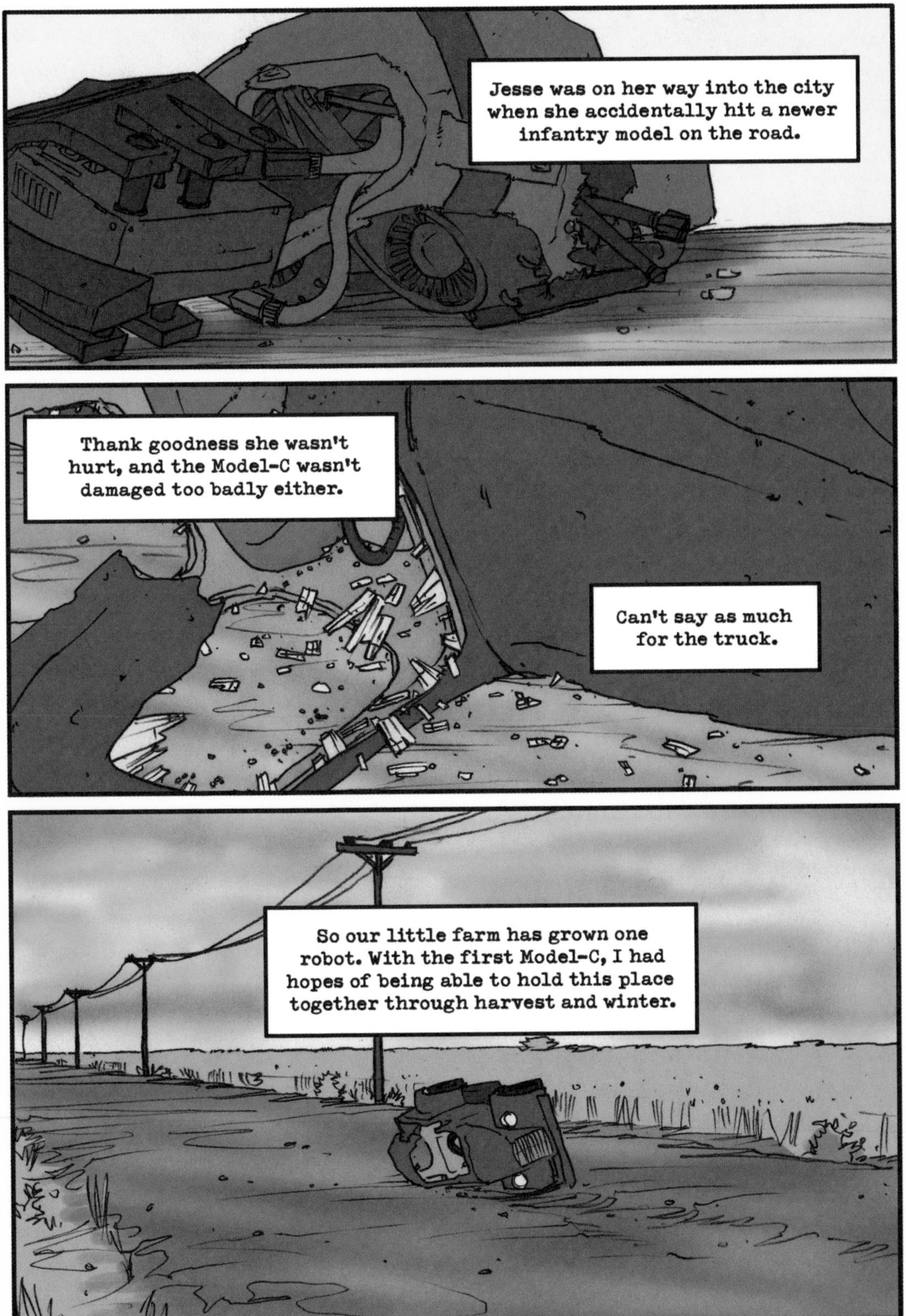
Jesse was on her way into the city when she accidentally hit a newer infantry model on the road.
Thank goodness she wasn't hurt, and the Model-C wasn't damaged too badly either.
Can't say as much for the truck.
So our little farm has grown one robot. With the first Model-C, I had hopes of being able to hold this place together through harvest and winter.

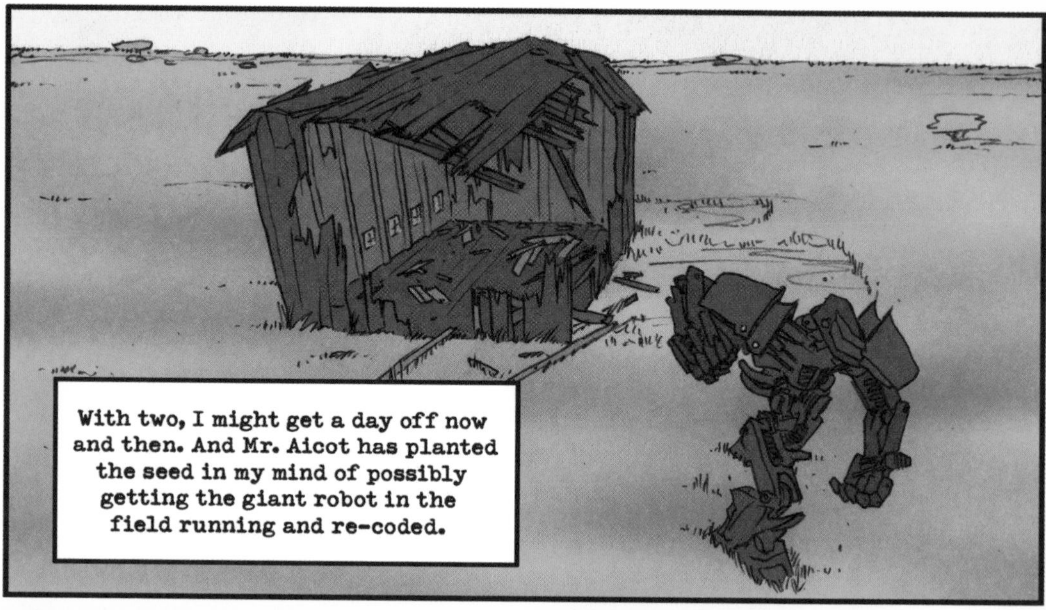
With two, I might get a day off now and then. And Mr. Aicot has planted the seed in my mind of possibly getting the giant robot in the field running and re-coded.

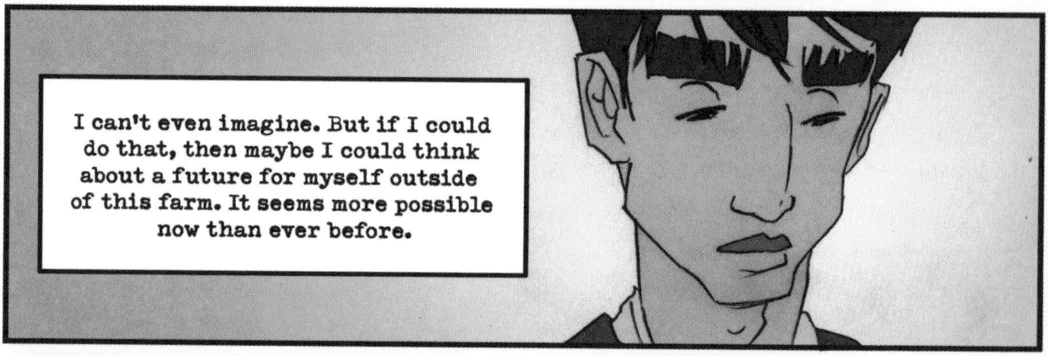
I can't even imagine. But if I could do that, then maybe I could think about a future for myself outside of this farm. It seems more possible now than ever before.

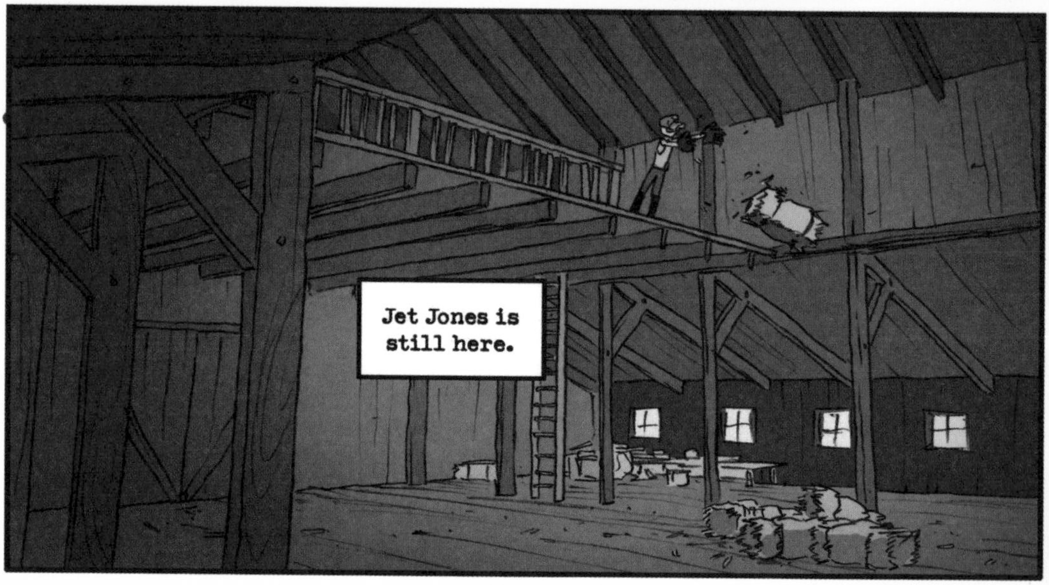
Jet Jones is still here.

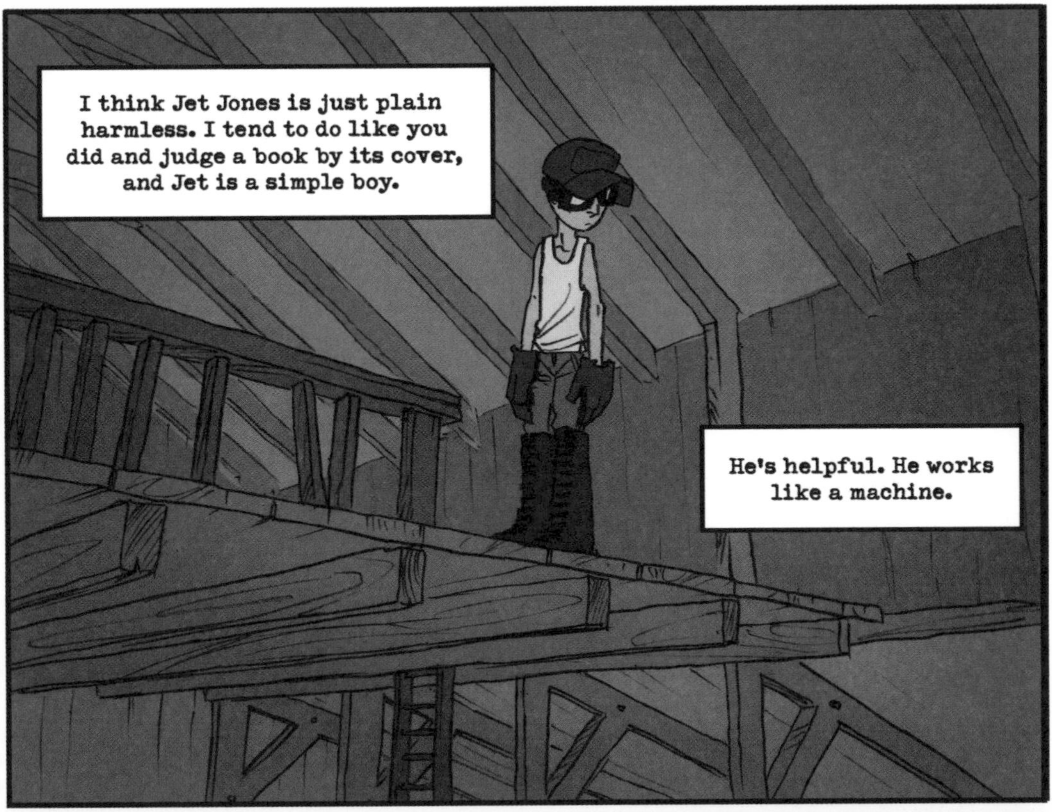
I think Jet Jones is just plain harmless. I tend to do like you did and judge a book by its cover, and Jet is a simple boy.
He's helpful. He works like a machine.

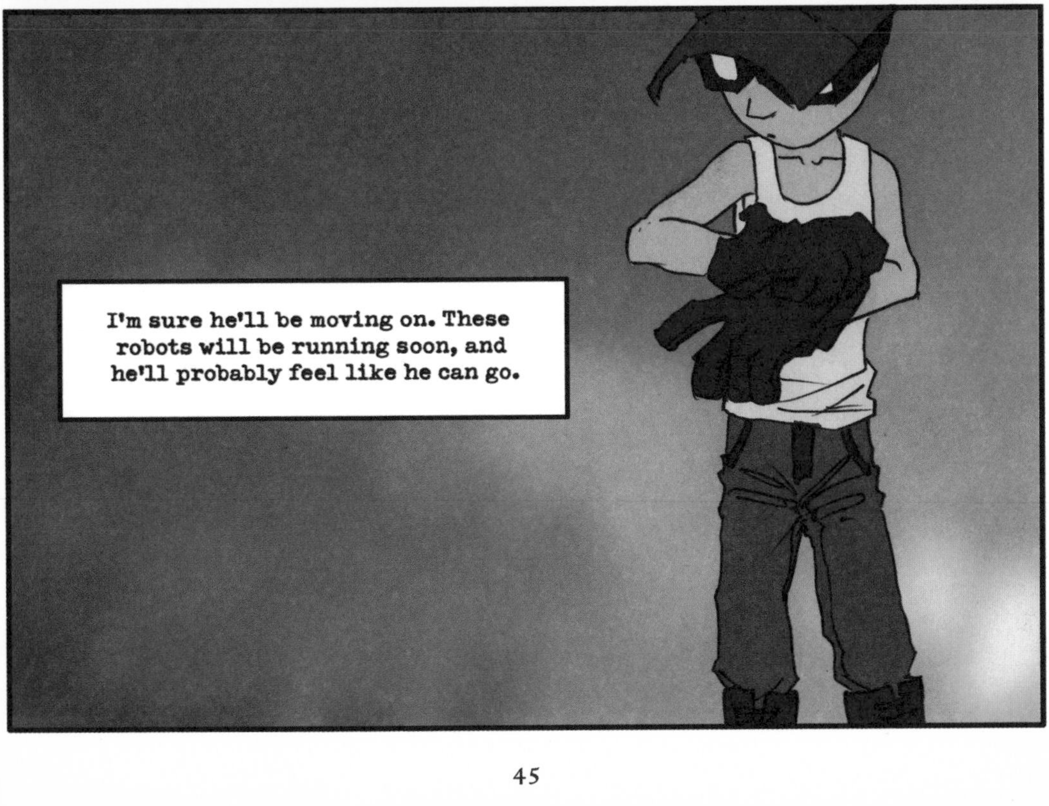
I'm sure he'll be moving on. These robots will be running soon, and he'll probably feel like he can go.

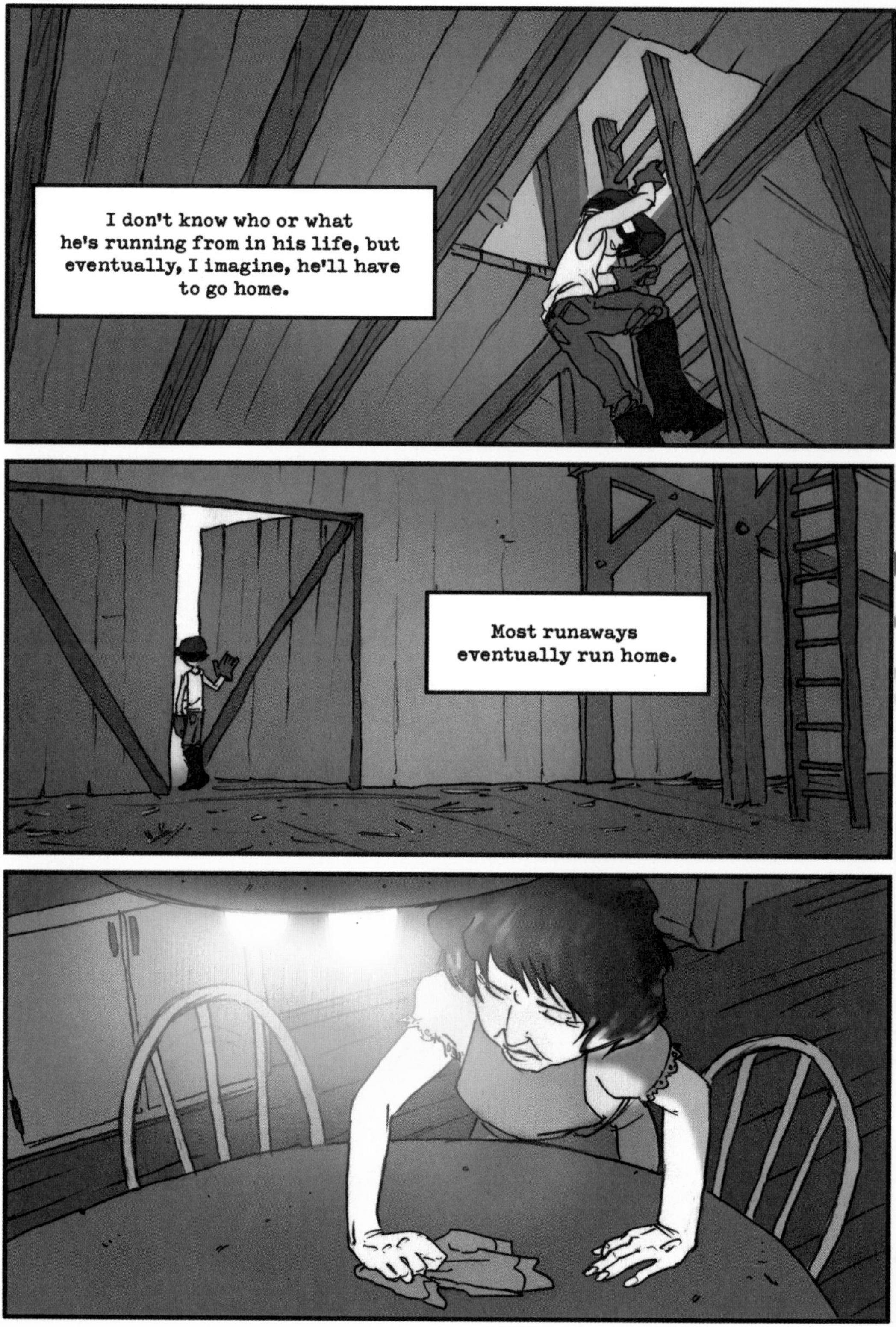
I don't know who or what he's running from in his life, but eventually, I imagine, he'll have to go home.
Most runaways eventually run home.

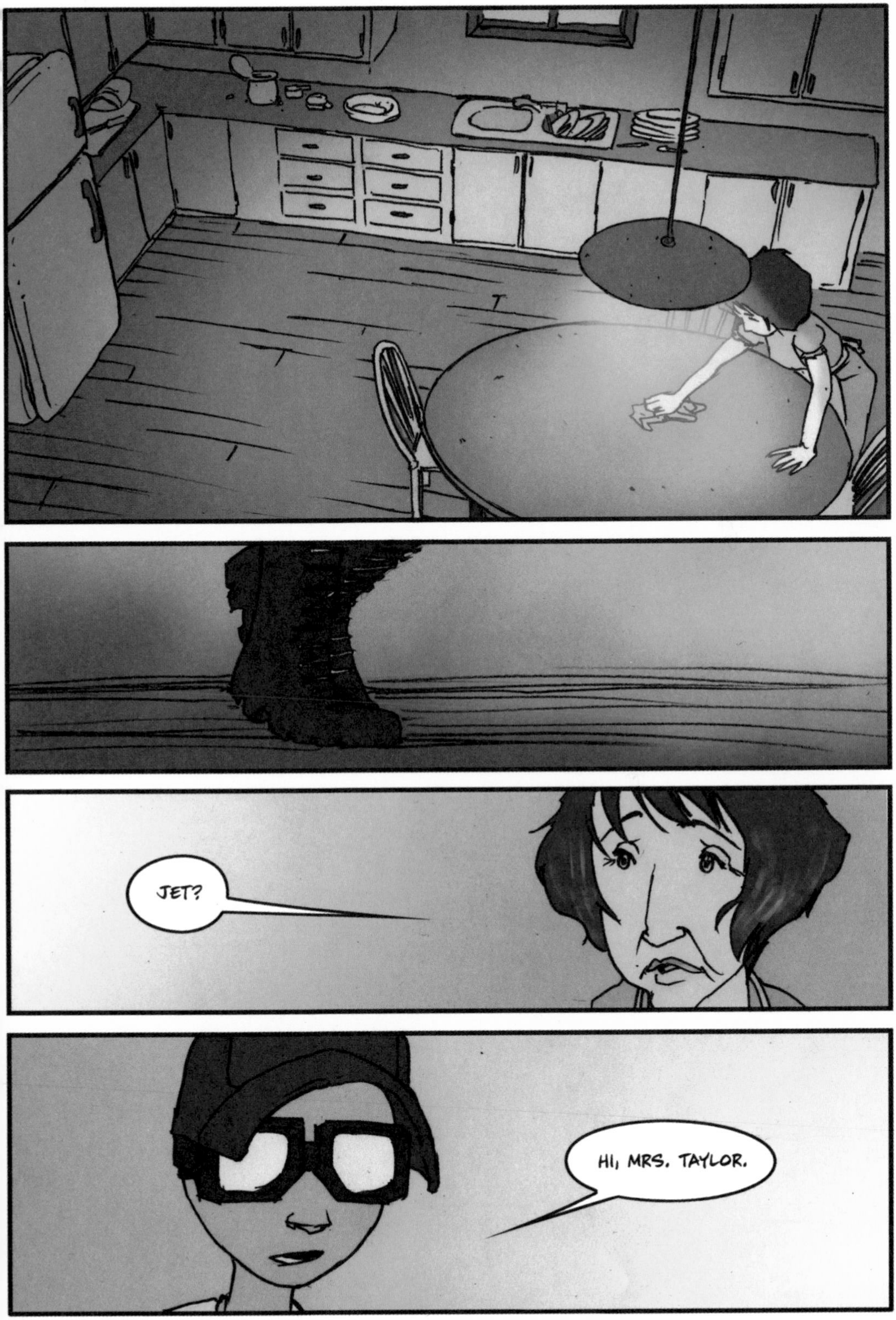
JET?
HI, MRS. TAYLOR.

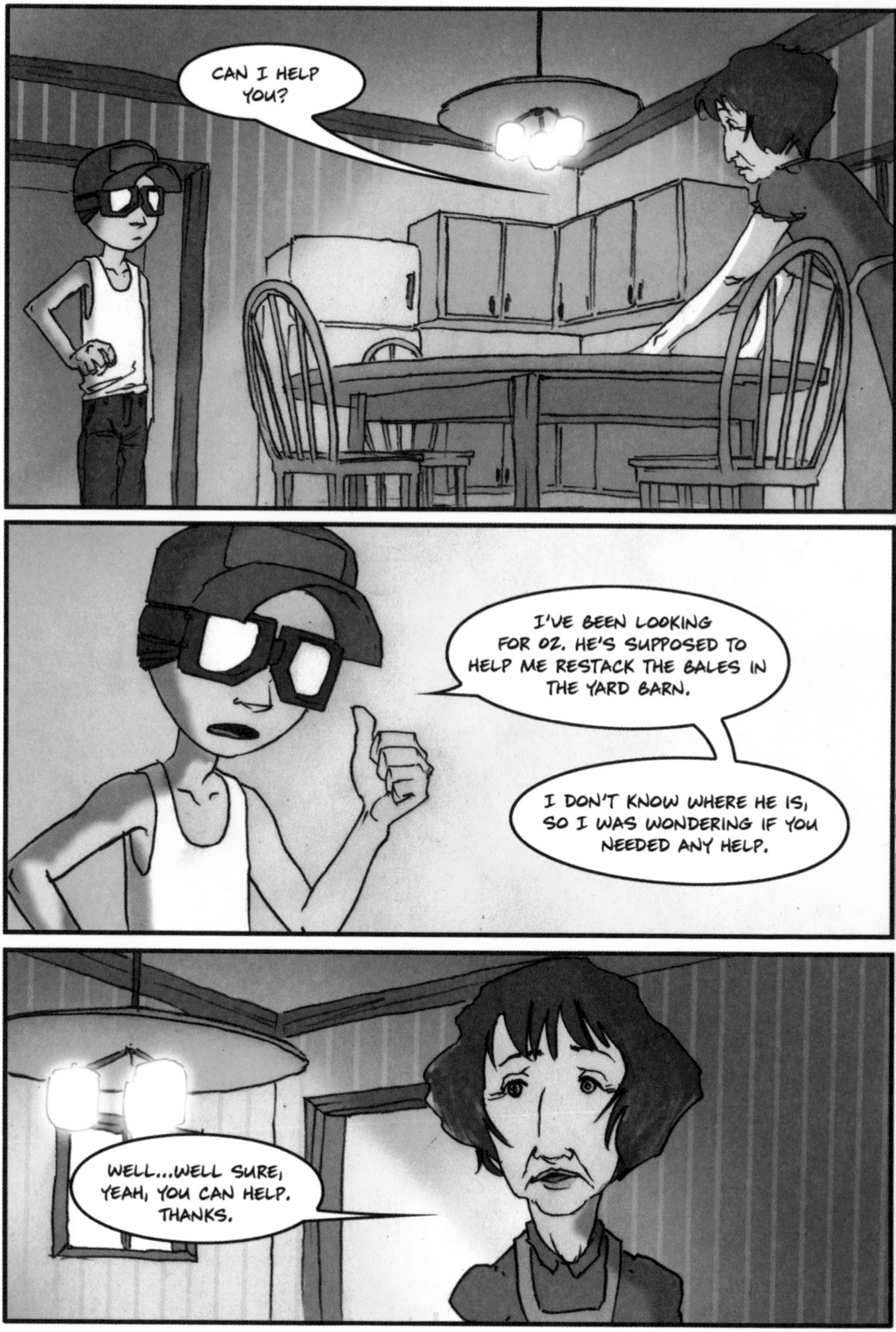
CAN I HELP YOU?
I'VE BEEN LOOKING FOR OZ. HE'S SUPPOSED TO HELP ME RESTACK THE BALES IN THE YARD BARN.
I DON'T KNOW WHERE HE IS, SO I WAS WONDERING IF YOU NEEDED ANY HELP.
WELL...WELL SURE, YEAH, YOU CAN HELP. THANKS.

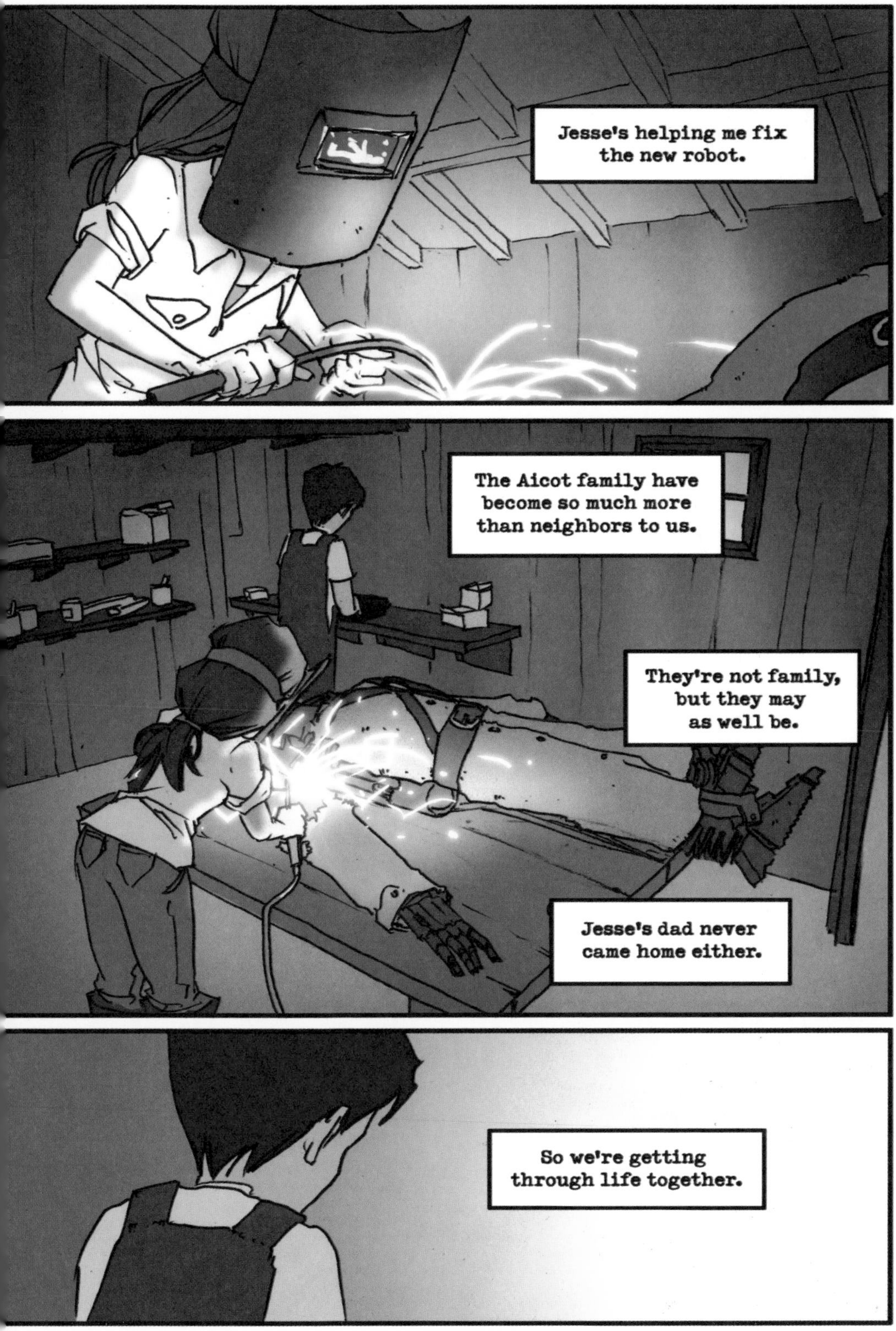
Jesse's helping me fix the new robot.
The Aicot family have become so much more than neighbors to us.
They're not family, but they may as well be.
Jesse's dad never came home either.
So we're getting through life together.

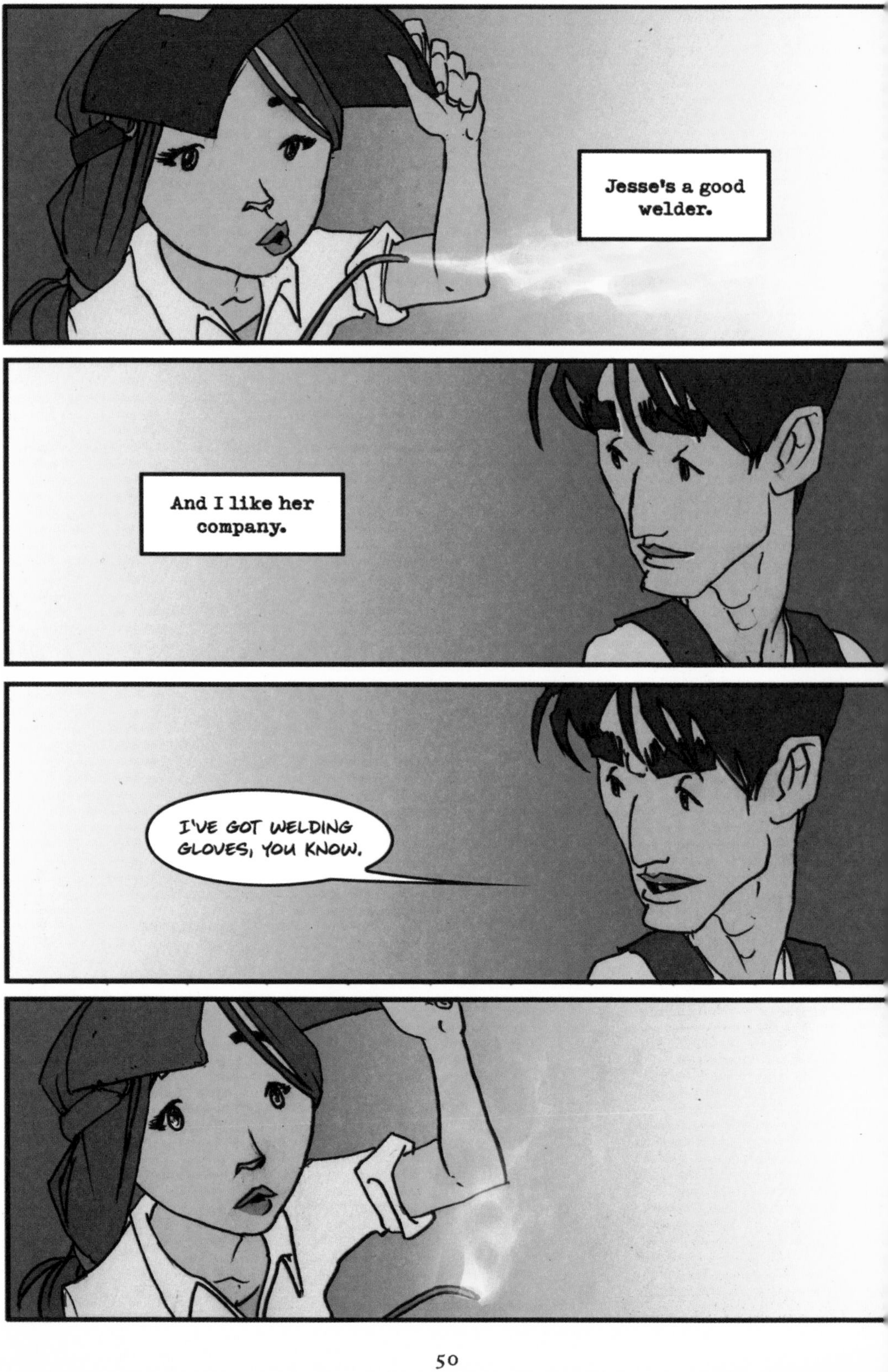
Jesse's a good welder.
And I like her company.
I'VE GOT WELDING GLOVES, YOU KNOW.

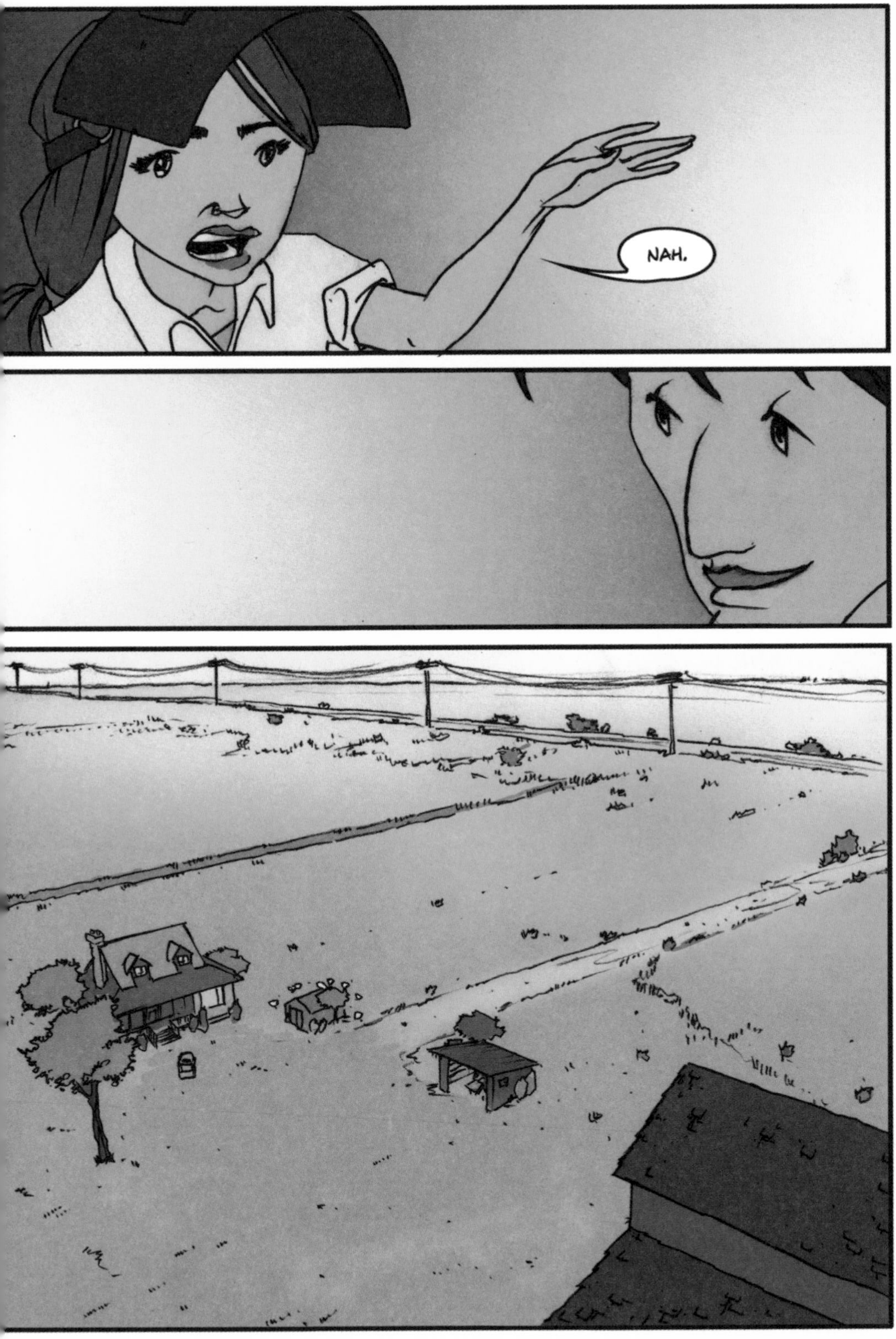
NAH.

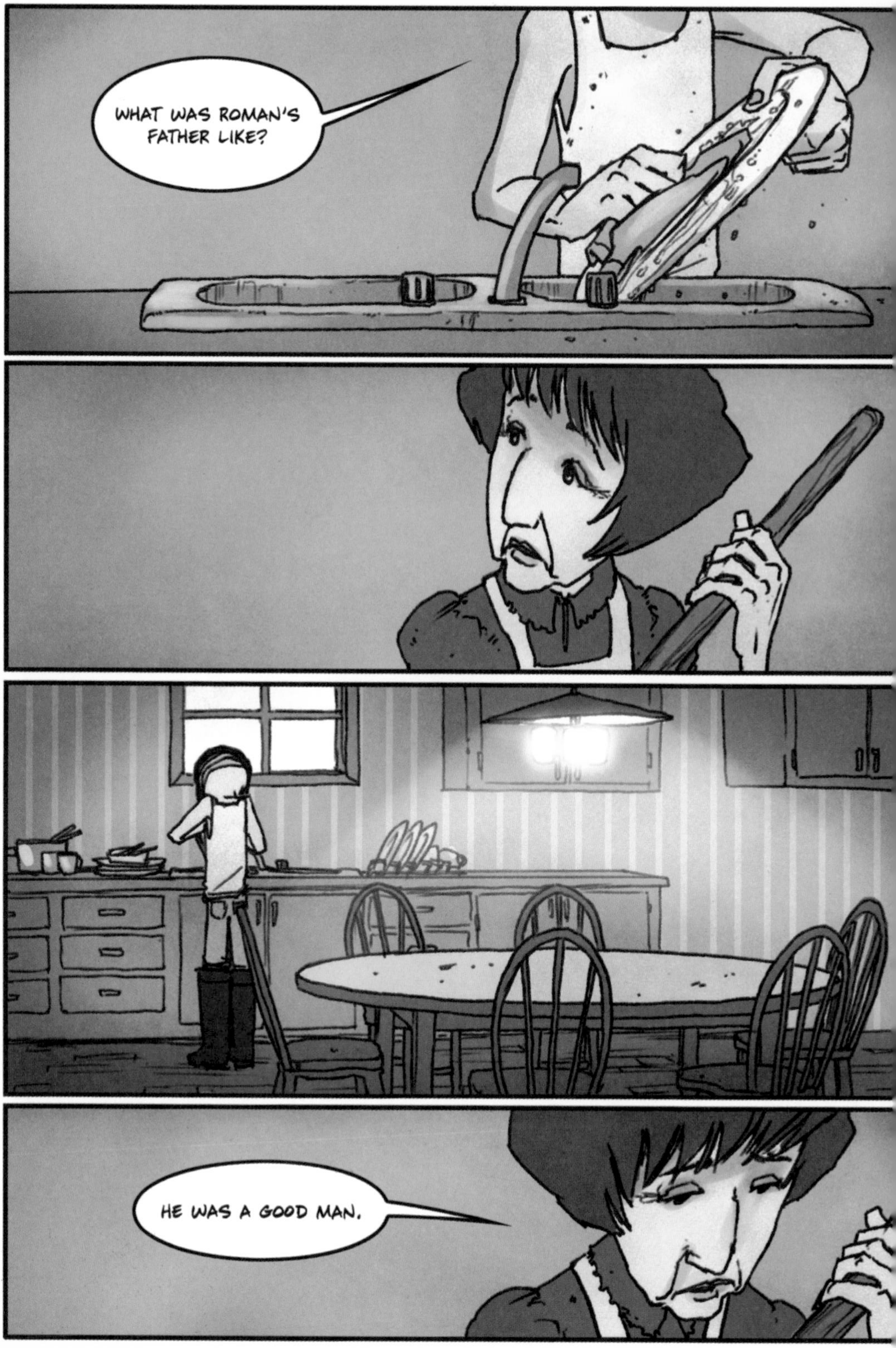
WHAT WAS ROMAN'S FATHER LIKE?
HE WAS A GOOD MAN.

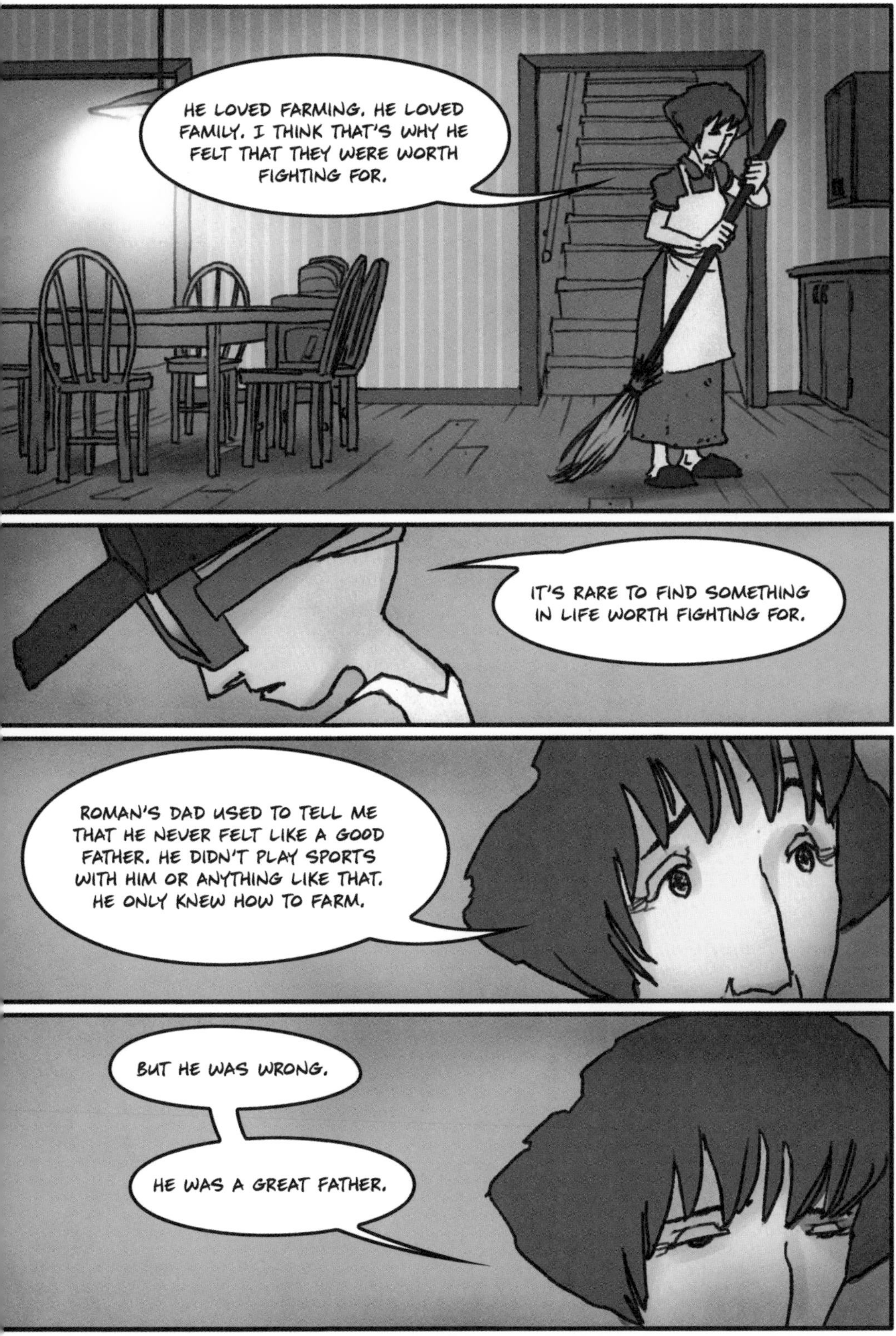
HE LOVED FARMING. HE LOVED FAMILY. I THINK THAT'S WHY HE FELT THAT THEY WERE WORTH FIGHTING FOR.
IT'S RARE TO FIND SOMETHING IN LIFE WORTH FIGHTING FOR.
ROMAN'S DAD USED TO TELL ME THAT HE NEVER FELT LIKE A GOOD FATHER. HE DIDN'T PLAY SPORTS WITH HIM OR ANYTHING LIKE THAT. HE ONLY KNEW HOW TO FARM.
BUT HE WAS WRONG.
HE WAS A GREAT FATHER.

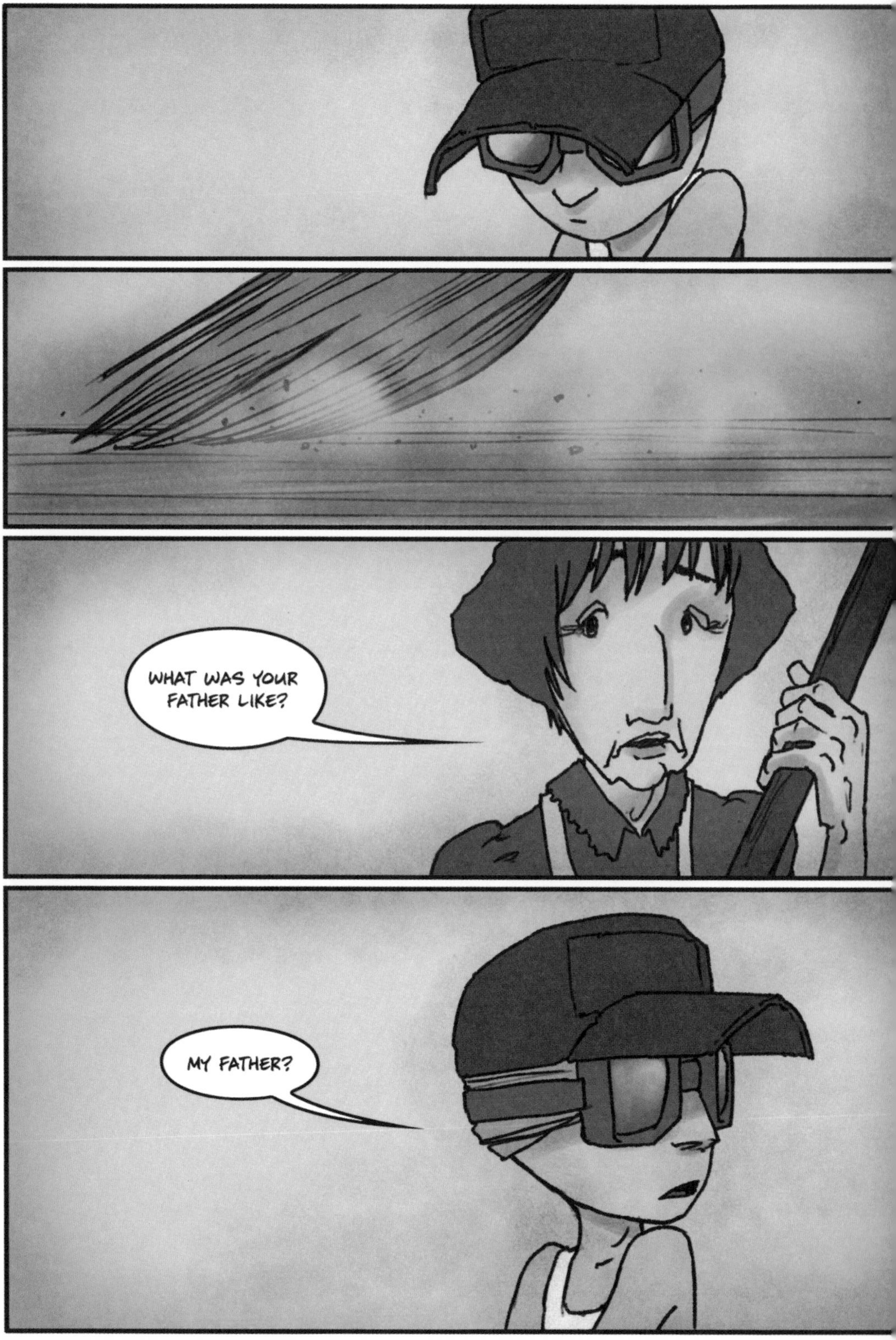
WHAT WAS YOUR FATHER LIKE?
MY FATHER?

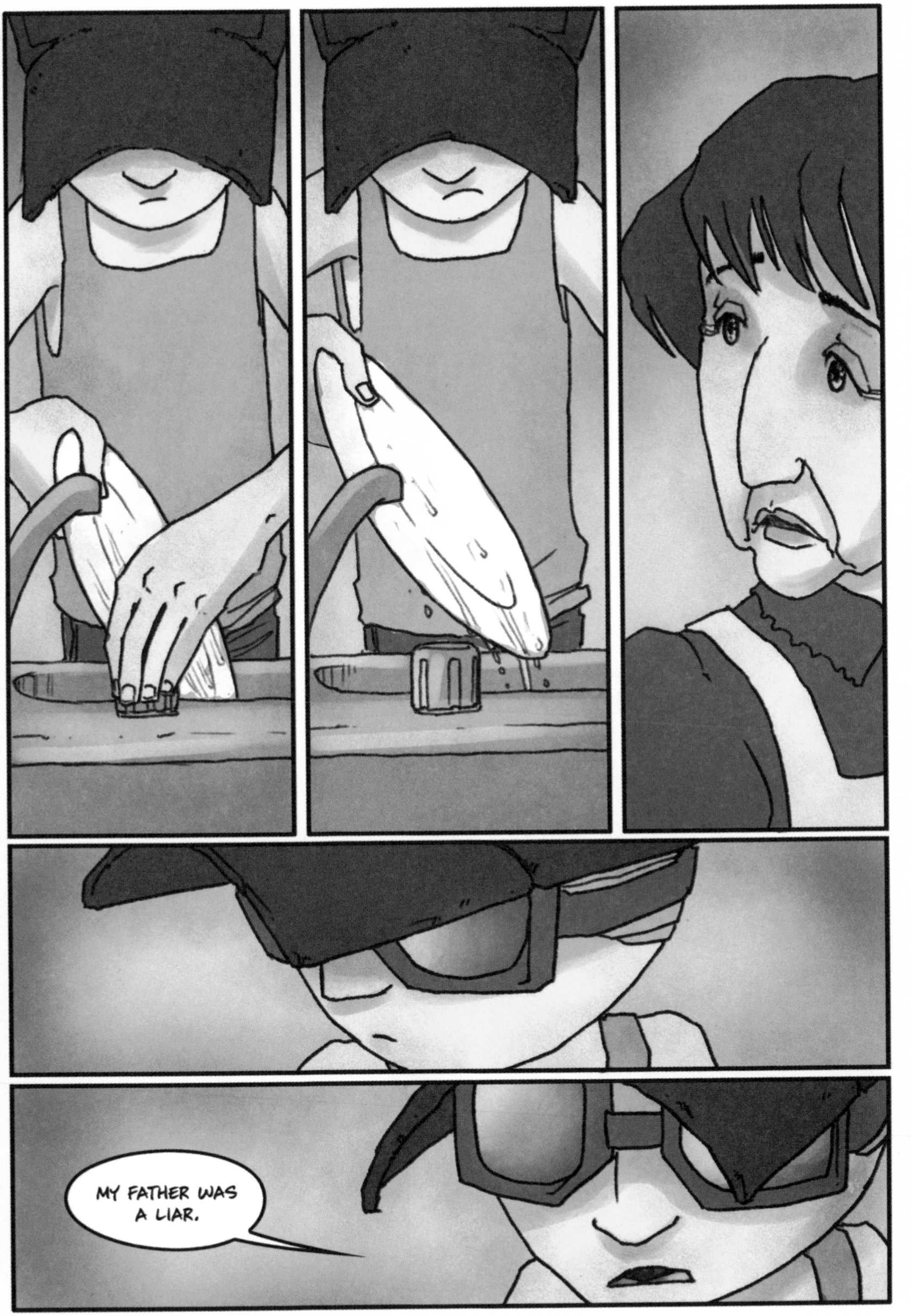
MY FATHER WAS
A LIAR.

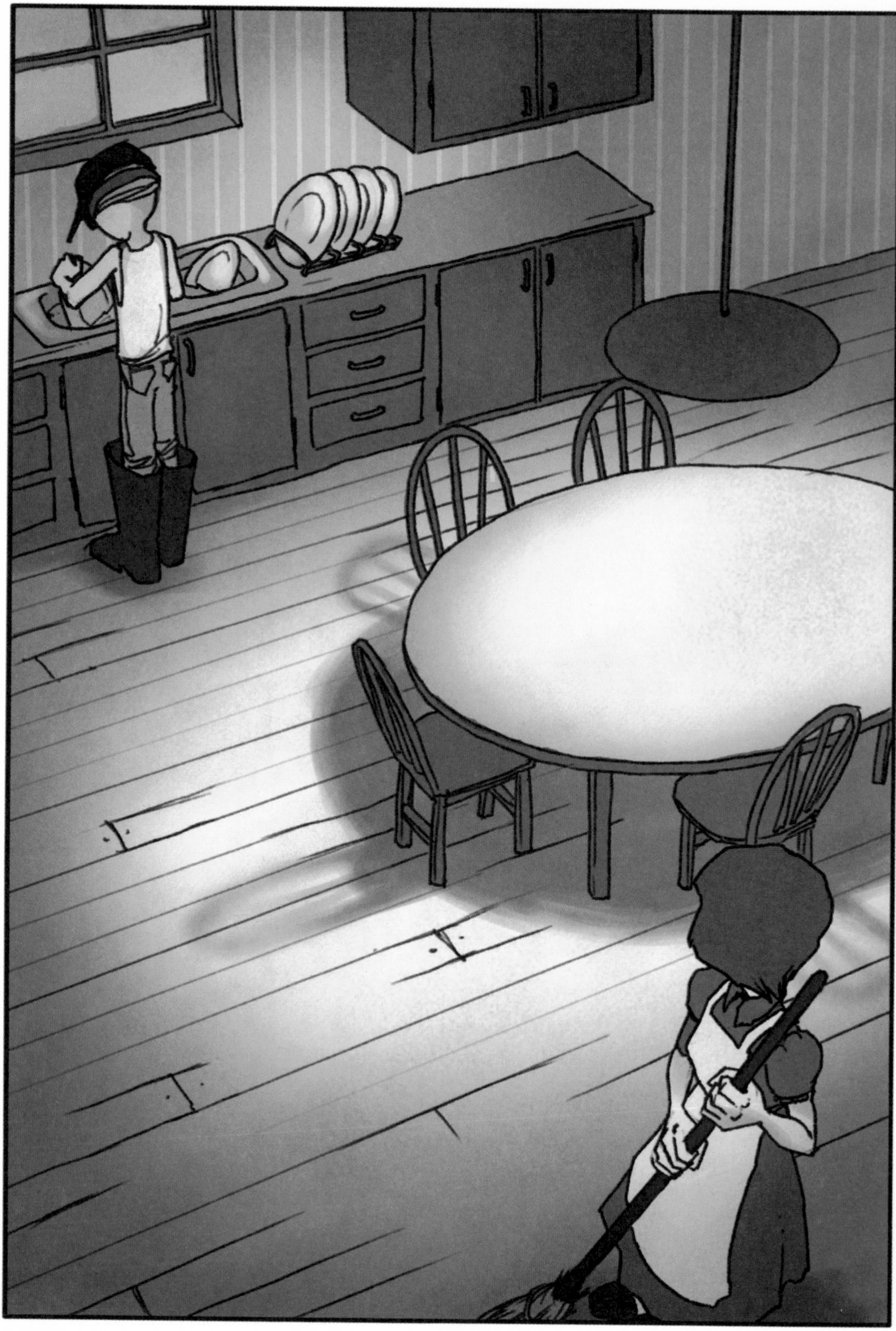

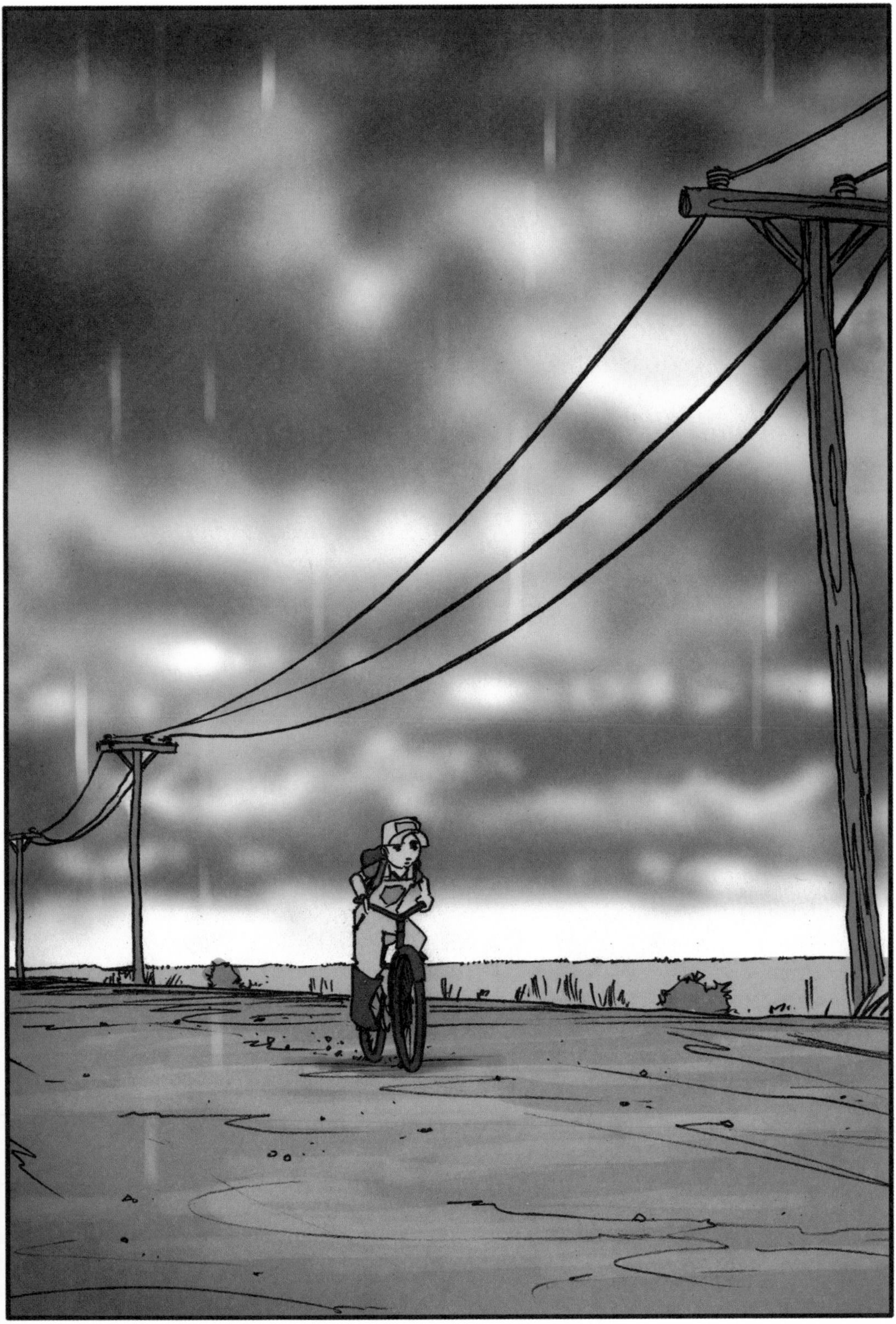

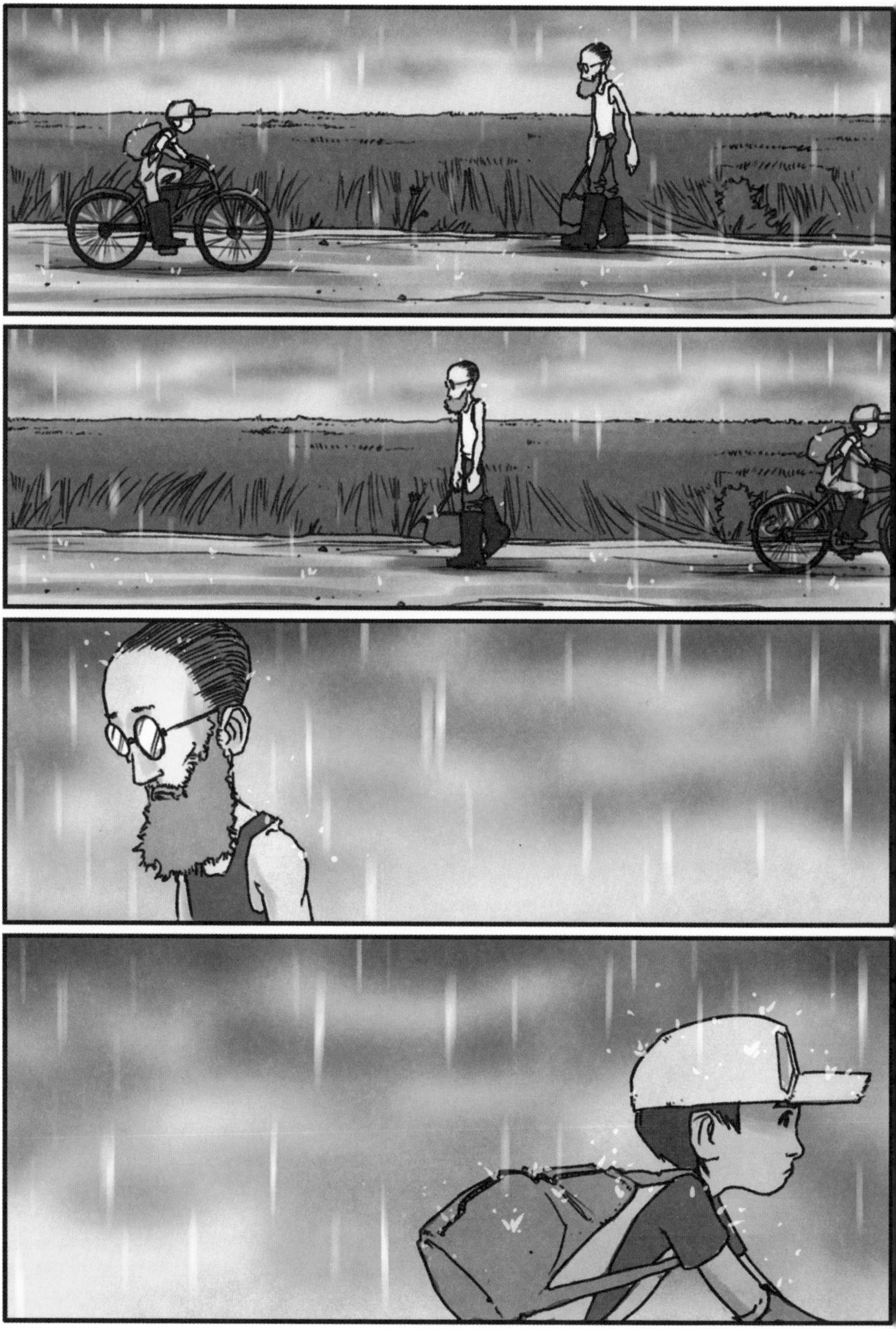

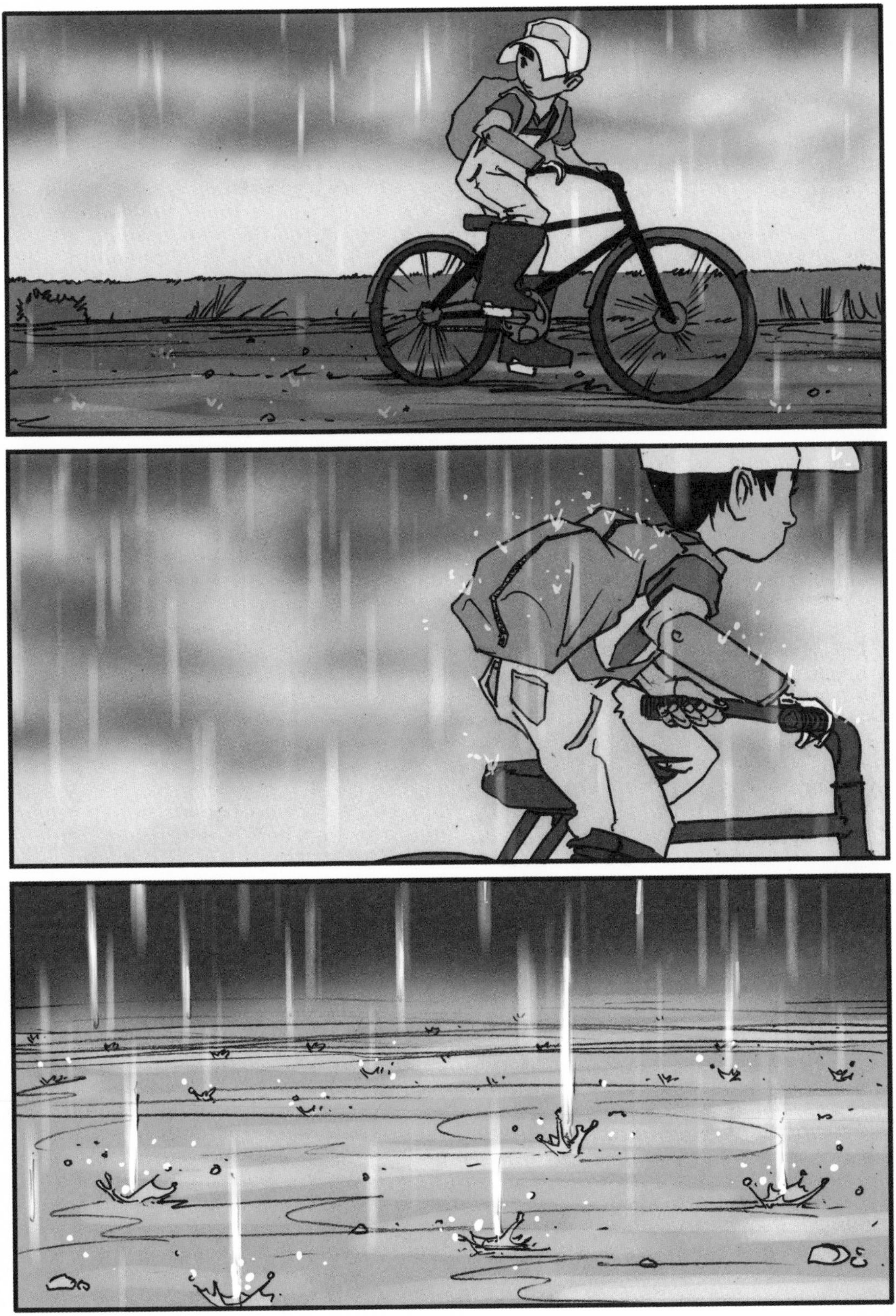

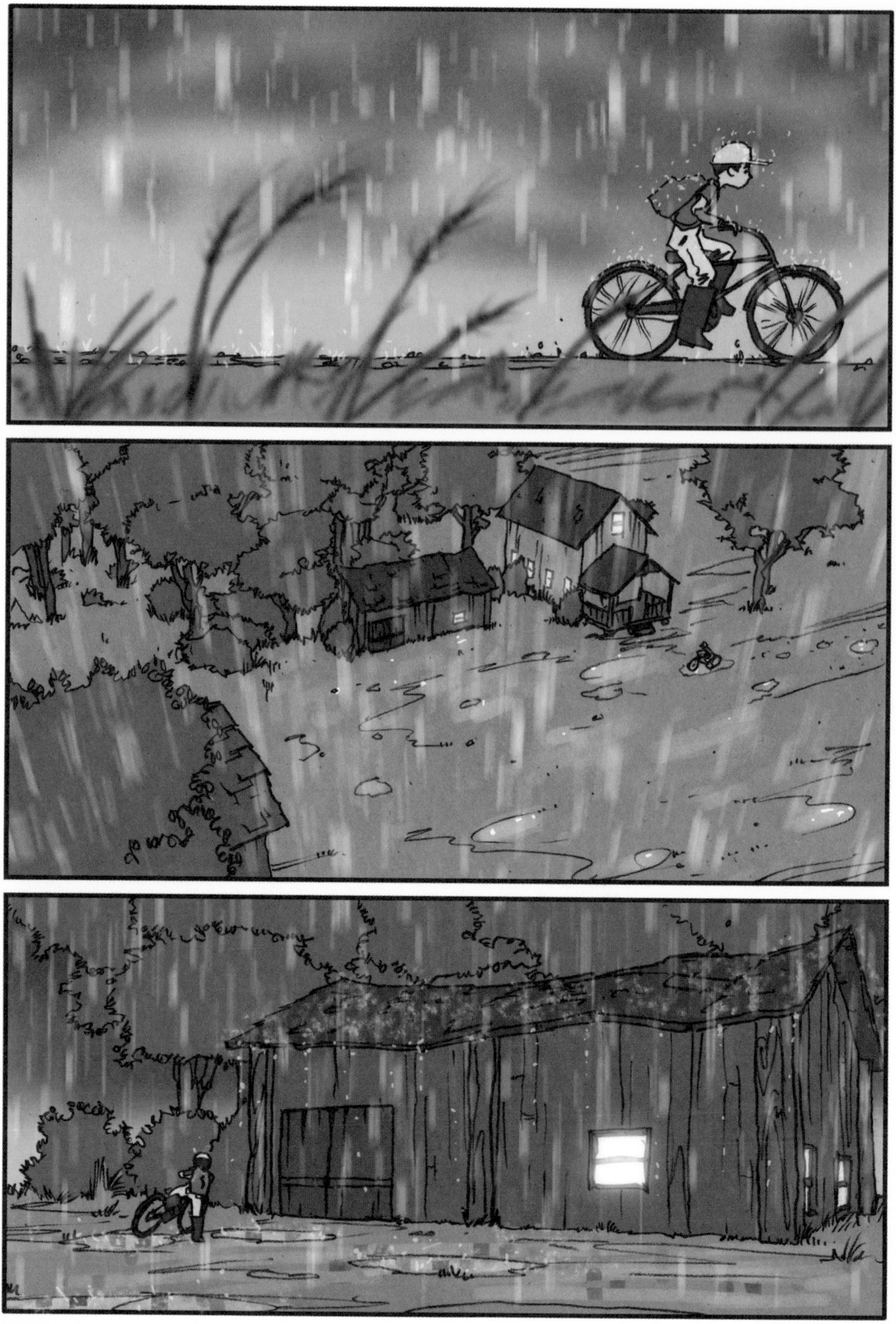

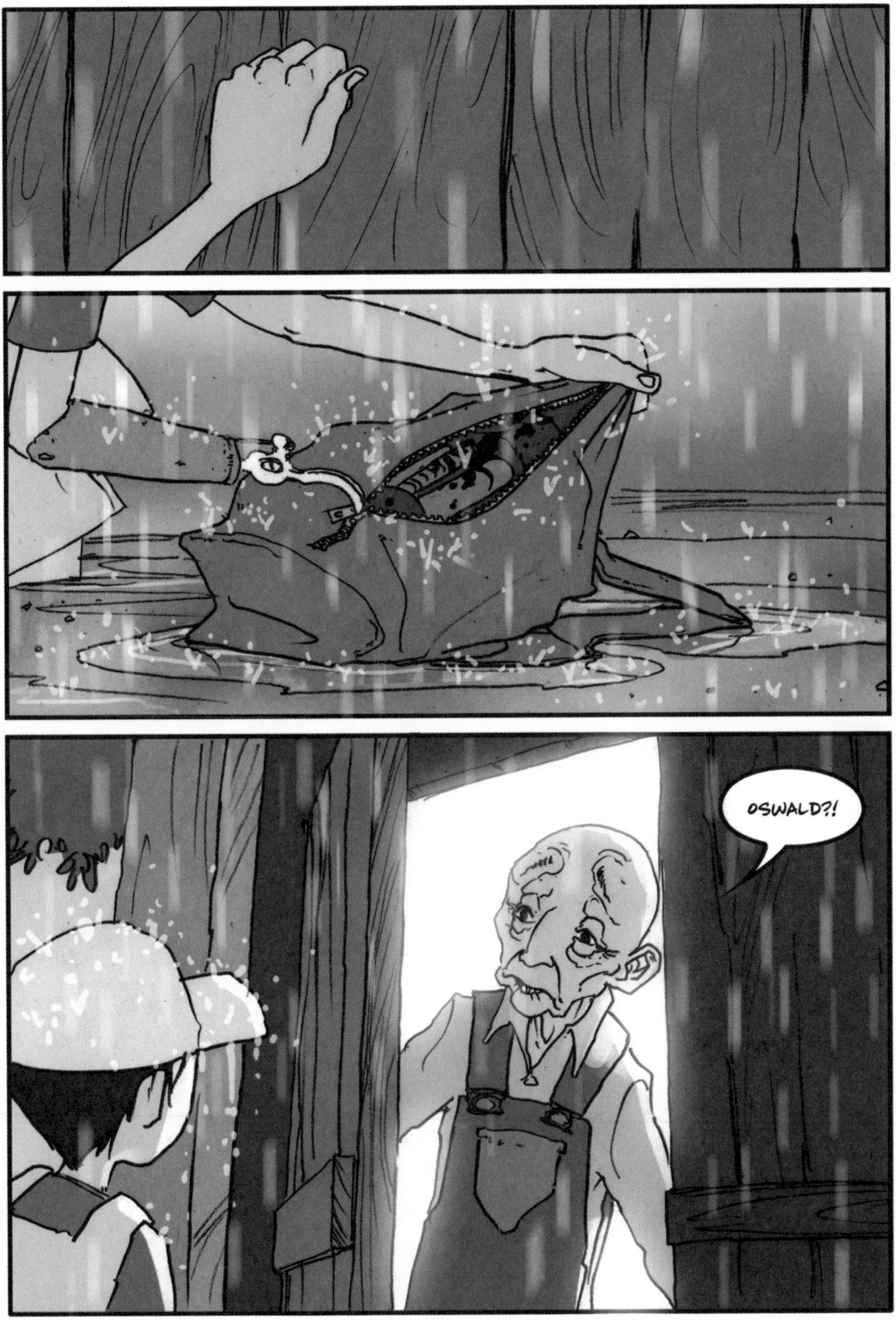
OSWALD?!

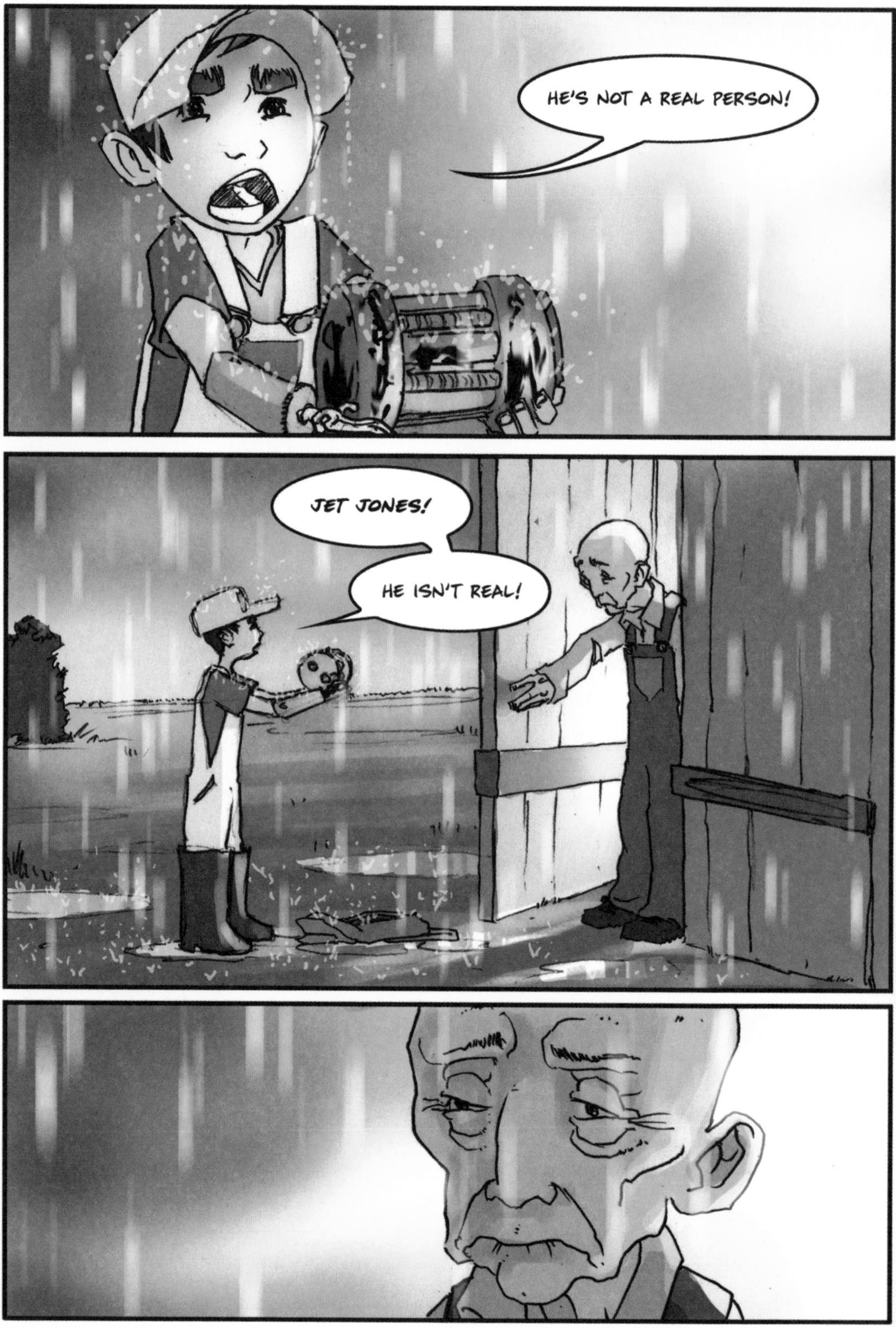
HE'S NOT A REAL PERSON!
JET JONES!
HE ISN'T REAL!

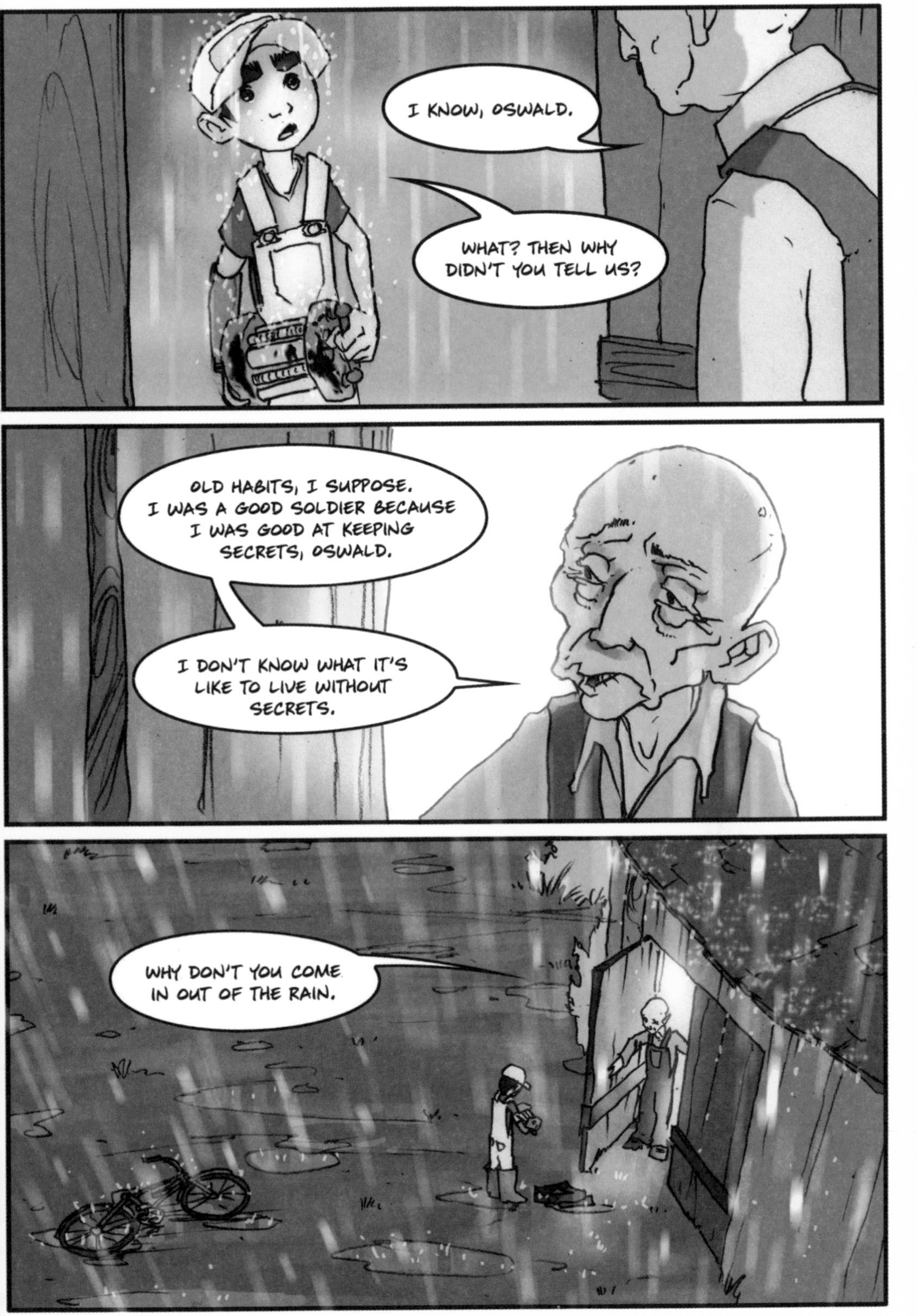
I KNOW, OSWALD.
WHAT? THEN WHY DIDN'T YOU TELL US?
OLD HABITS, I SUPPOSE. I WAS A GOOD SOLDIER BECAUSE I WAS GOOD AT KEEPING SECRETS, OSWALD.
I DON'T KNOW WHAT IT'S LIKE TO LIVE WITHOUT SECRETS.
WHY DON'T YOU COME IN OUT OF THE RAIN.

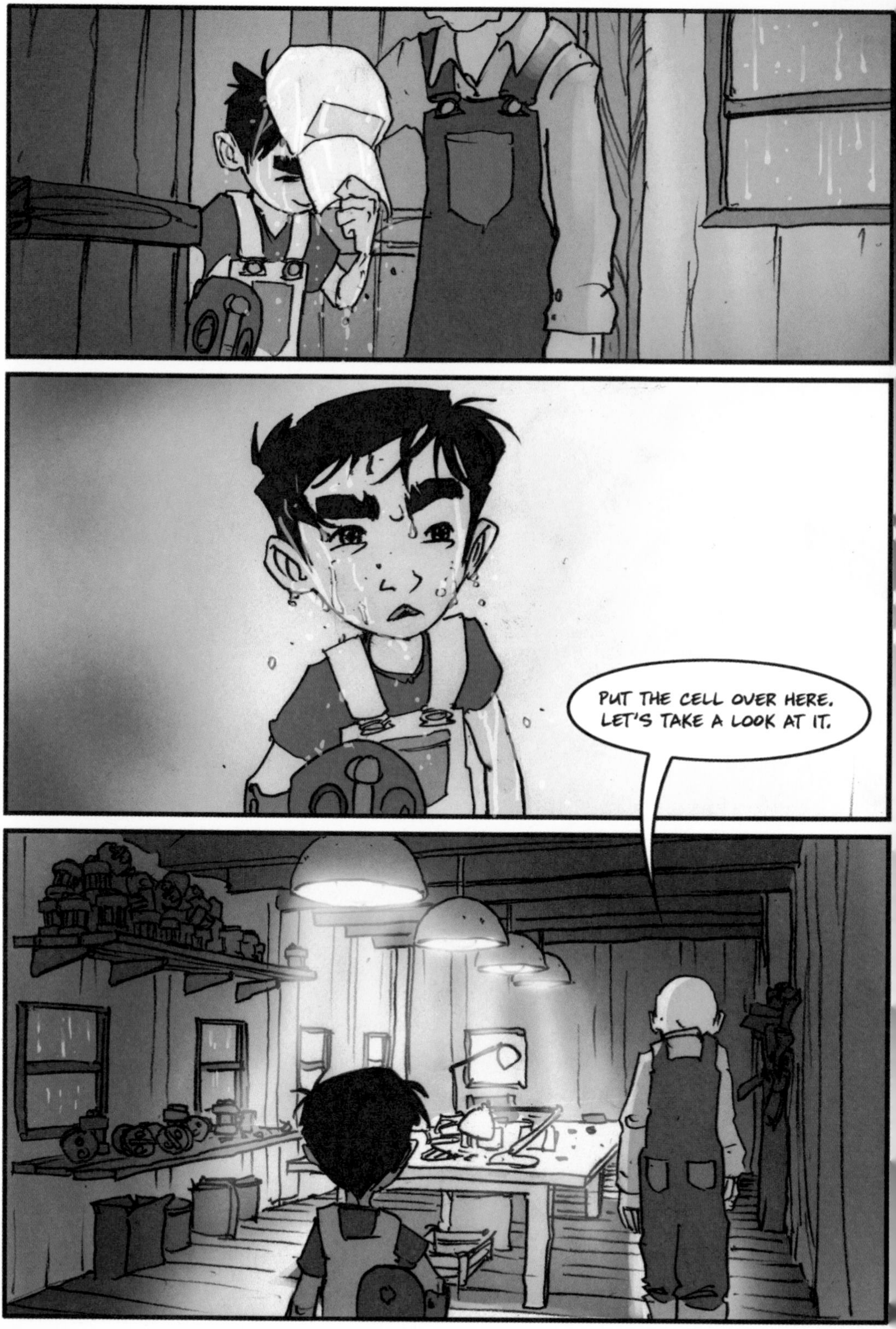
PUT THE CELL OVER HERE.
LET'S TAKE A LOOK AT IT.

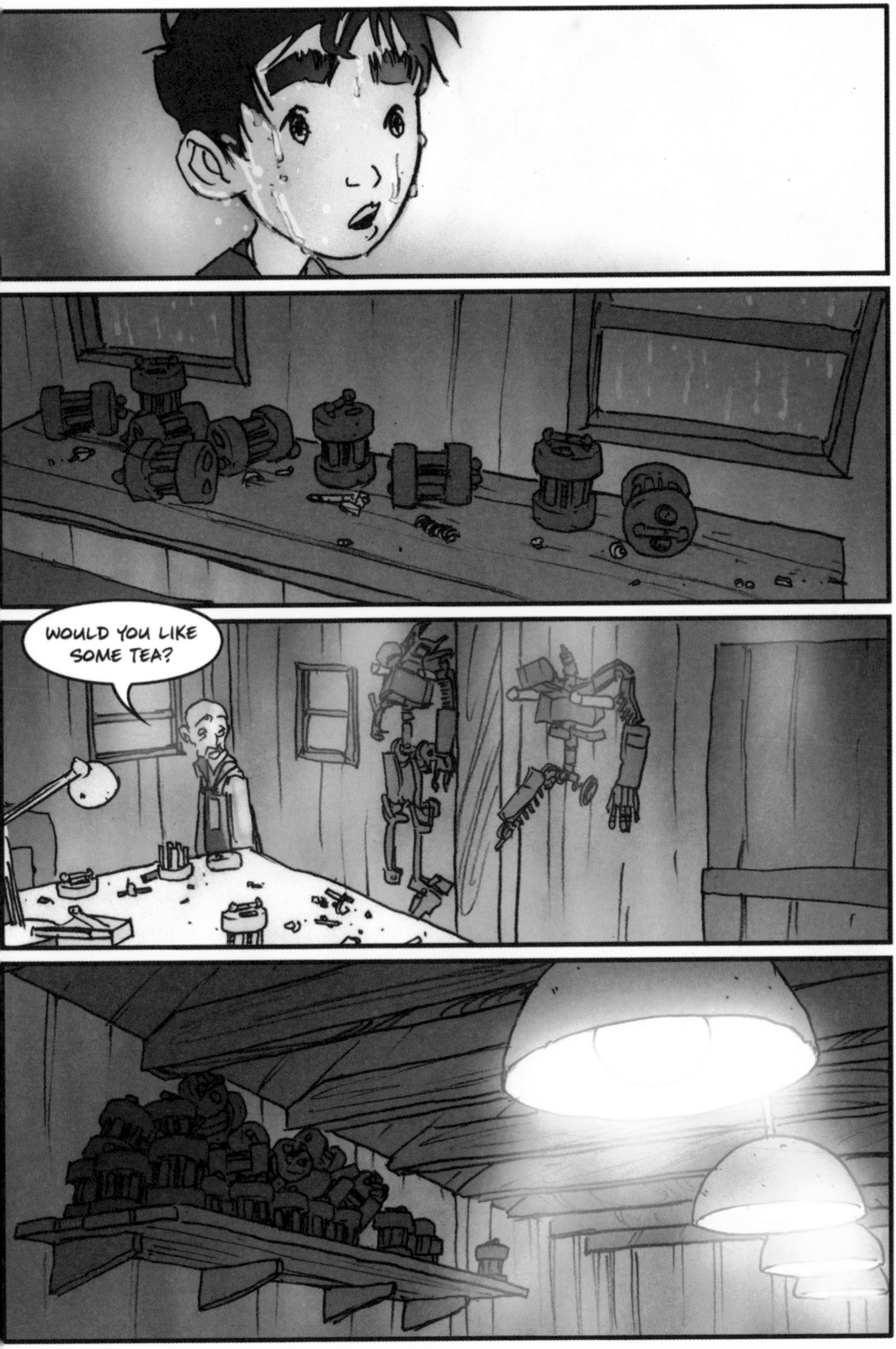
WOULD YOU LIKE SOME TEA?

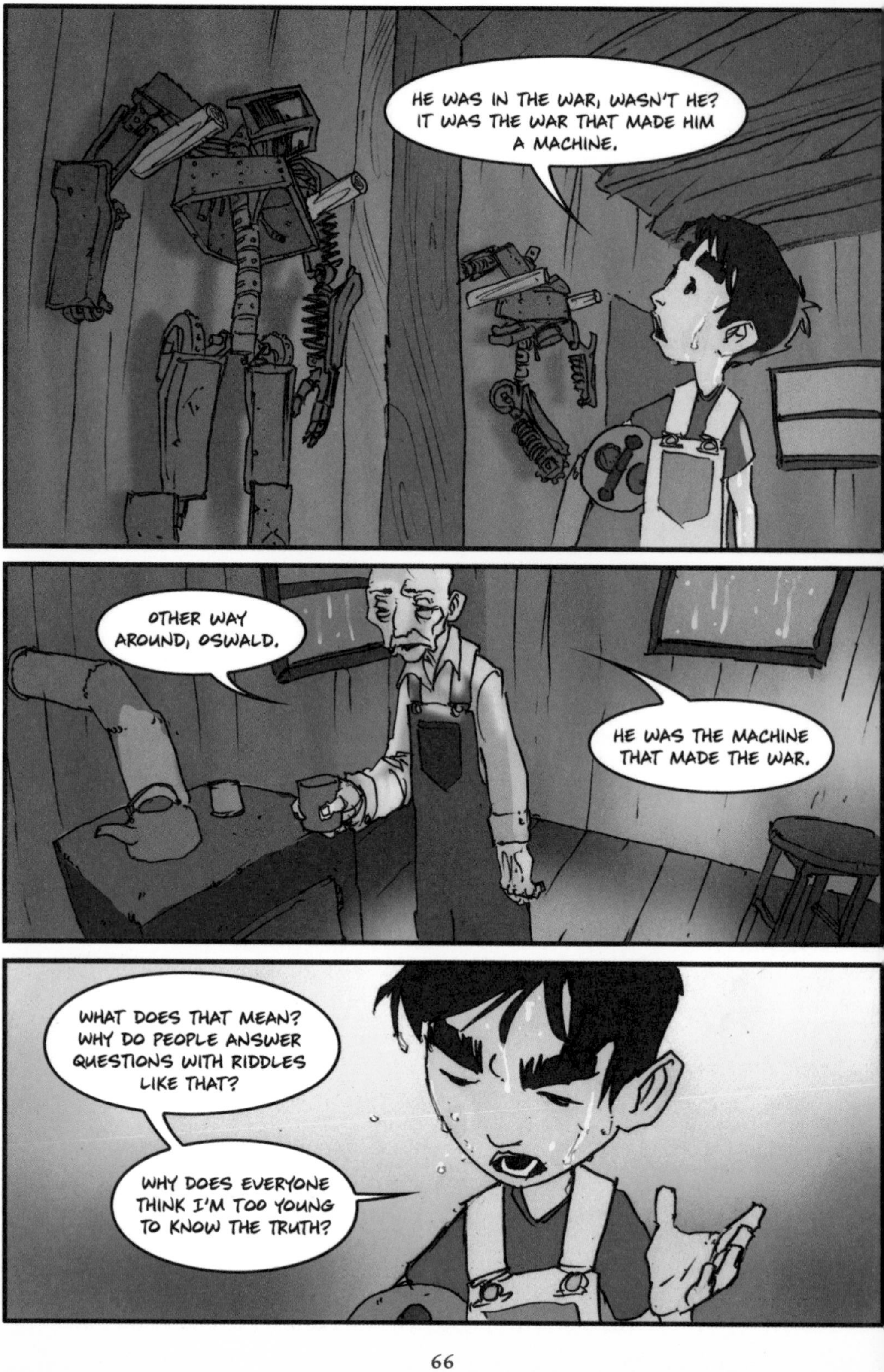
HE WAS IN THE WAR, WASN'T HE? IT WAS THE WAR THAT MADE HIM A MACHINE.
OTHER WAY AROUND, OSWALD.
HE WAS THE MACHINE THAT MADE THE WAR.
WHAT DOES THAT MEAN? WHY DO PEOPLE ANSWER QUESTIONS WITH RIDDLES LIKE THAT?
WHY DOES EVERYONE THINK I'M TOO YOUNG TO KNOW THE TRUTH?

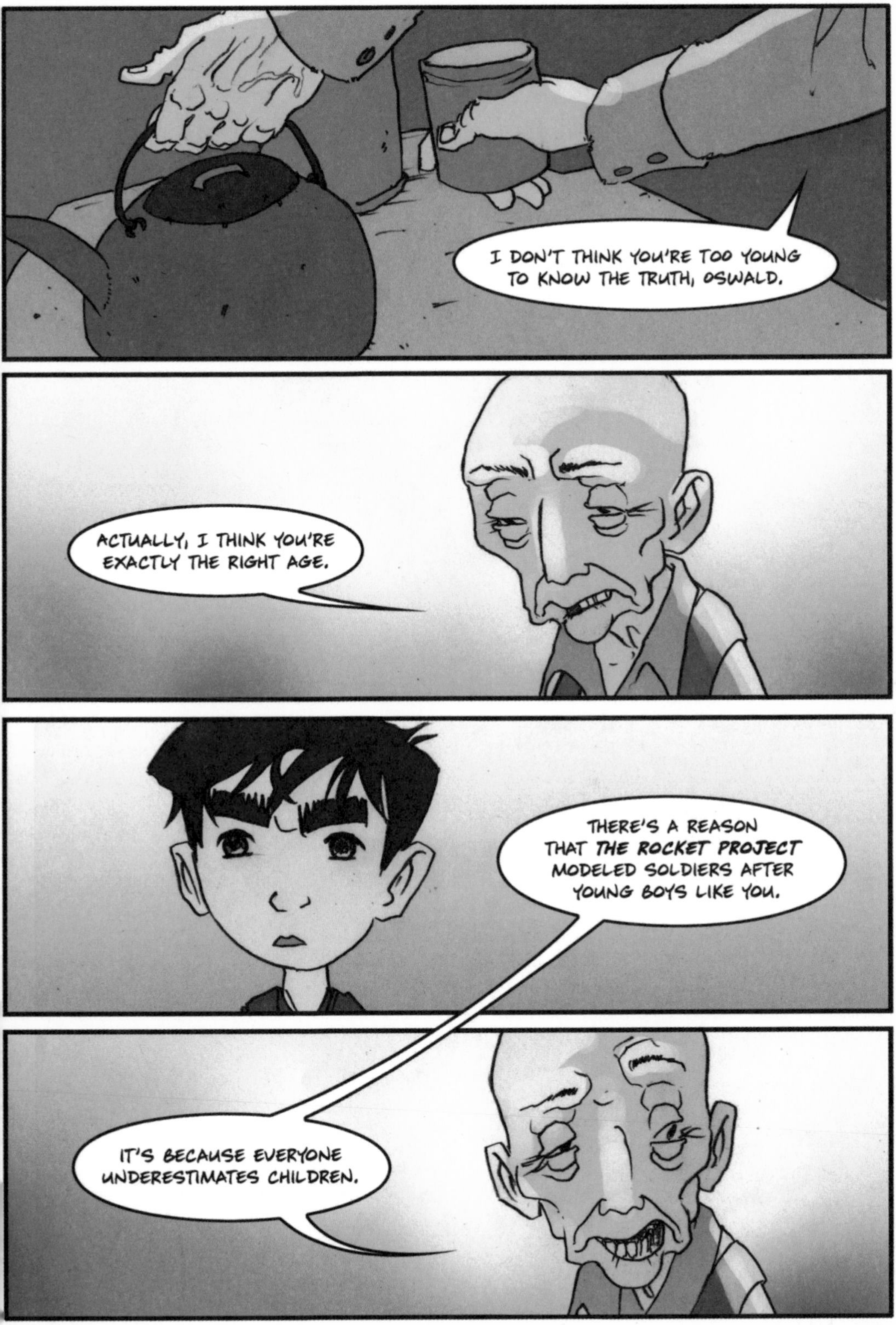
I DON'T THINK YOU'RE TOO YOUNG TO KNOW THE TRUTH, OSWALD.
ACTUALLY, I THINK YOU'RE EXACTLY THE RIGHT AGE.
THERE'S A REASON THAT THE ROCKET PROJECT MODELED SOLDIERS AFTER YOUNG BOYS LIKE YOU.
IT'S BECAUSE EVERYONE UNDERESTIMATES CHILDREN.

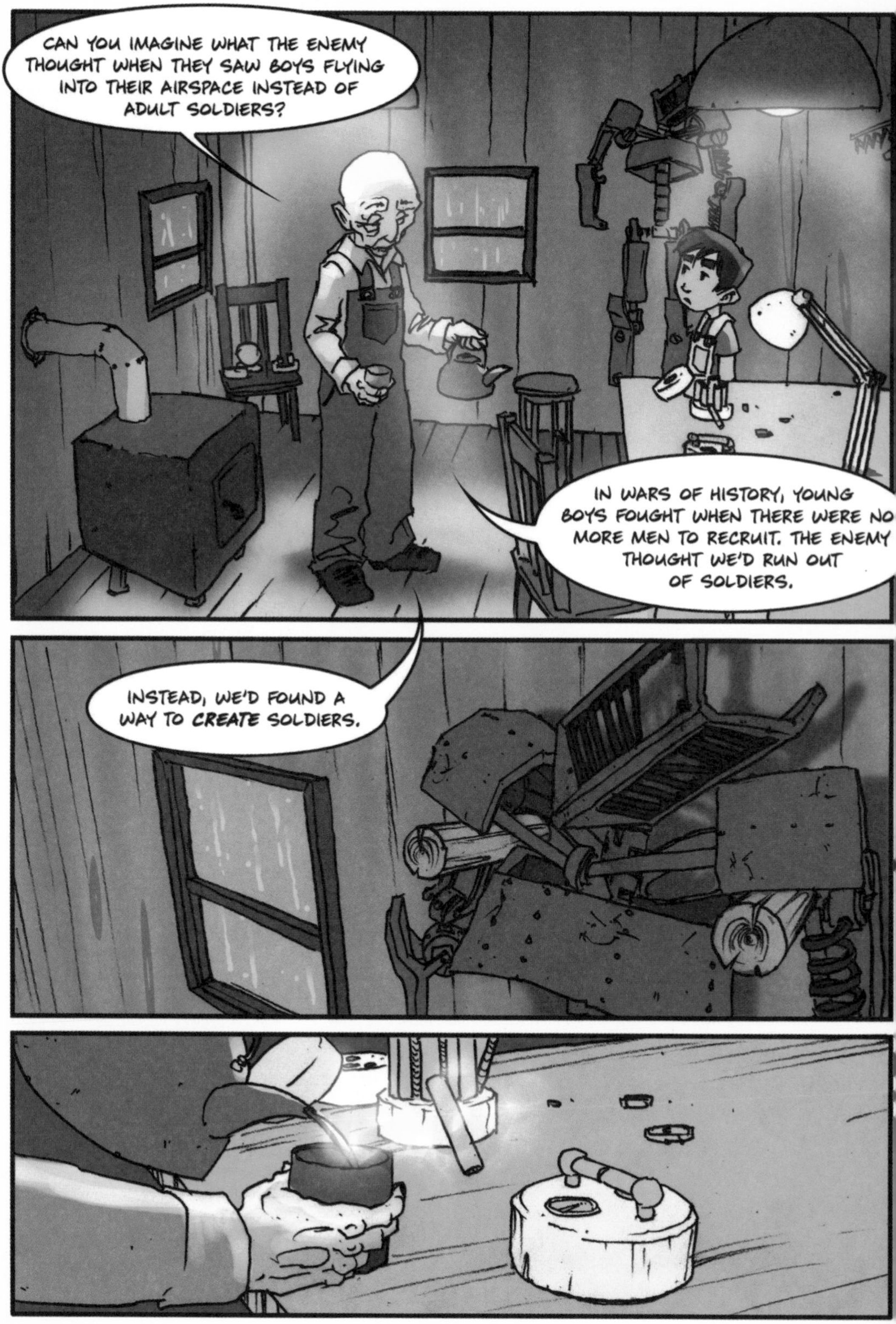
CAN YOU IMAGINE WHAT THE ENEMY THOUGHT WHEN THEY SAW BOYS FLYING INTO THEIR AIRSPACE INSTEAD OF ADULT SOLDIERS?
IN WARS OF HISTORY, YOUNG BOYS FOUGHT WHEN THERE WERE NO MORE MEN TO RECRUIT. THE ENEMY THOUGHT WE'D RUN OUT OF SOLDIERS.
INSTEAD, WE'D FOUND A WAY TO *CREATE* SOLDIERS.

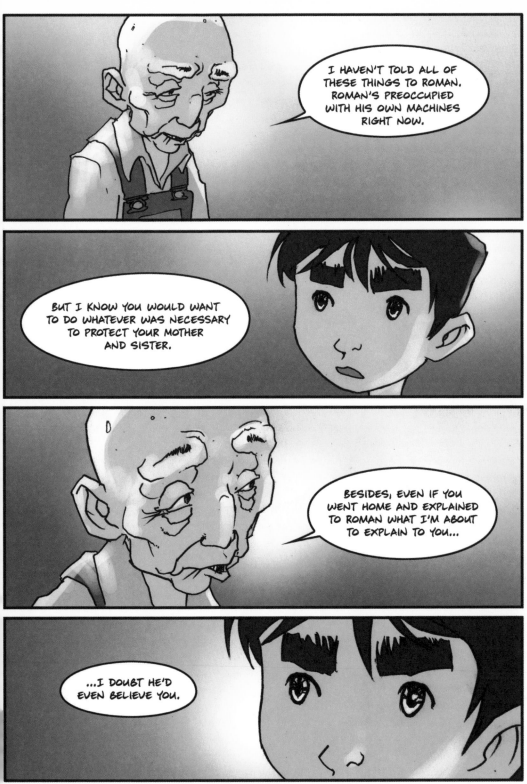

I HAVEN'T TOLD ALL OF THESE THINGS TO ROMAN. ROMAN'S PREOCCUPIED WITH HIS OWN MACHINES RIGHT NOW.

BUT I KNOW YOU WOULD WANT TO DO WHATEVER WAS NECESSARY TO PROTECT YOUR MOTHER AND SISTER.

BESIDES, EVEN IF YOU WENT HOME AND EXPLAINED TO ROMAN WHAT I'M ABOUT TO EXPLAIN TO YOU...

...I DOUBT HE'D EVEN BELIEVE YOU.

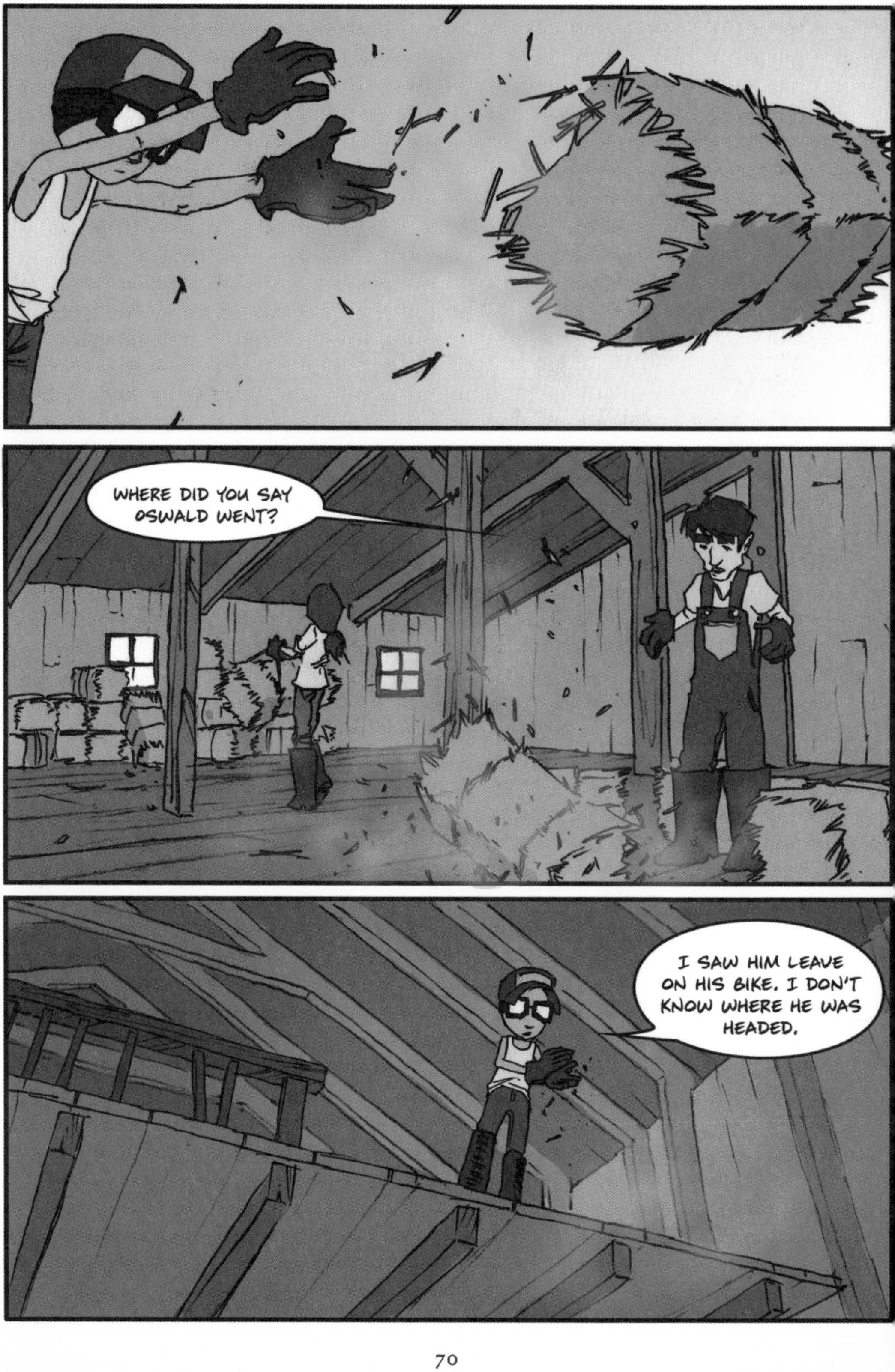
WHERE DID YOU SAY OSWALD WENT?
I SAW HIM LEAVE ON HIS BIKE. I DON'T KNOW WHERE HE WAS HEADED.

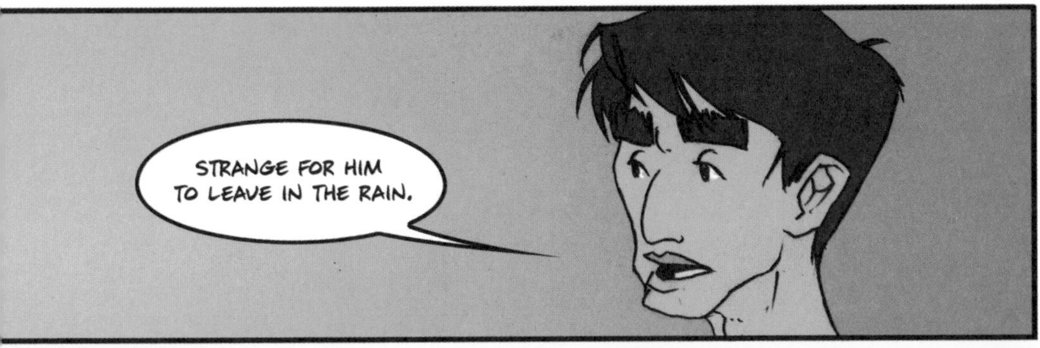
STRANGE FOR HIM TO LEAVE IN THE RAIN.

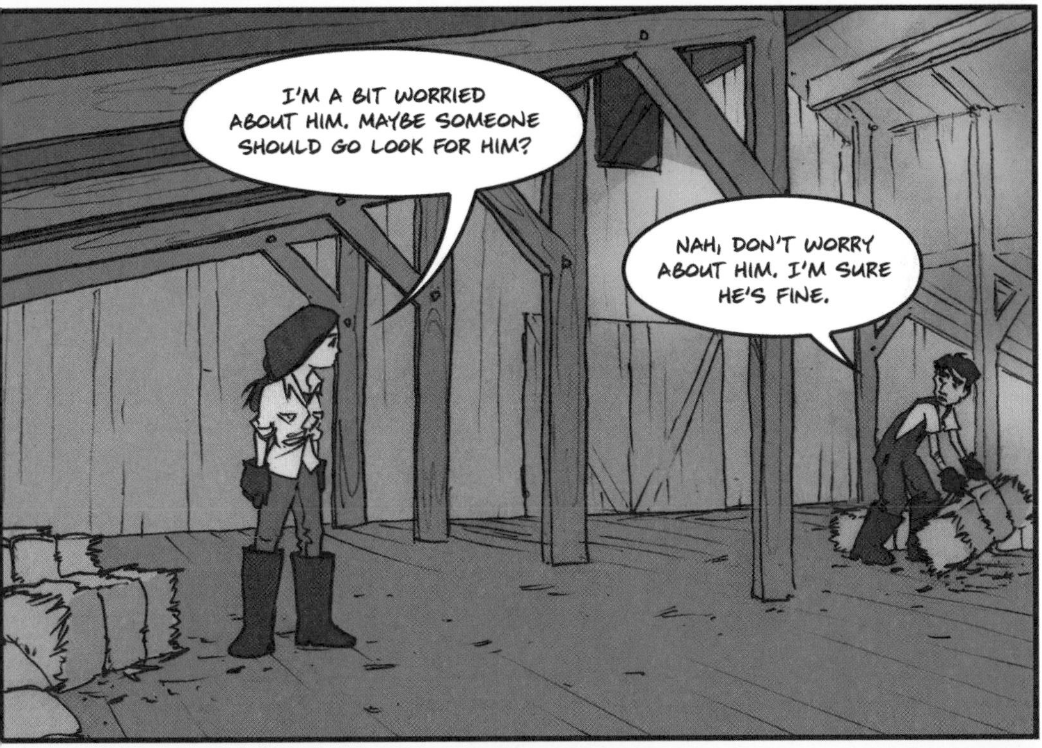
I'M A BIT WORRIED ABOUT HIM. MAYBE SOMEONE SHOULD GO LOOK FOR HIM?
NAH, DON'T WORRY ABOUT HIM. I'M SURE HE'S FINE.

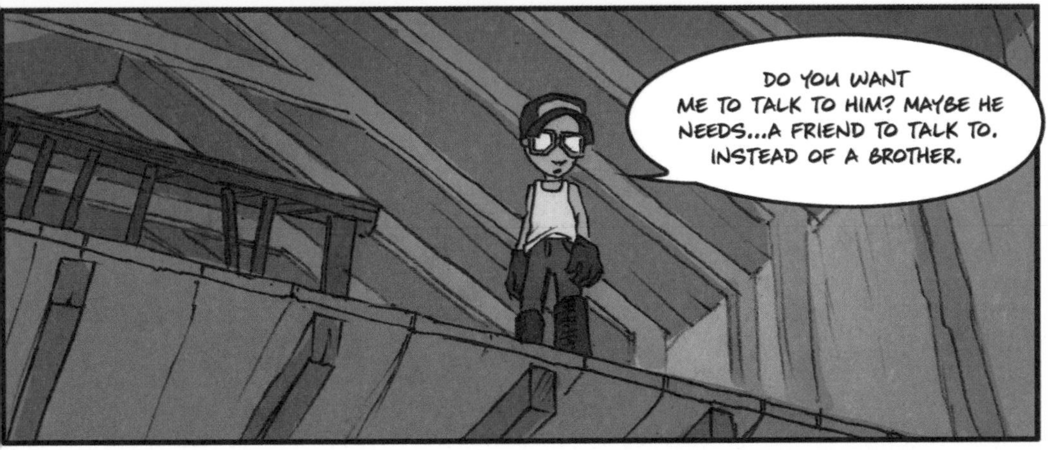
DO YOU WANT ME TO TALK TO HIM? MAYBE HE NEEDS...A FRIEND TO TALK TO. INSTEAD OF A BROTHER.

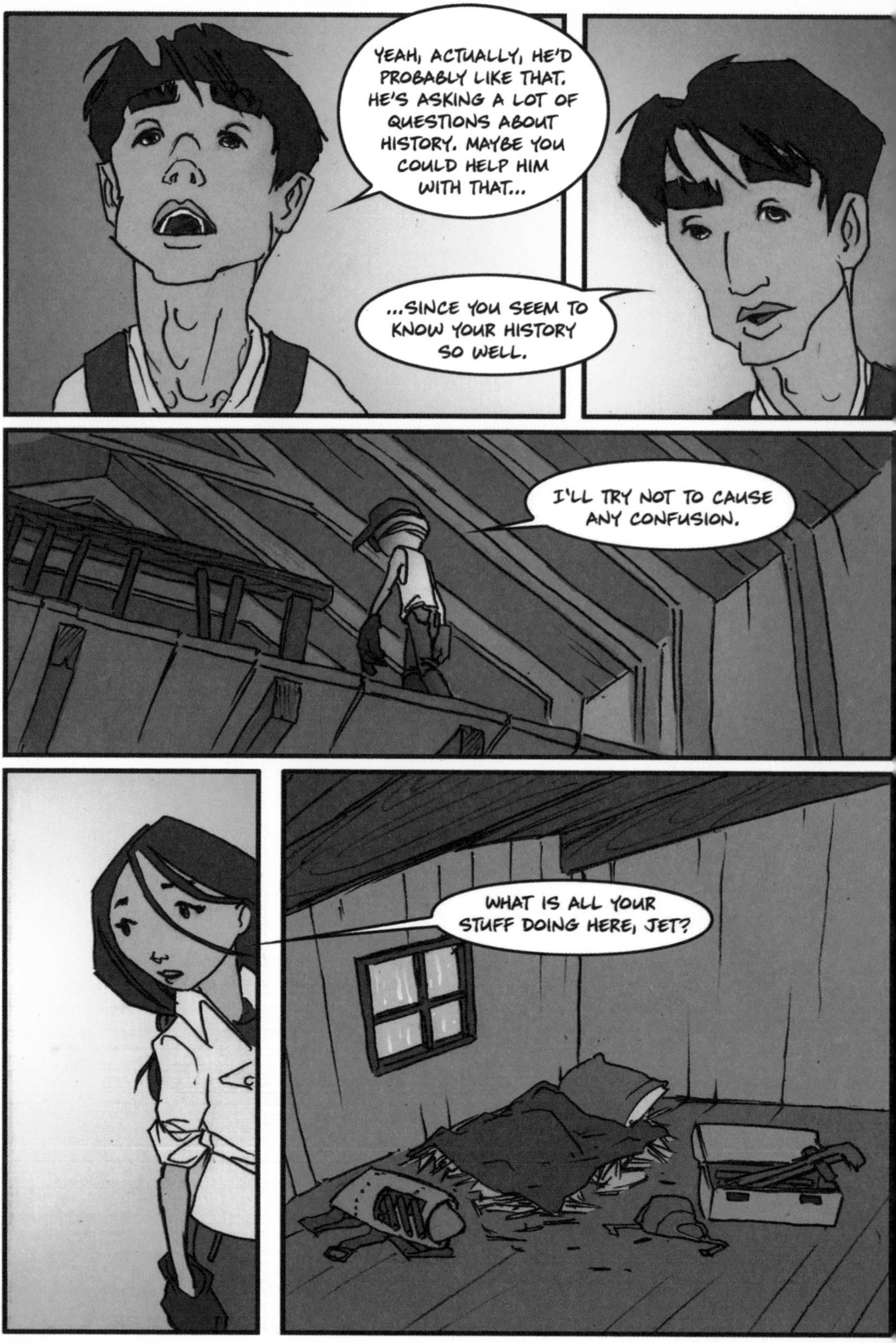
YEAH, ACTUALLY, HE'D PROBABLY LIKE THAT. HE'S ASKING A LOT OF QUESTIONS ABOUT HISTORY. MAYBE YOU COULD HELP HIM WITH THAT...
...SINCE YOU SEEM TO KNOW YOUR HISTORY SO WELL.
I'LL TRY NOT TO CAUSE ANY CONFUSION.
WHAT IS ALL YOUR STUFF DOING HERE, JET?

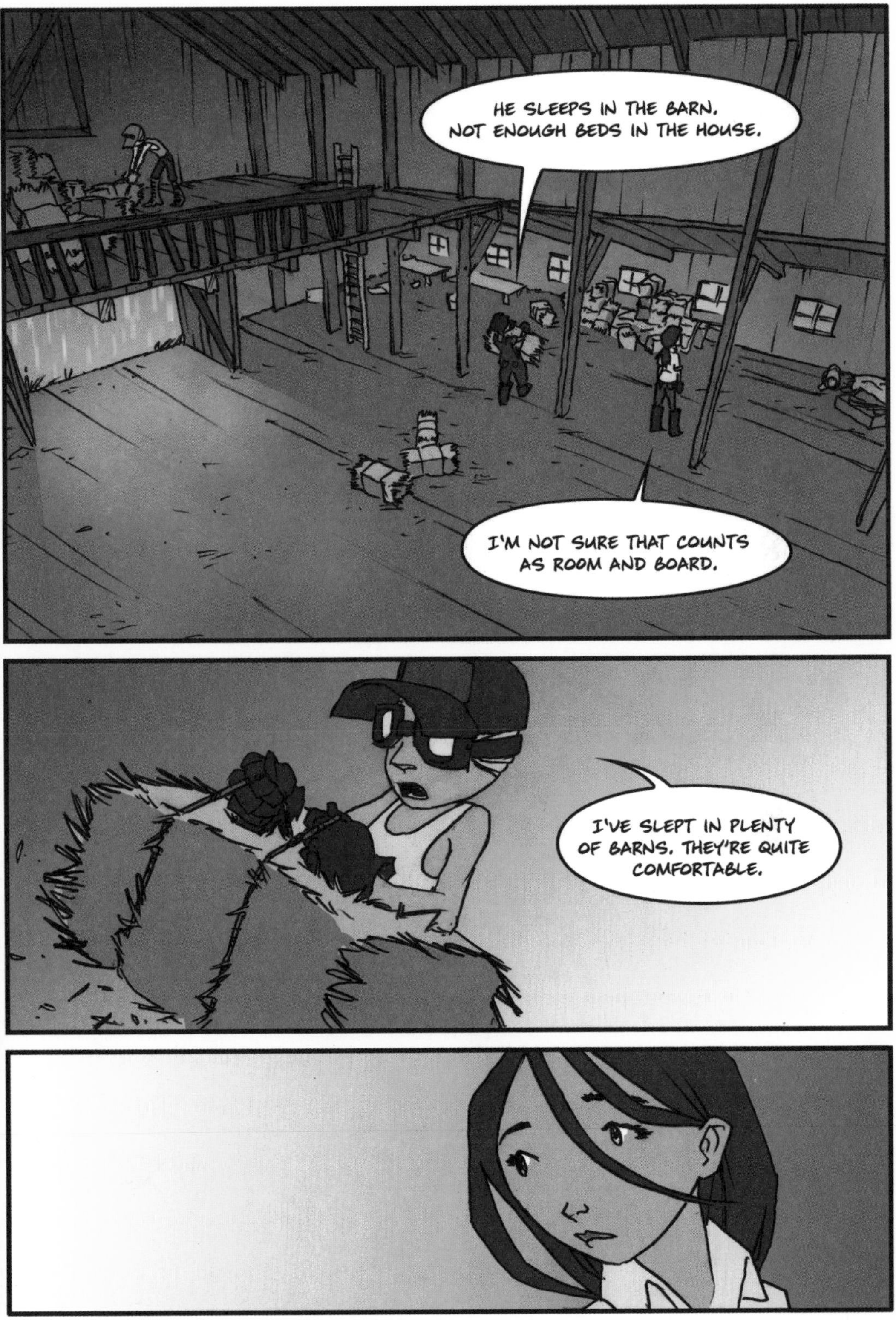
HE SLEEPS IN THE BARN. NOT ENOUGH BEDS IN THE HOUSE.
I'M NOT SURE THAT COUNTS AS ROOM AND BOARD.
I'VE SLEPT IN PLENTY OF BARNS. THEY'RE QUITE COMFORTABLE.

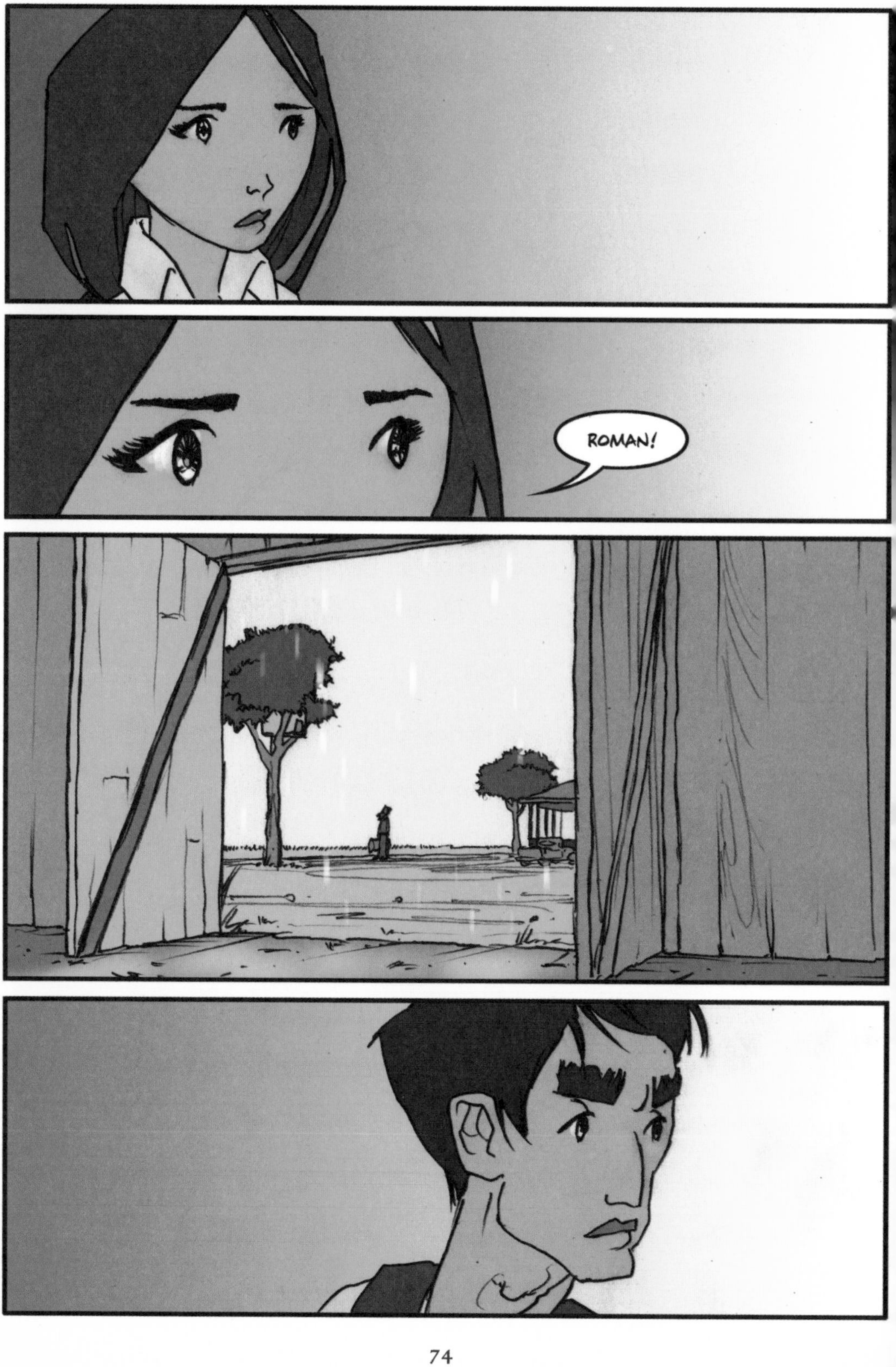
ROMAN!

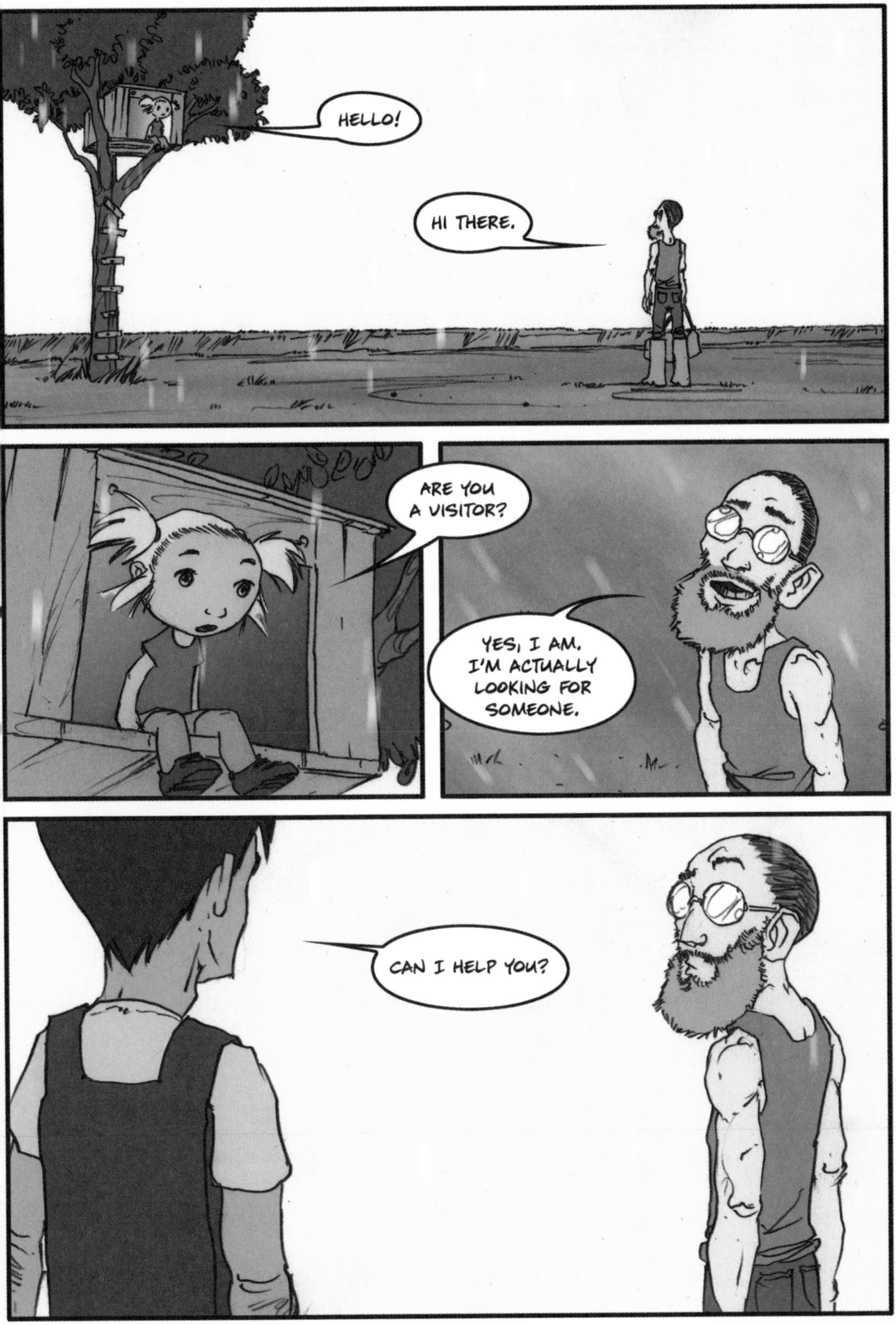
HELLO!
HI THERE.
ARE YOU A VISITOR?
YES, I AM. I'M ACTUALLY LOOKING FOR SOMEONE.
CAN I HELP YOU?

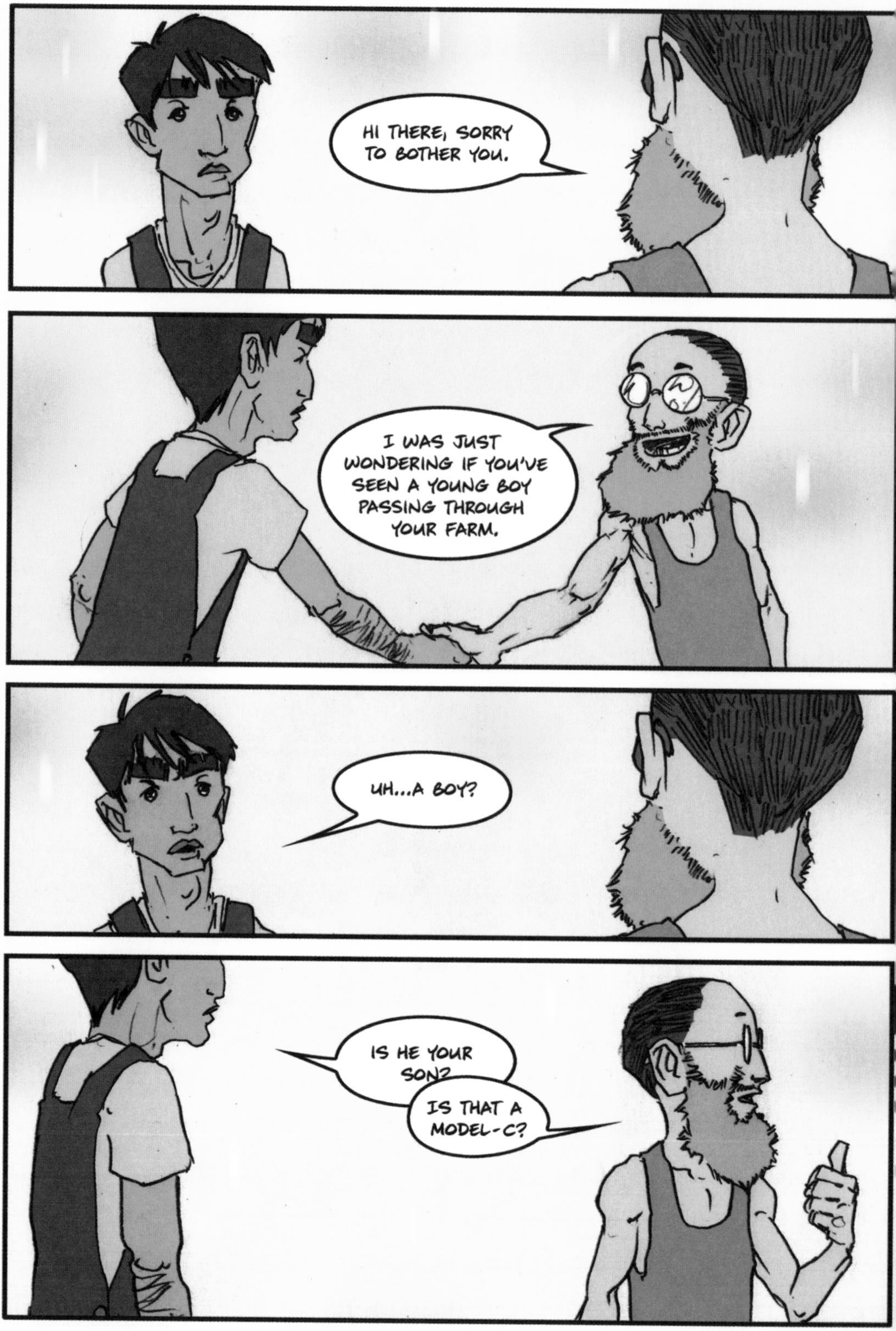
HI THERE, SORRY TO BOTHER YOU.
I WAS JUST WONDERING IF YOU'VE SEEN A YOUNG BOY PASSING THROUGH YOUR FARM.
UH...A BOY?
IS HE YOUR SON?
IS THAT A MODEL-C?

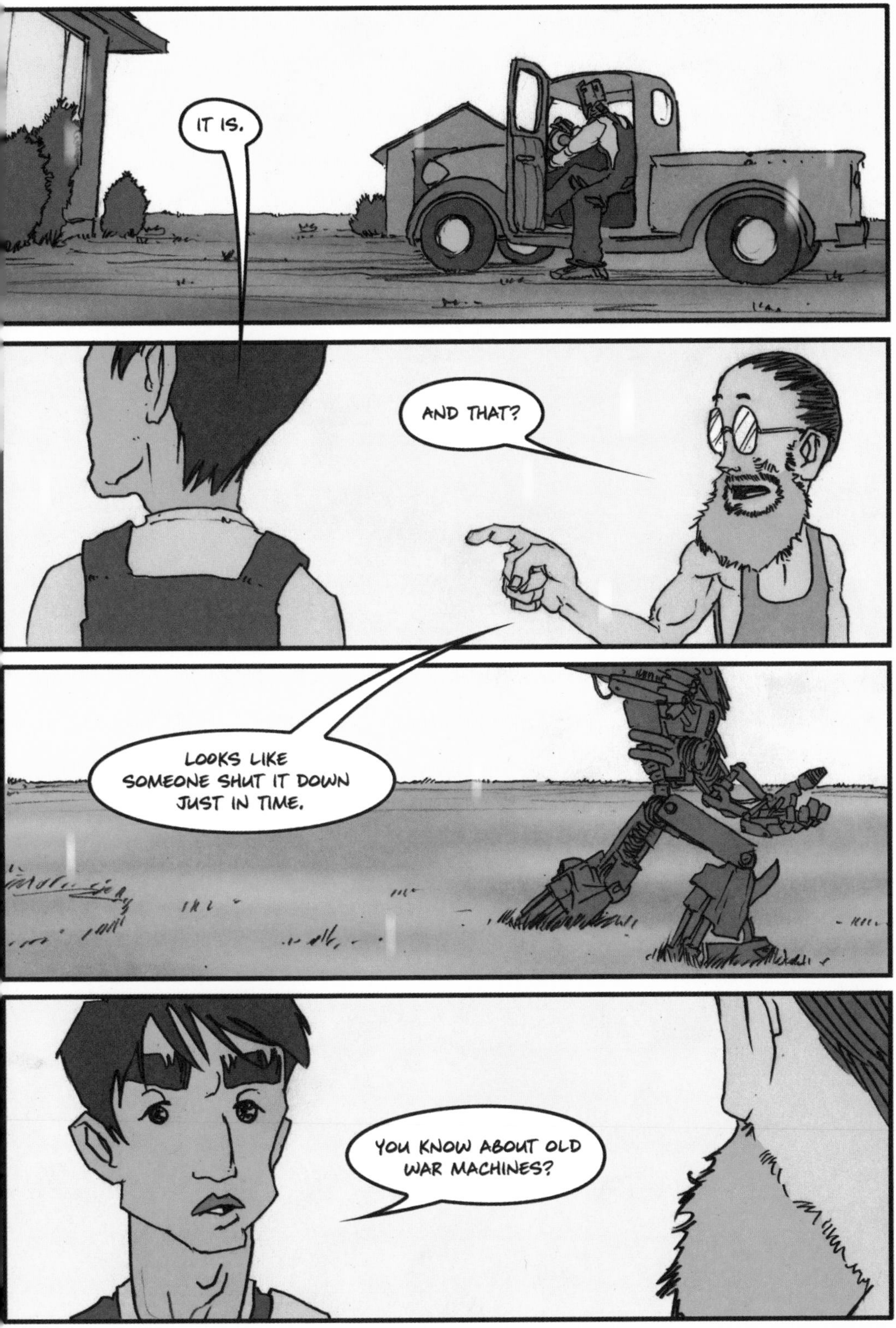
IT IS.
AND THAT?
LOOKS LIKE SOMEONE SHUT IT DOWN JUST IN TIME.
YOU KNOW ABOUT OLD WAR MACHINES?

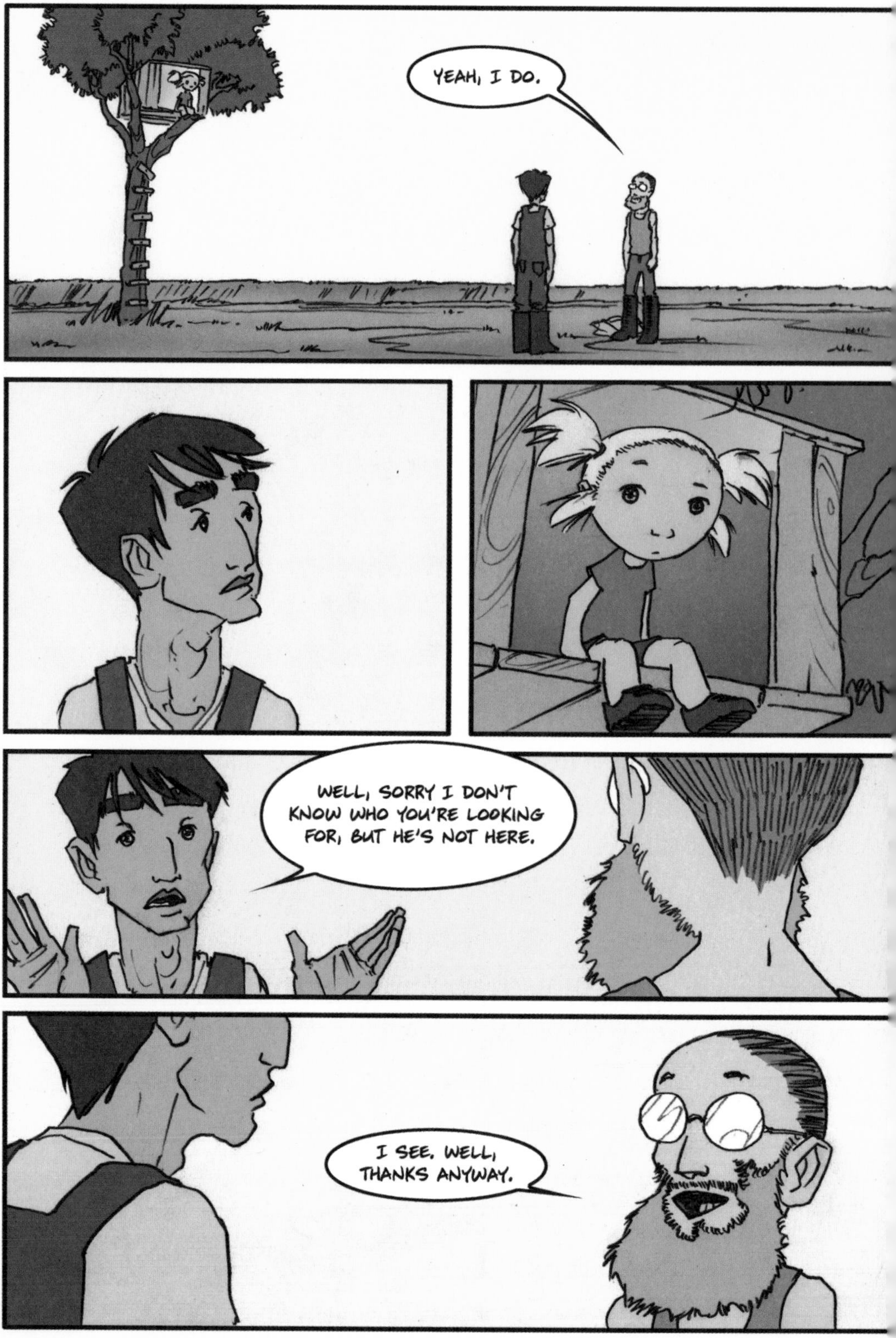
YEAH, I DO.
WELL, SORRY I DON'T KNOW WHO YOU'RE LOOKING FOR, BUT HE'S NOT HERE.
I SEE. WELL, THANKS ANYWAY.

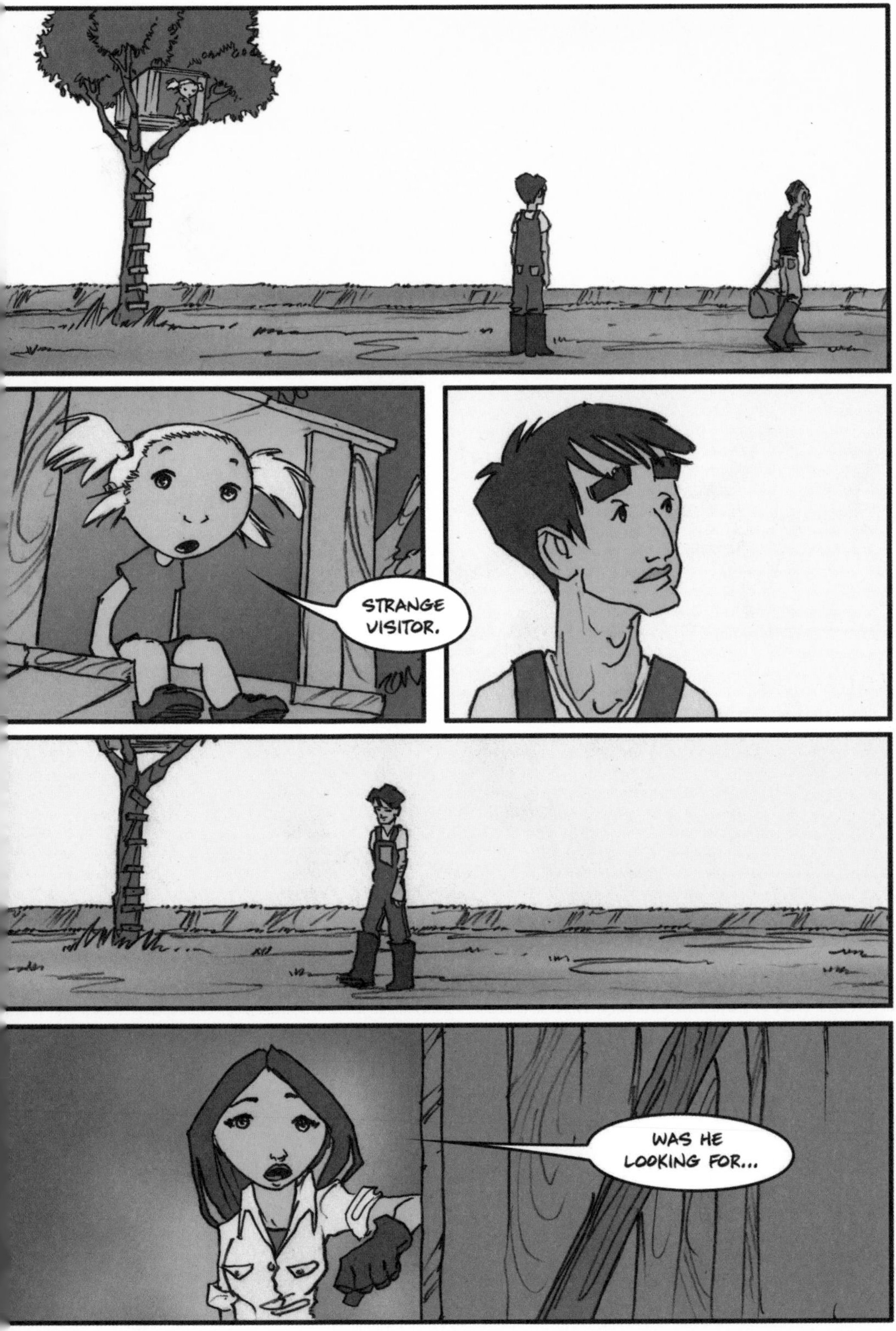
STRANGE VISITOR.
WAS HE LOOKING FOR...

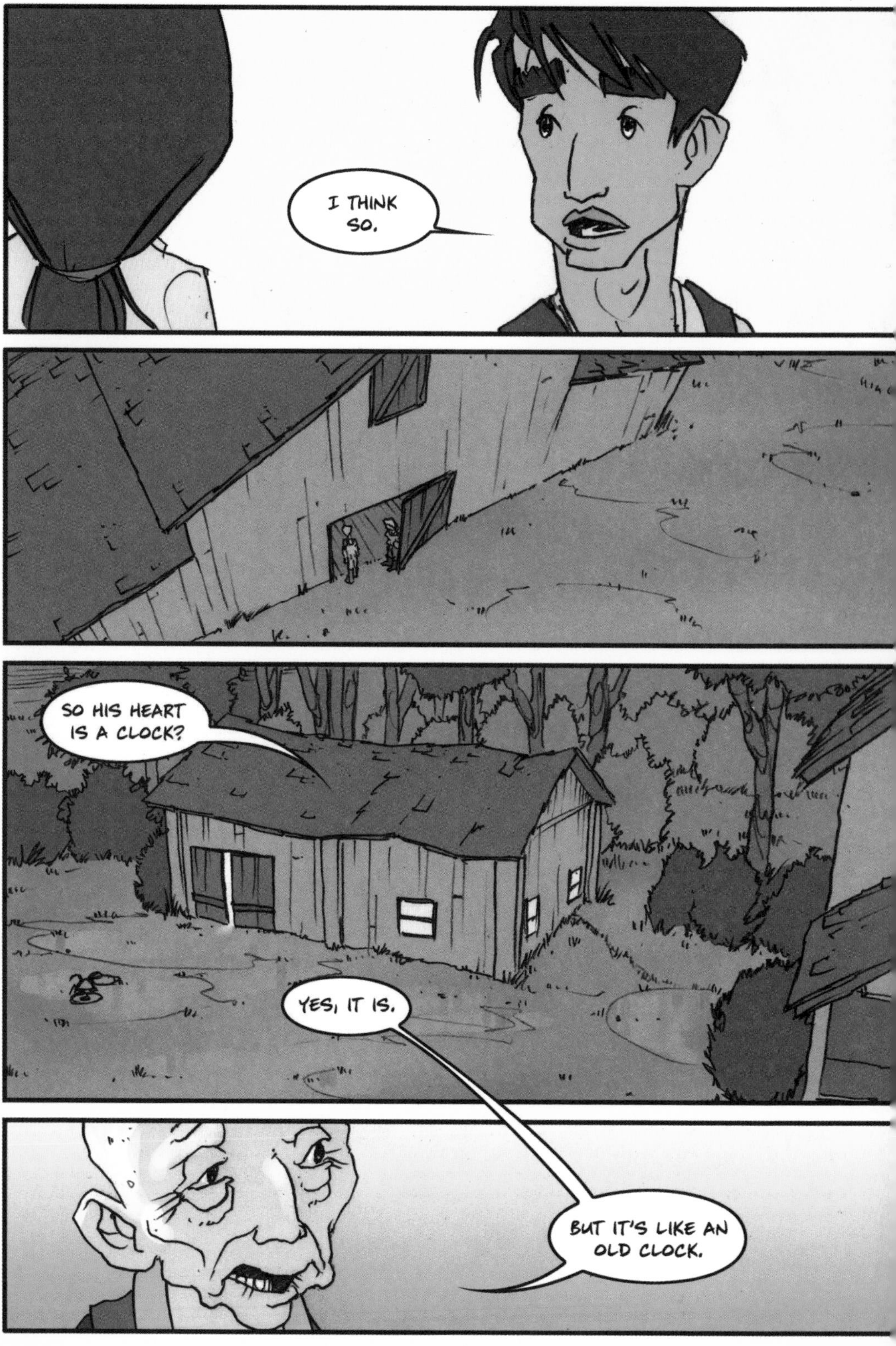
I THINK SO.
SO HIS HEART IS A CLOCK?
YES, IT IS.
BUT IT'S LIKE AN OLD CLOCK.

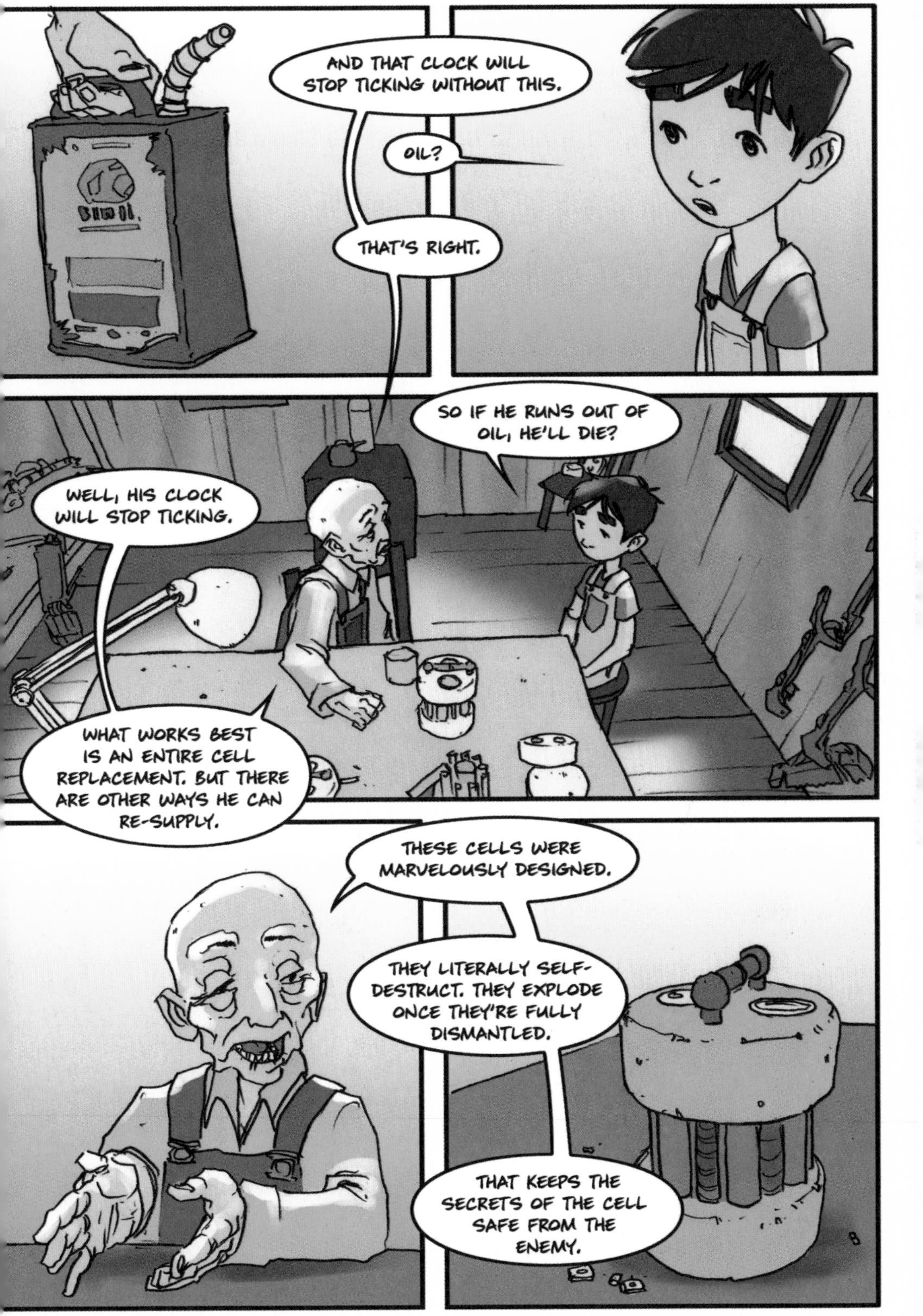
AND THAT CLOCK WILL STOP TICKING WITHOUT THIS.
OIL?
THAT'S RIGHT.
SO IF HE RUNS OUT OF OIL, HE'LL DIE?
WELL, HIS CLOCK WILL STOP TICKING.
WHAT WORKS BEST IS AN ENTIRE CELL REPLACEMENT. BUT THERE ARE OTHER WAYS HE CAN RE-SUPPLY.
THESE CELLS WERE MARVELOUSLY DESIGNED.
THEY LITERALLY SELF-DESTRUCT. THEY EXPLODE ONCE THEY'RE FULLY DISMANTLED.
THAT KEEPS THE SECRETS OF THE CELL SAFE FROM THE ENEMY.

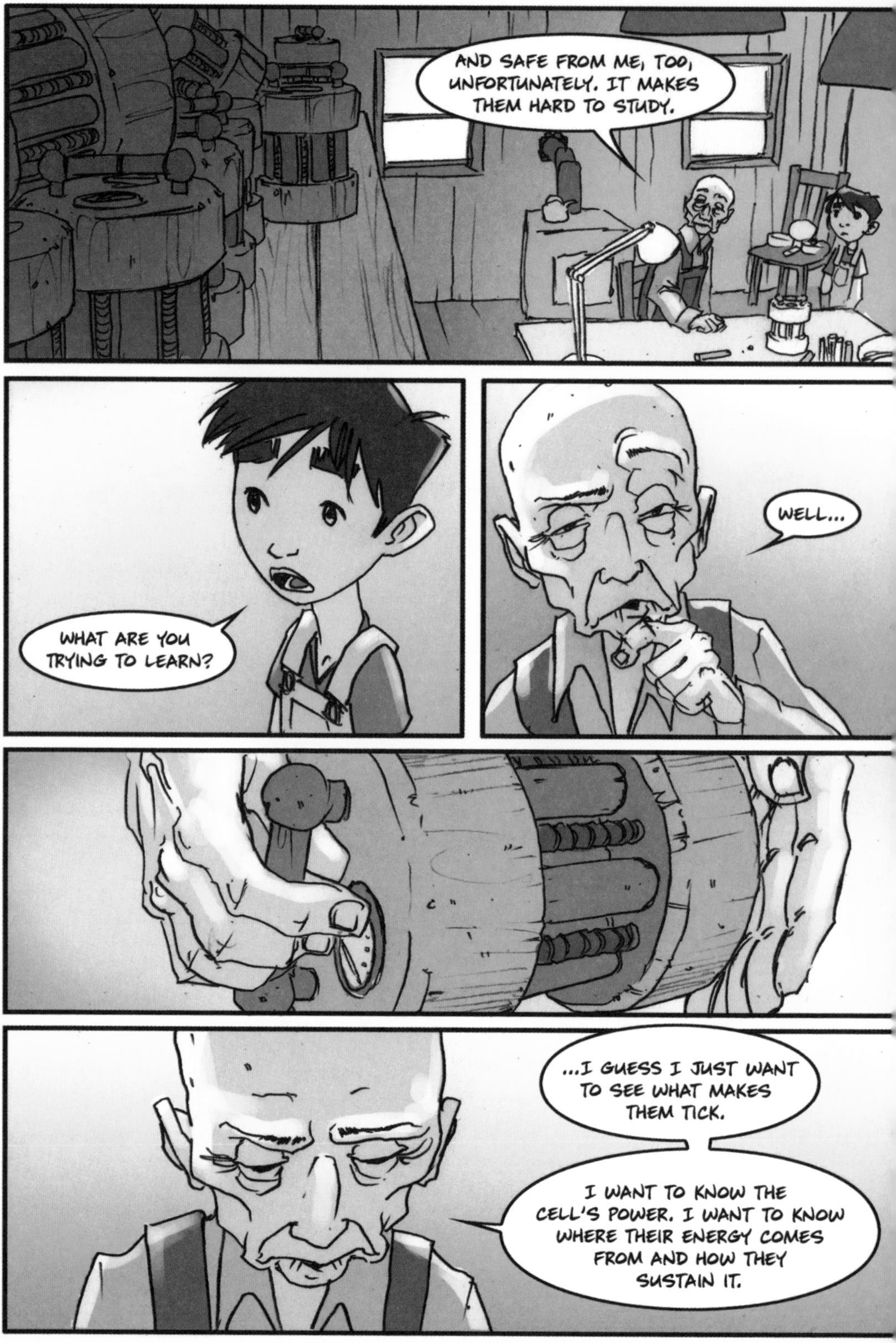
AND SAFE FROM ME, TOO, UNFORTUNATELY. IT MAKES THEM HARD TO STUDY.
WHAT ARE YOU TRYING TO LEARN?
WELL...
...I GUESS I JUST WANT TO SEE WHAT MAKES THEM TICK.
I WANT TO KNOW THE CELL'S POWER. I WANT TO KNOW WHERE THEIR ENERGY COMES FROM AND HOW THEY SUSTAIN IT.

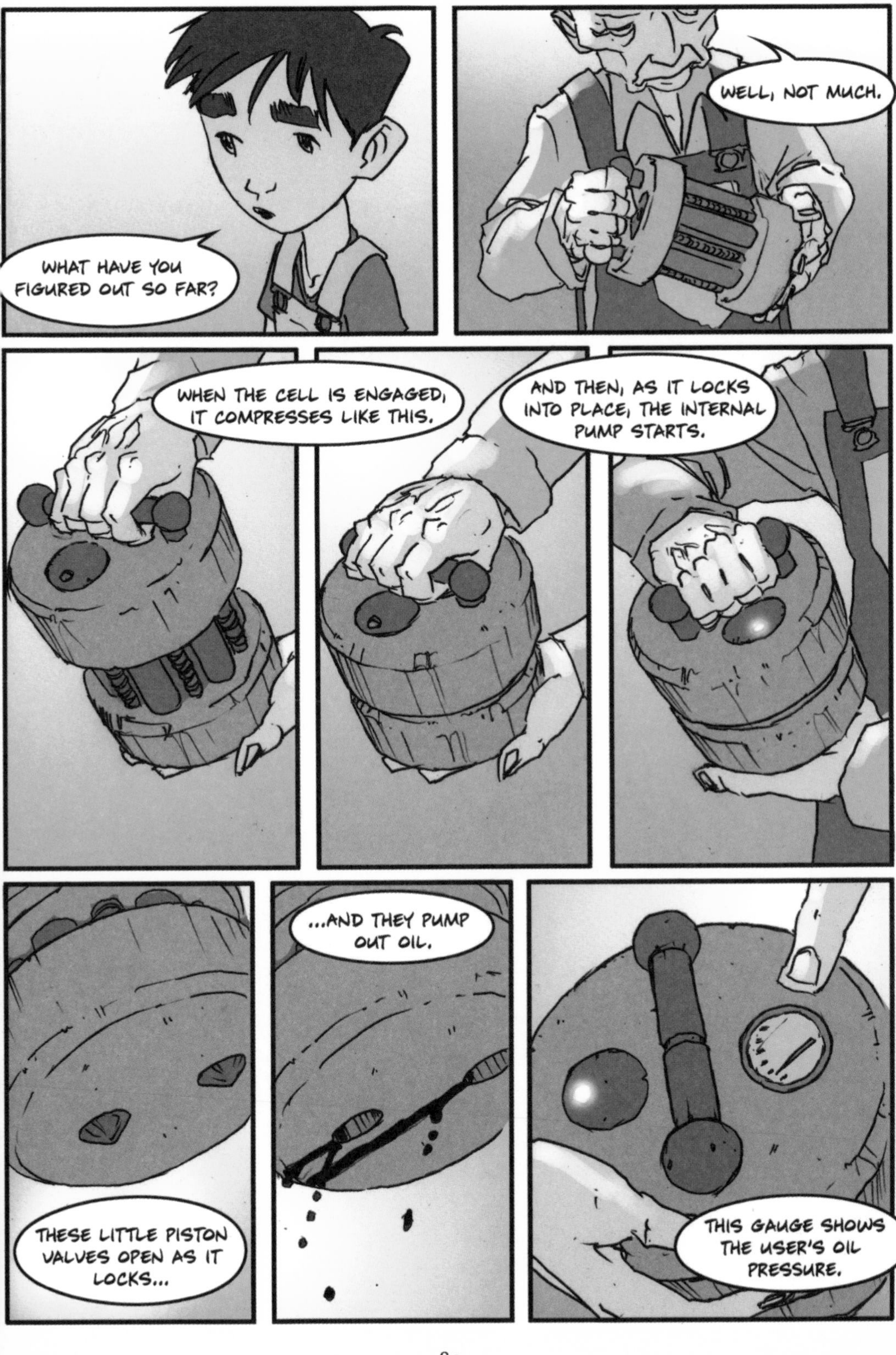
WHAT HAVE YOU FIGURED OUT SO FAR?
WELL, NOT MUCH.
WHEN THE CELL IS ENGAGED, IT COMPRESSES LIKE THIS.
AND THEN, AS IT LOCKS INTO PLACE, THE INTERNAL PUMP STARTS.
THESE LITTLE PISTON VALVES OPEN AS IT LOCKS...
...AND THEY PUMP OUT OIL.
THIS GAUGE SHOWS THE USER'S OIL PRESSURE.

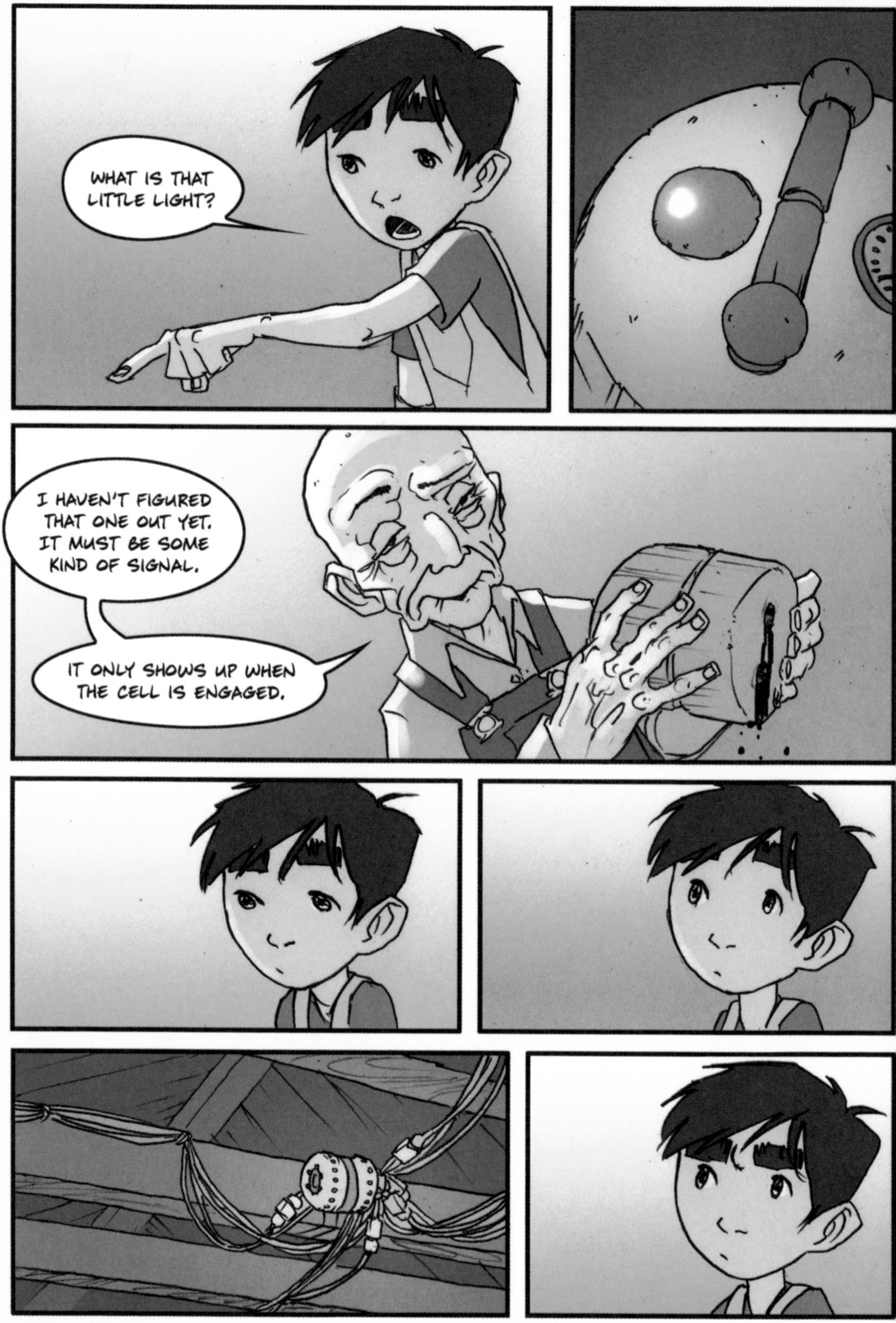
WHAT IS THAT LITTLE LIGHT?
I HAVEN'T FIGURED THAT ONE OUT YET. IT MUST BE SOME KIND OF SIGNAL.
IT ONLY SHOWS UP WHEN THE CELL IS ENGAGED.

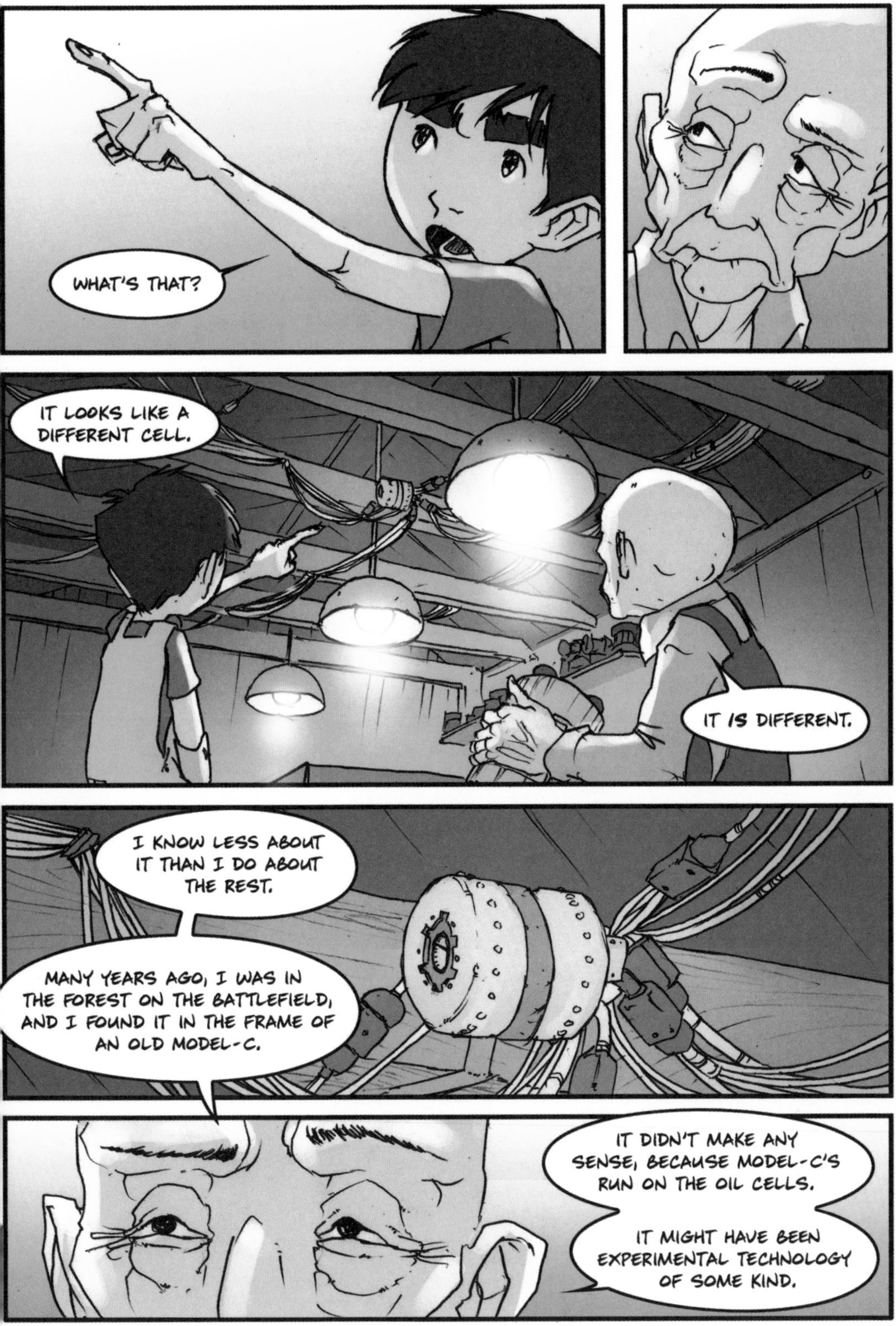
WHAT'S THAT?
IT LOOKS LIKE A DIFFERENT CELL.
IT IS DIFFERENT.
I KNOW LESS ABOUT IT THAN I DO ABOUT THE REST.
MANY YEARS AGO, I WAS IN THE FOREST ON THE BATTLEFIELD, AND I FOUND IT IN THE FRAME OF AN OLD MODEL-C.
IT DIDN'T MAKE ANY SENSE, BECAUSE MODEL-C'S RUN ON THE OIL CELLS.
IT MIGHT HAVE BEEN EXPERIMENTAL TECHNOLOGY OF SOME KIND.

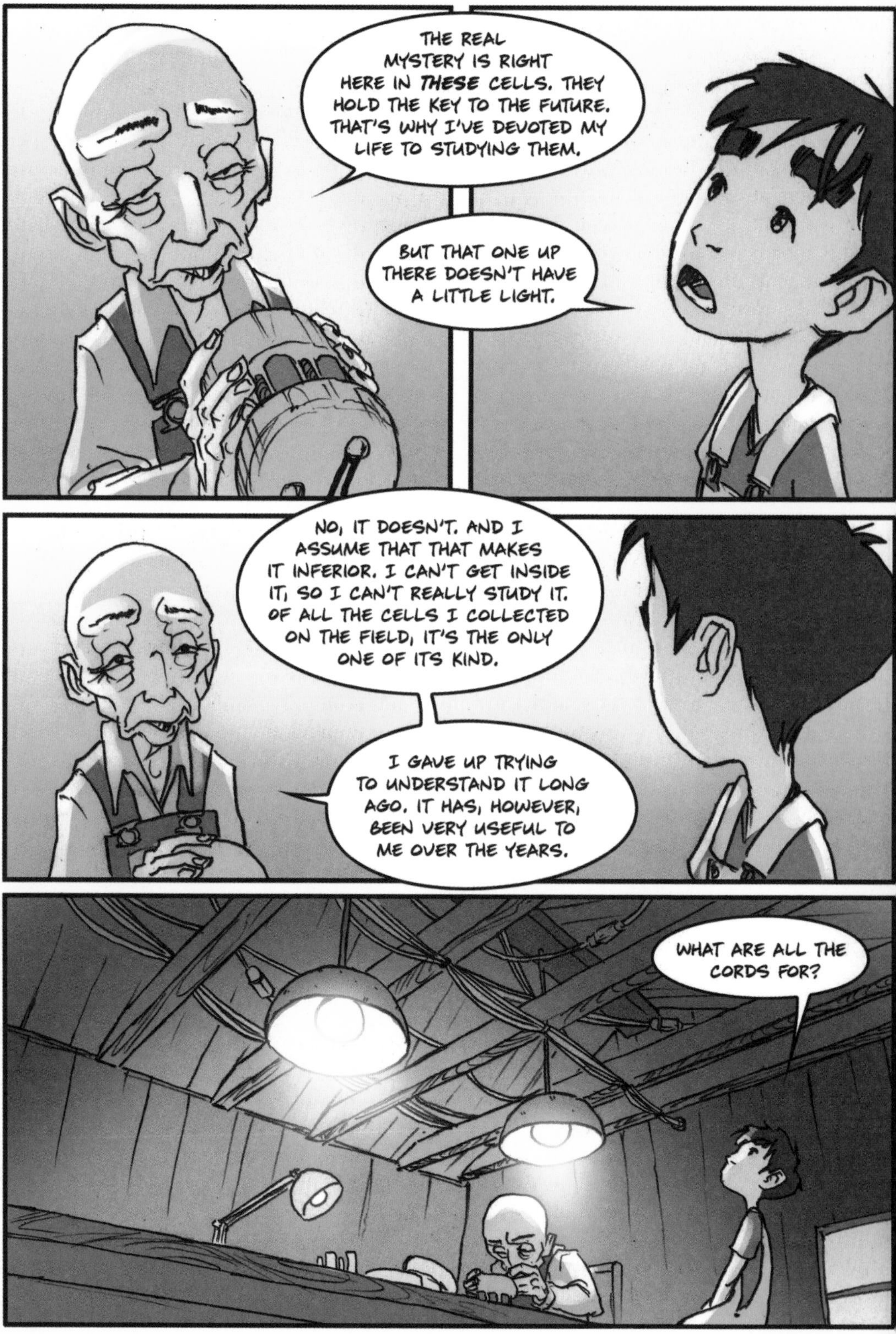
THE REAL MYSTERY IS RIGHT HERE IN THESE CELLS. THEY HOLD THE KEY TO THE FUTURE. THAT'S WHY I'VE DEVOTED MY LIFE TO STUDYING THEM.
BUT THAT ONE UP THERE DOESN'T HAVE A LITTLE LIGHT.
NO, IT DOESN'T. AND I ASSUME THAT THAT MAKES IT INFERIOR. I CAN'T GET INSIDE IT, SO I CAN'T REALLY STUDY IT. OF ALL THE CELLS I COLLECTED ON THE FIELD, IT'S THE ONLY ONE OF ITS KIND.
I GAVE UP TRYING TO UNDERSTAND IT LONG AGO. IT HAS, HOWEVER, BEEN VERY USEFUL TO ME OVER THE YEARS.
WHAT ARE ALL THE CORDS FOR?

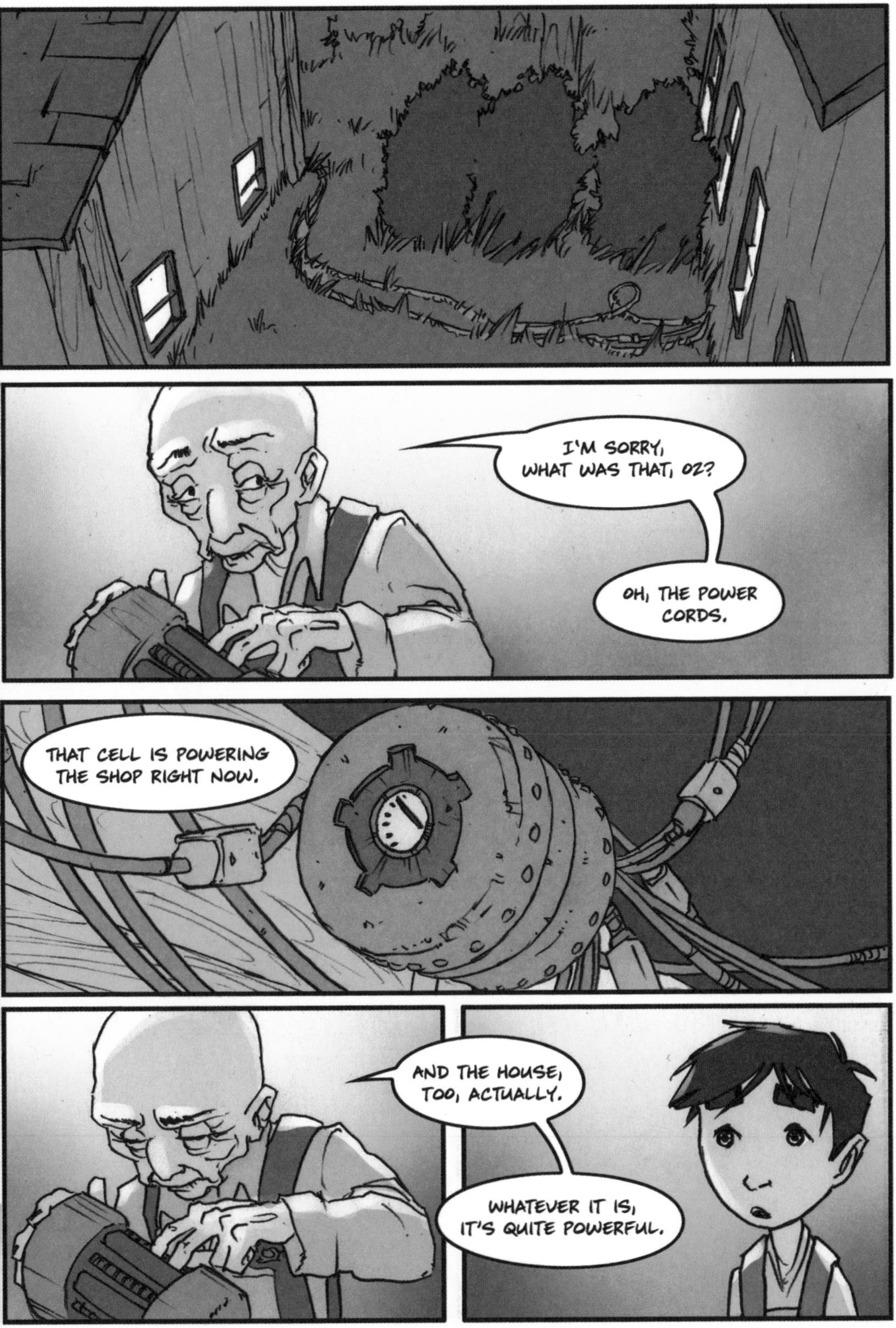
I'M SORRY, WHAT WAS THAT, OZ?
OH, THE POWER CORDS.
THAT CELL IS POWERING THE SHOP RIGHT NOW.
AND THE HOUSE, TOO, ACTUALLY.
WHATEVER IT IS, IT'S QUITE POWERFUL.

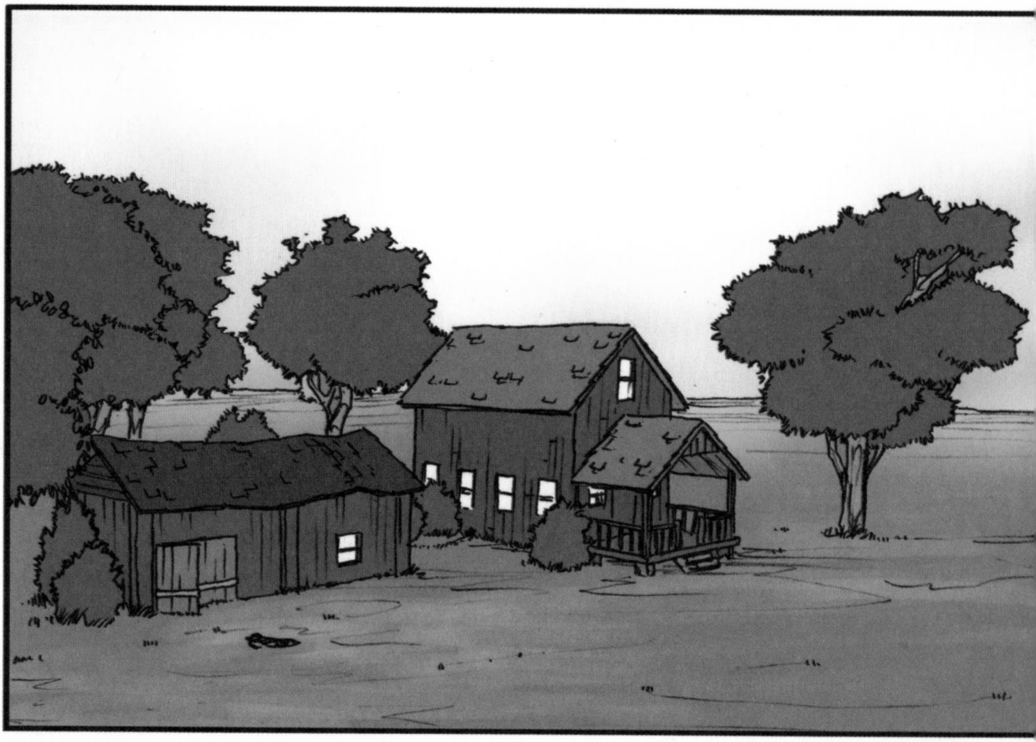

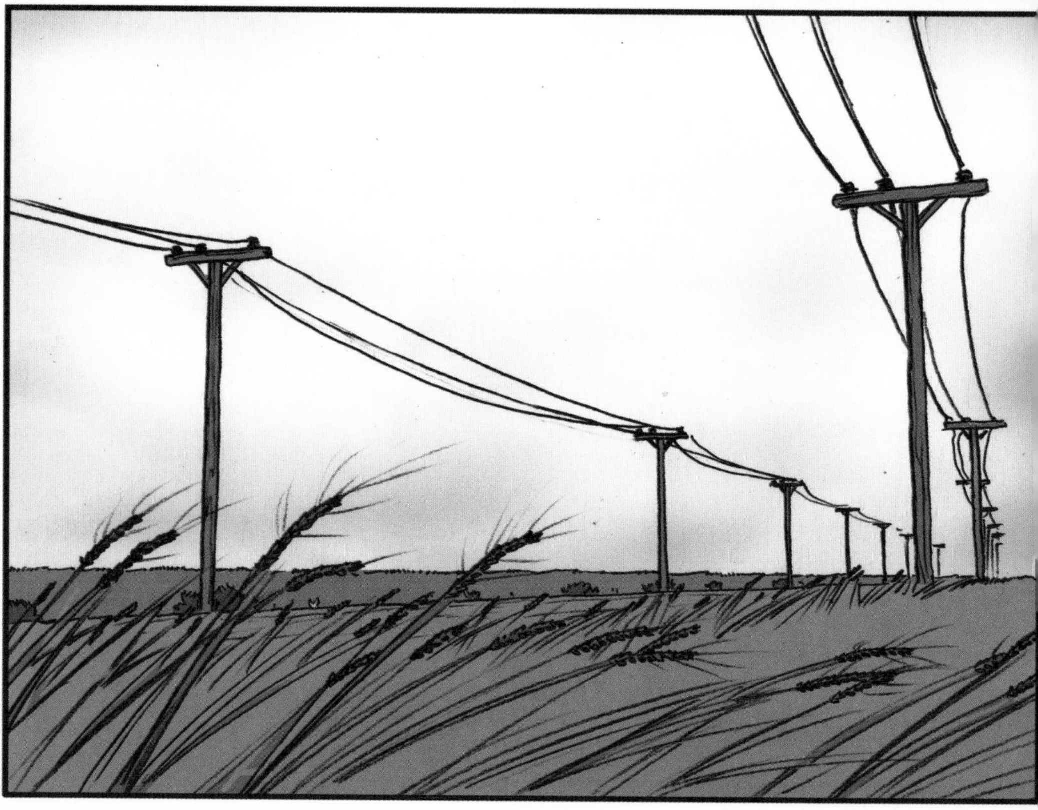

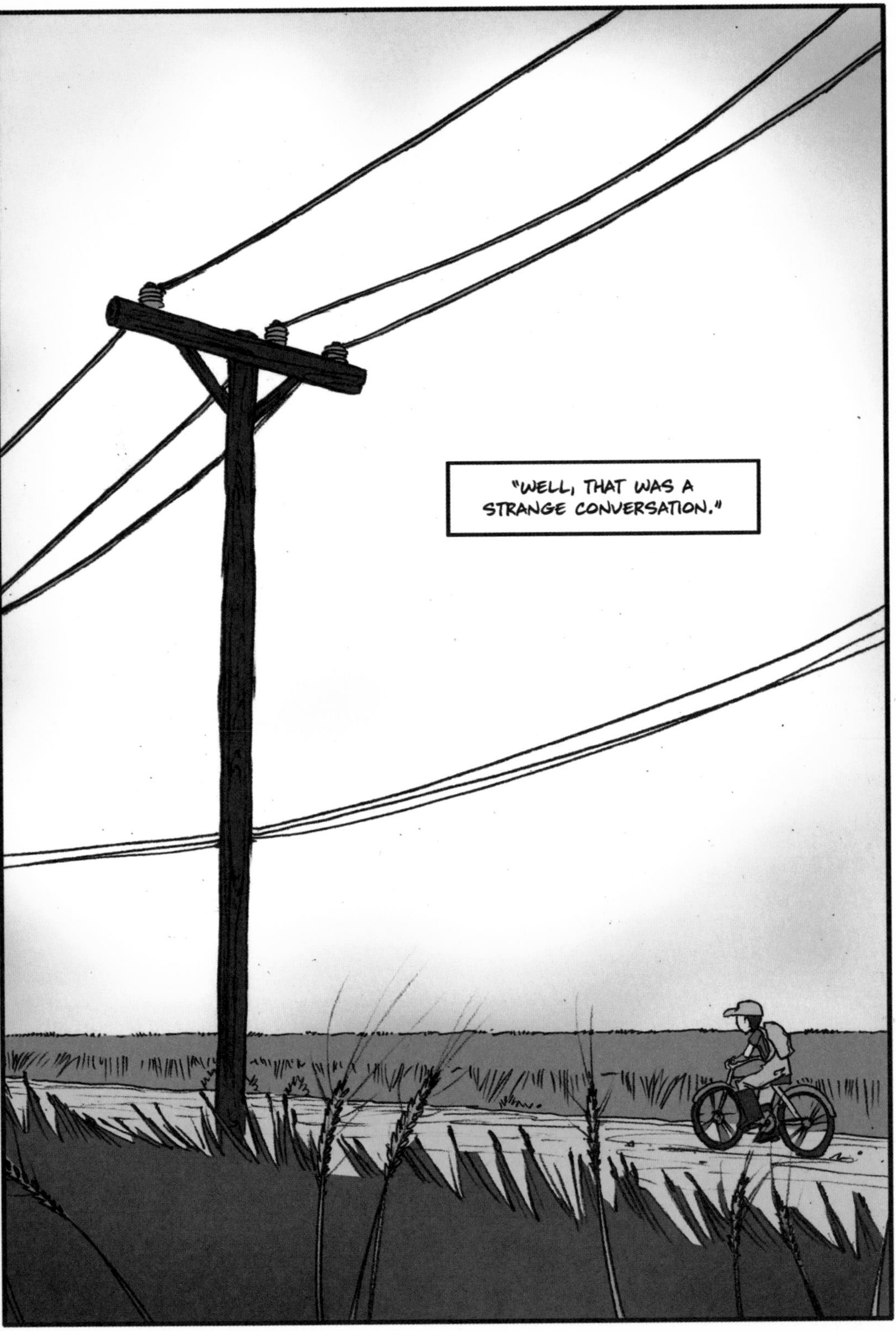
"WELL, THAT WAS A STRANGE CONVERSATION."

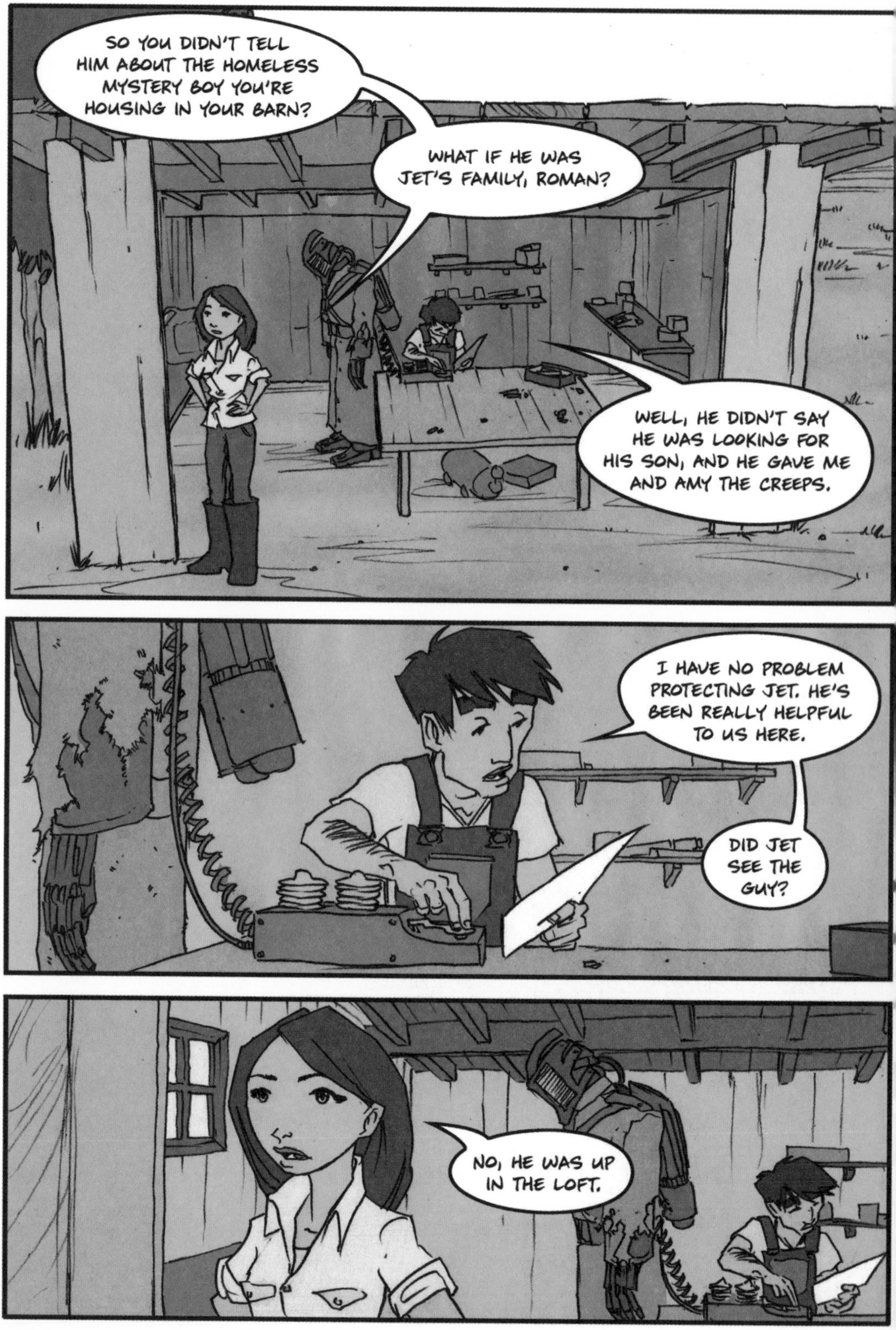
SO YOU DIDN'T TELL HIM ABOUT THE HOMELESS MYSTERY BOY YOU'RE HOUSING IN YOUR BARN?
WHAT IF HE WAS JET'S FAMILY, ROMAN?
WELL, HE DIDN'T SAY HE WAS LOOKING FOR HIS SON, AND HE GAVE ME AND AMY THE CREEPS.
I HAVE NO PROBLEM PROTECTING JET. HE'S BEEN REALLY HELPFUL TO US HERE.
DID JET SEE THE GUY?
NO, HE WAS UP IN THE LOFT.

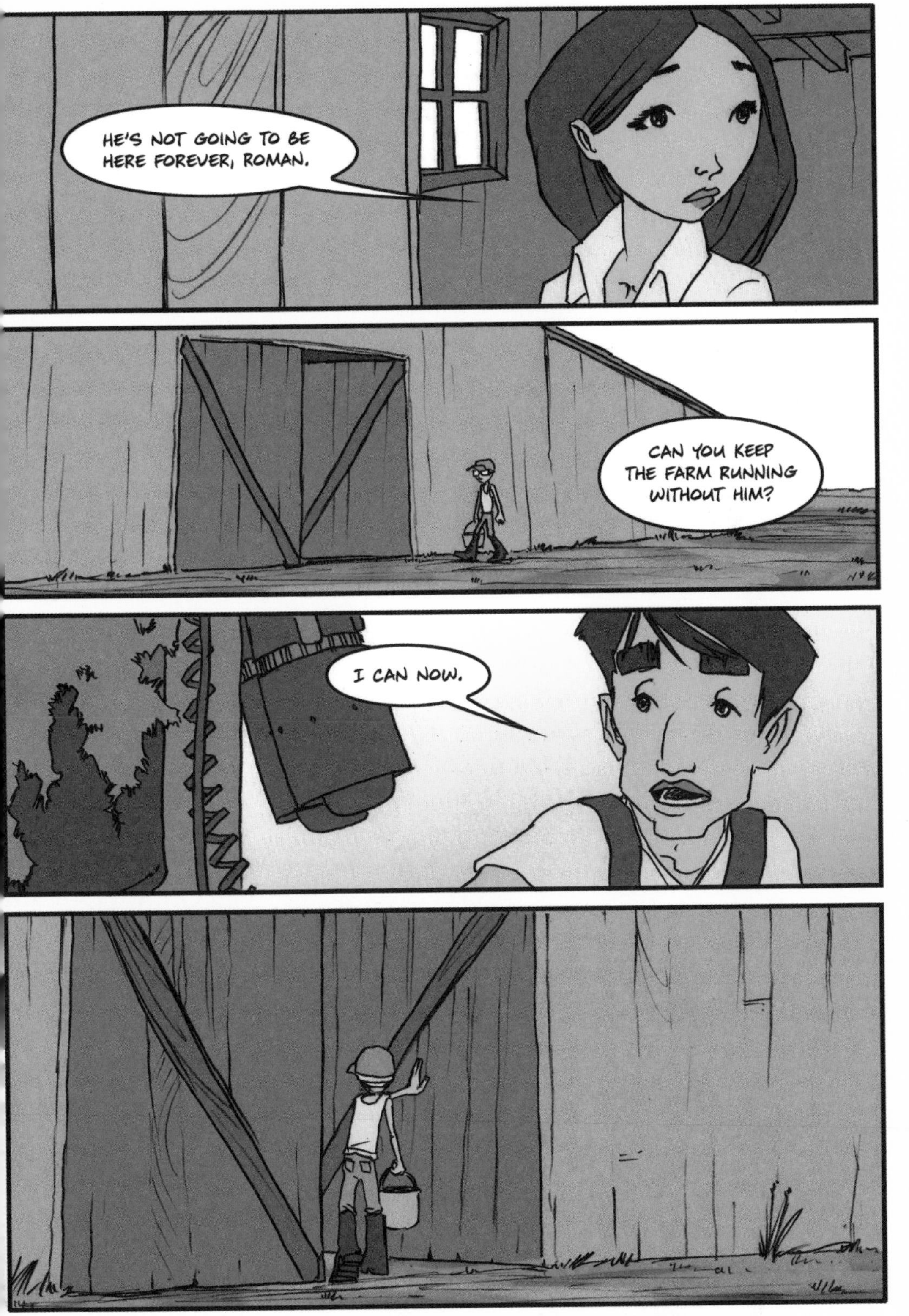
HE'S NOT GOING TO BE HERE FOREVER, ROMAN.
CAN YOU KEEP THE FARM RUNNING WITHOUT HIM?
I CAN NOW.

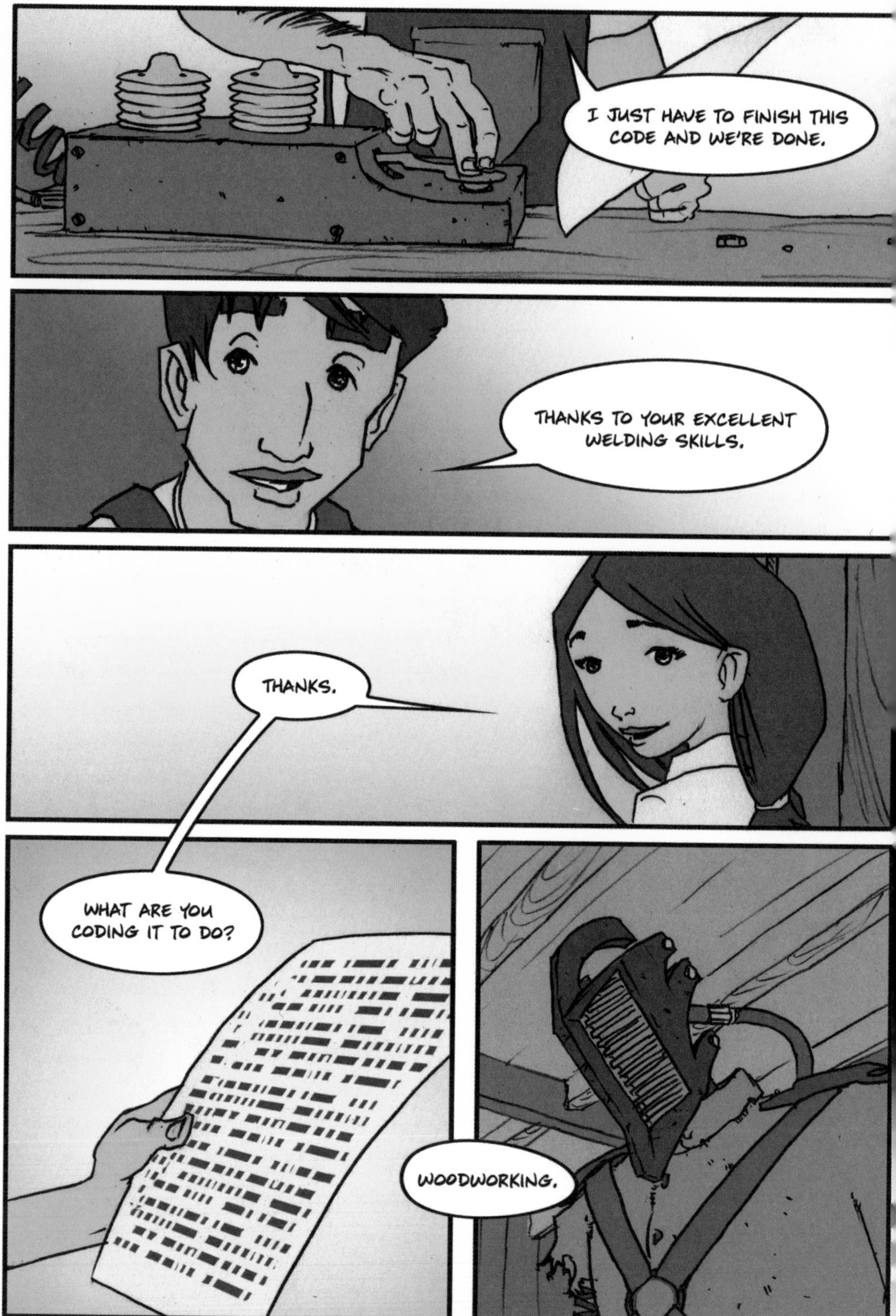
I JUST HAVE TO FINISH THIS CODE AND WE'RE DONE.
THANKS TO YOUR EXCELLENT WELDING SKILLS.
THANKS.
WHAT ARE YOU CODING IT TO DO?
WOODWORKING.

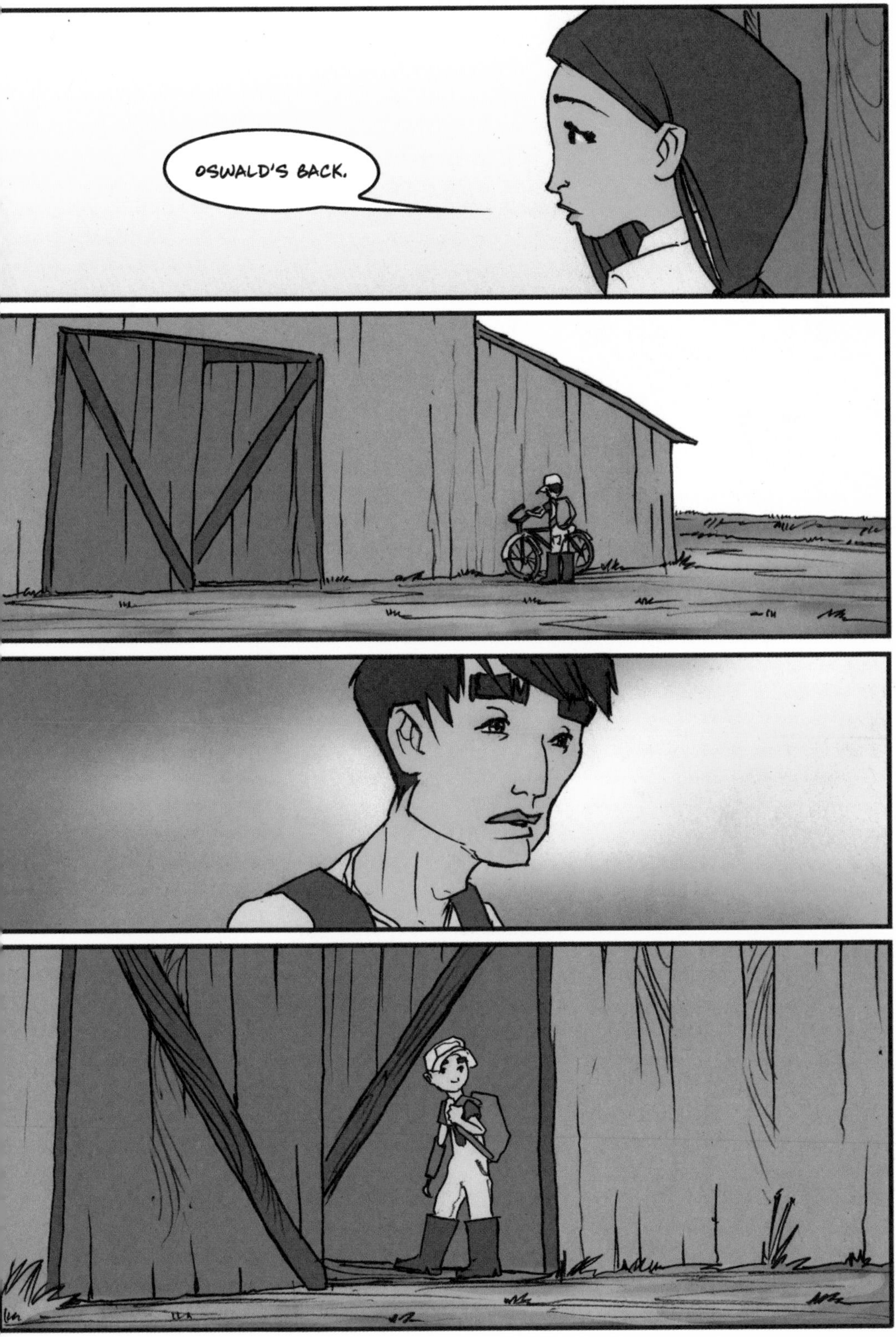
OSWALD'S BACK.

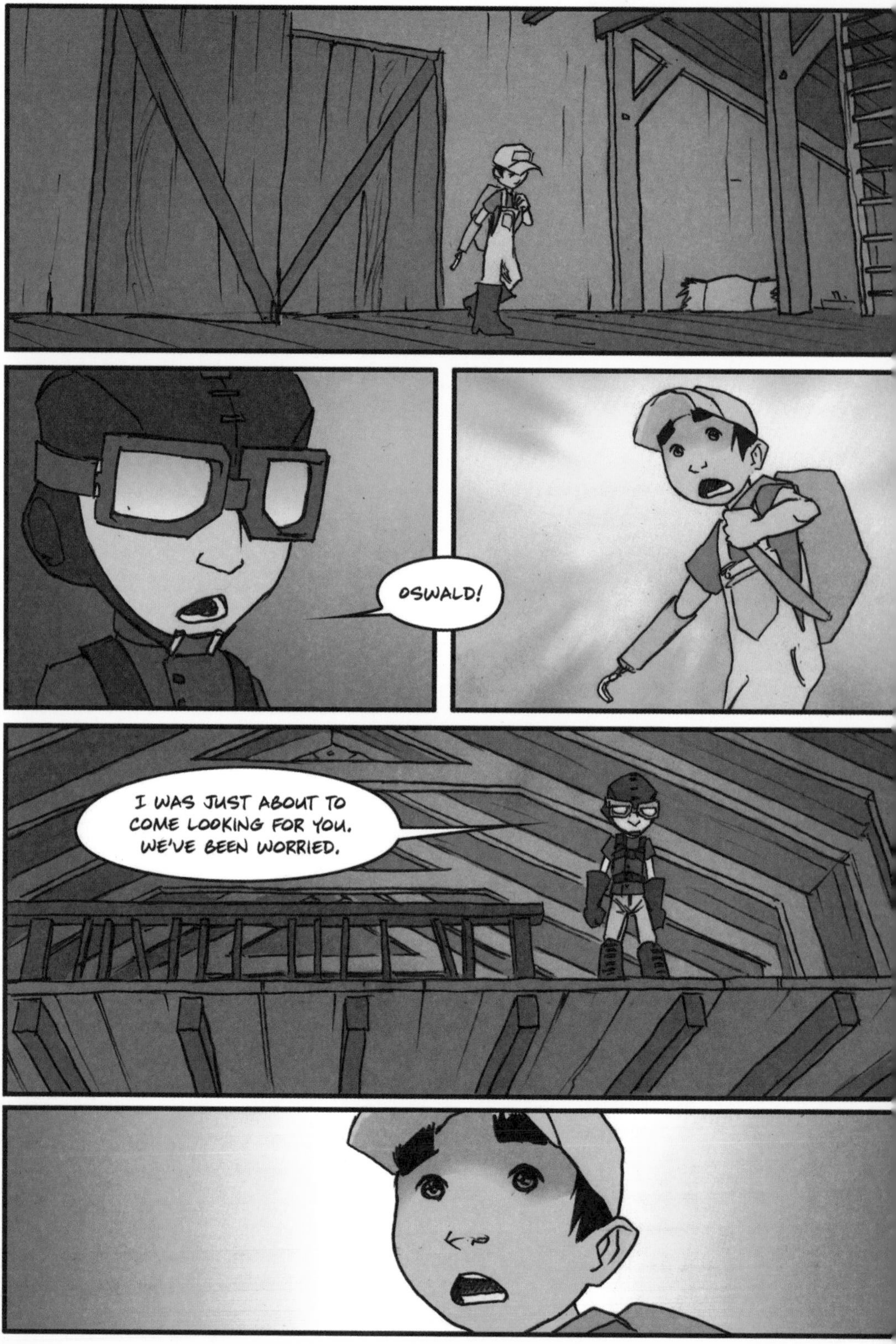
OSWALD!
I WAS JUST ABOUT TO COME LOOKING FOR YOU. WE'VE BEEN WORRIED.

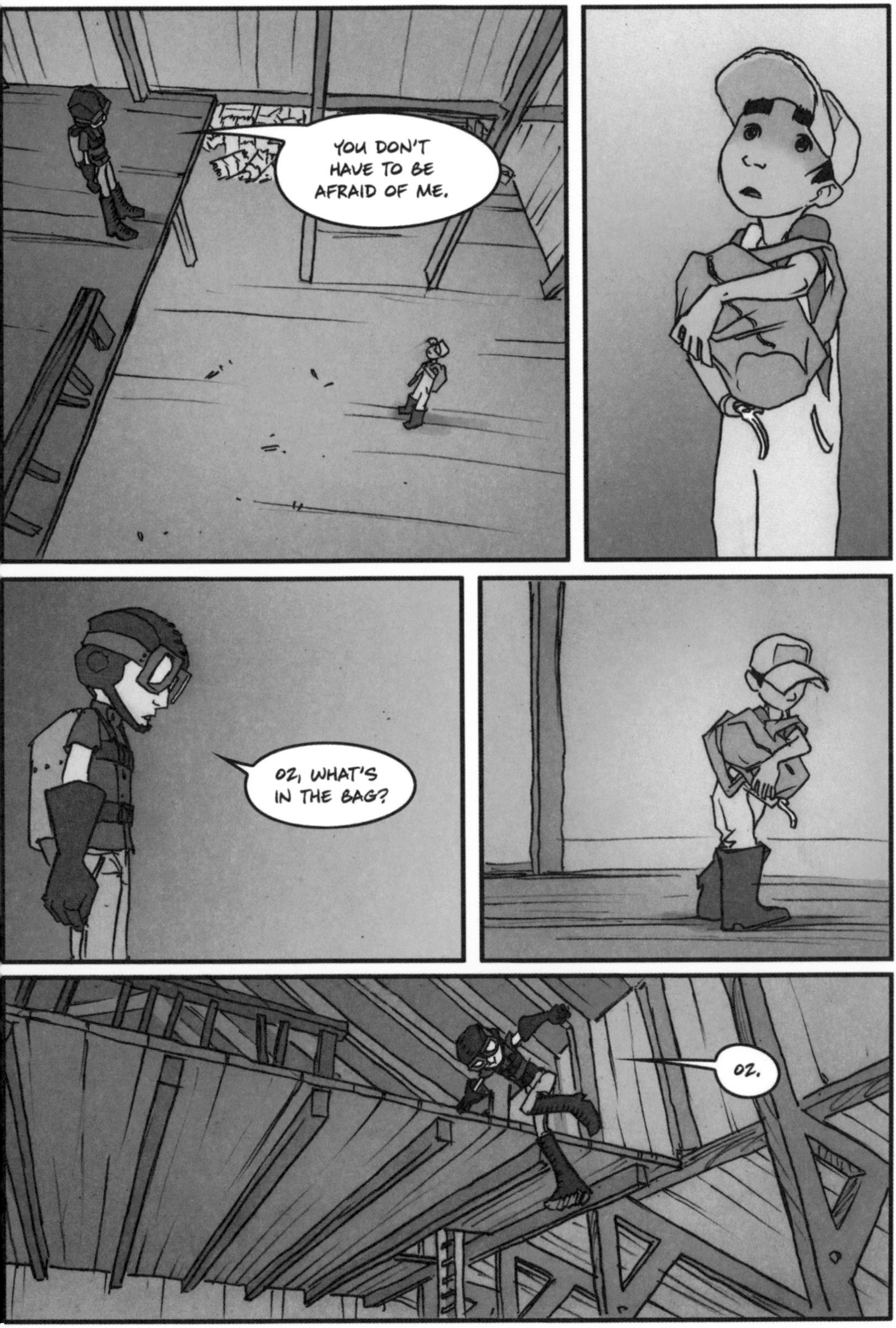
YOU DON'T HAVE TO BE AFRAID OF ME.
OZ, WHAT'S IN THE BAG?
OZ.

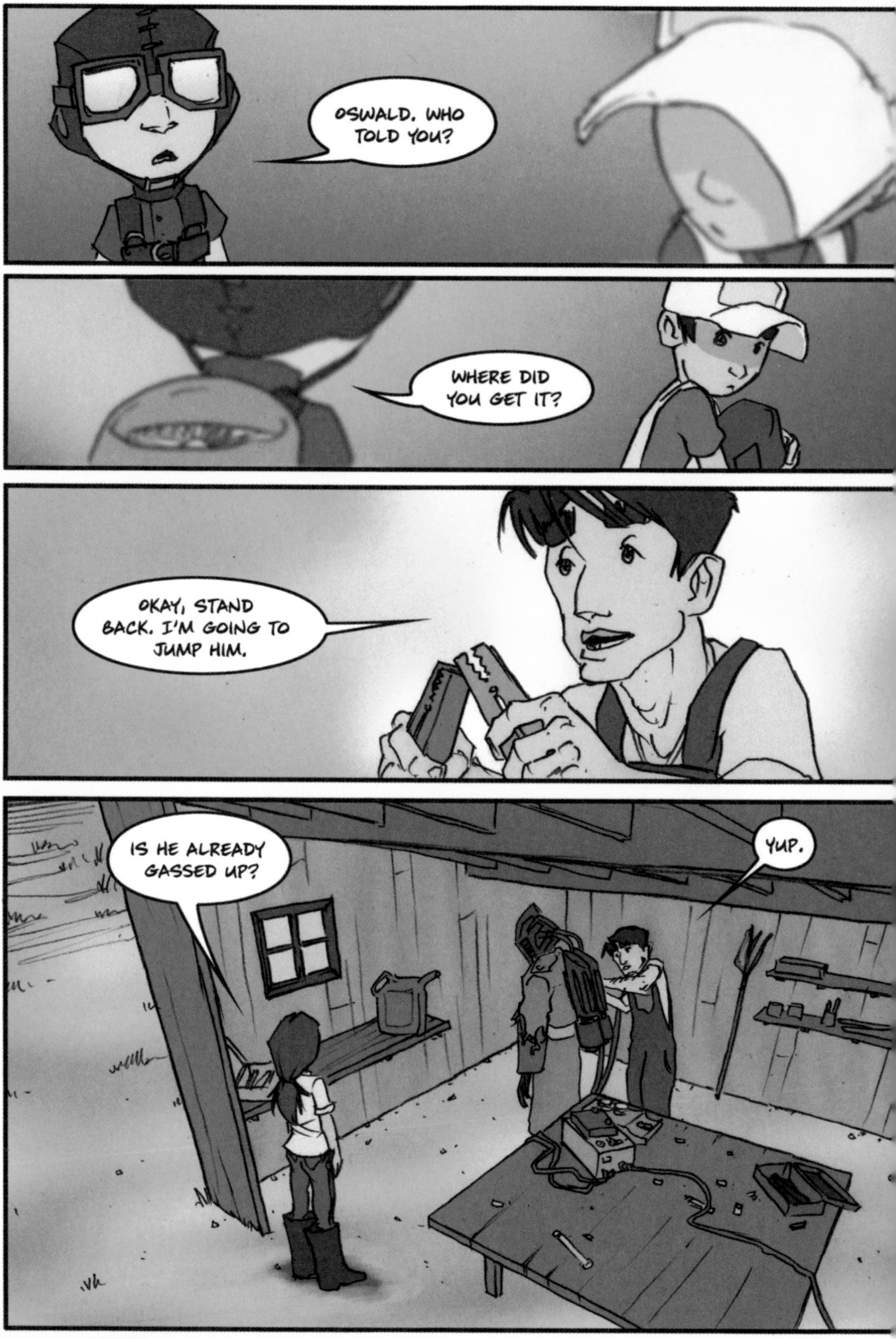
OSWALD. WHO TOLD YOU?
WHERE DID YOU GET IT?
OKAY, STAND BACK. I'M GOING TO JUMP HIM.
IS HE ALREADY GASSED UP?
YUP.

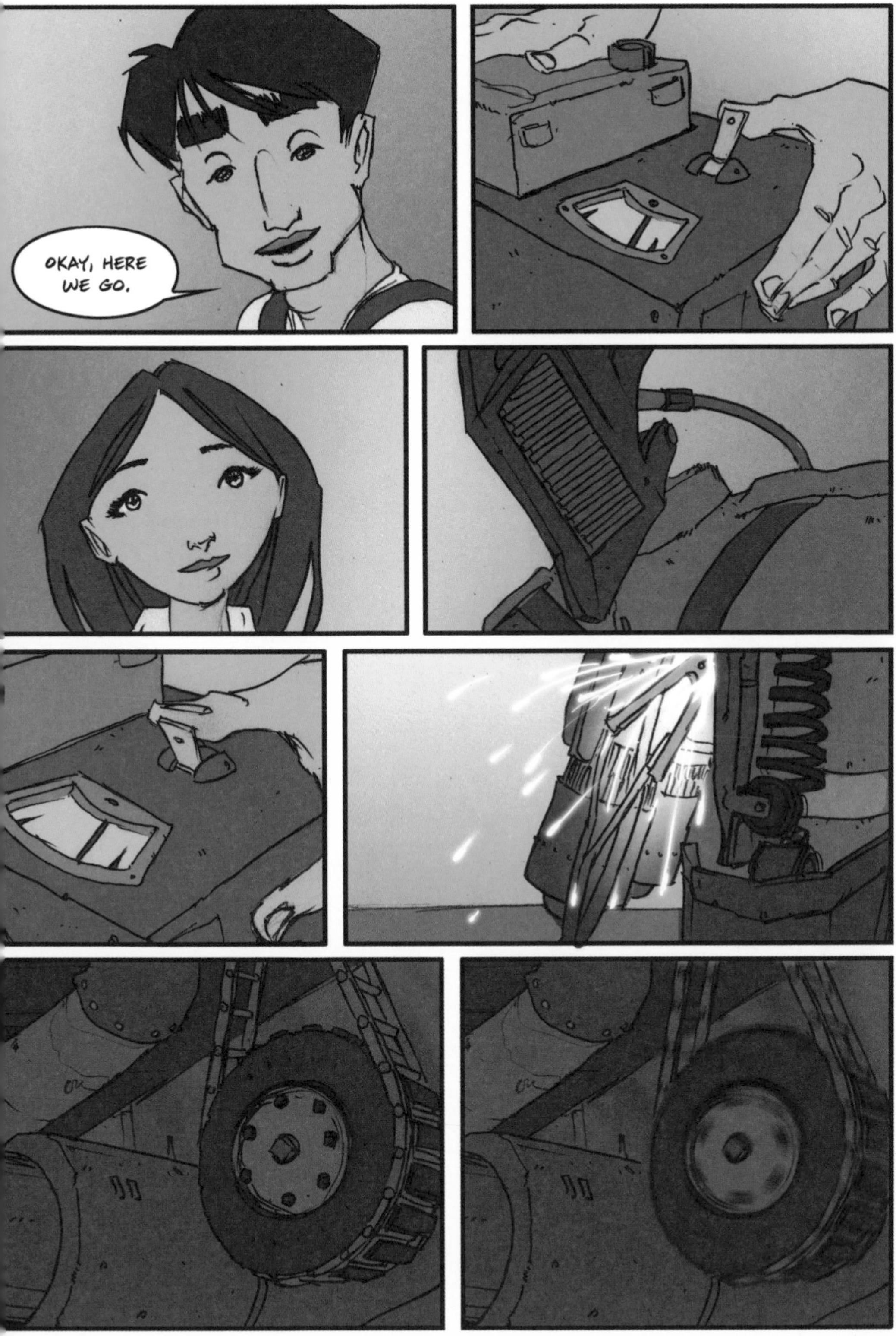
OKAY, HERE WE GO.

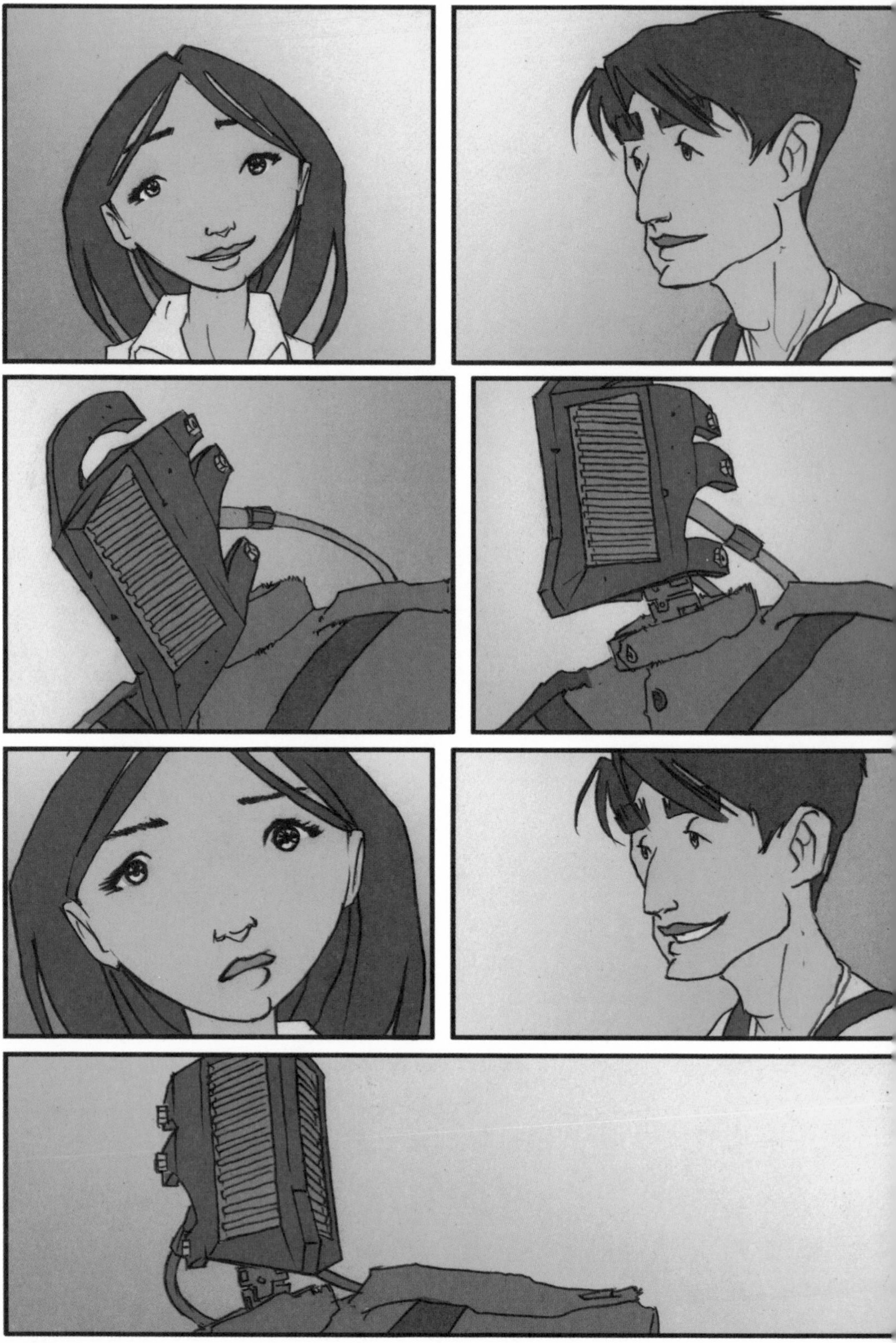

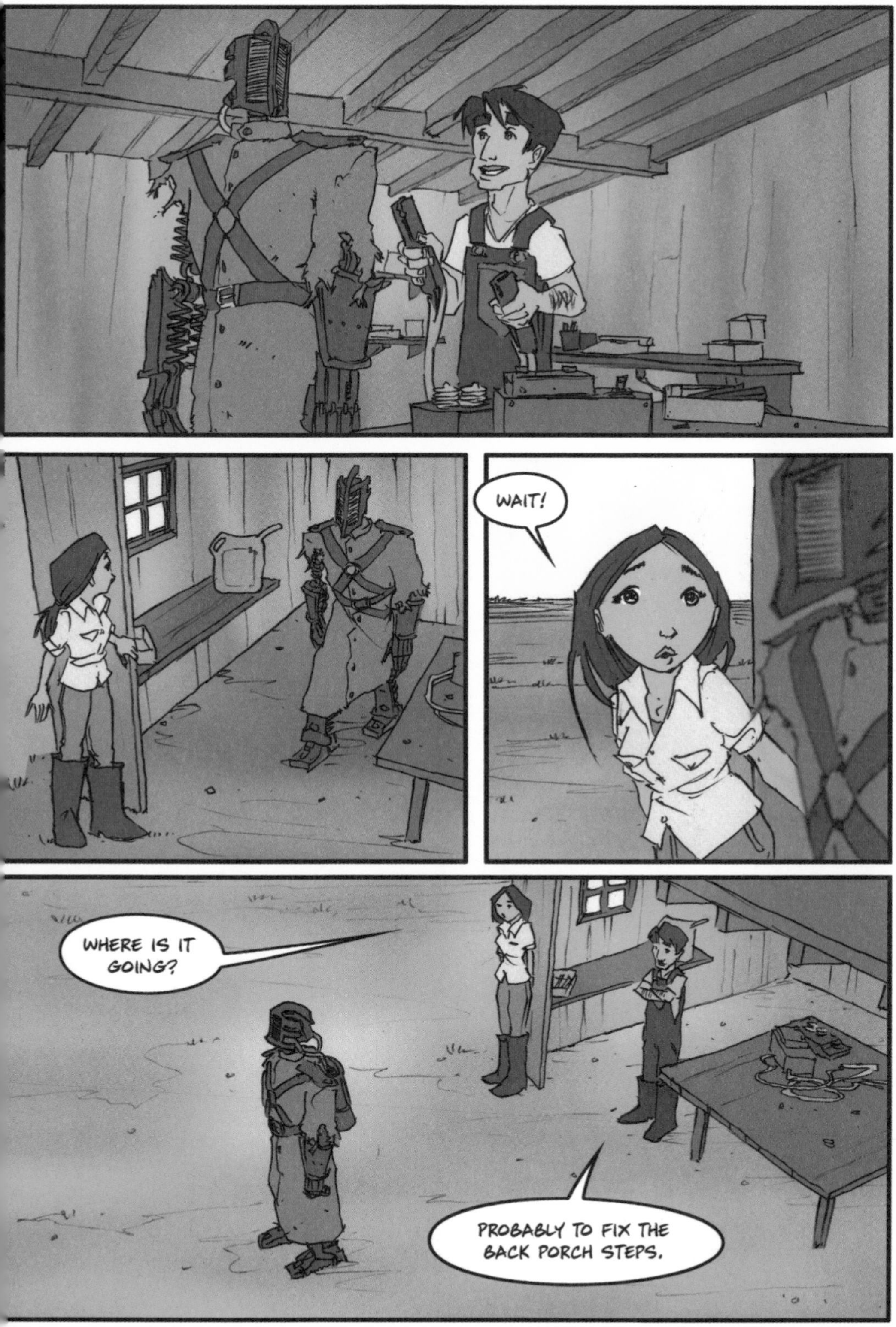
WAIT!
WHERE IS IT GOING?
PROBABLY TO FIX THE BACK PORCH STEPS.

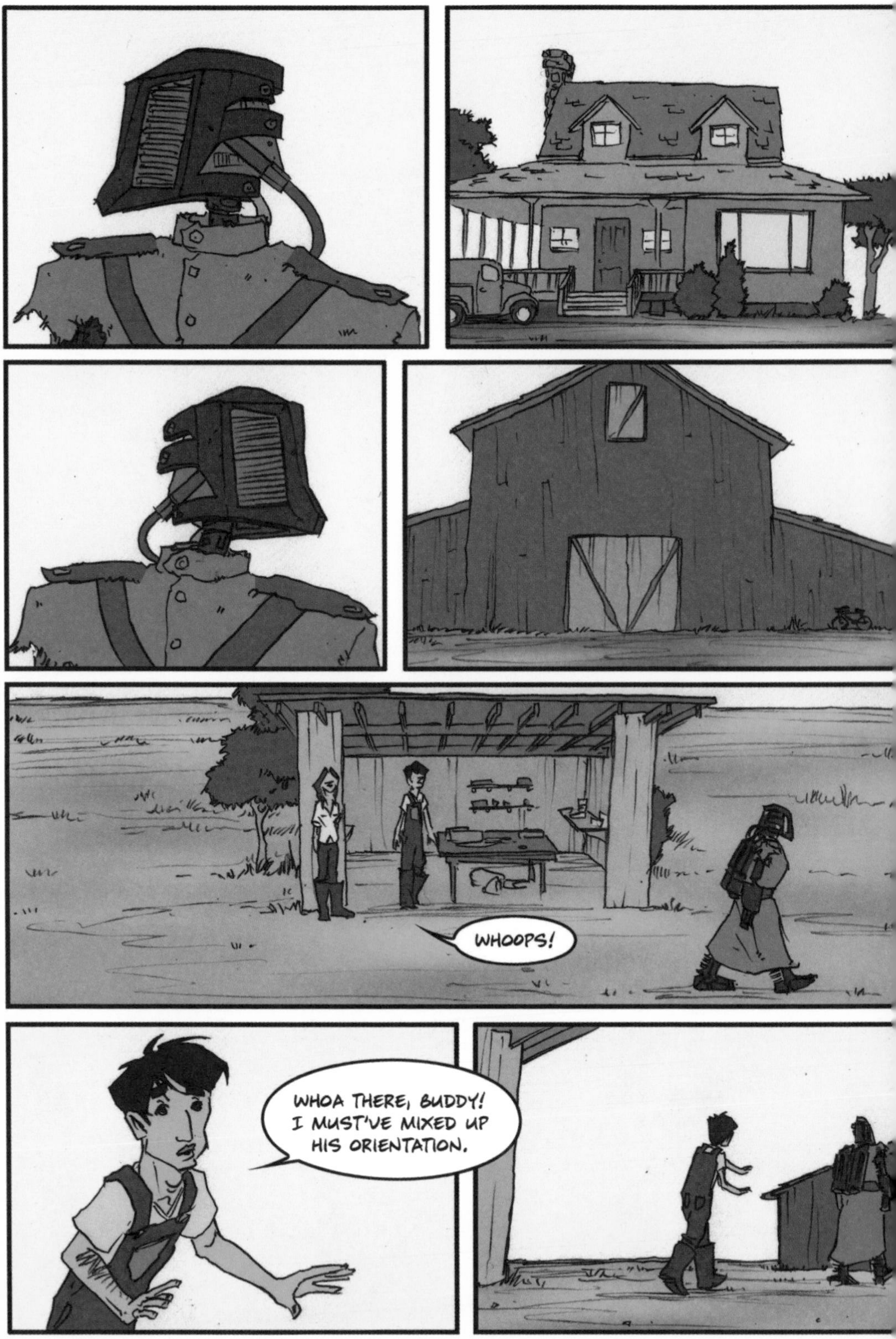
WHOOPS!
WHOA THERE, BUDDY! I MUST'VE MIXED UP HIS ORIENTATION.

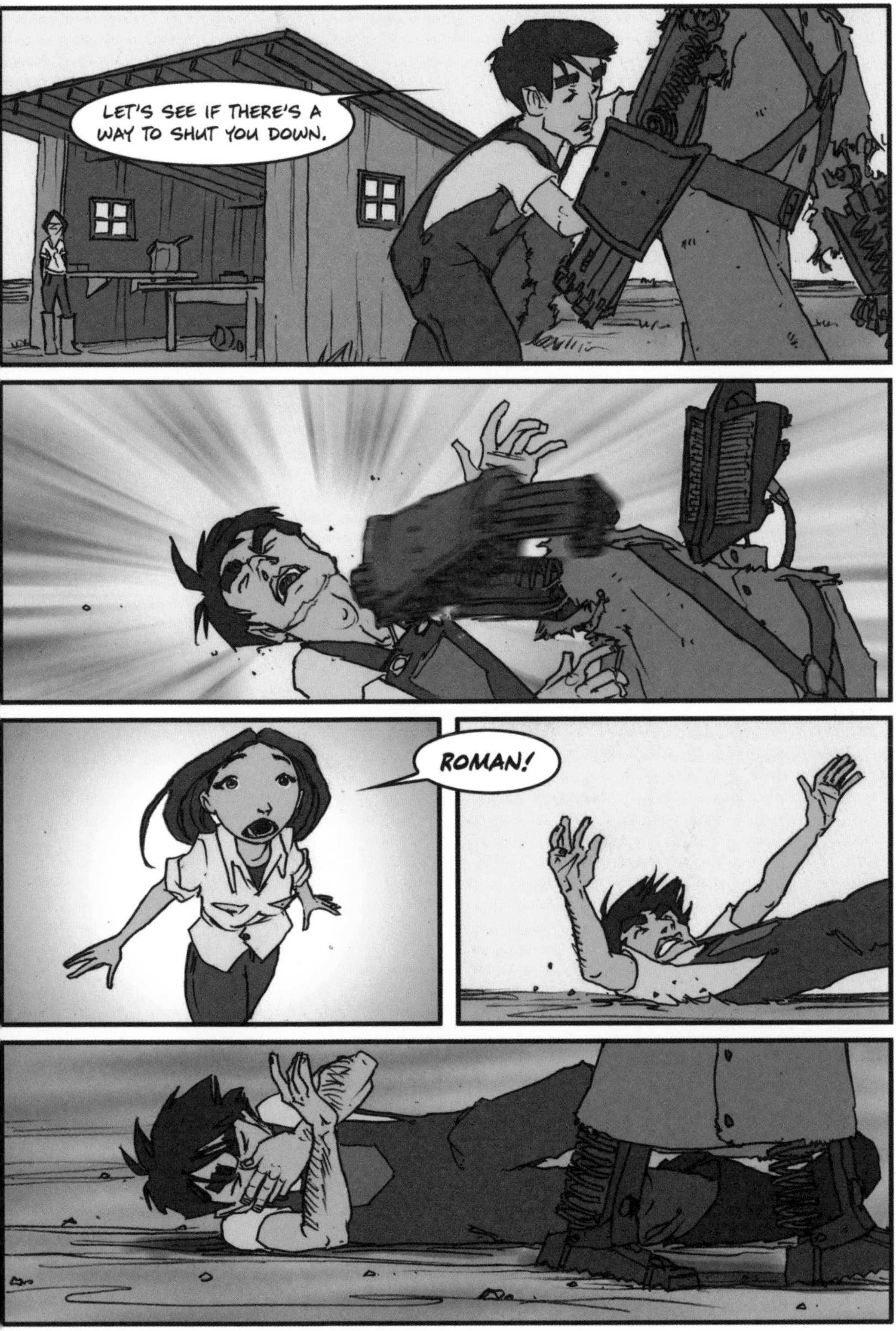
LET'S SEE IF THERE'S A WAY TO SHUT YOU DOWN.
ROMAN!

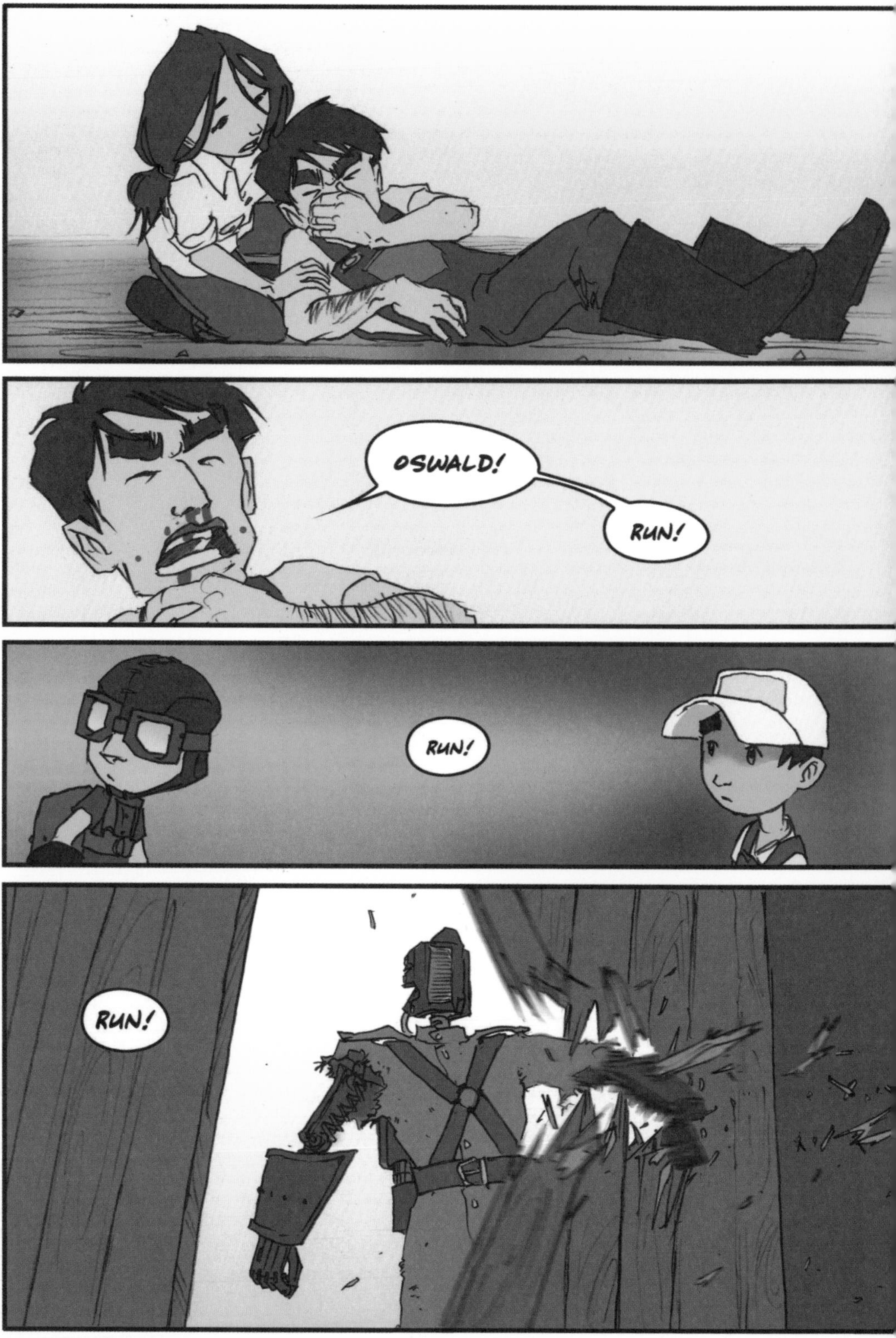
OSWALD!
RUN!
RUN!
RUN!

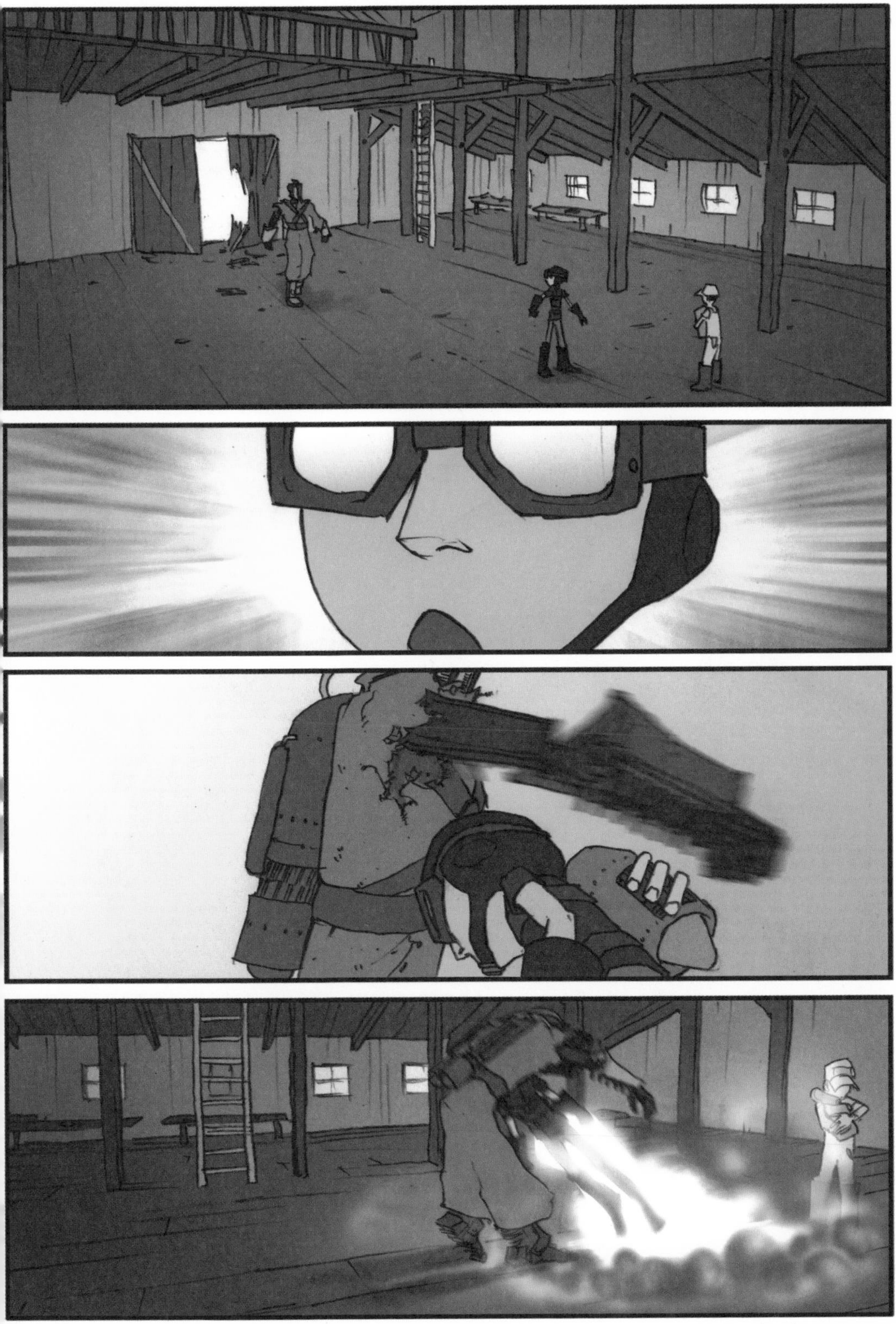

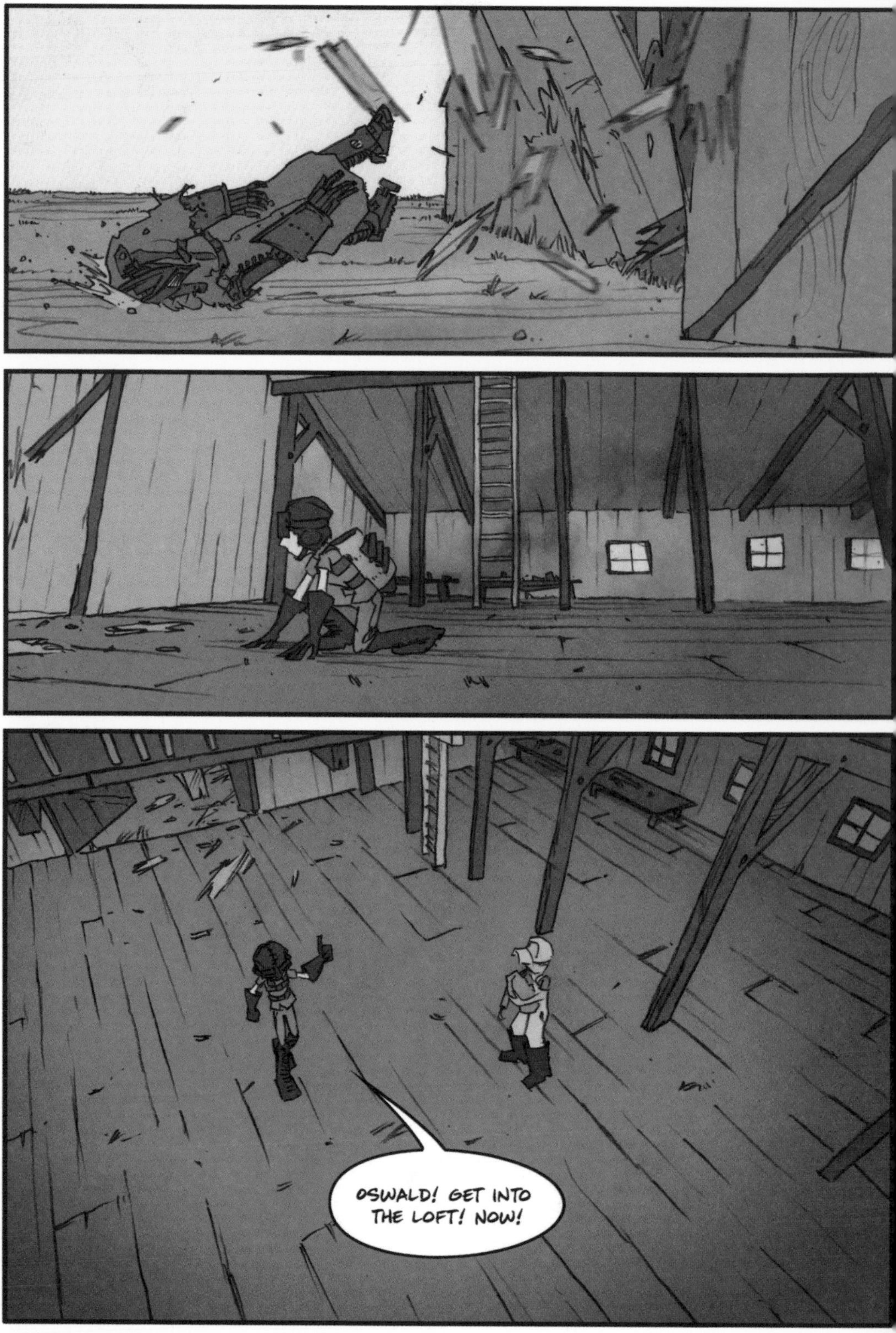
OSWALD! GET INTO
THE LOFT! NOW!

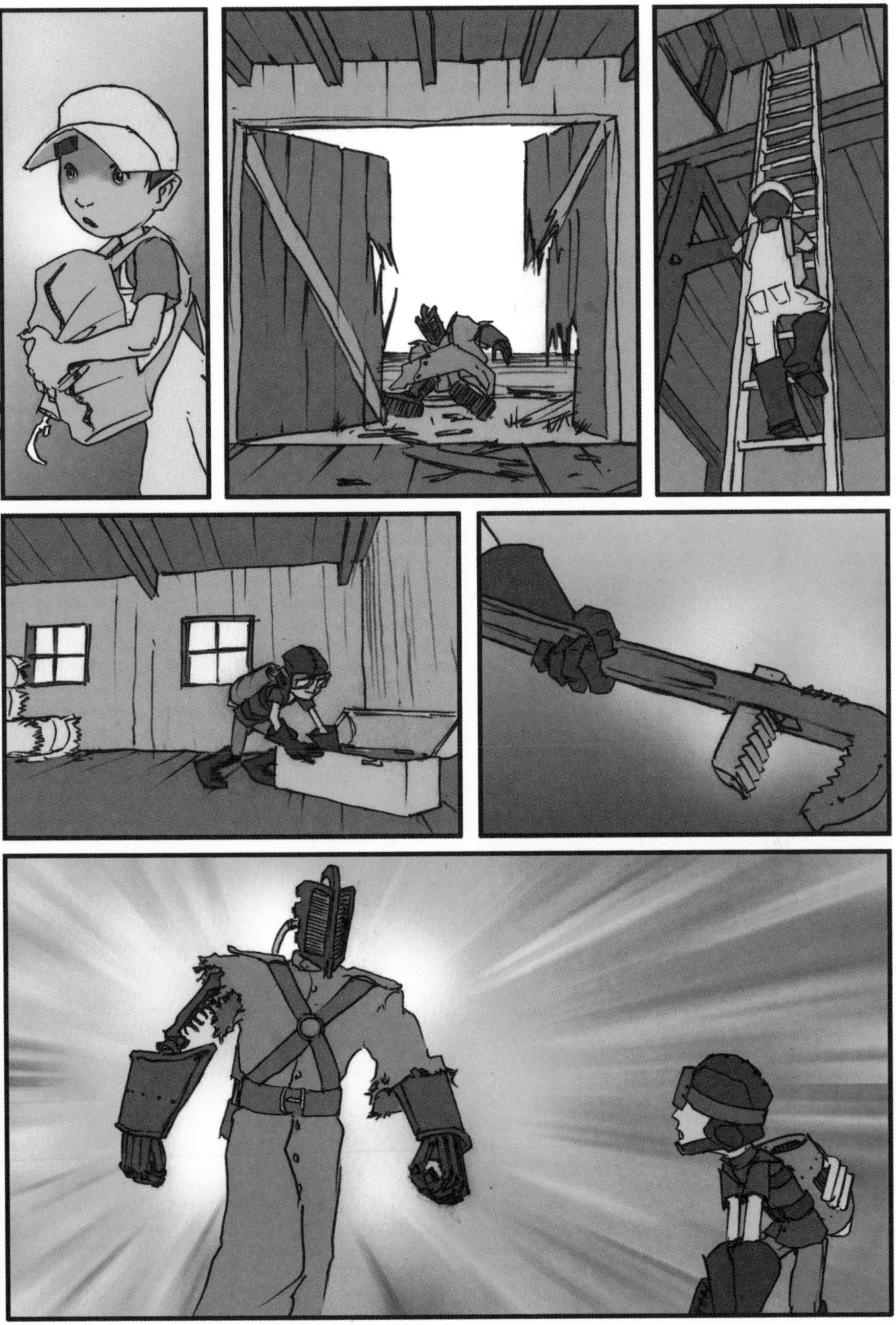

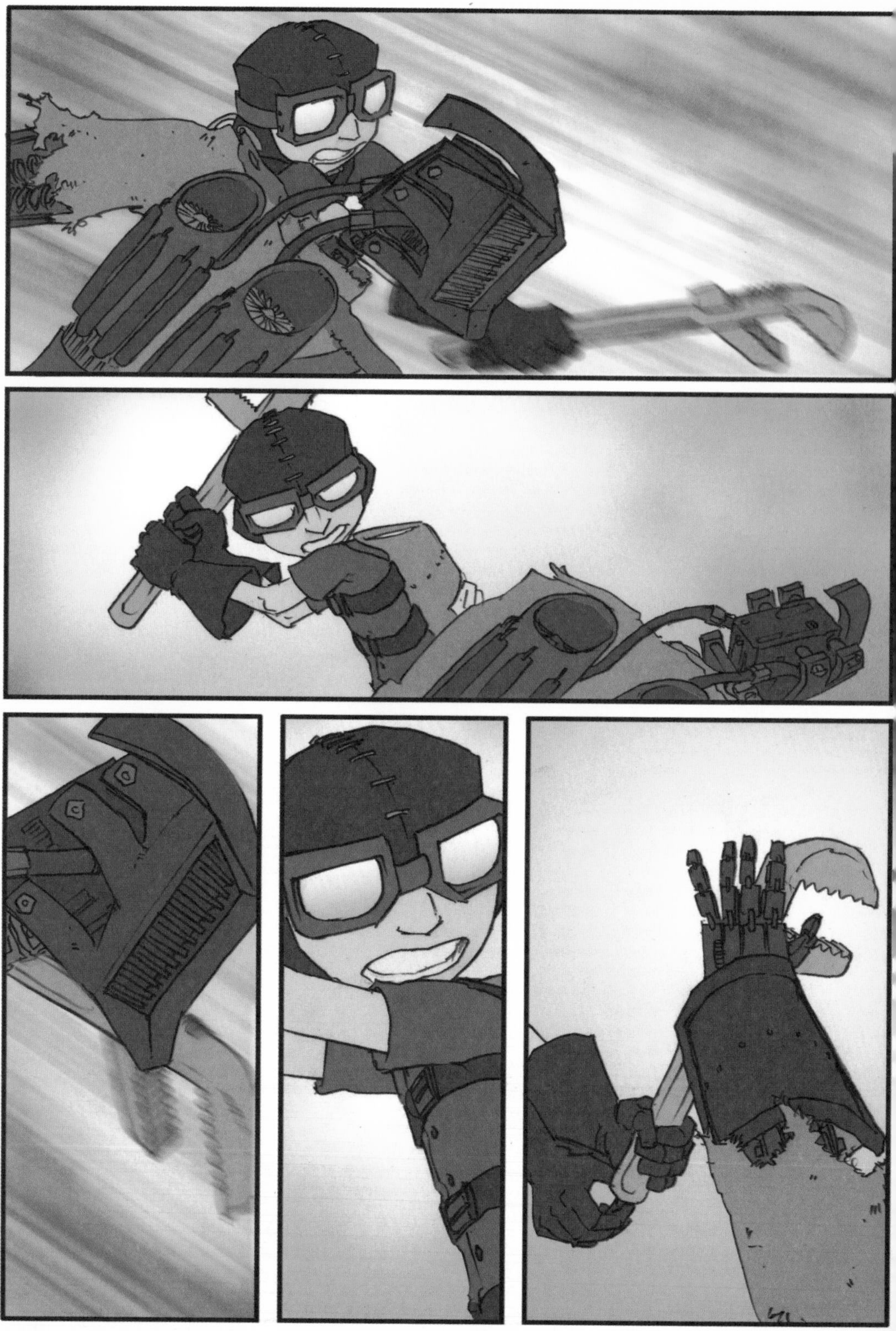

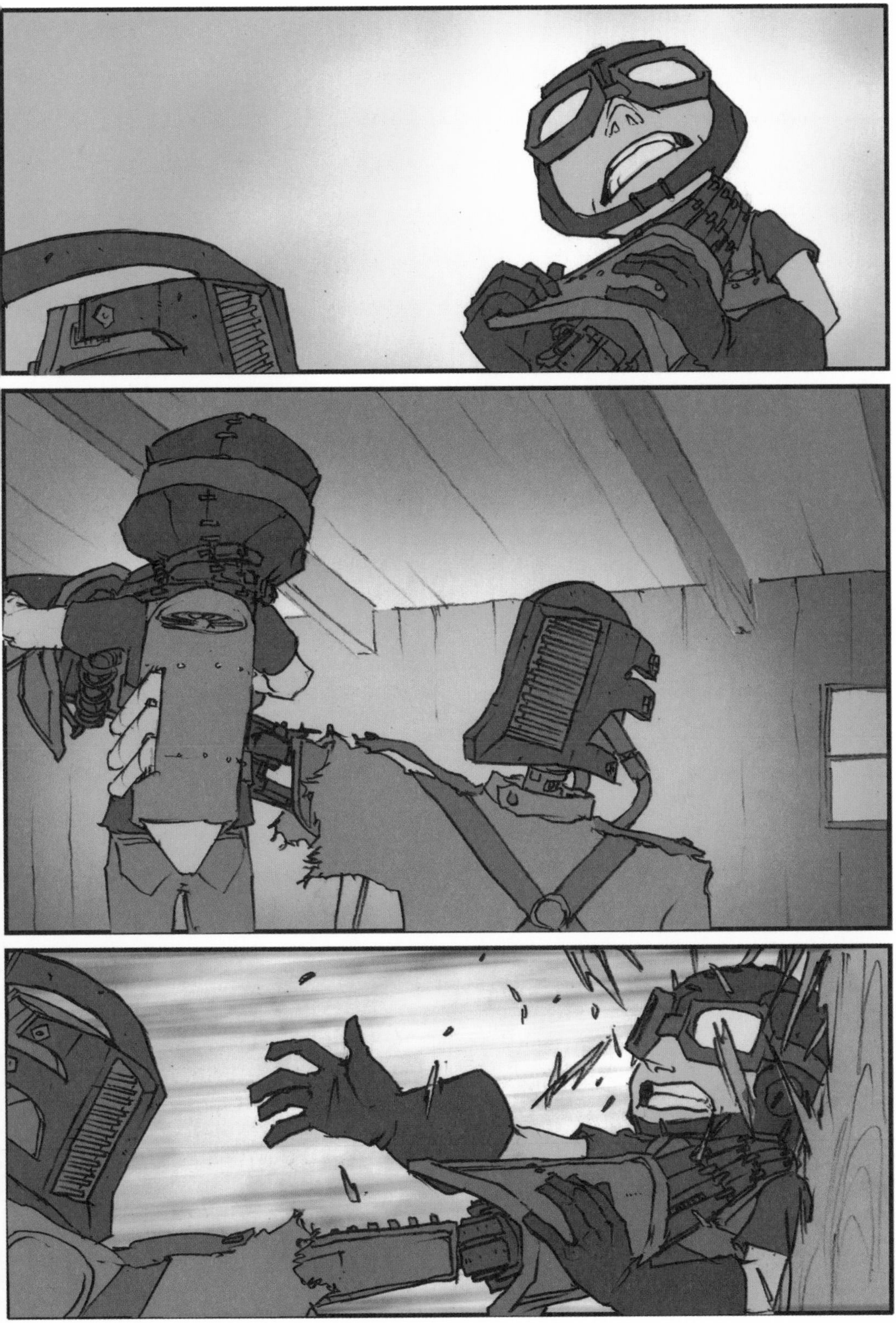

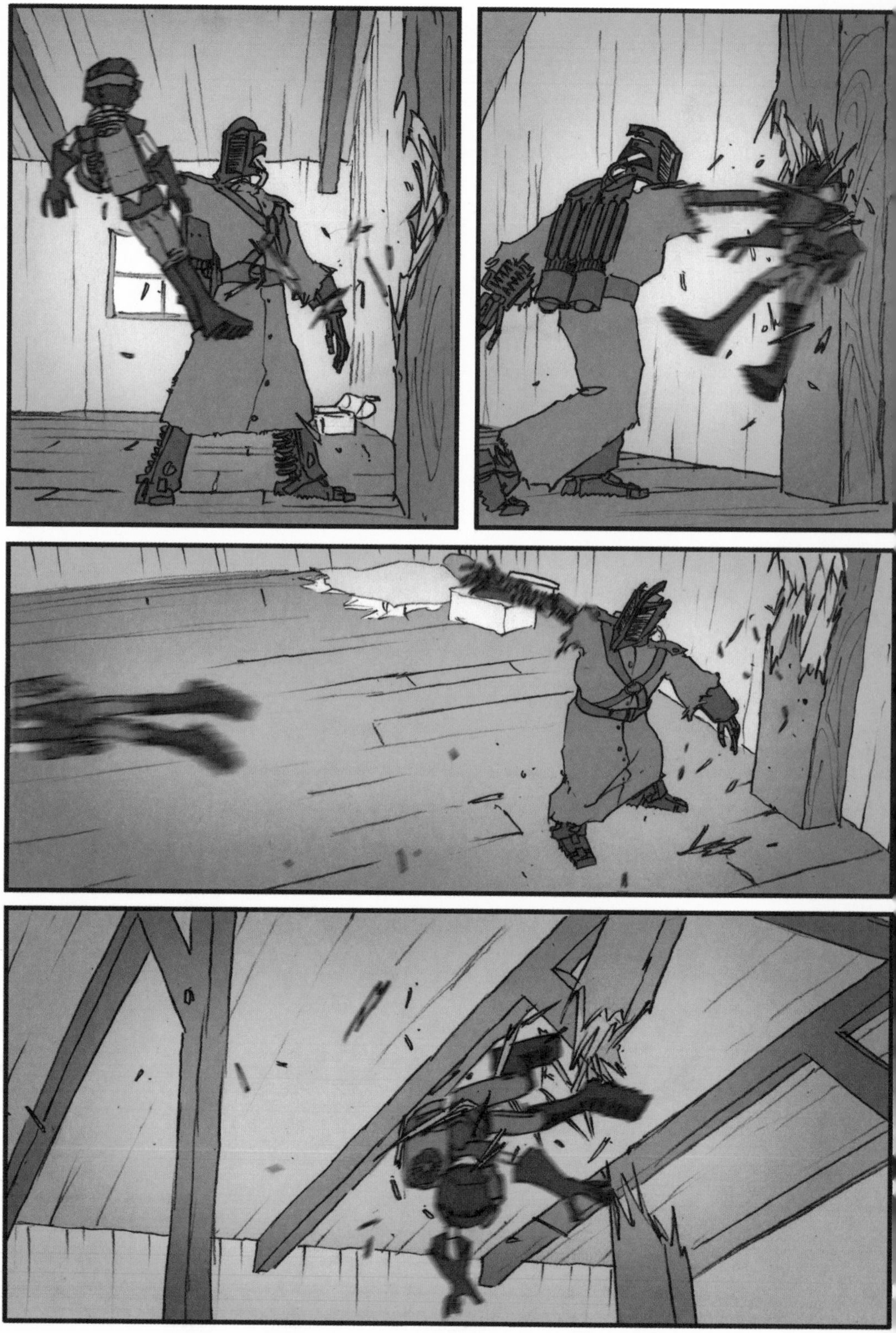

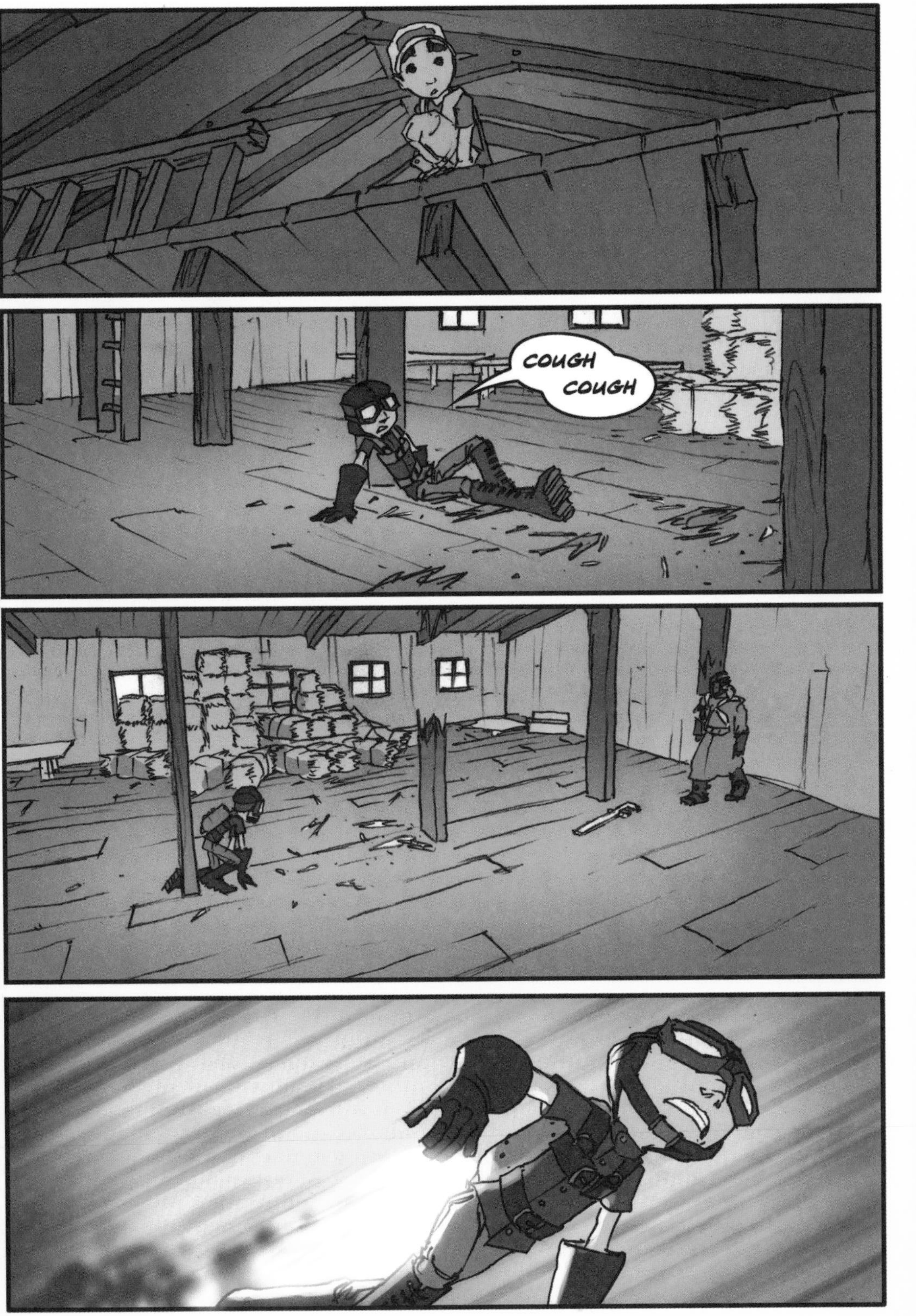
COUGH
COUGH

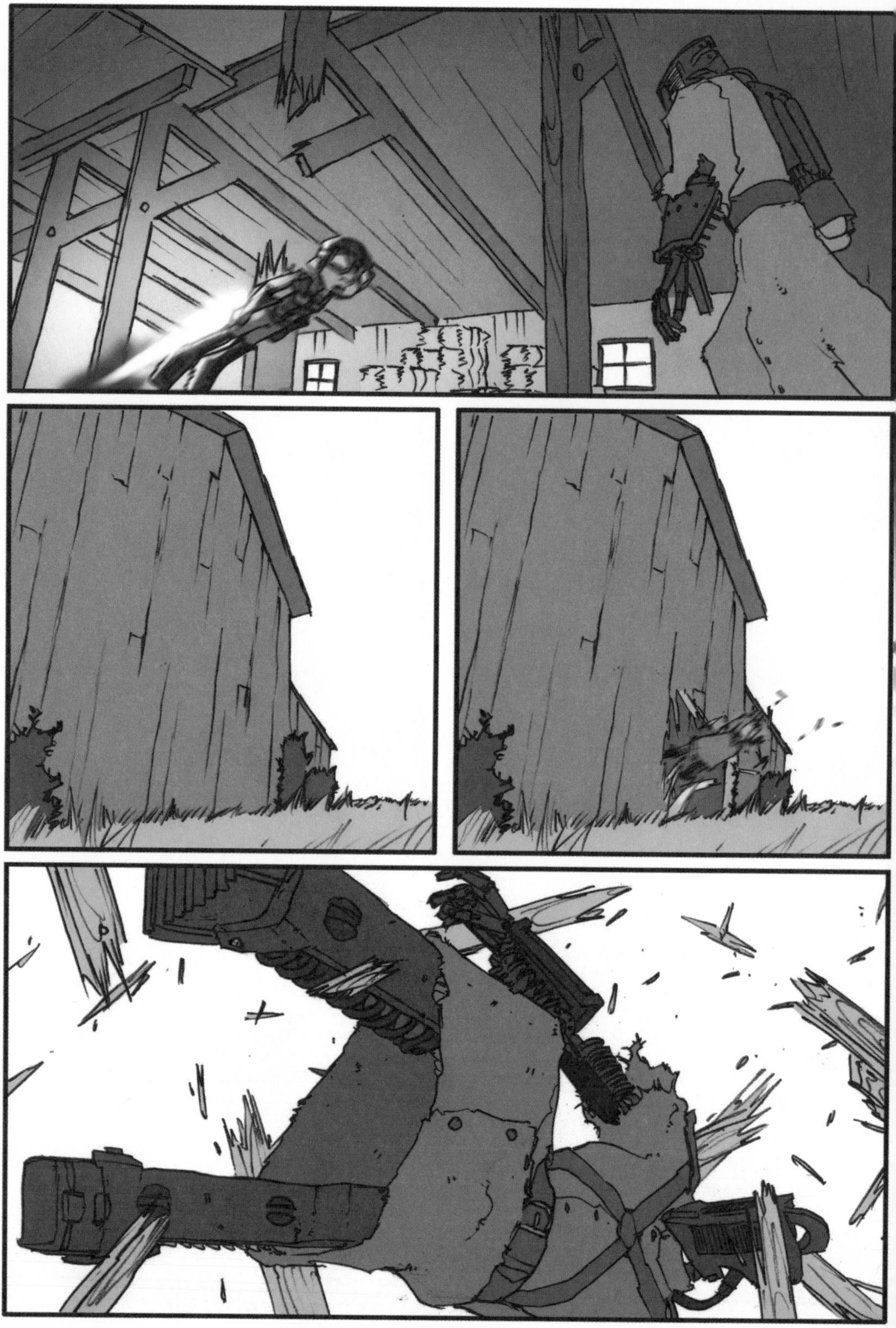

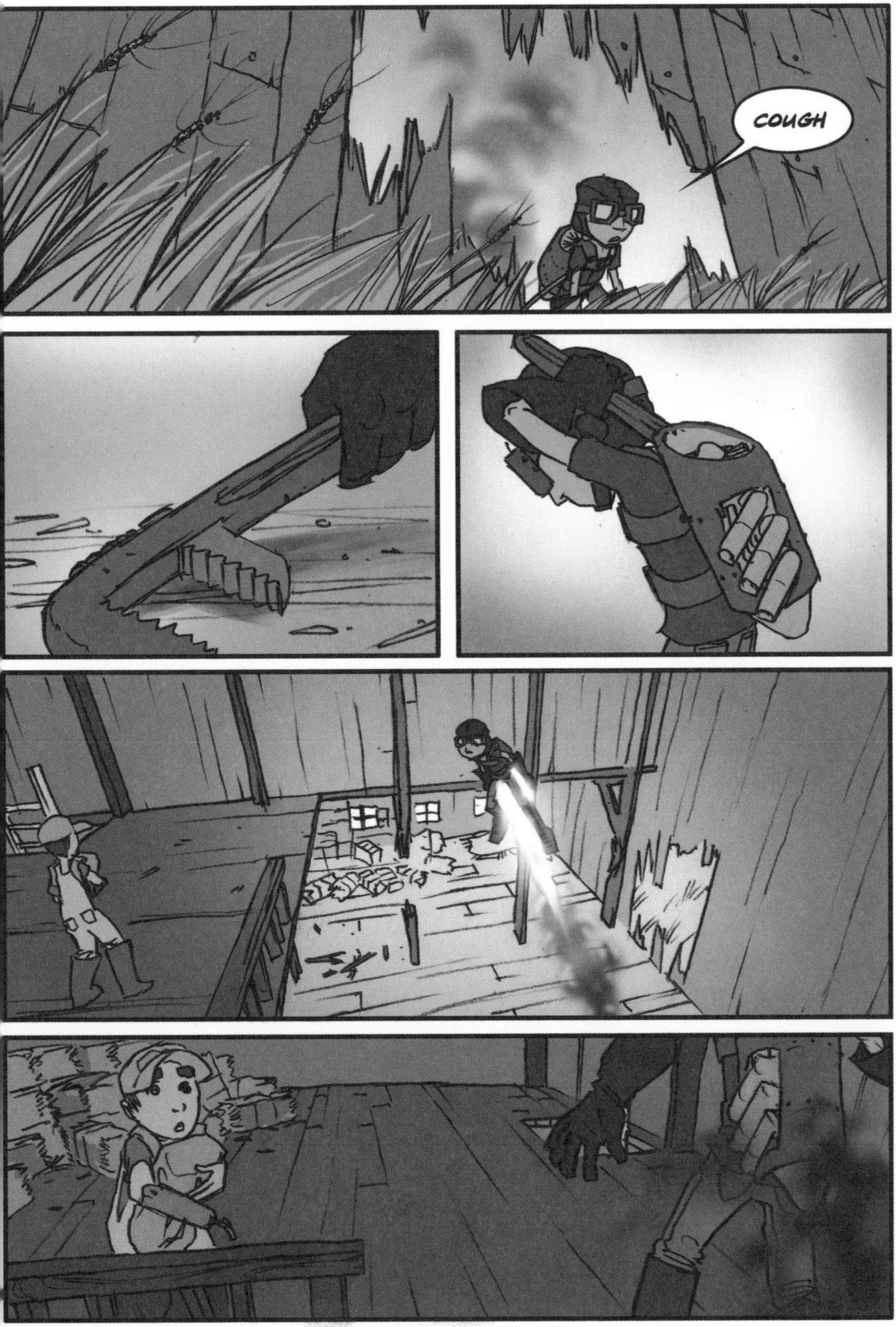
COUGH

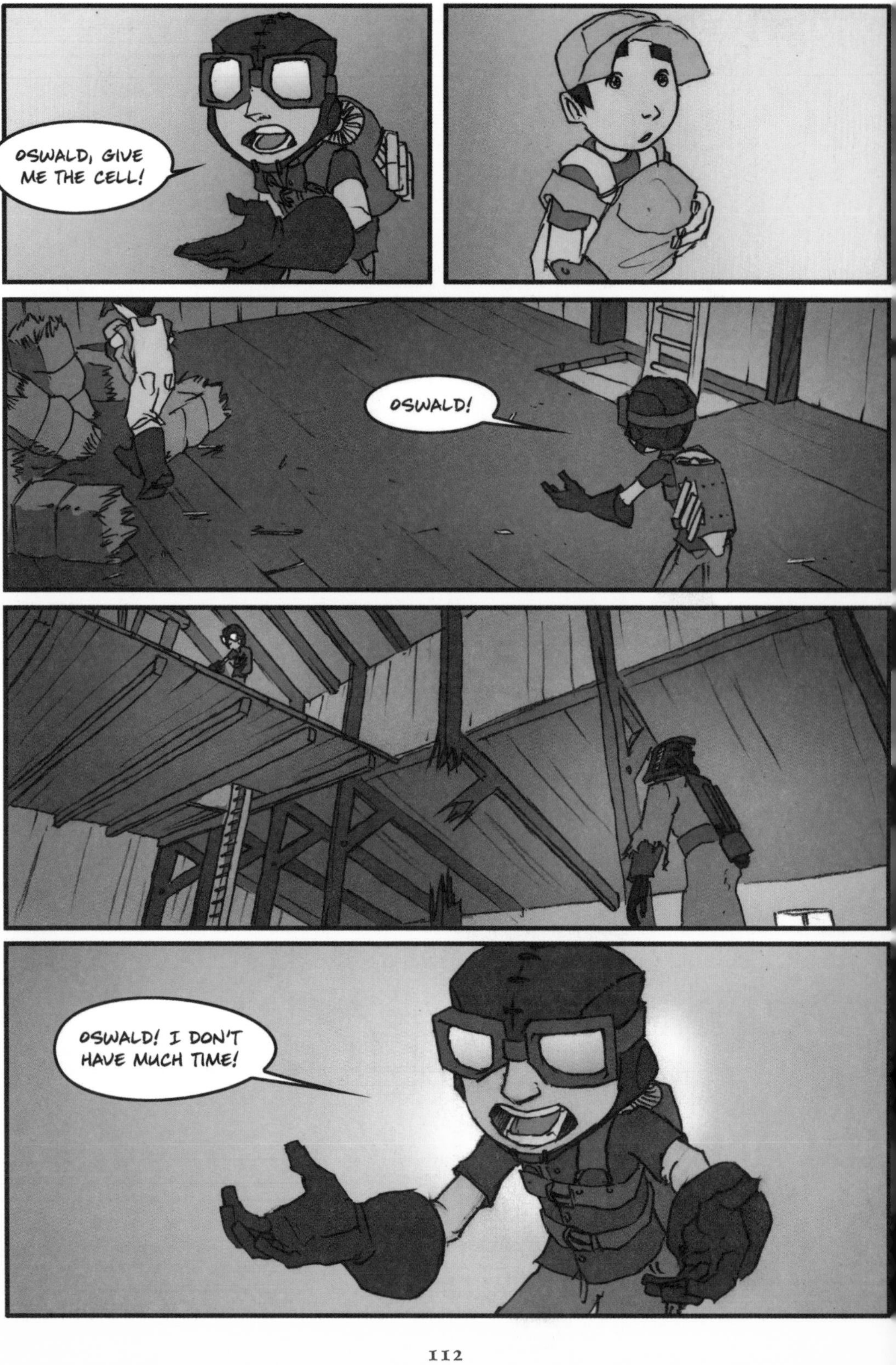
OSWALD, GIVE ME THE CELL!
OSWALD!
OSWALD! I DON'T HAVE MUCH TIME!

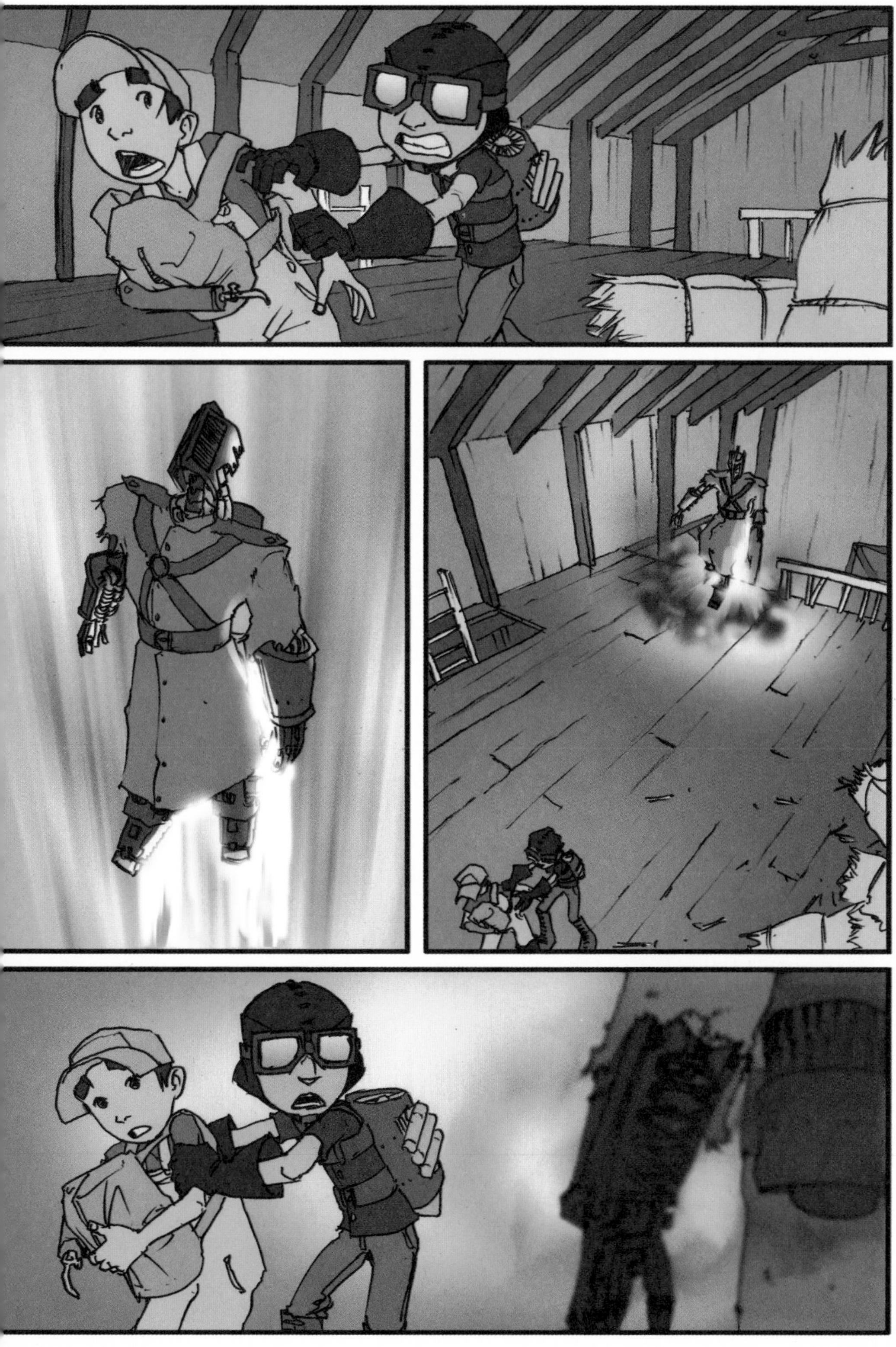

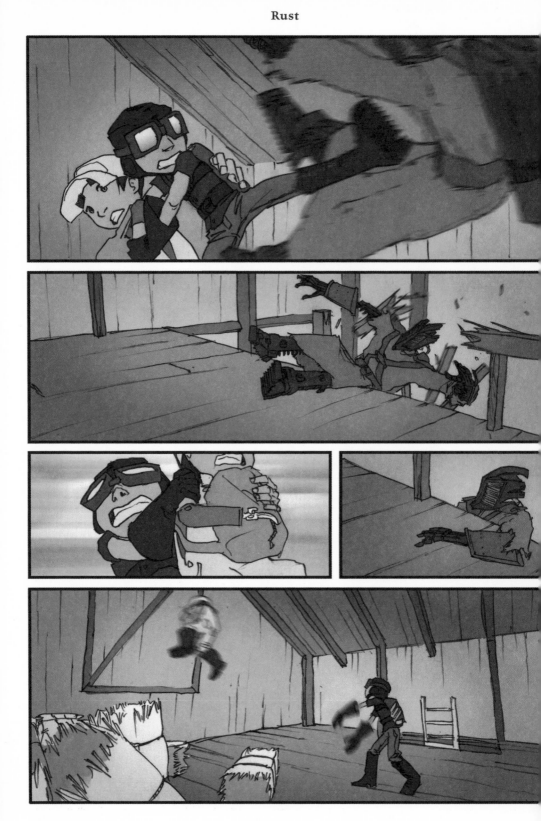

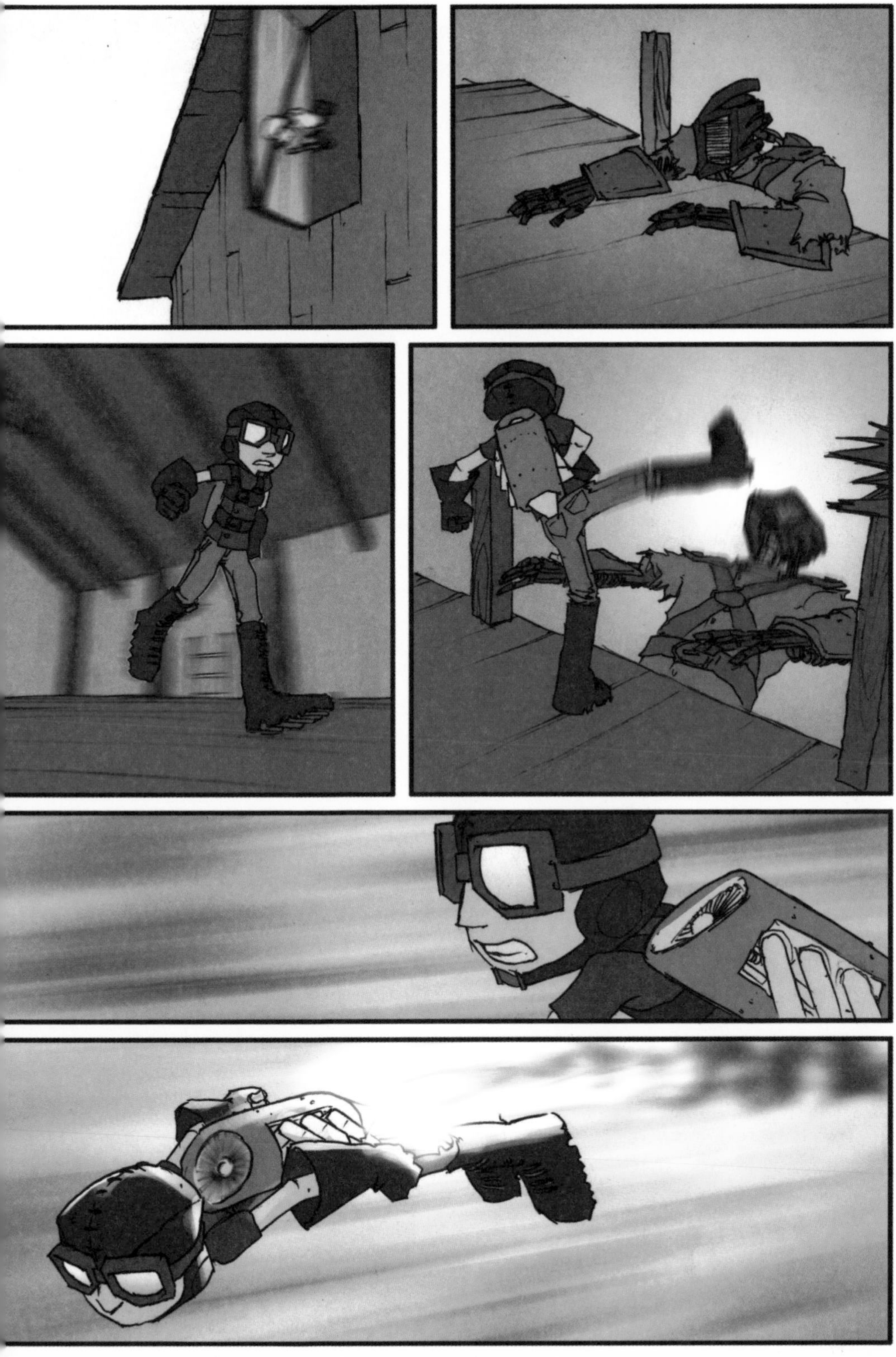

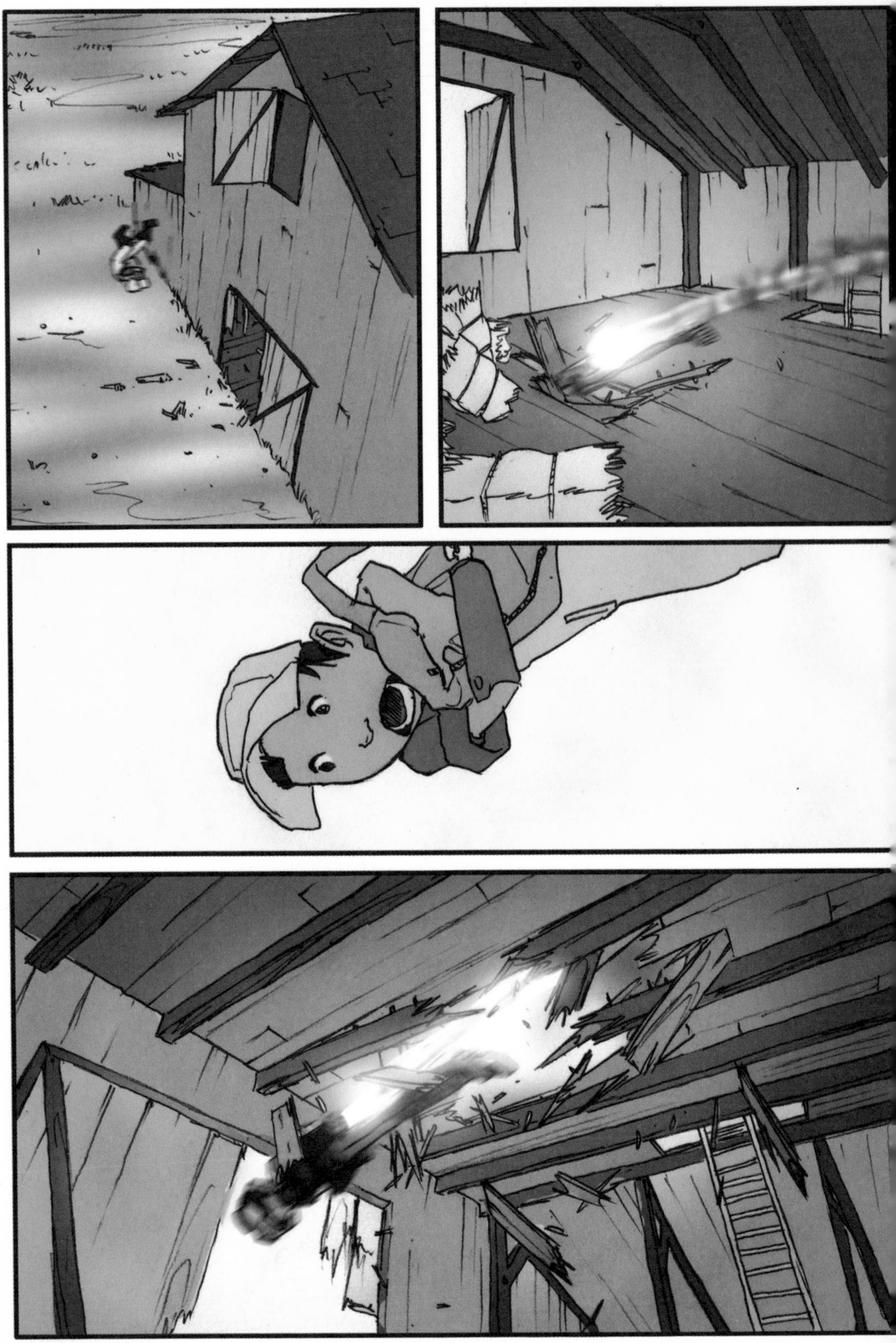

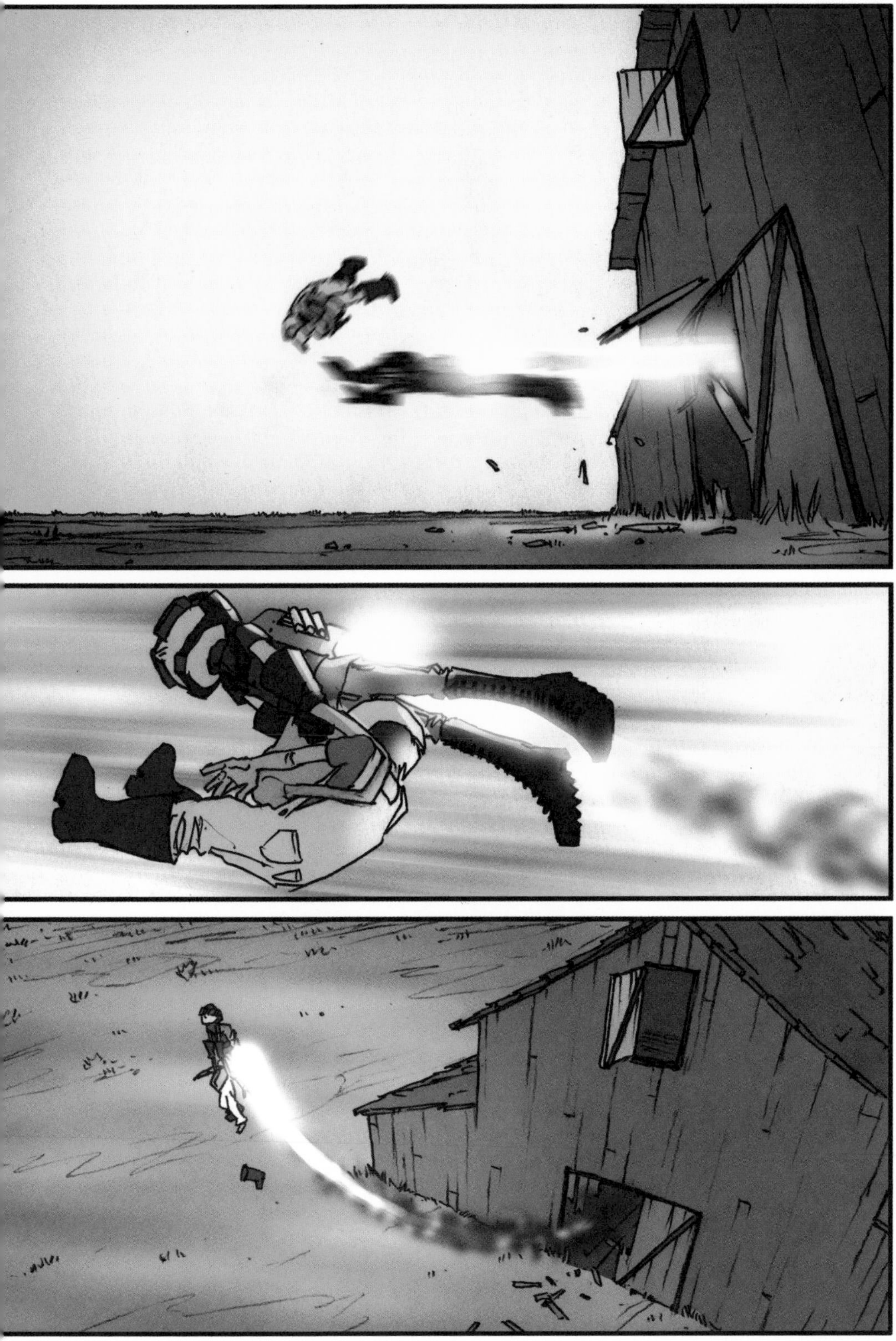

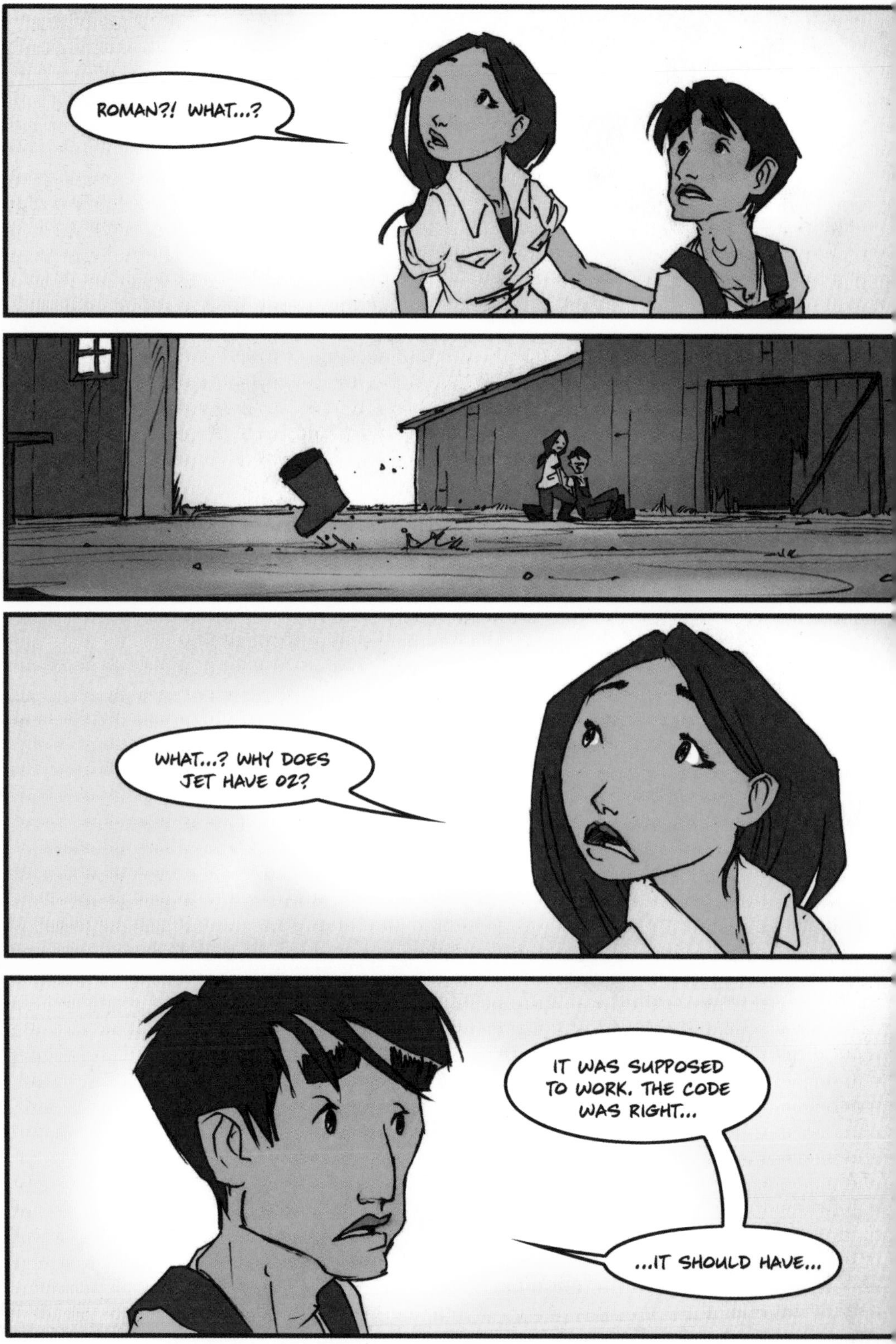
ROMAN?! WHAT...?
WHAT...? WHY DOES JET HAVE O2?
IT WAS SUPPOSED TO WORK. THE CODE WAS RIGHT...
...IT SHOULD HAVE...

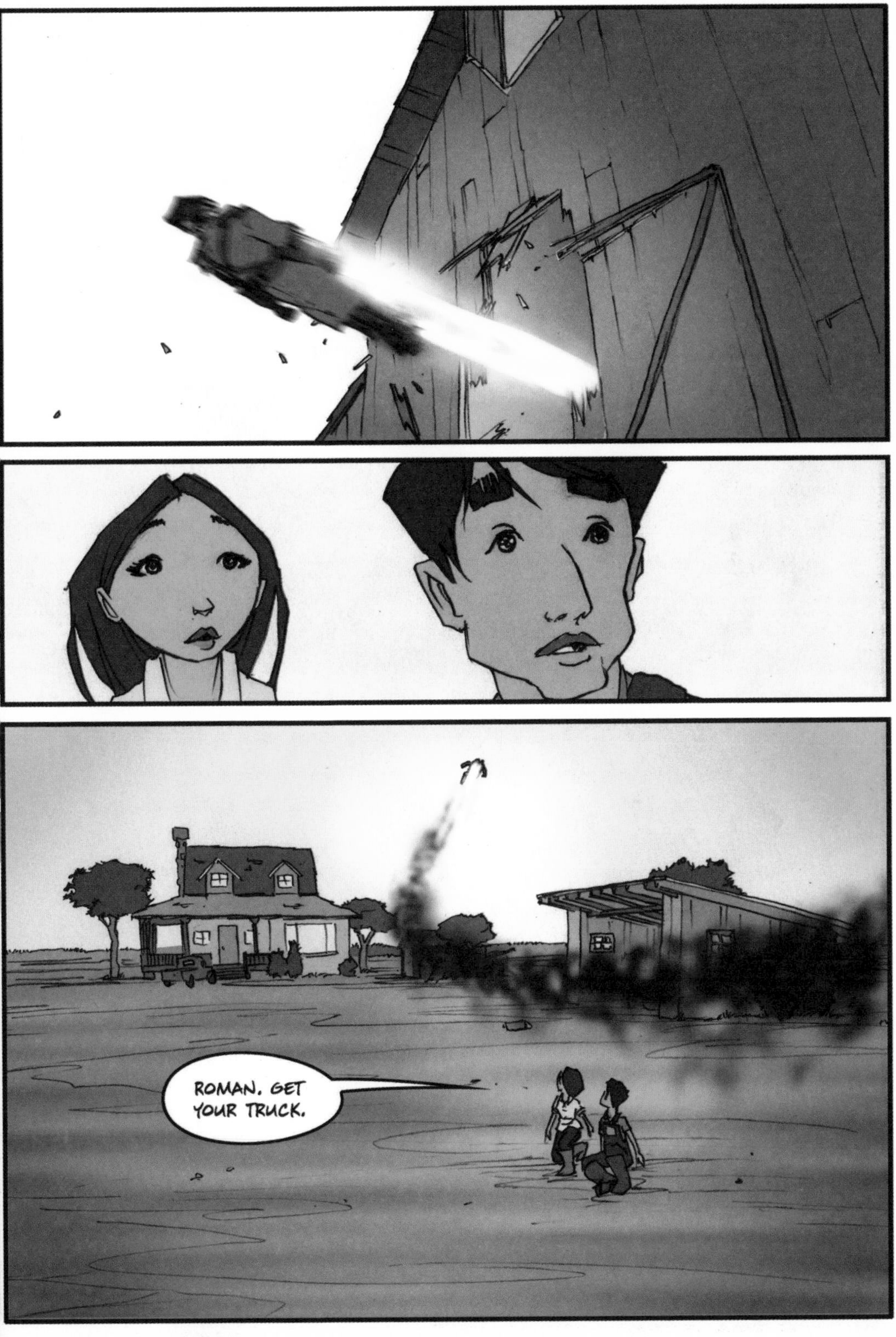
ROMAN. GET
YOUR TRUCK.

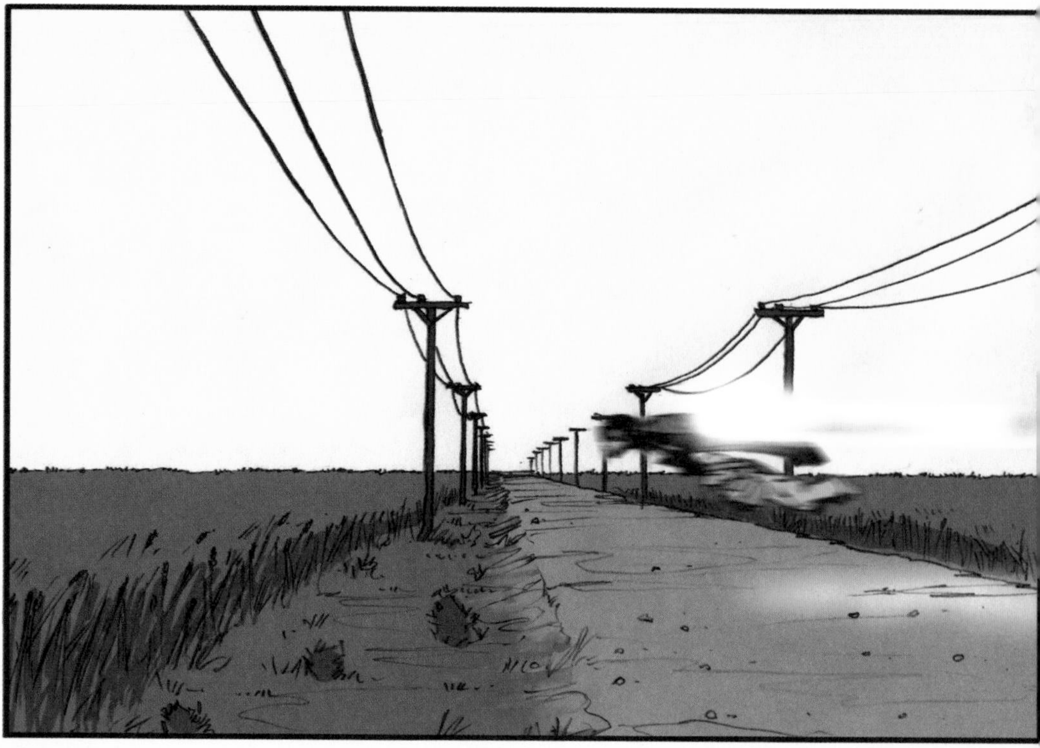

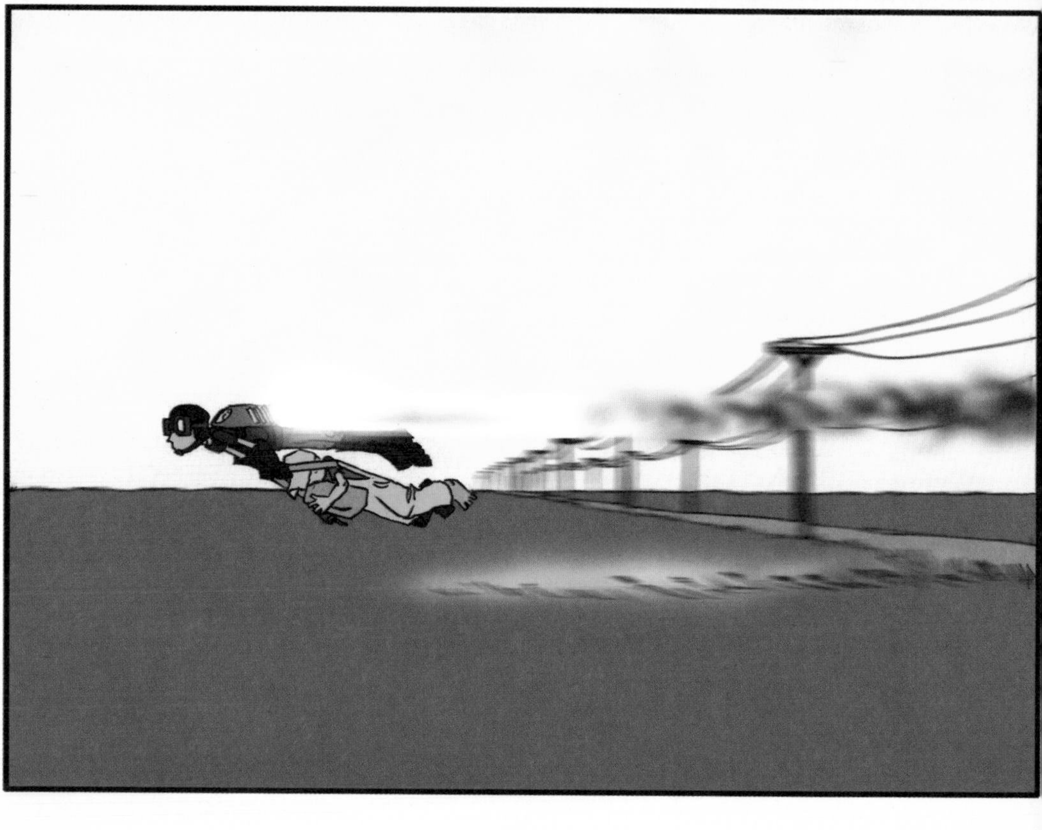

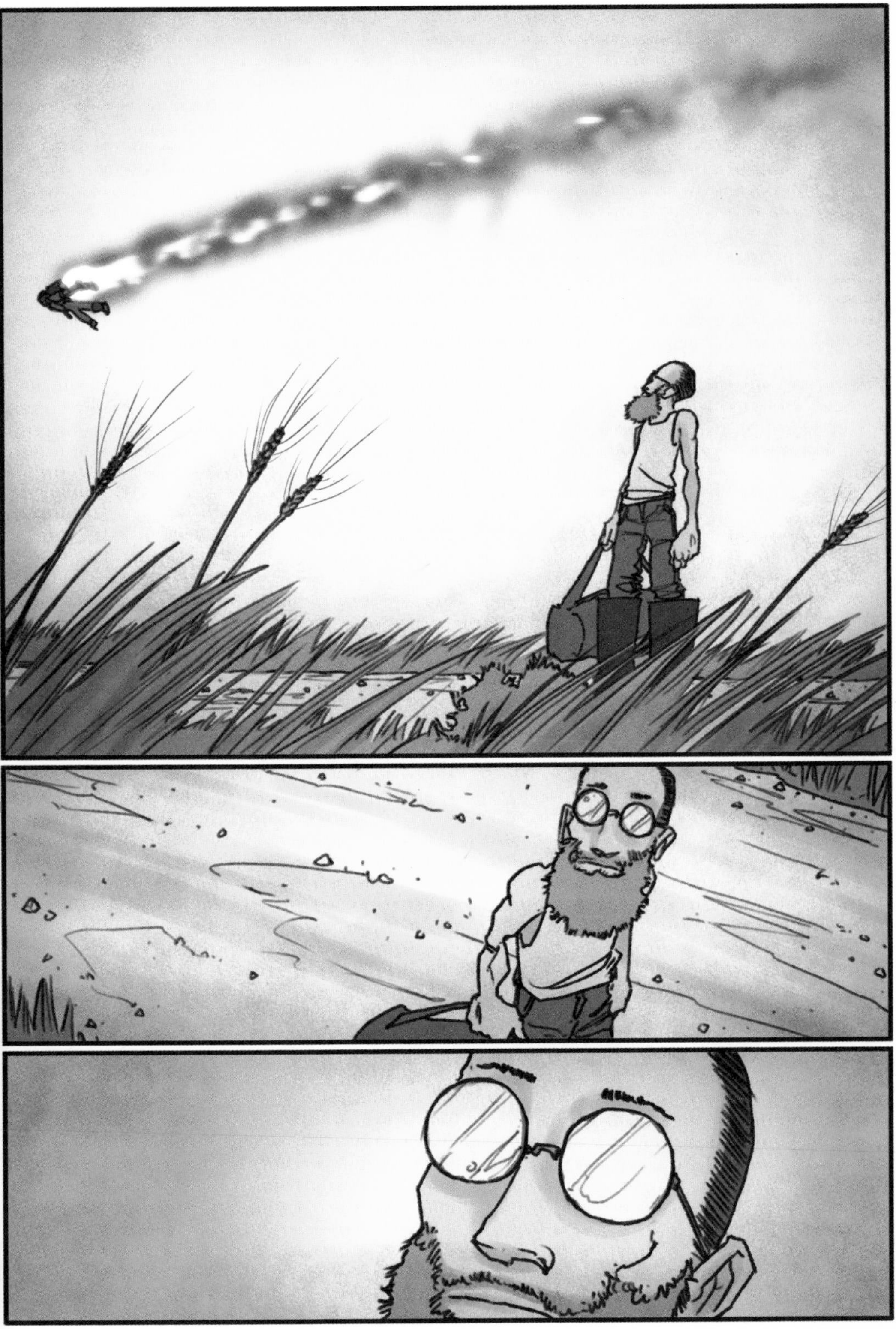

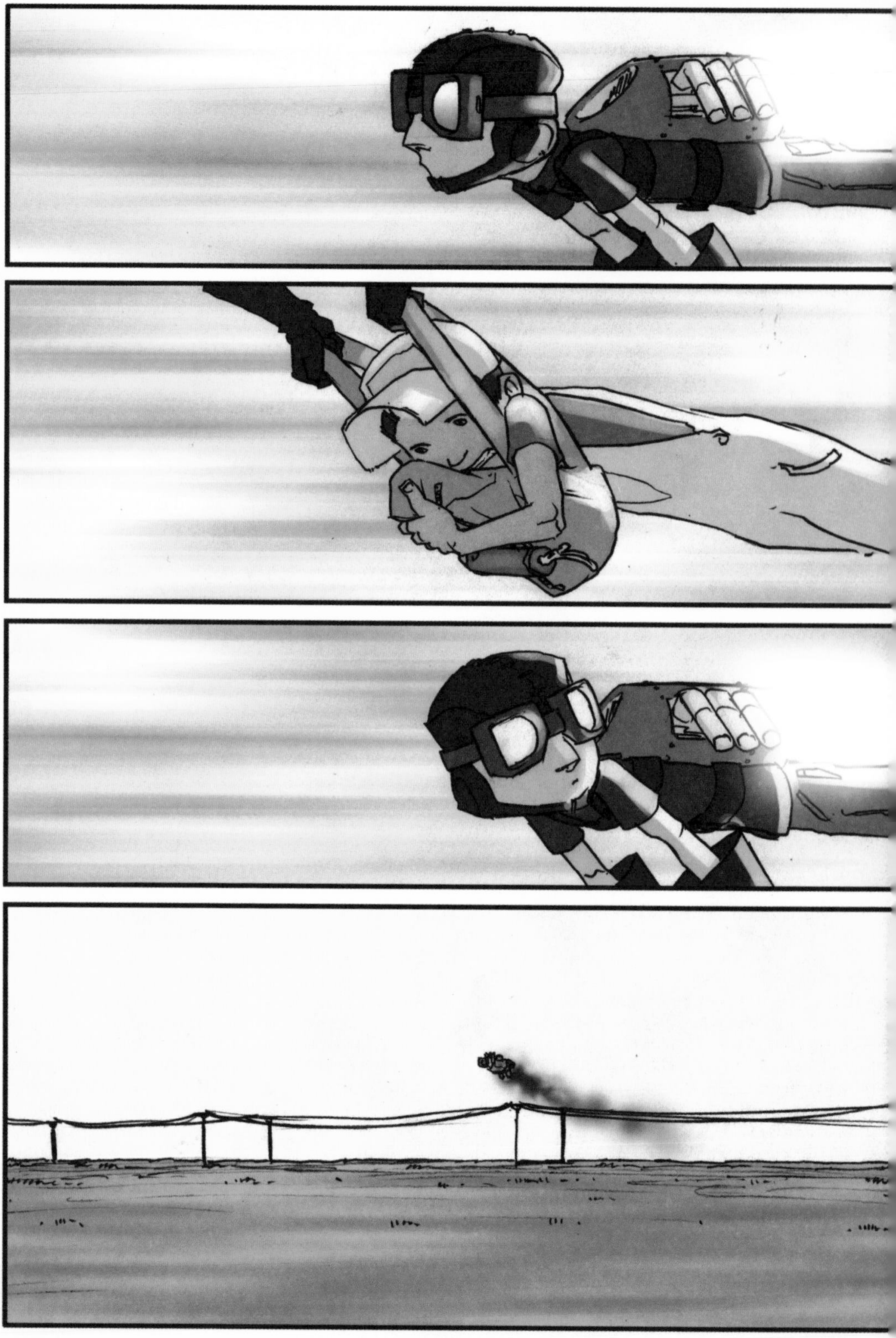

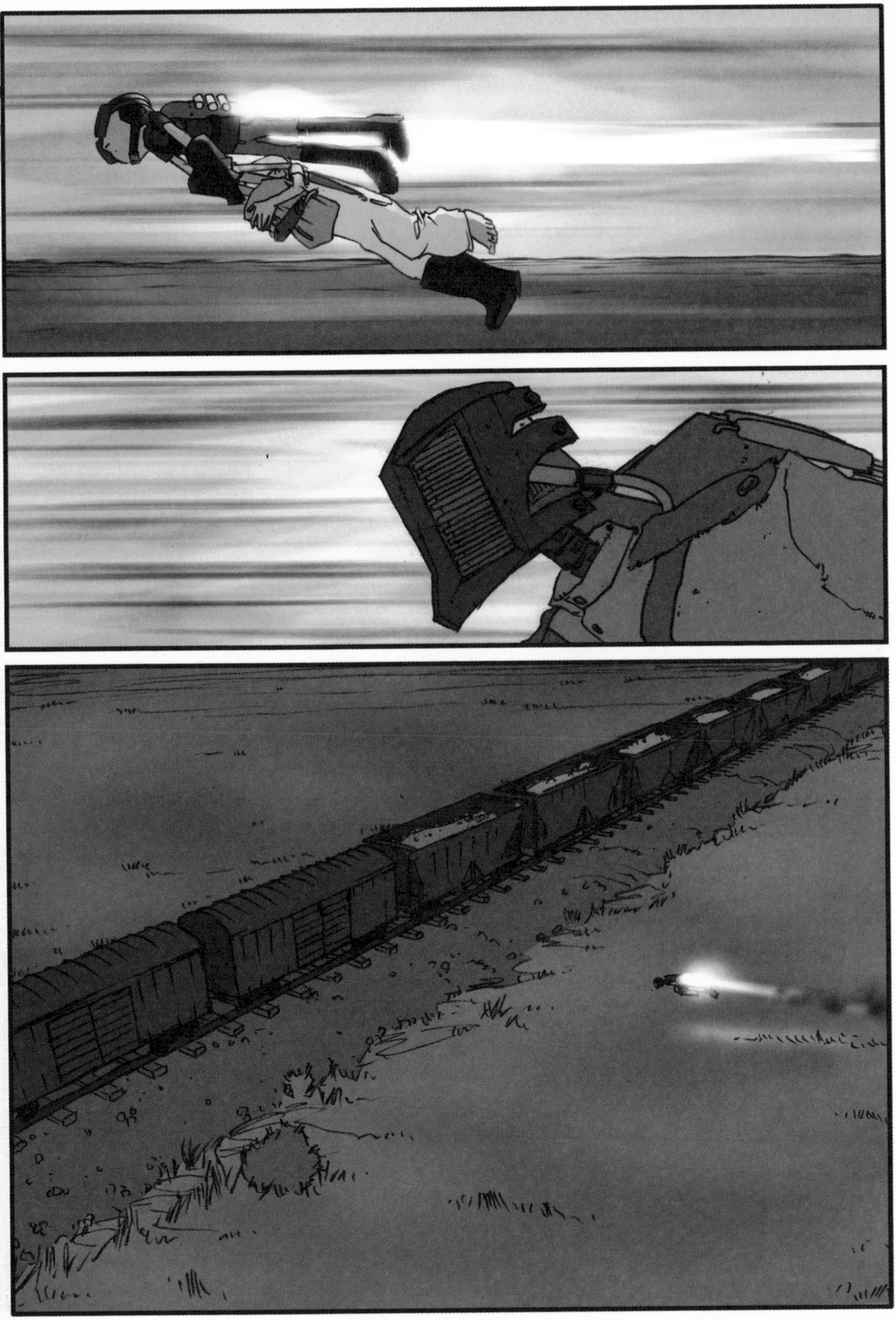

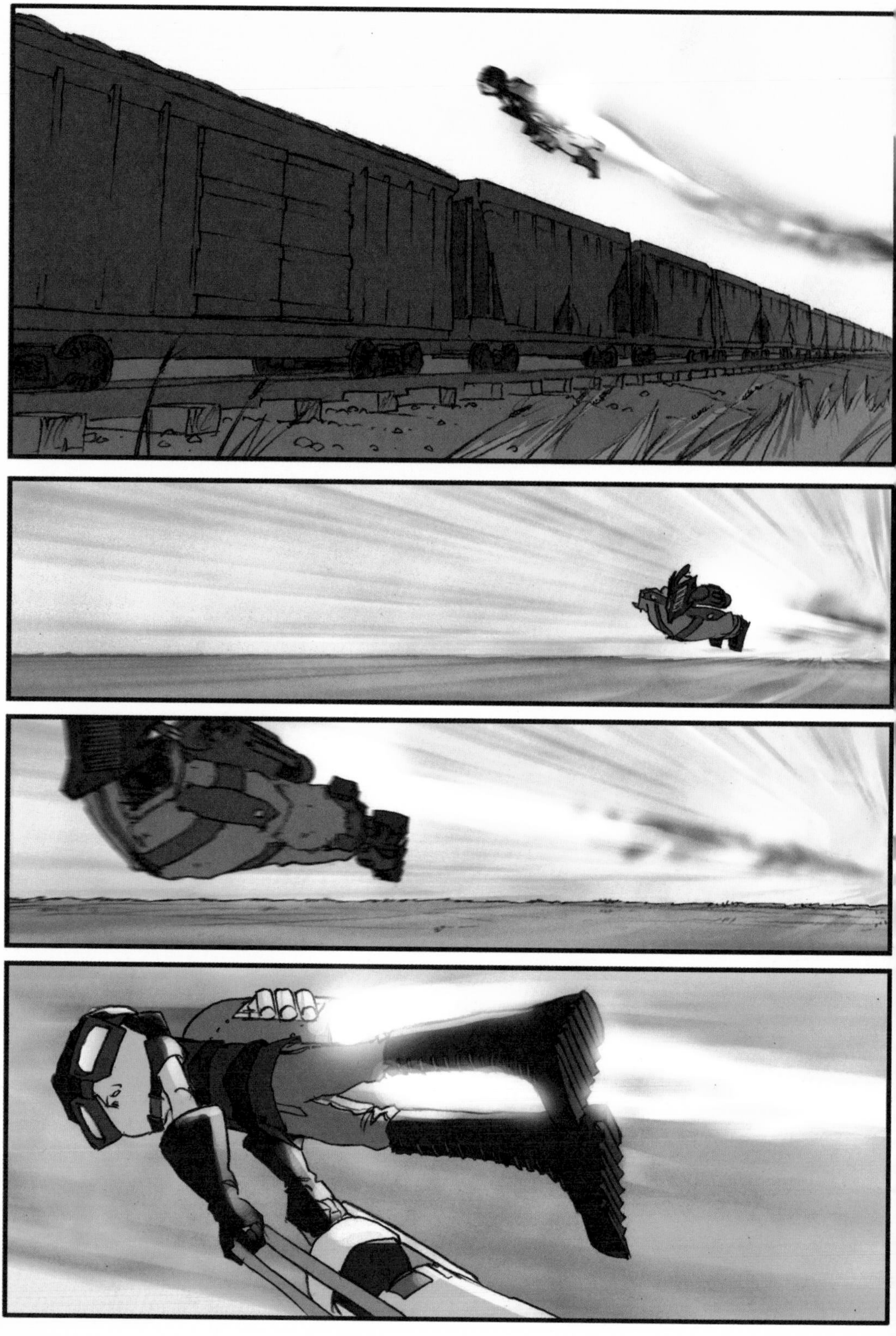

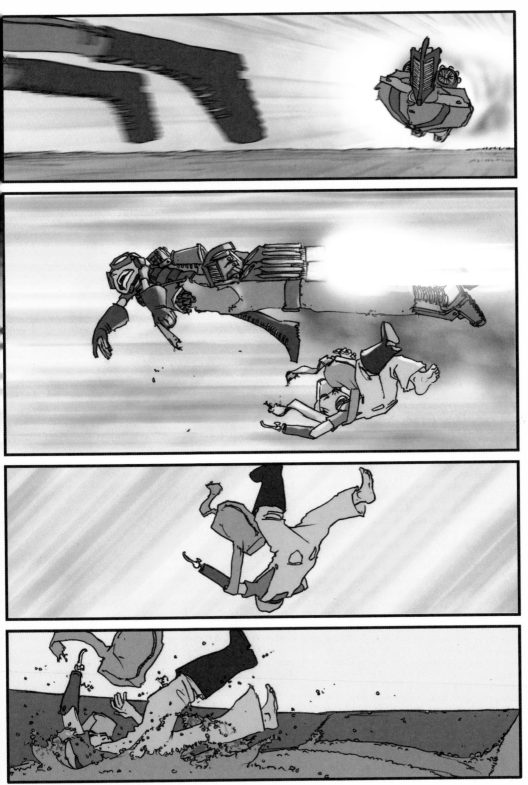

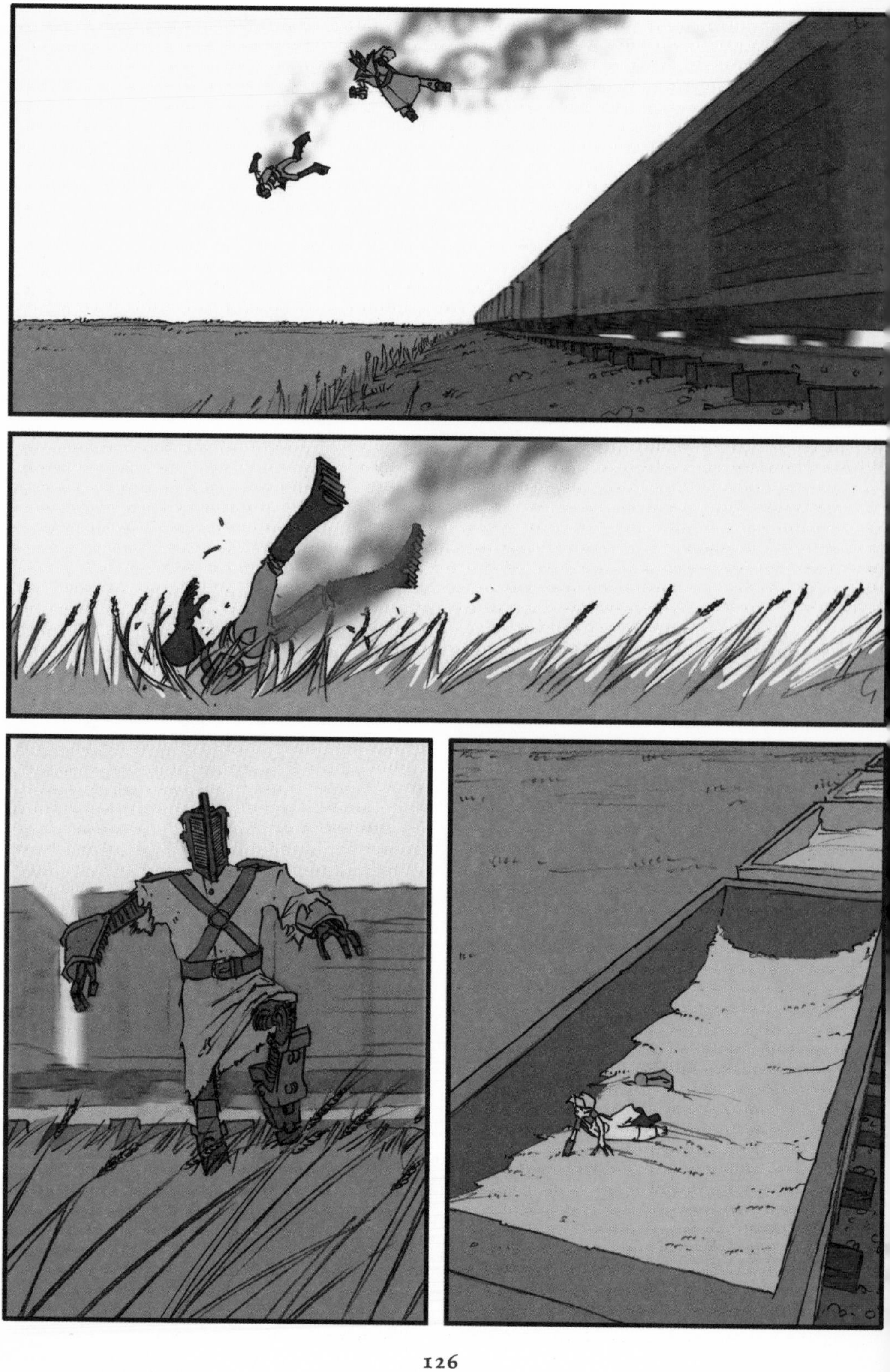

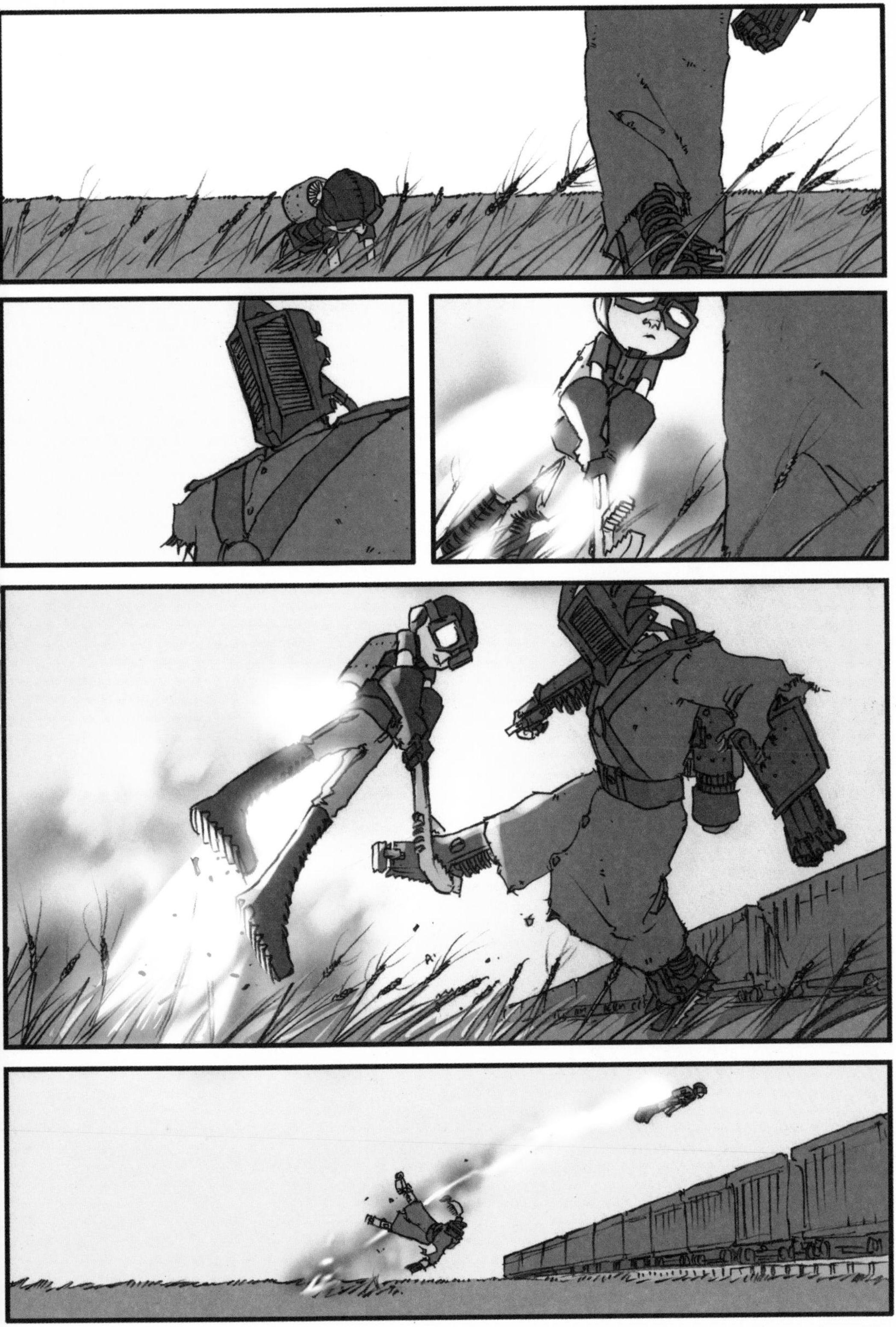

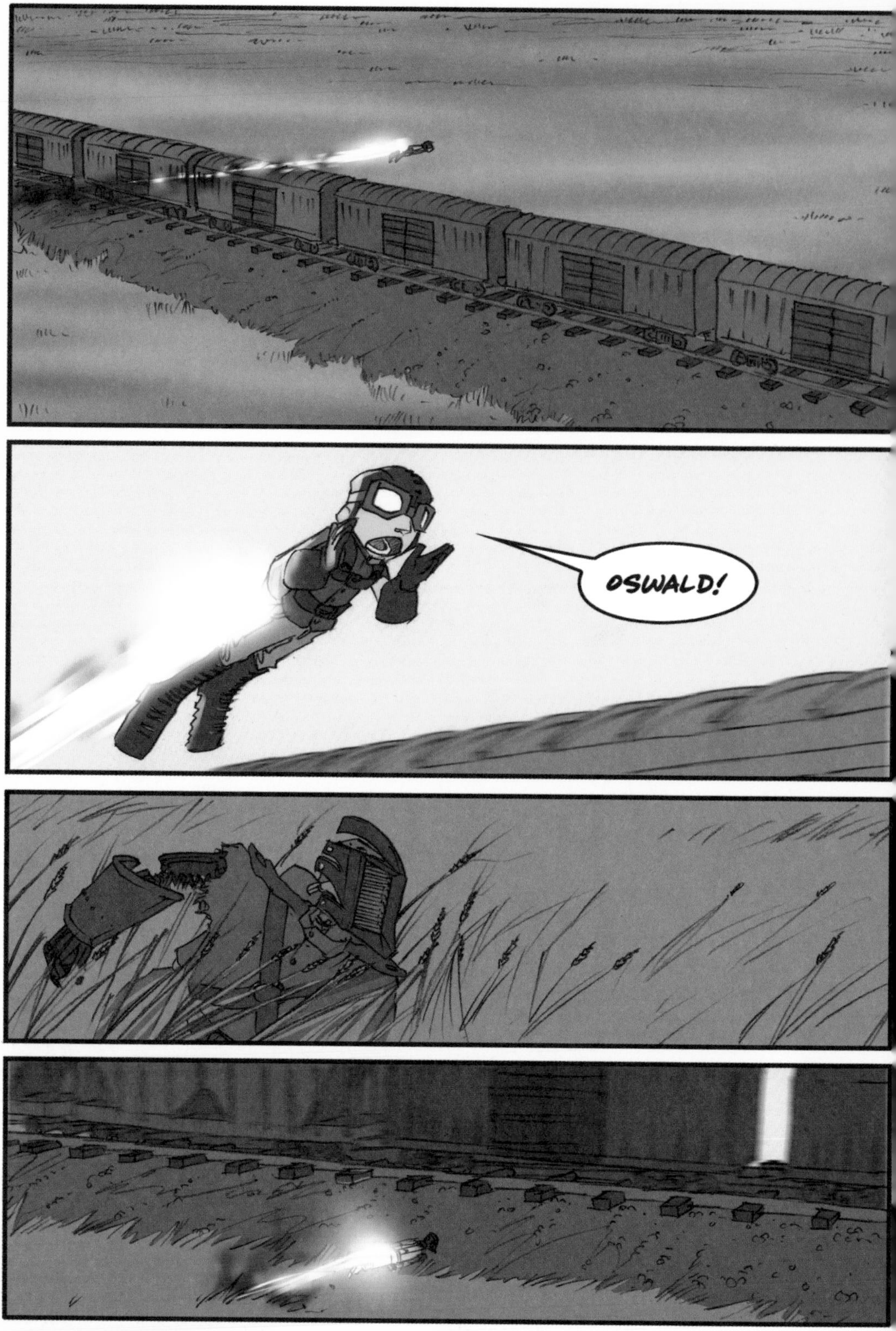
OSWALD!

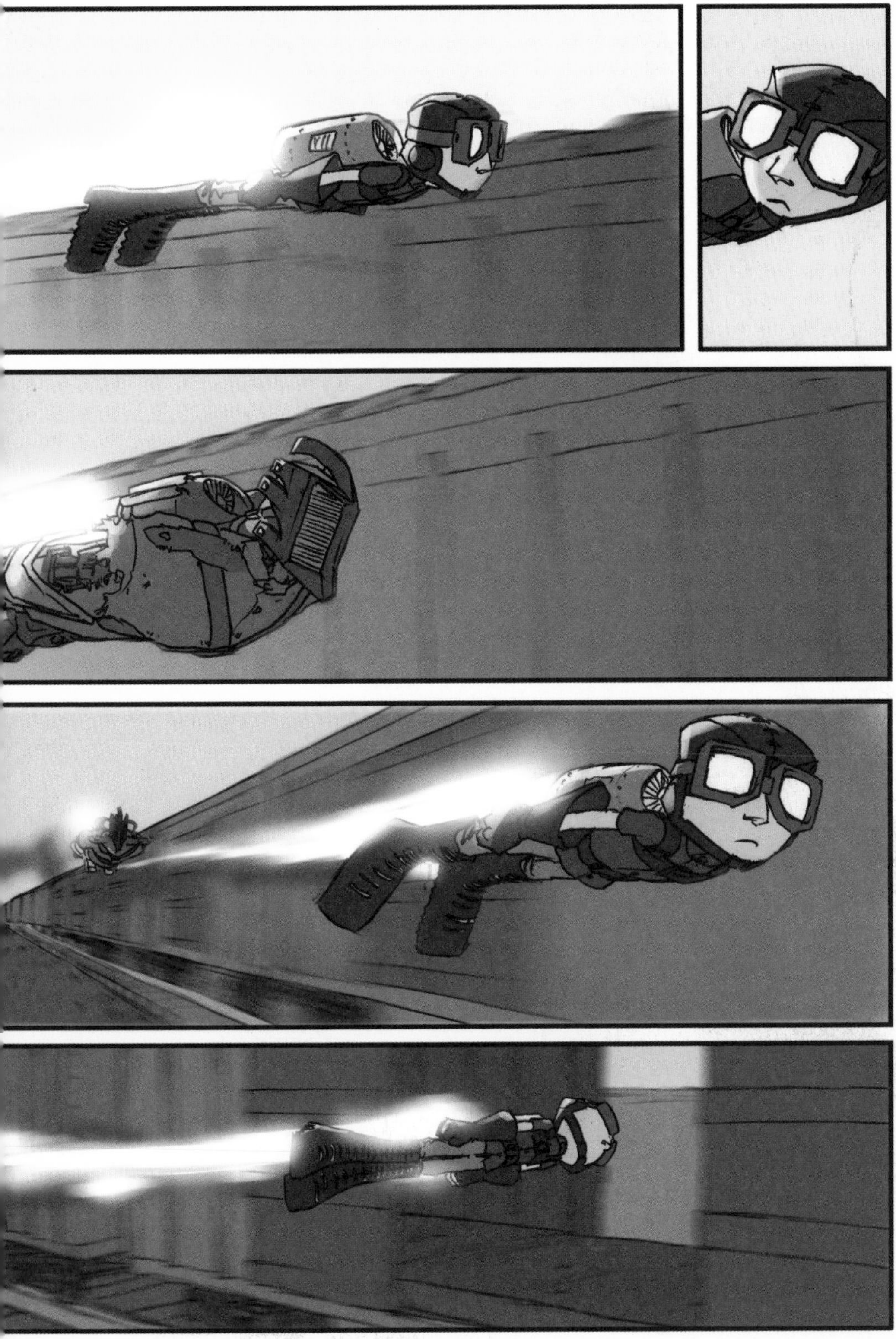

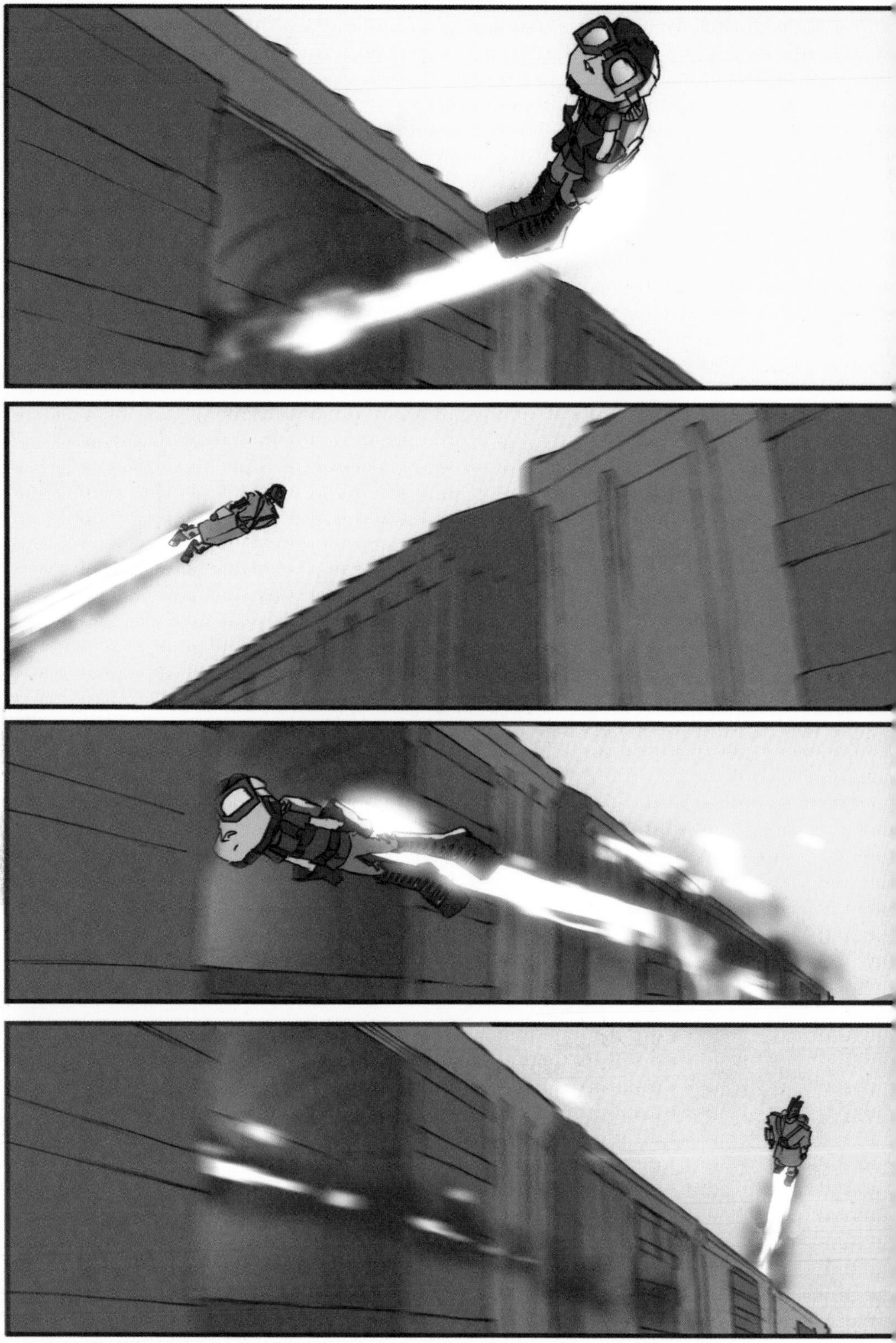

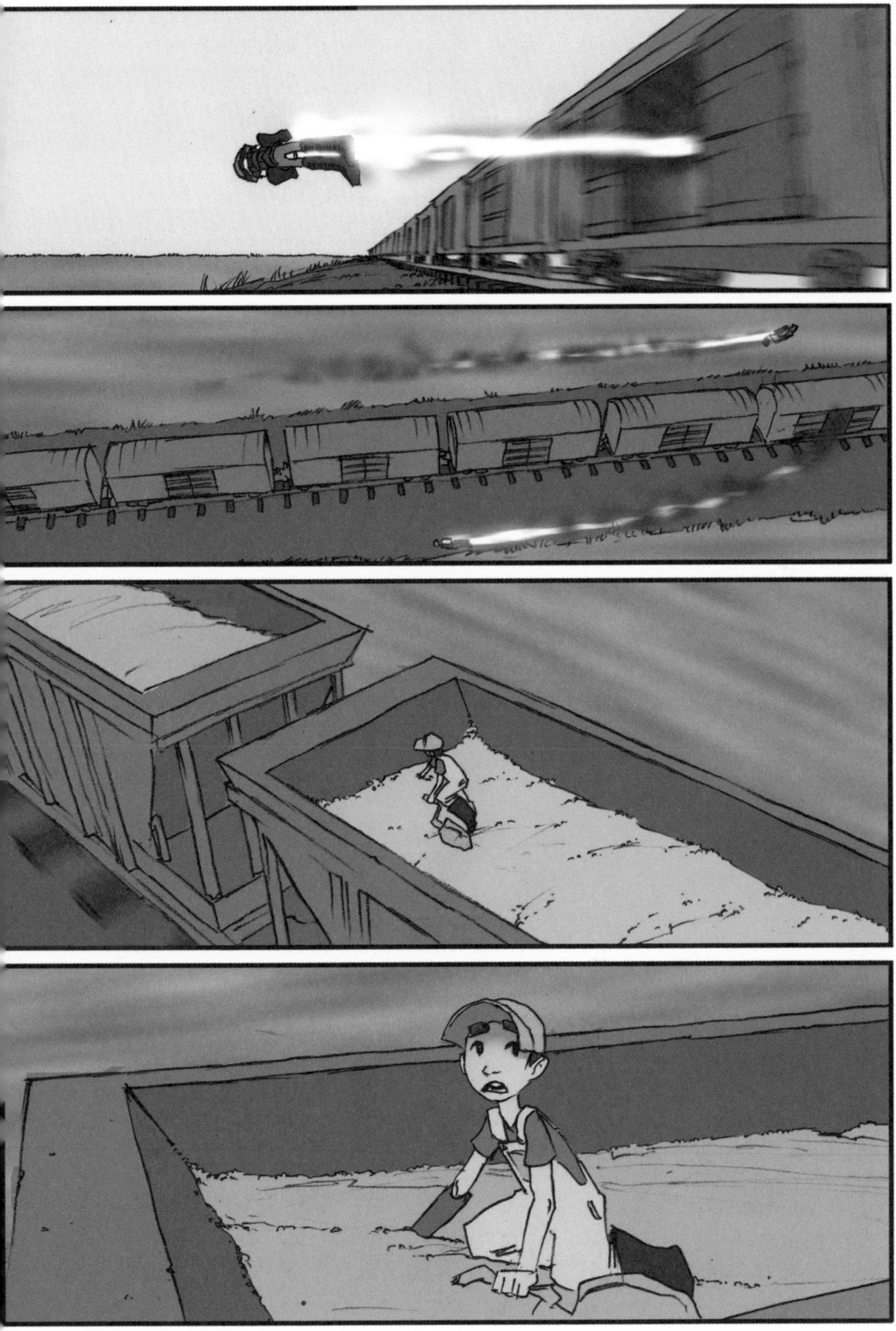

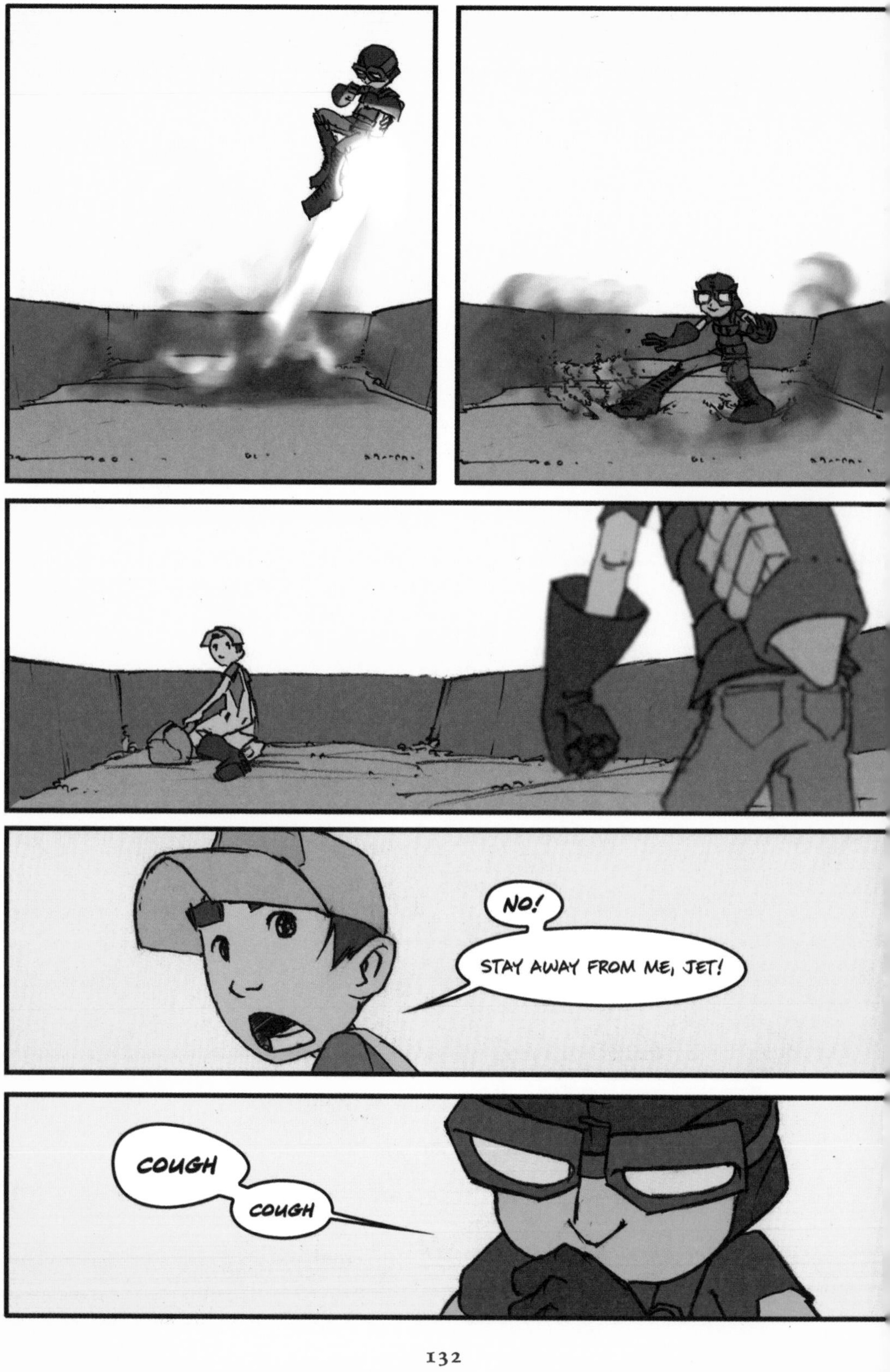
NO!
STAY AWAY FROM ME, JET!
COUGH
COUGH

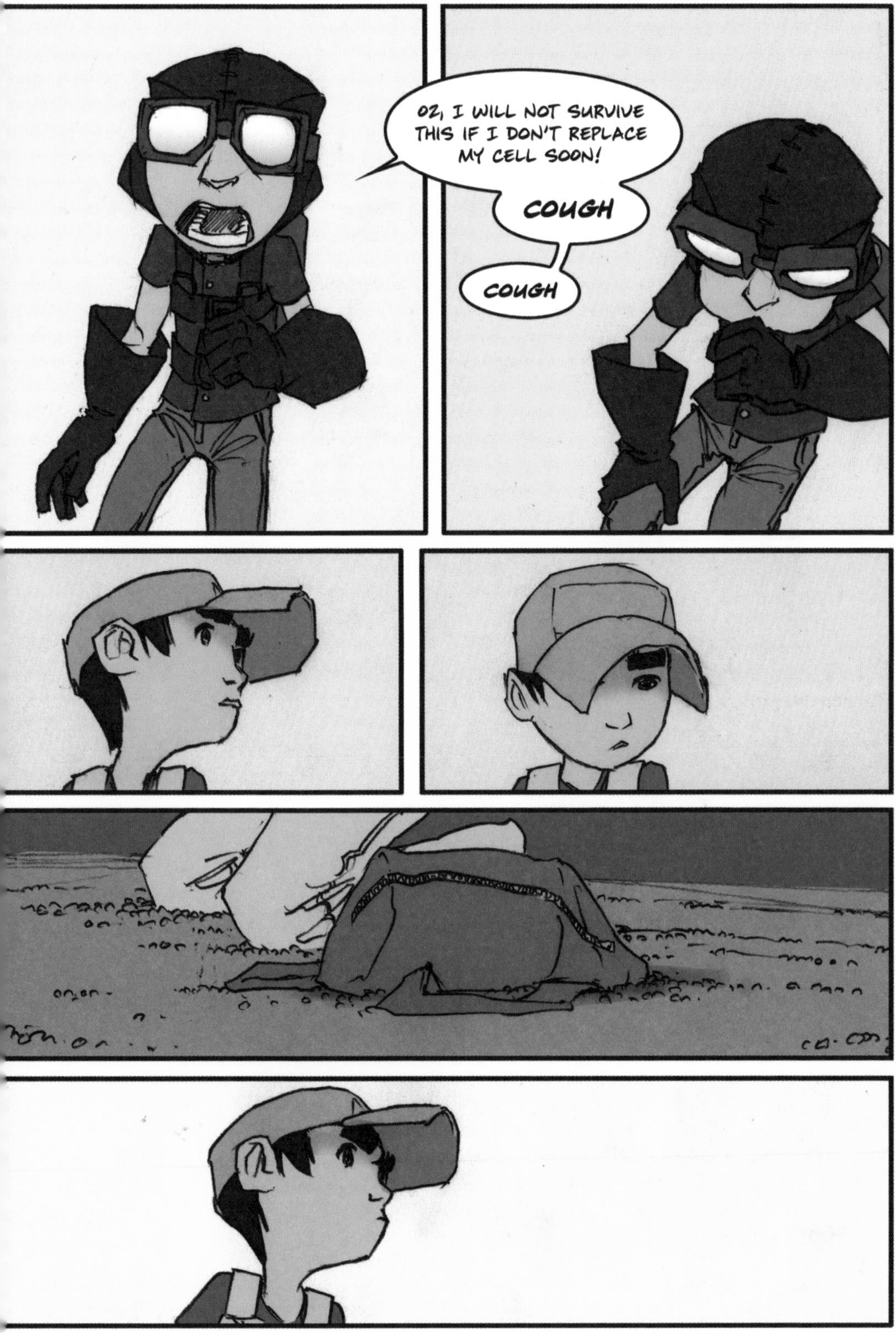
OZ, I WILL NOT SURVIVE THIS IF I DON'T REPLACE MY CELL SOON!
COUGH
COUGH

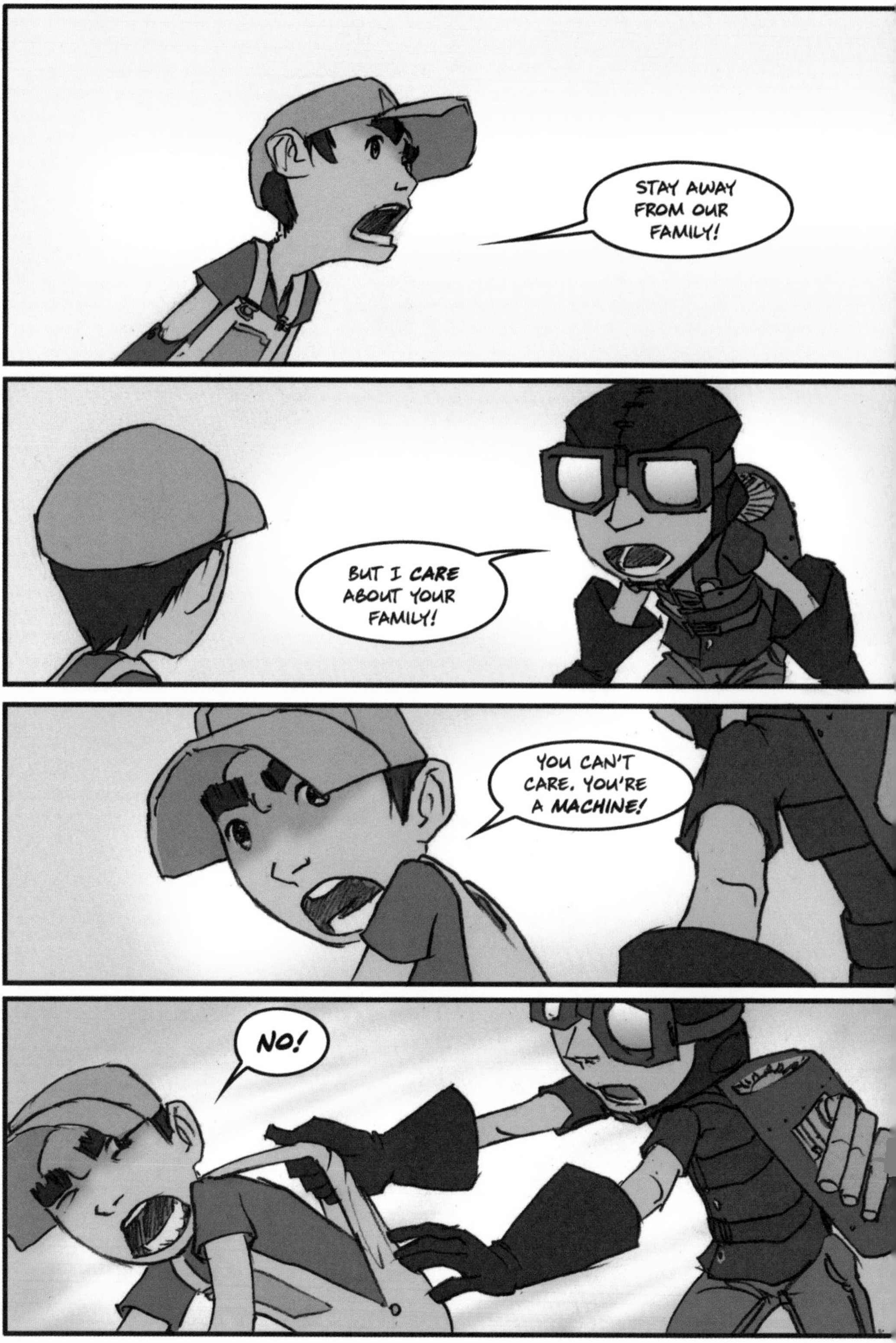
STAY AWAY FROM OUR FAMILY!
BUT I CARE ABOUT YOUR FAMILY!
YOU CAN'T CARE. YOU'RE A MACHINE!
NO!

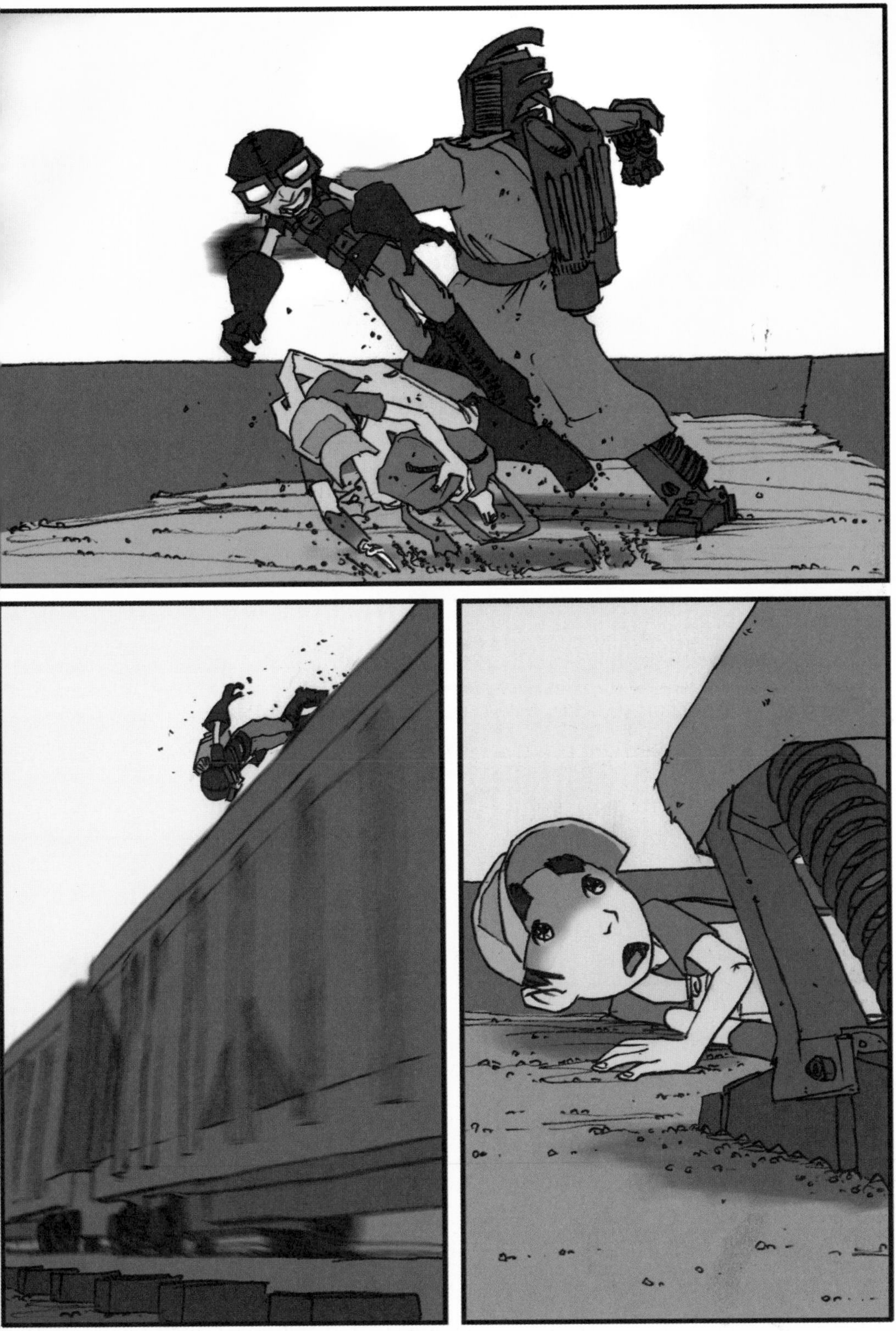

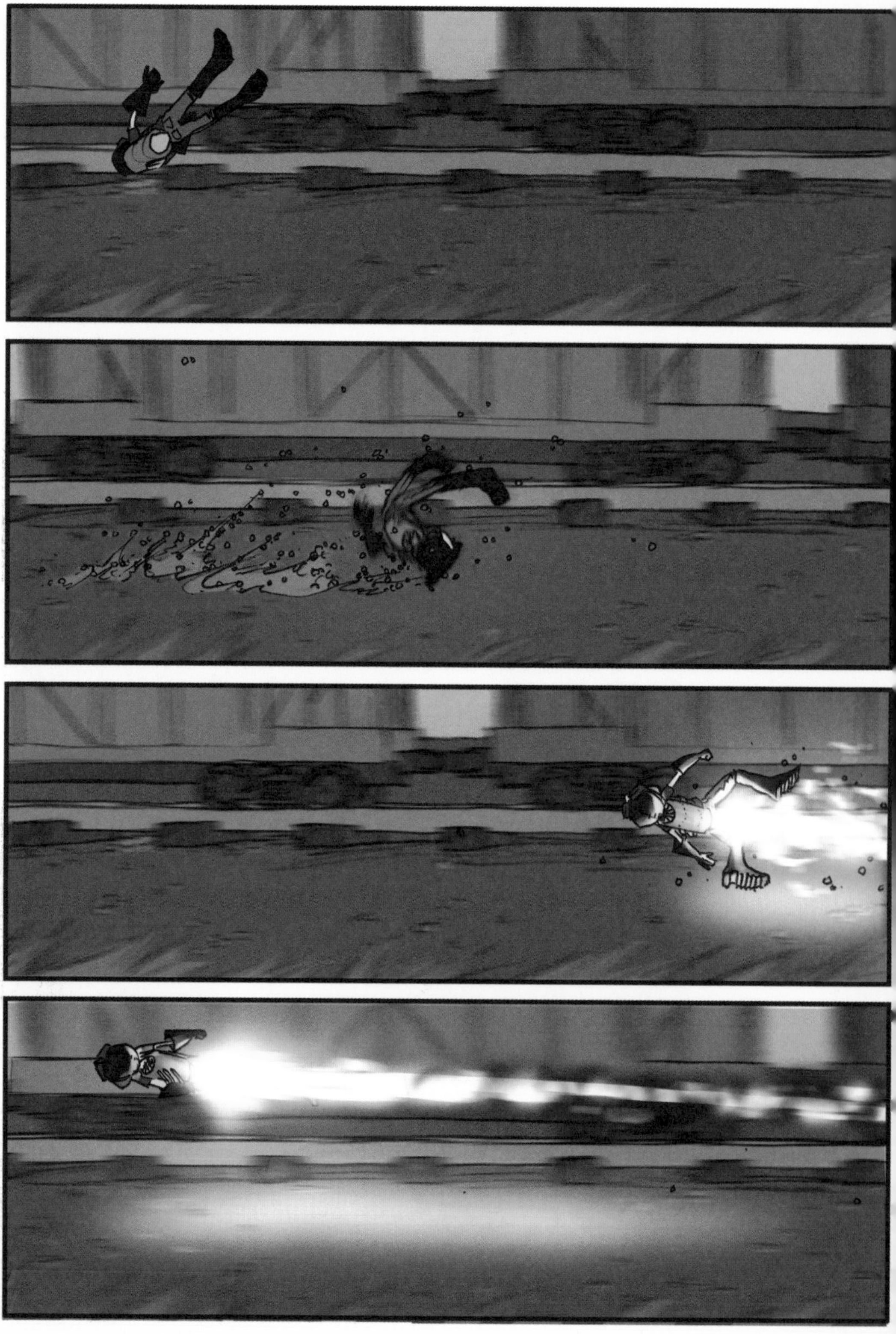

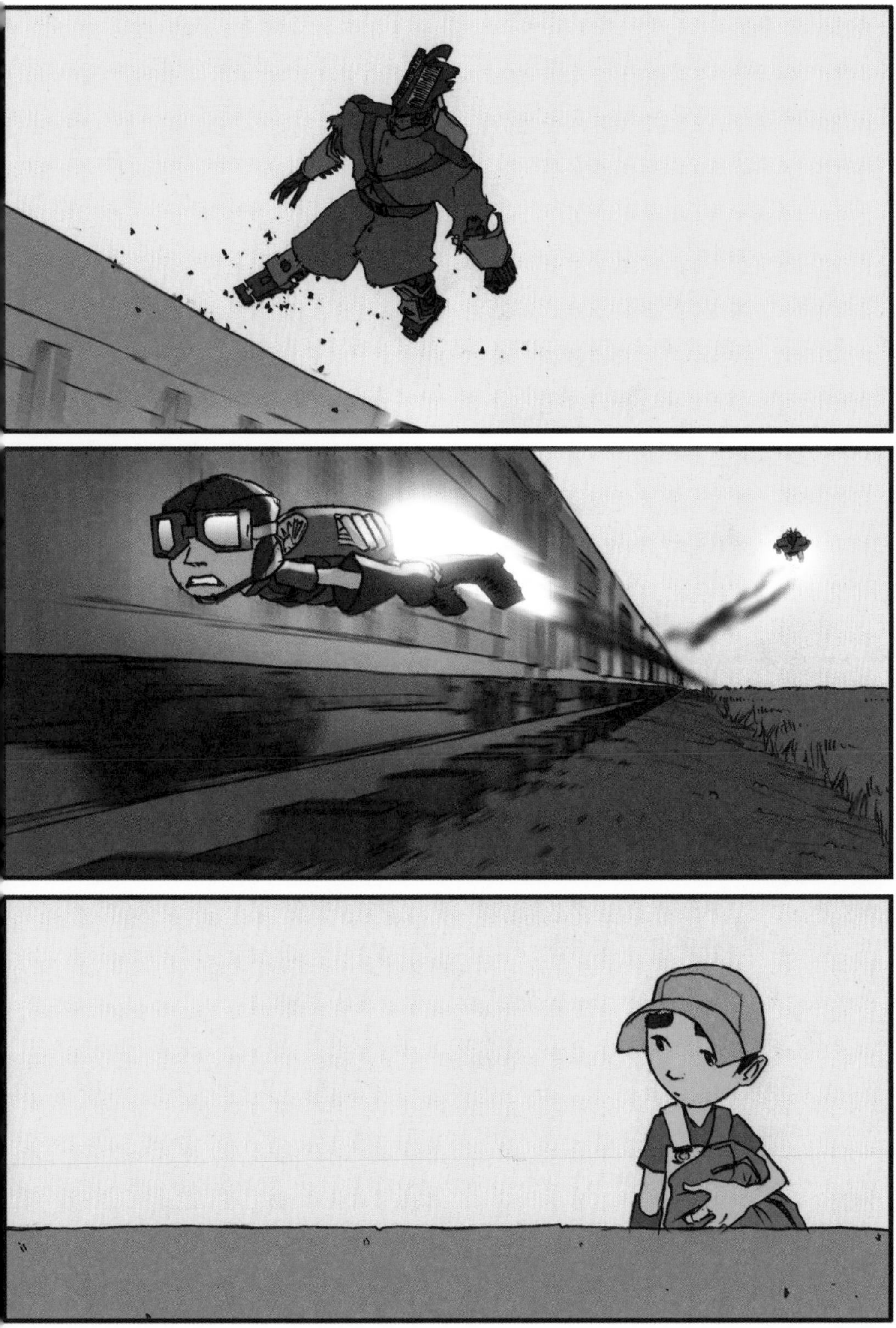

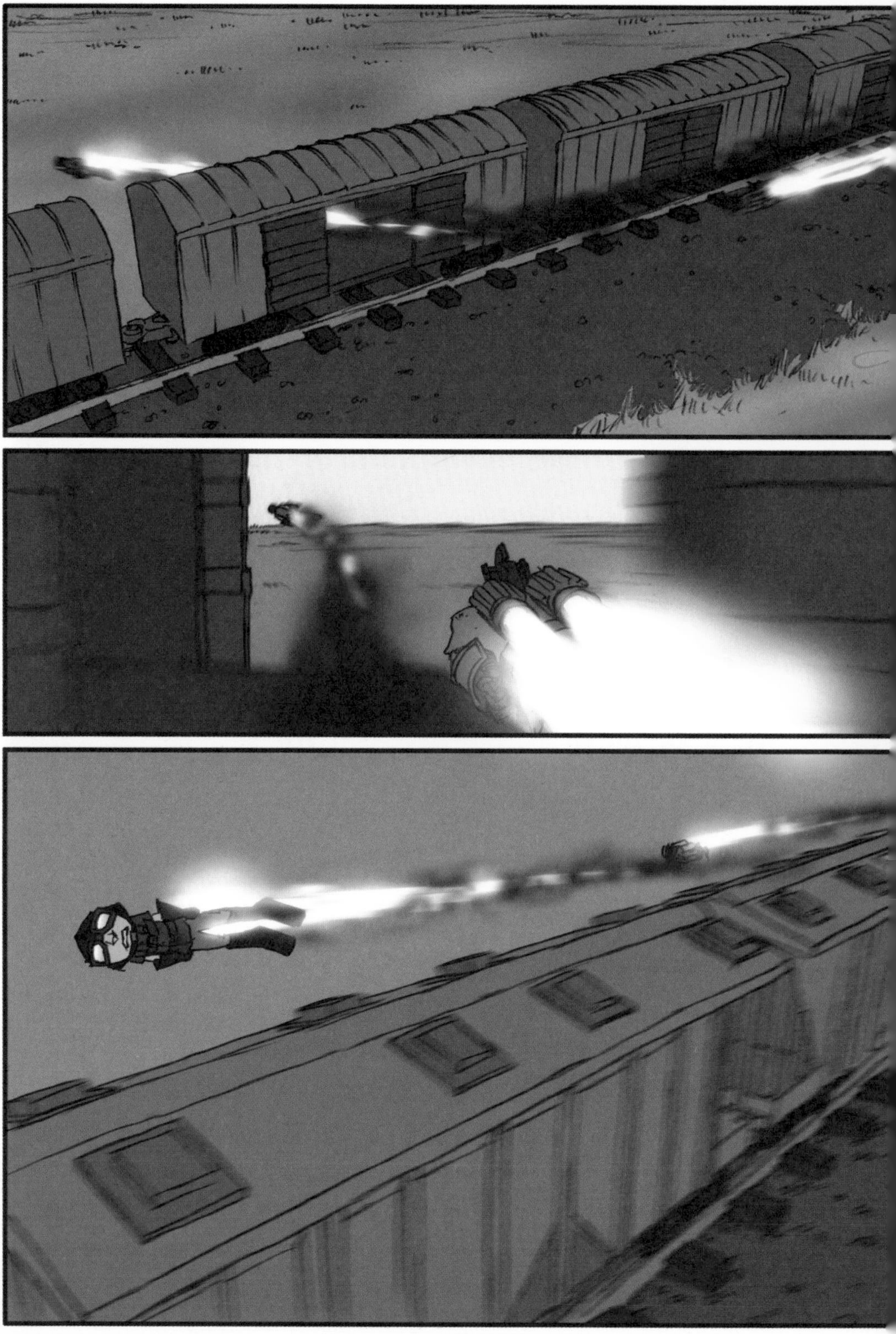

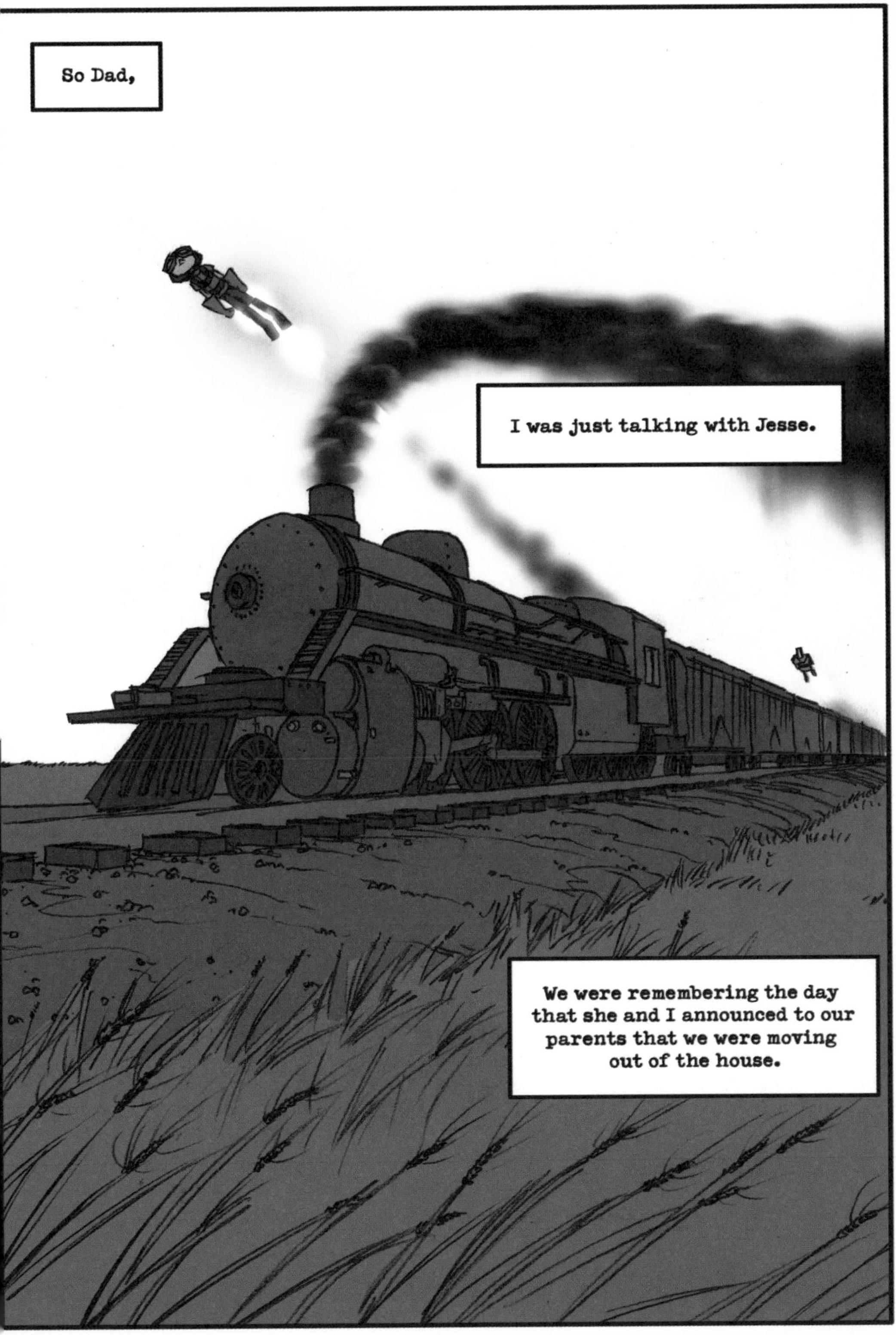
So Dad,
I was just talking with Jesse.
We were remembering the day that she and I announced to our parents that we were moving out of the house.

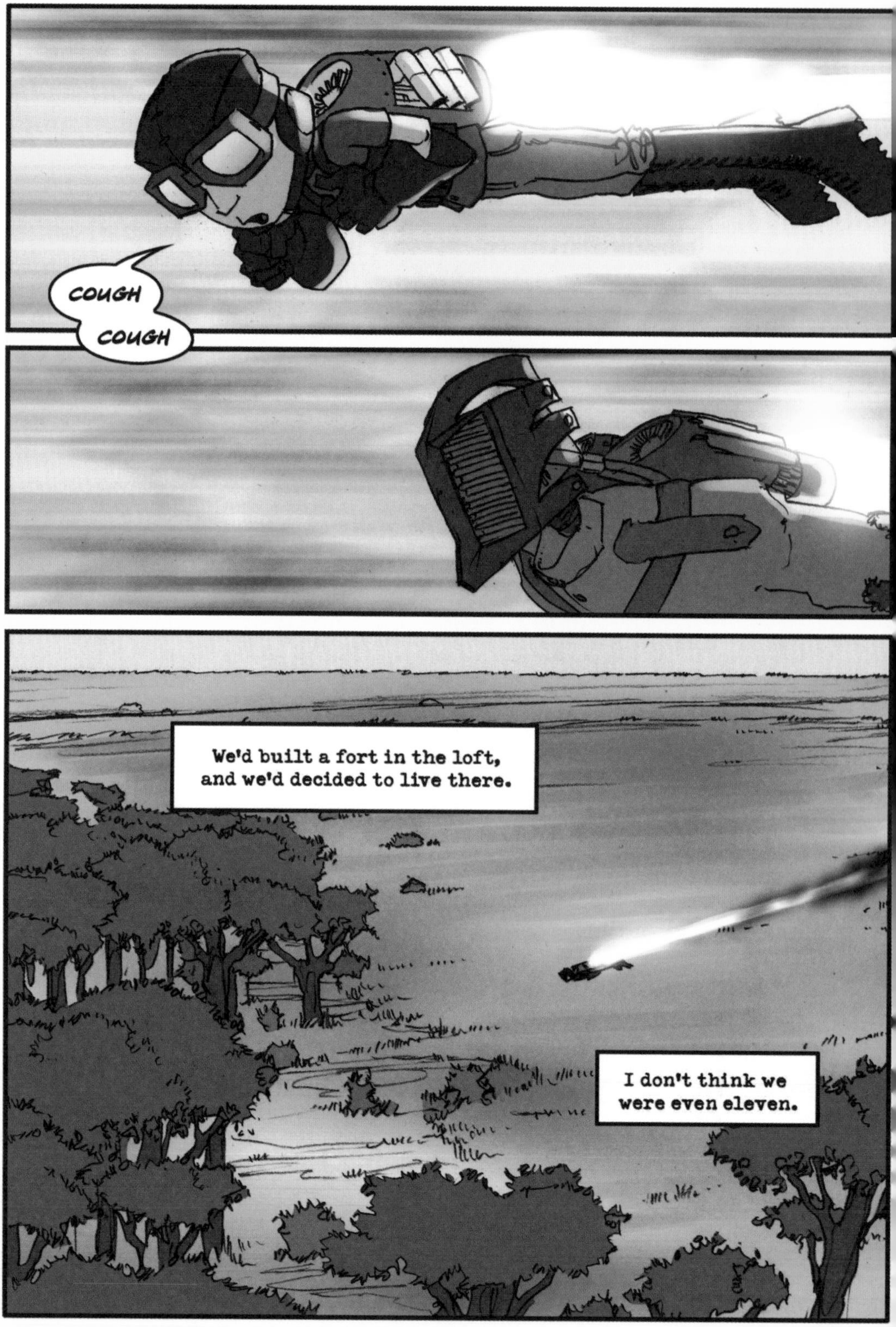
COUGH
COUGH
We'd built a fort in the loft, and we'd decided to live there.
I don't think we were even eleven.

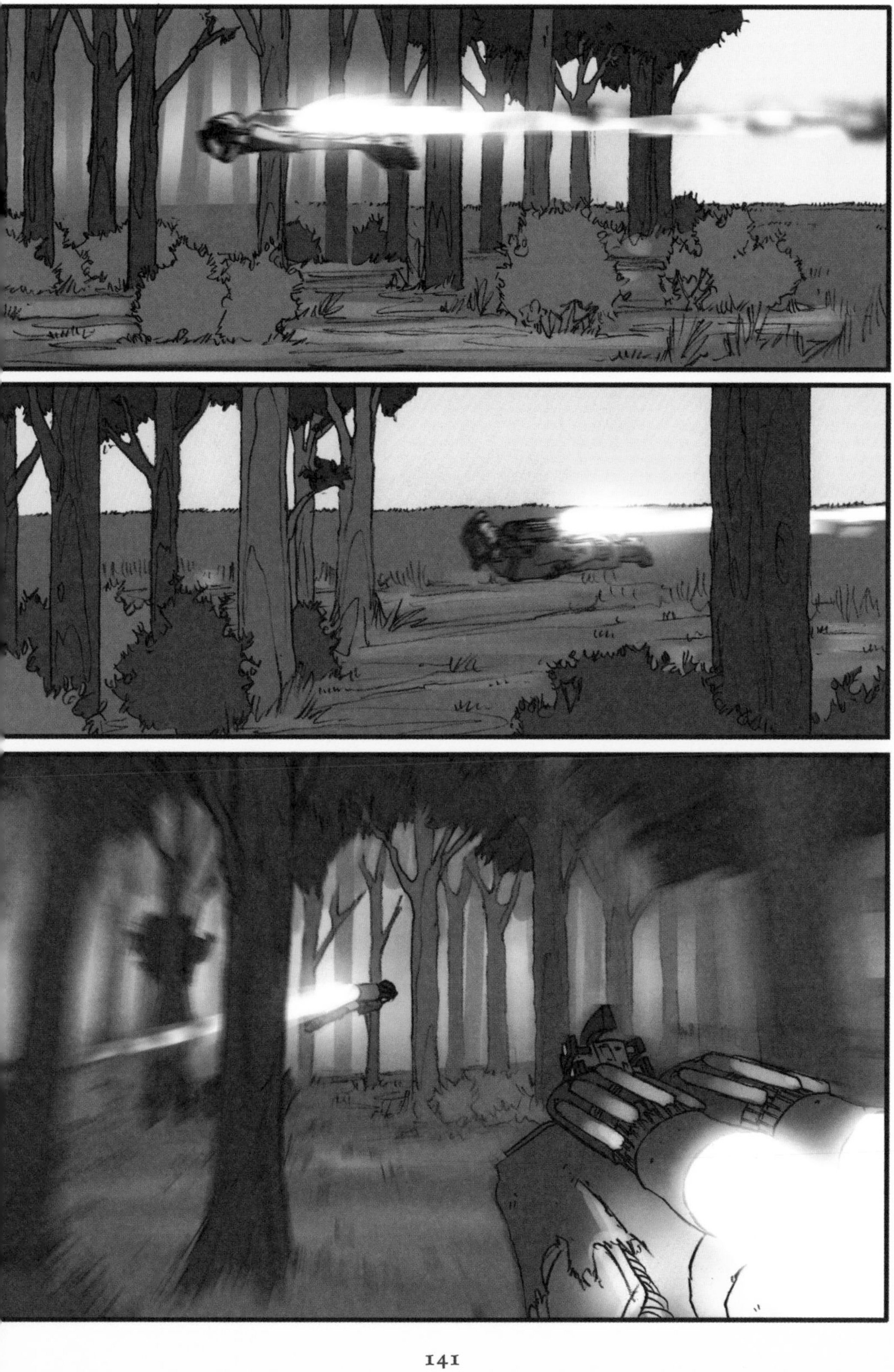

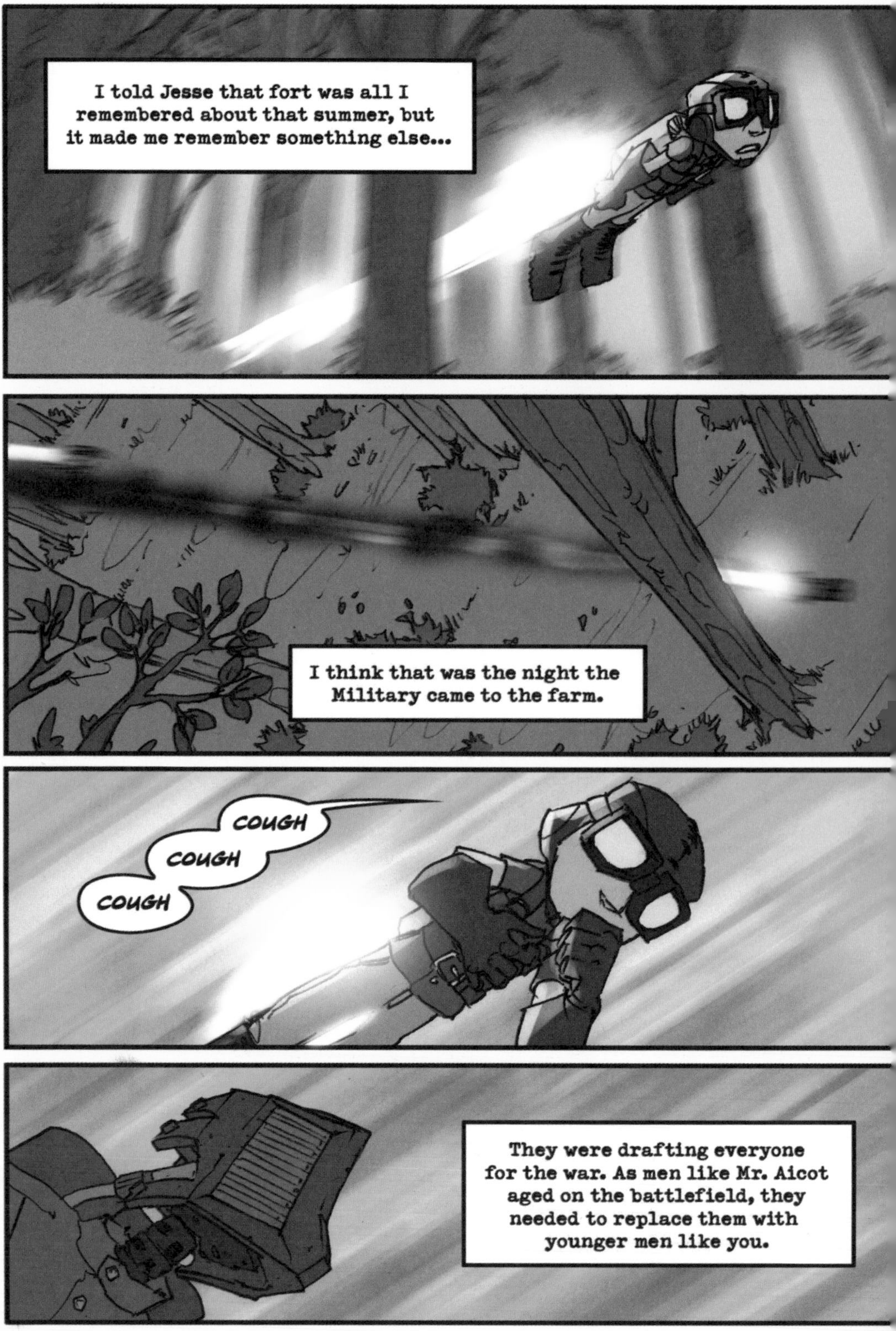
I told Jesse that fort was all I remembered about that summer, but it made me remember something else...
I think that was the night the Military came to the farm.
COUGH
COUGH
COUGH
They were drafting everyone for the war. As men like Mr. Aicot aged on the battlefield, they needed to replace them with younger men like you.

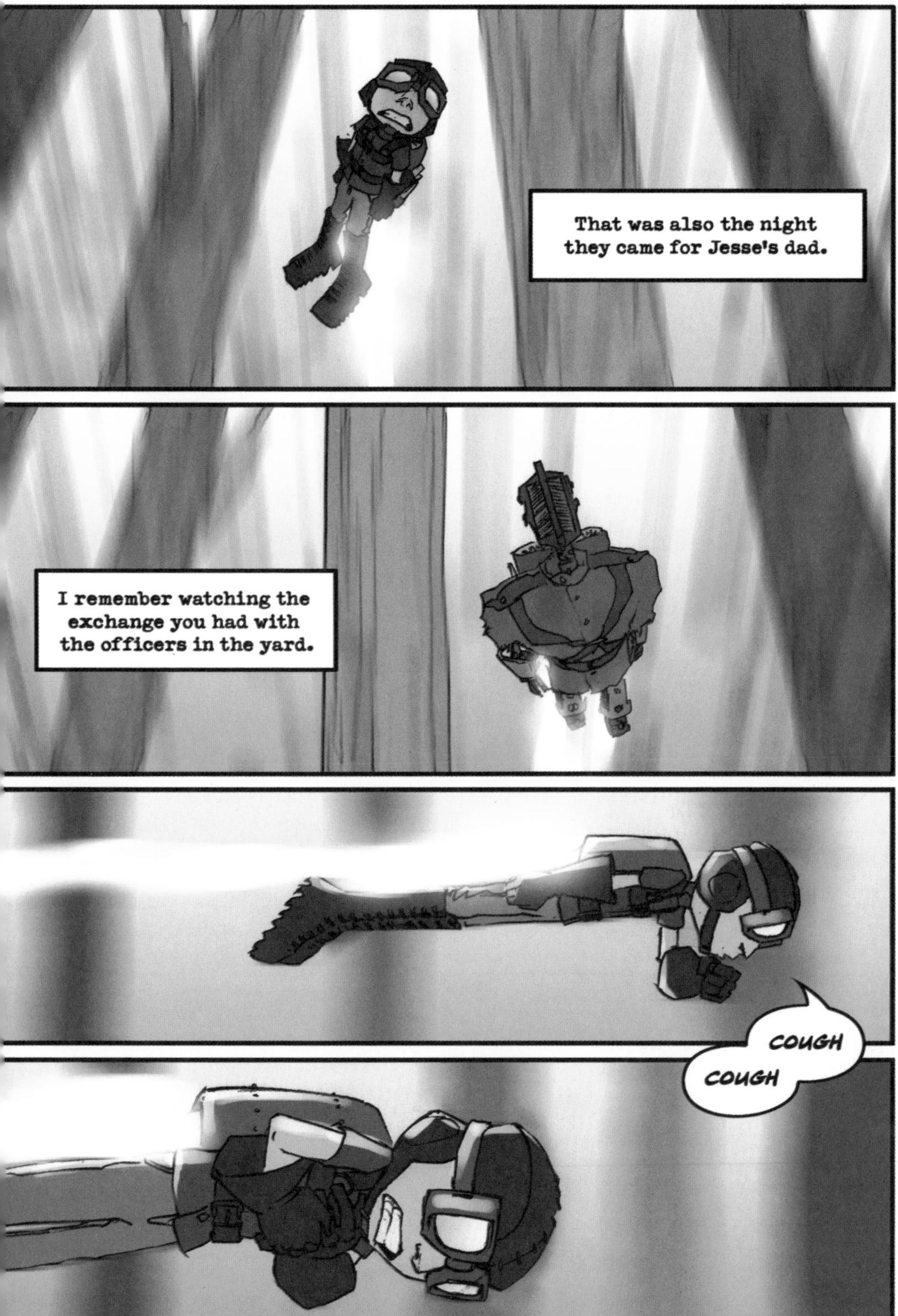
That was also the night
they came for Jesse's dad.
I remember watching the
exchange you had with
the officers in the yard.
COUGH
COUGH

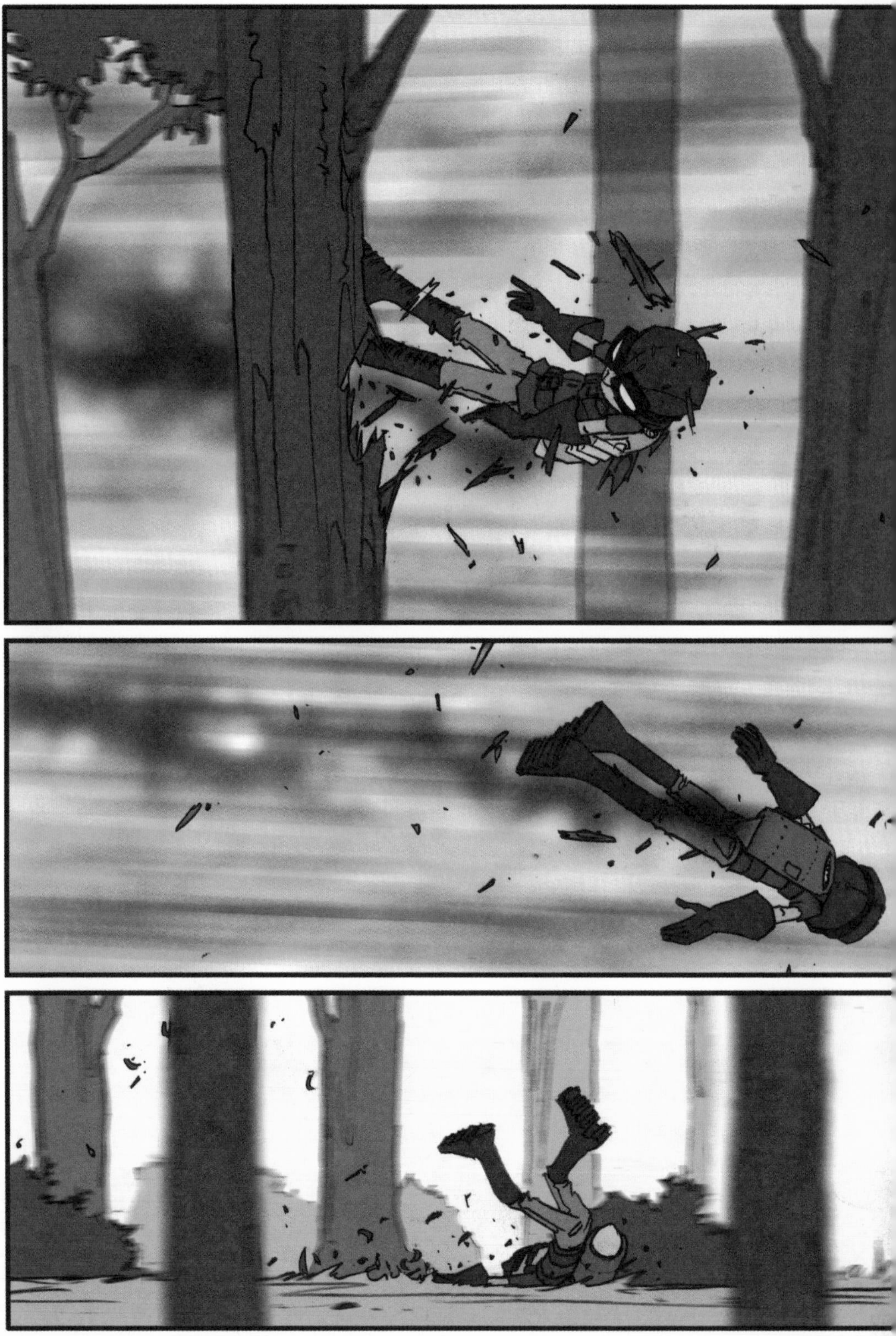

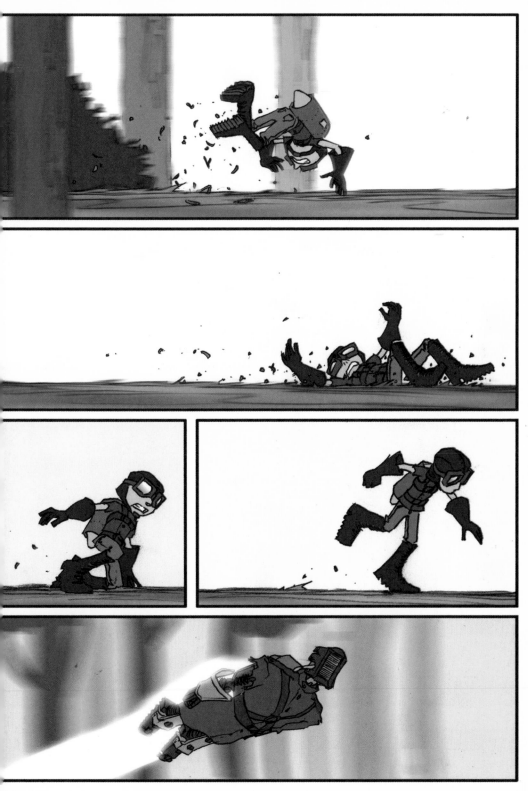

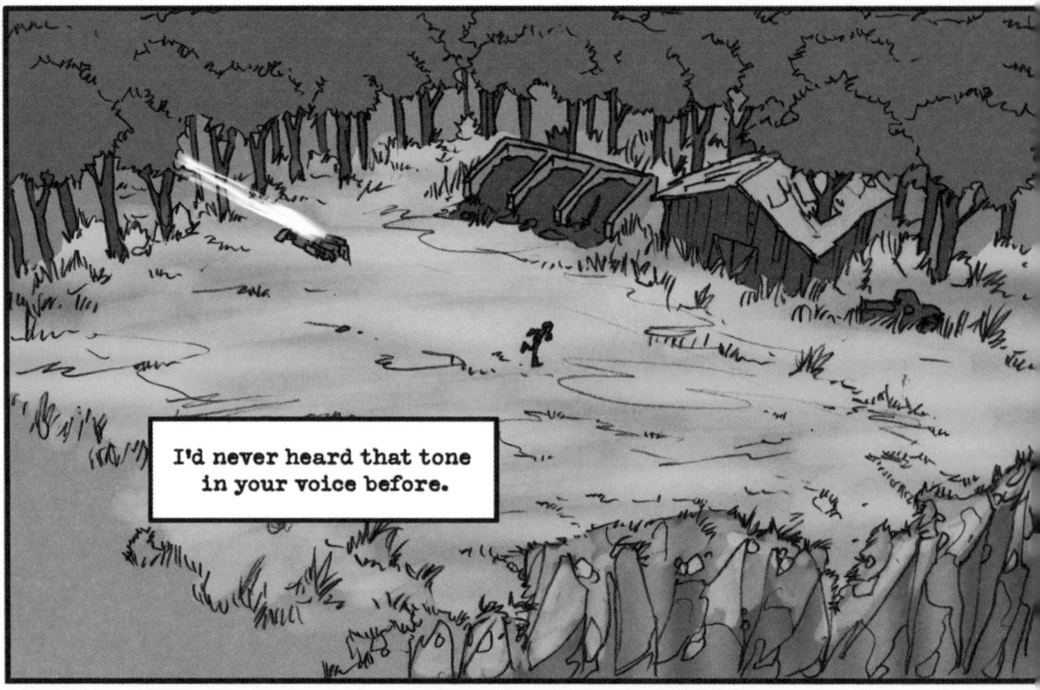
I'd never heard that tone
in your voice before.

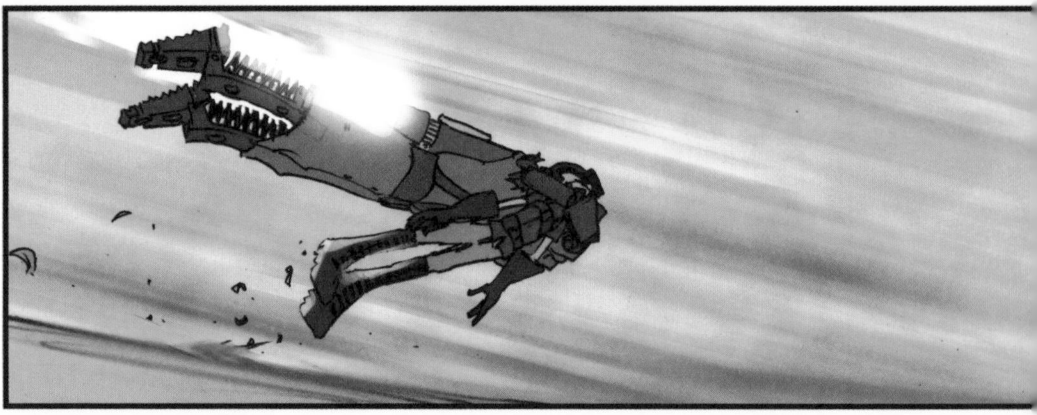

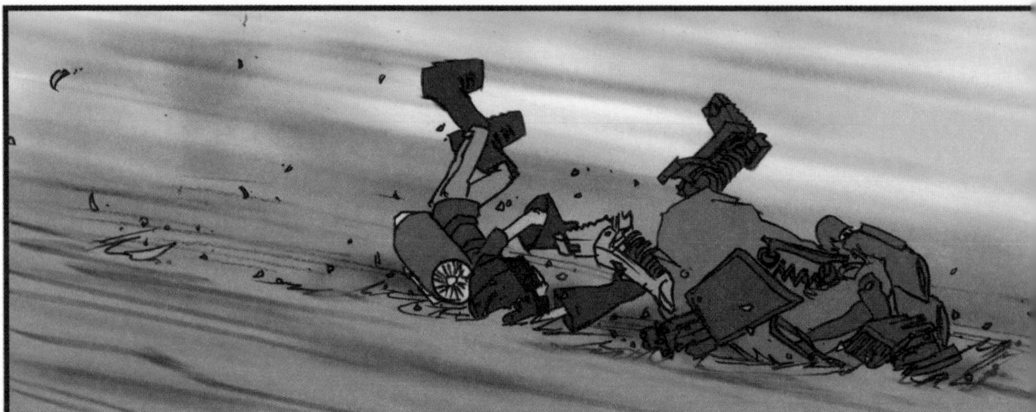

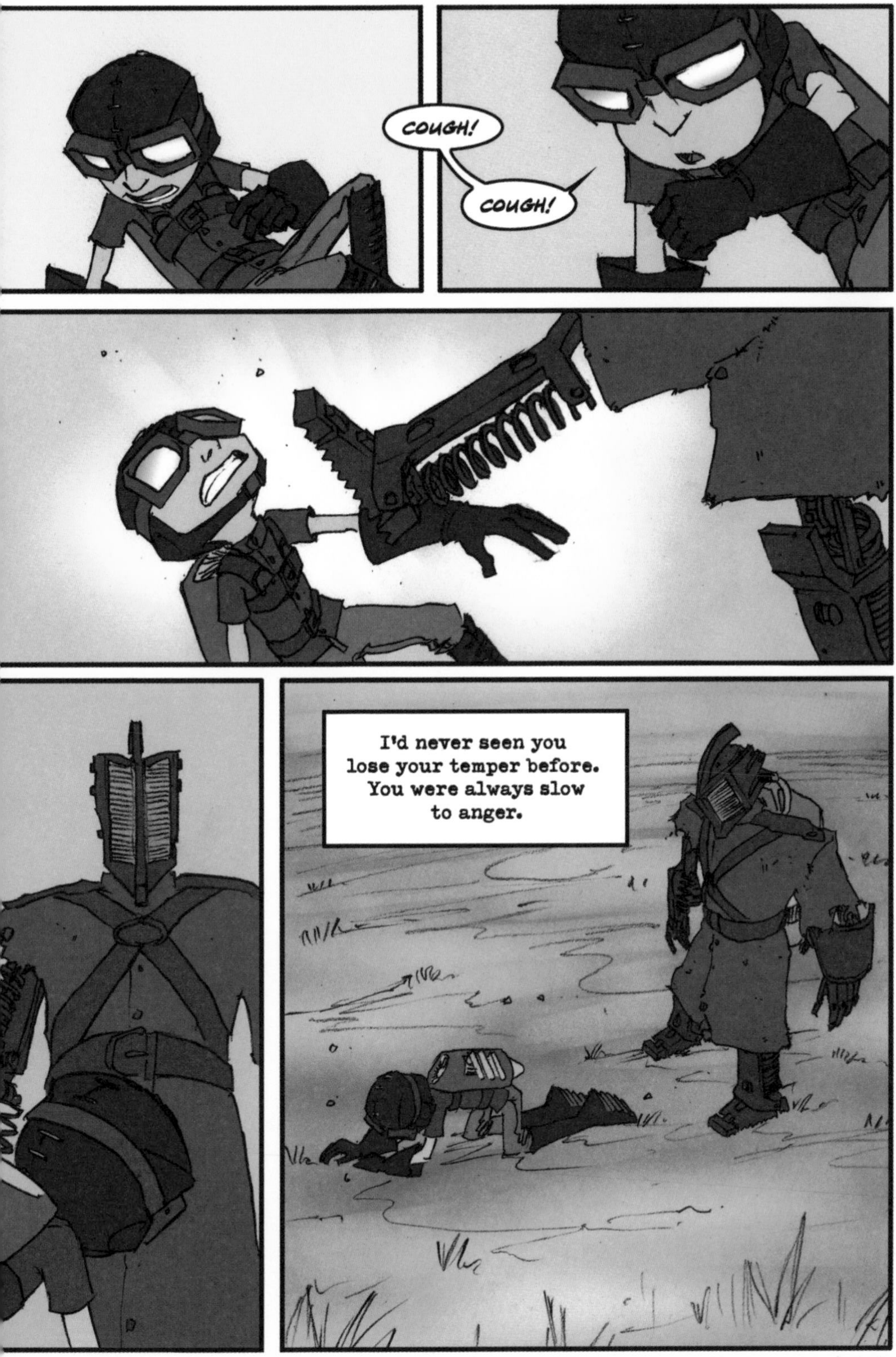
COUGH!
COUGH!
I'd never seen you lose your temper before. You were always slow to anger.

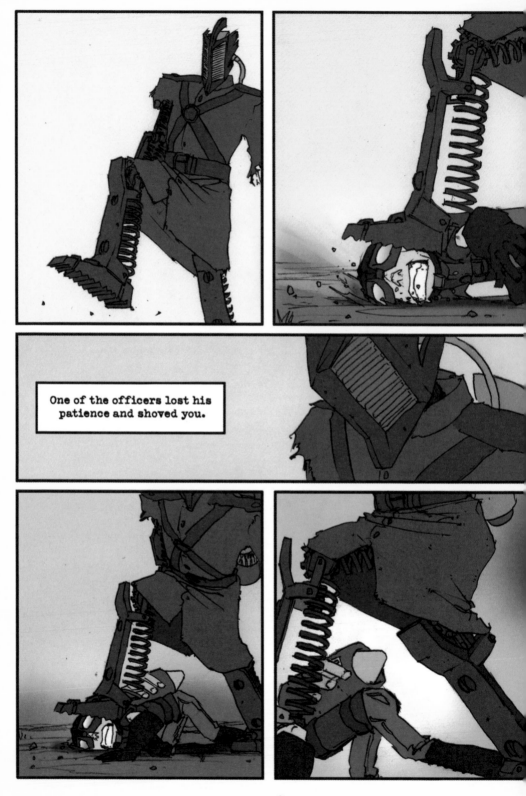

One of the officers lost his
patience and shoved you.

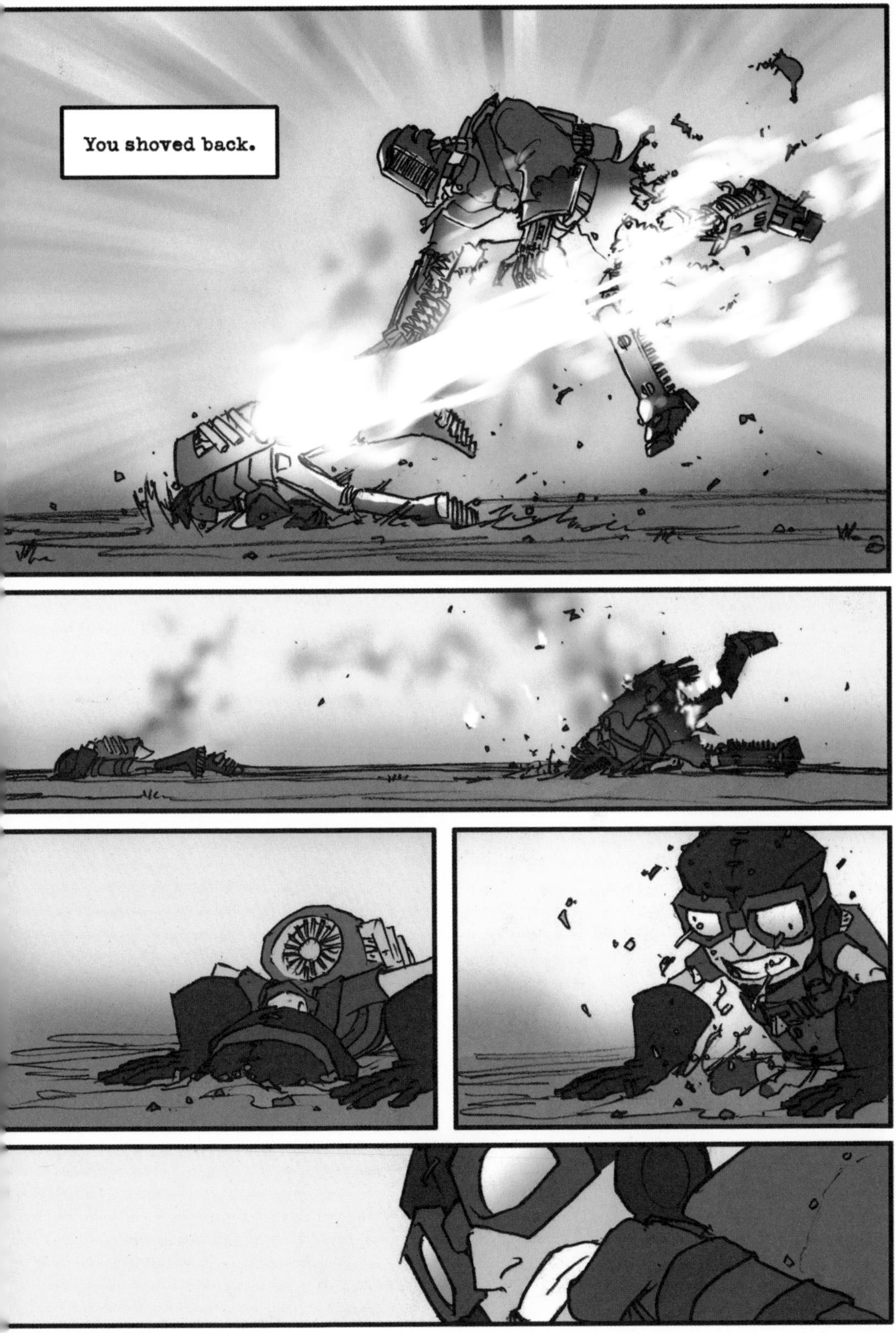
You shoved back.

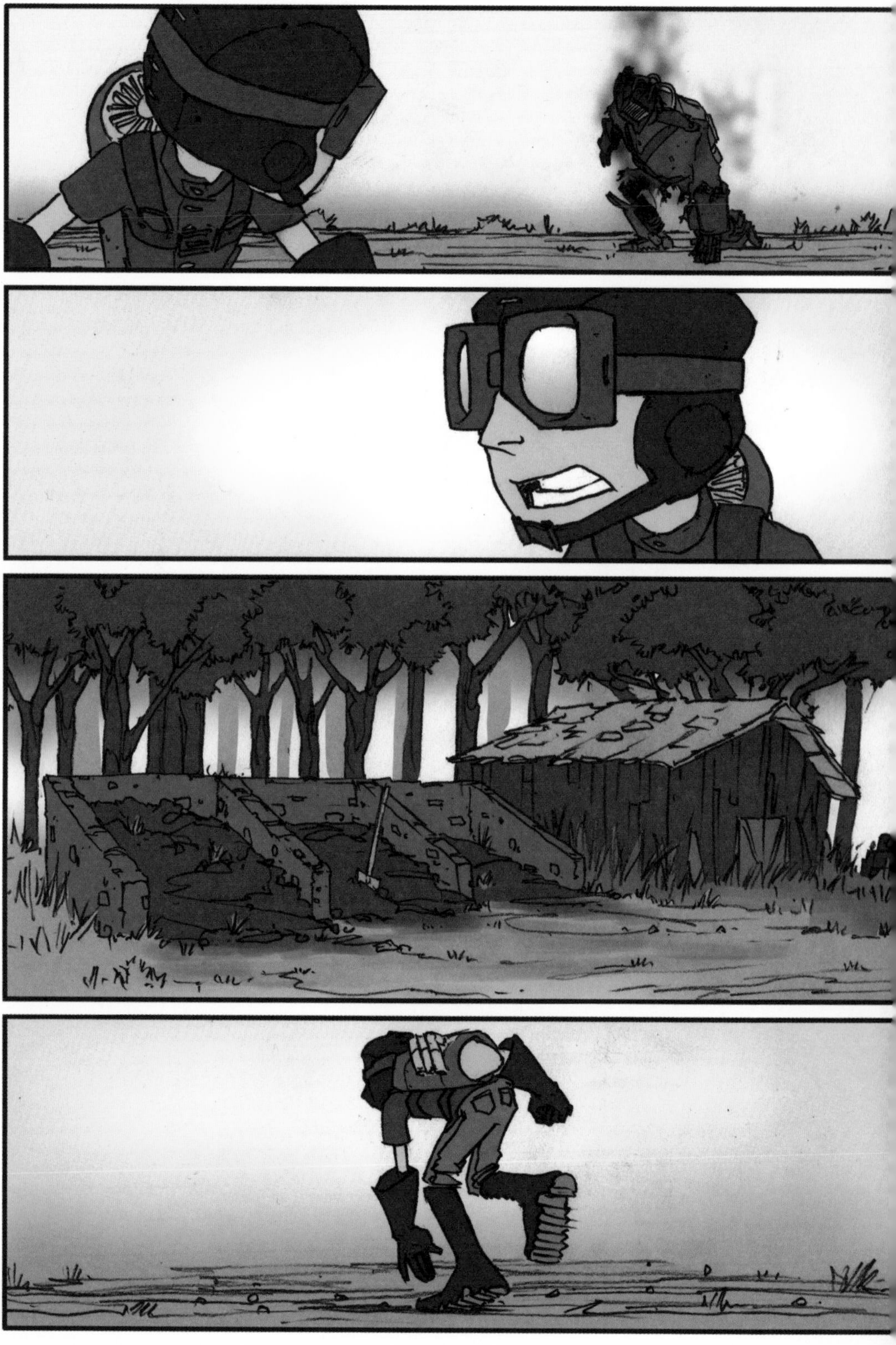

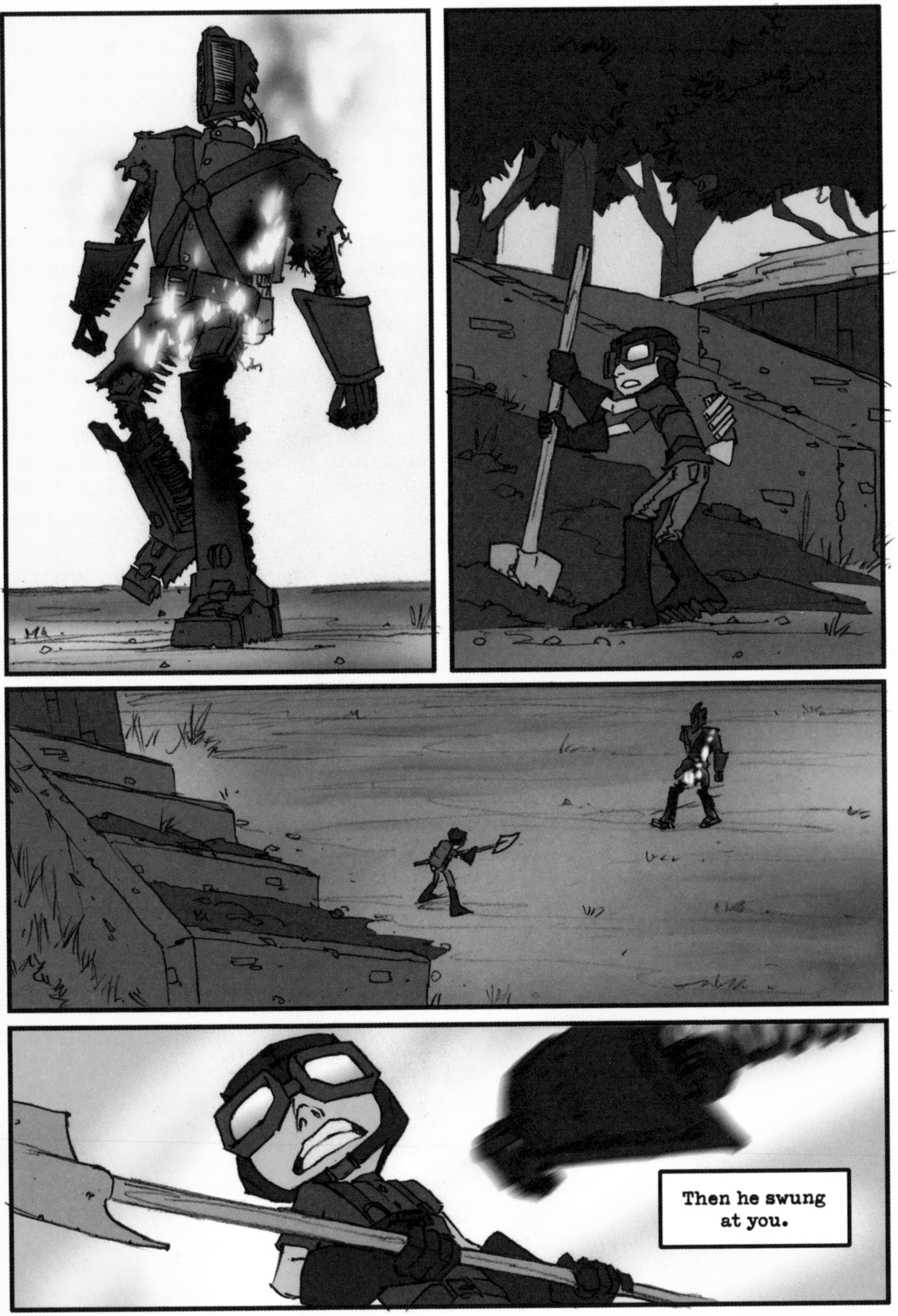
Then he swung
at you.

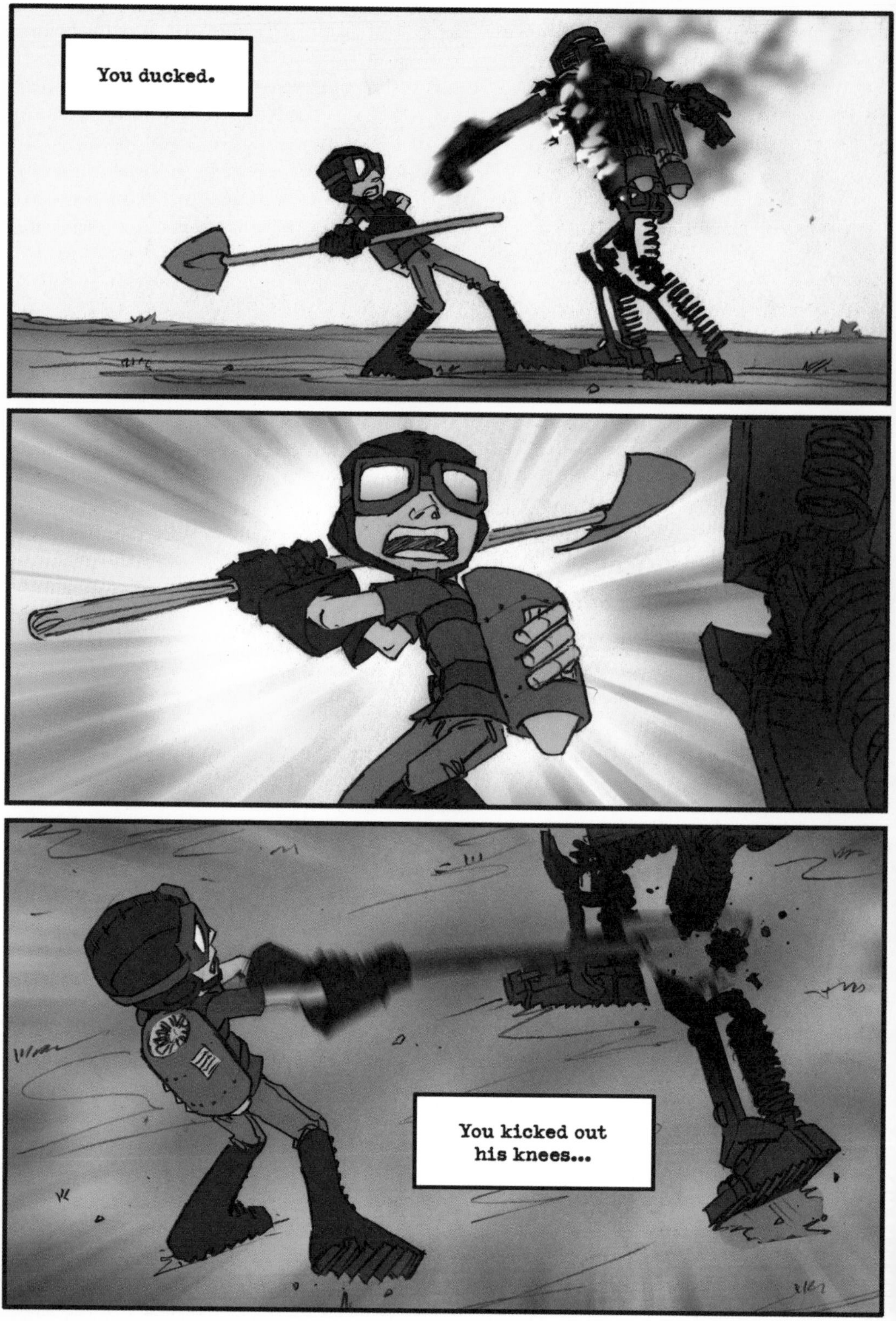
You ducked.
You kicked out his knees...

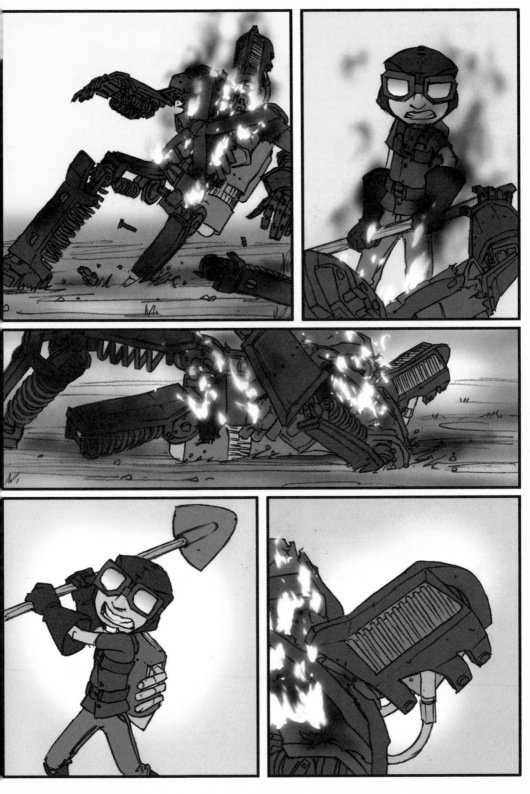

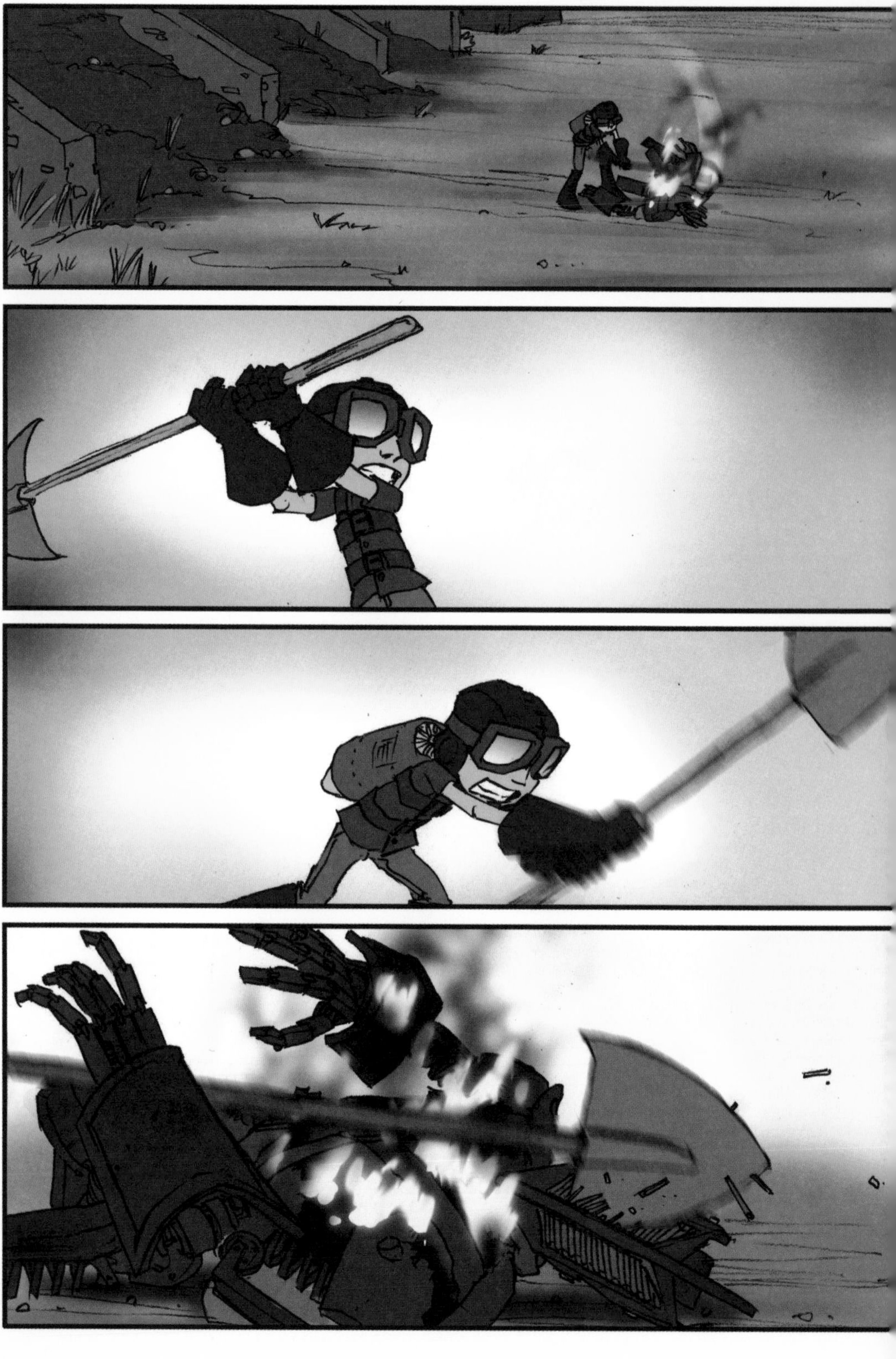

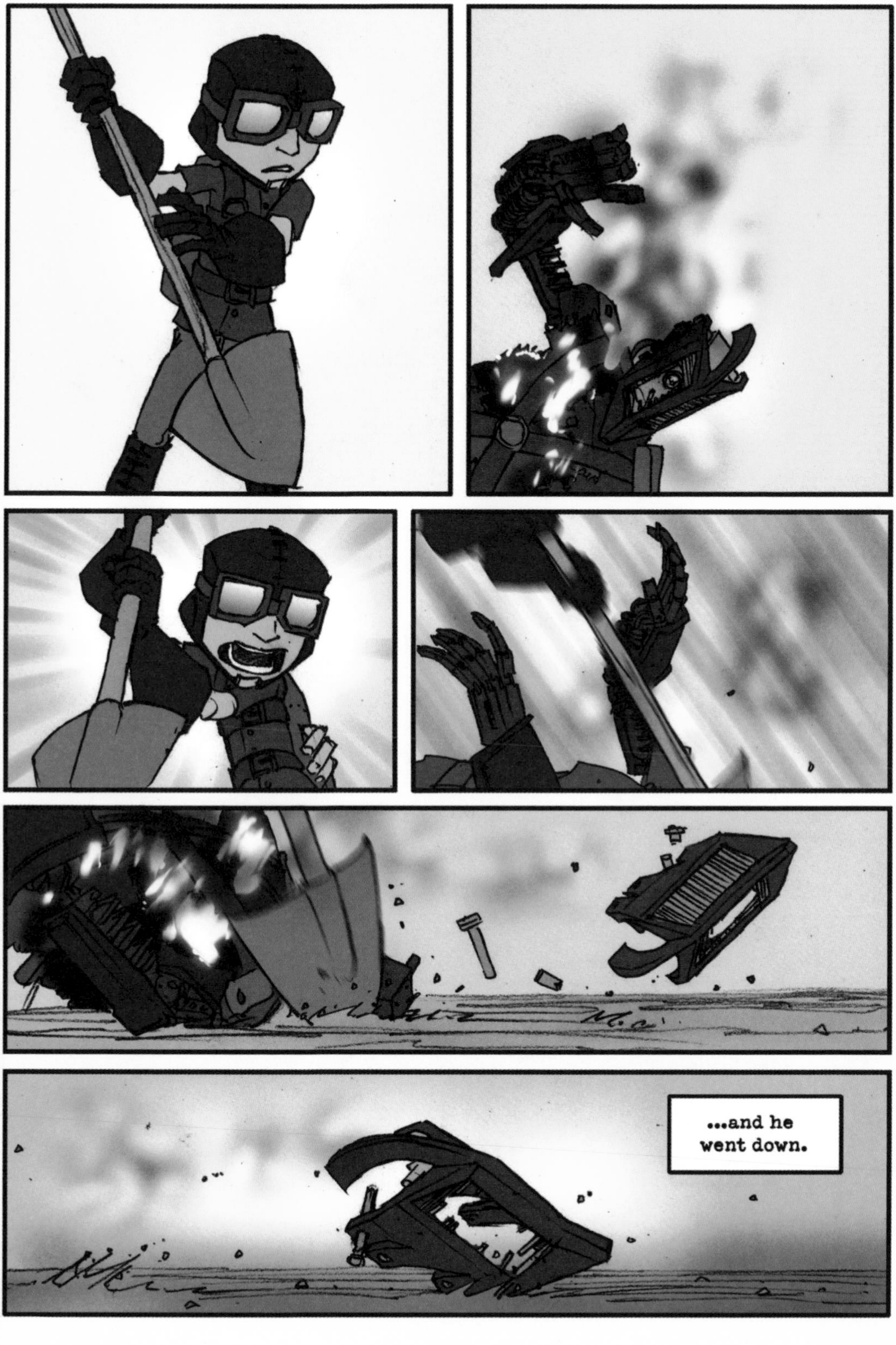
...and he
went down.

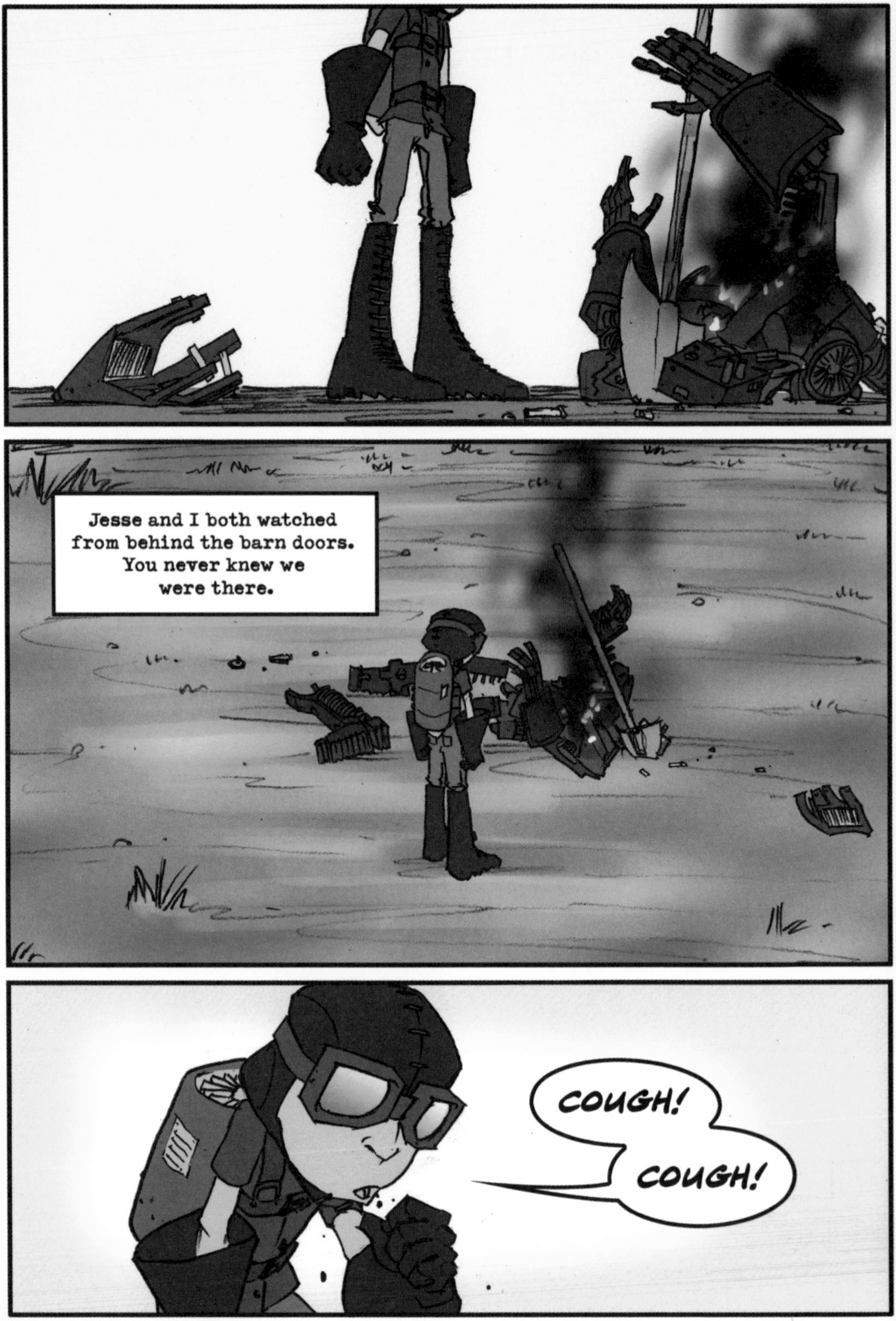
Jesse and I both watched from behind the barn doors. You never knew we were there.
COUGH!
COUGH!

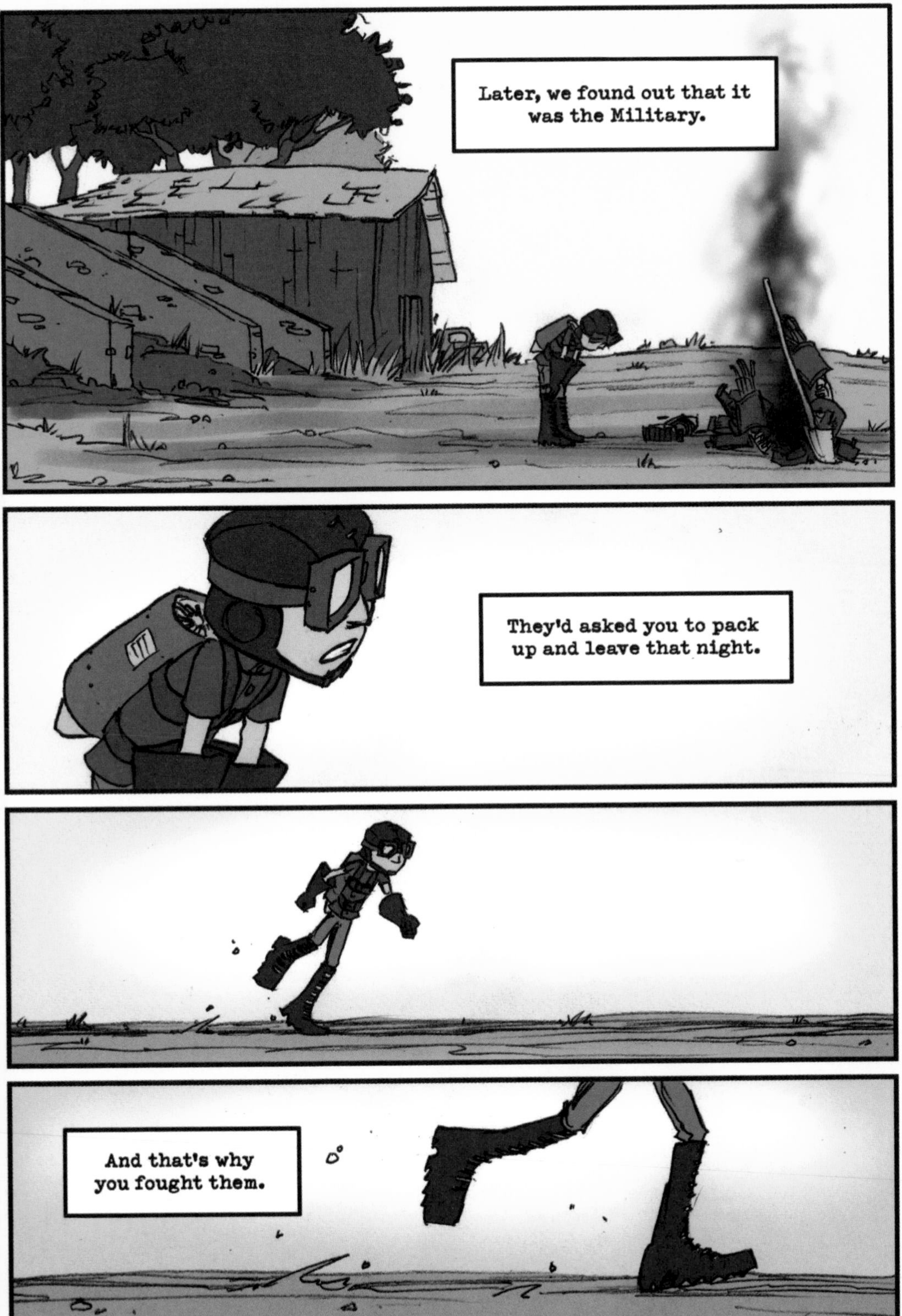
Later, we found out that it was the Military.
They'd asked you to pack up and leave that night.
And that's why you fought them.

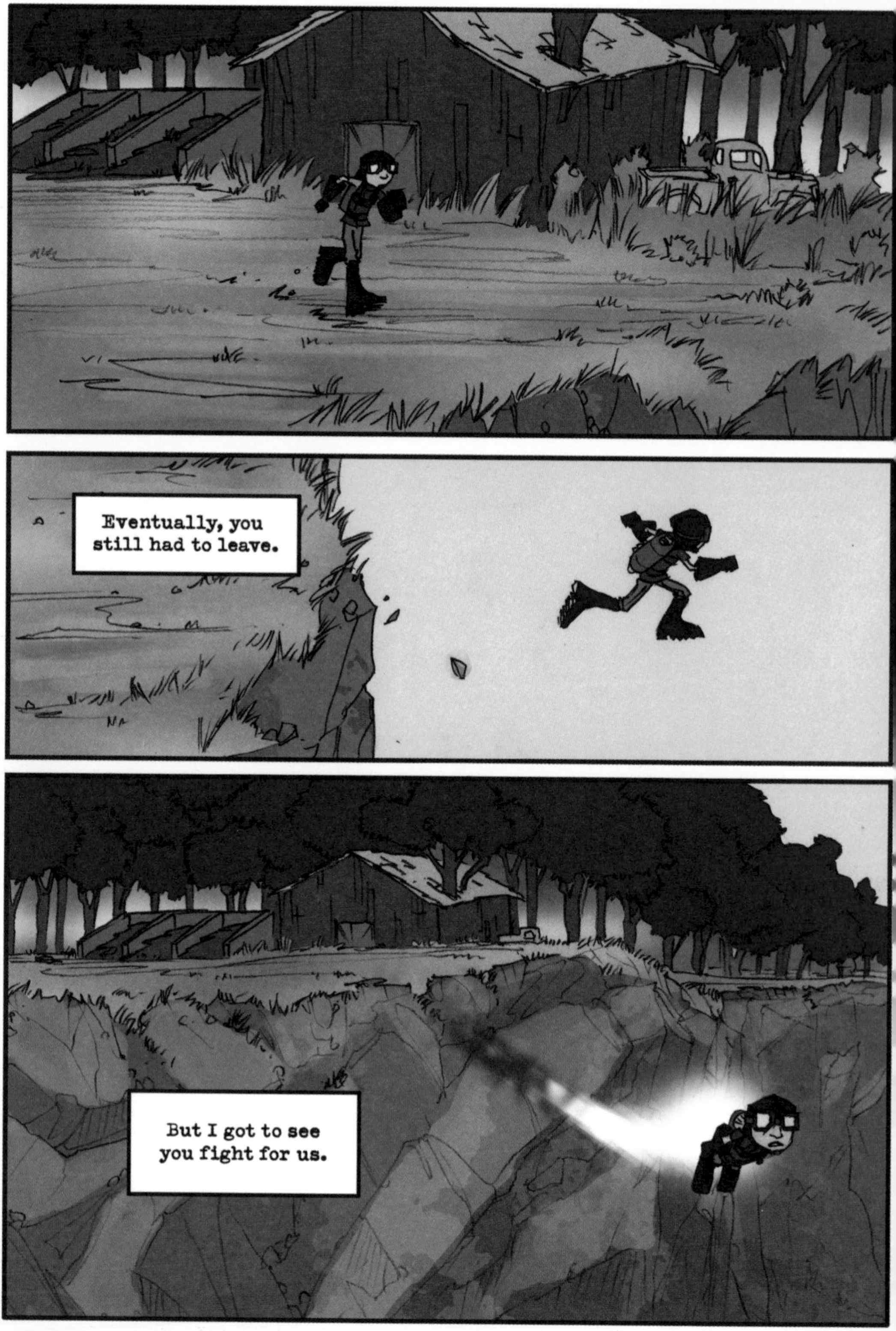
Eventually, you
still had to leave.
But I got to see
you fight for us.

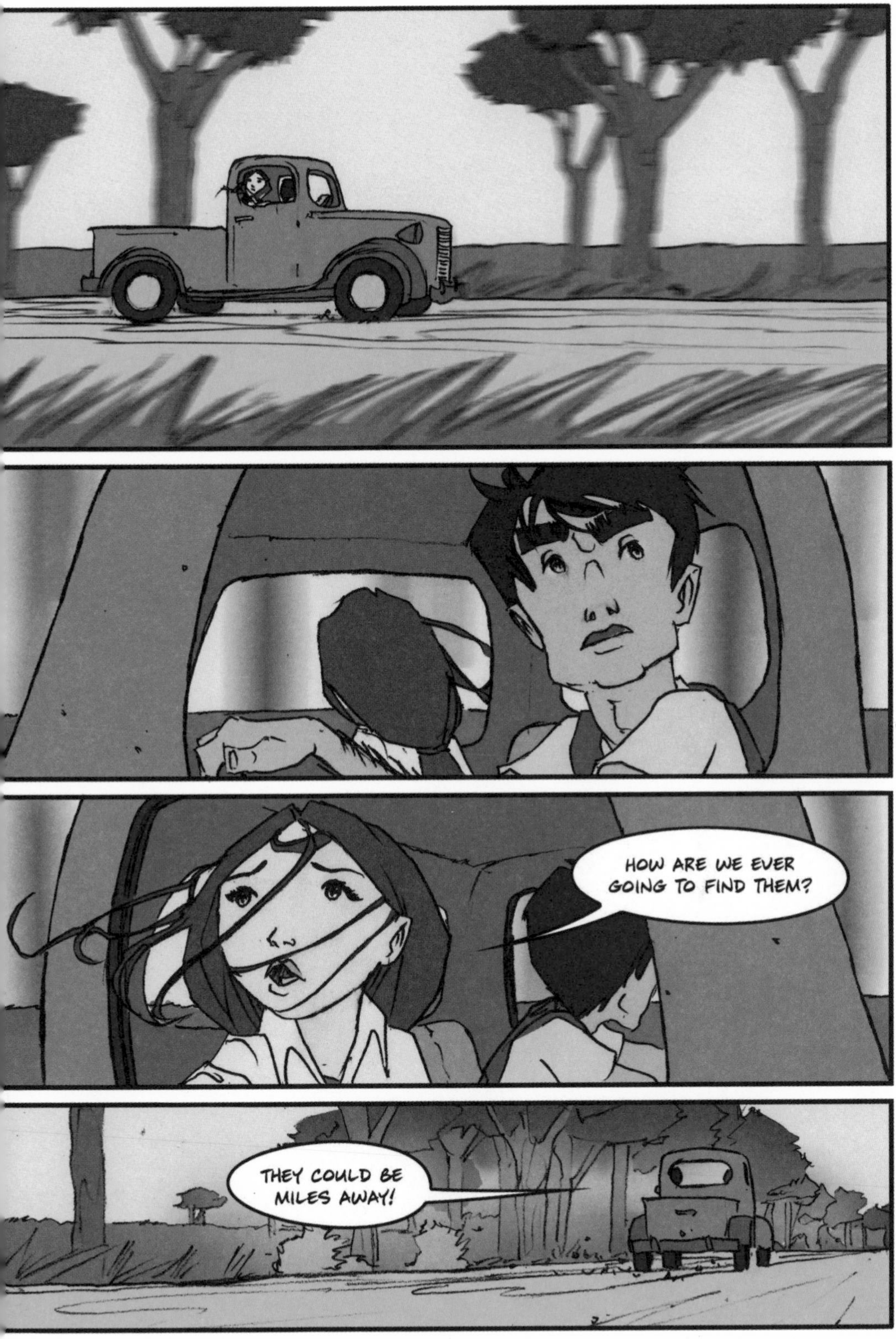
HOW ARE WE EVER GOING TO FIND THEM?
THEY COULD BE MILES AWAY!

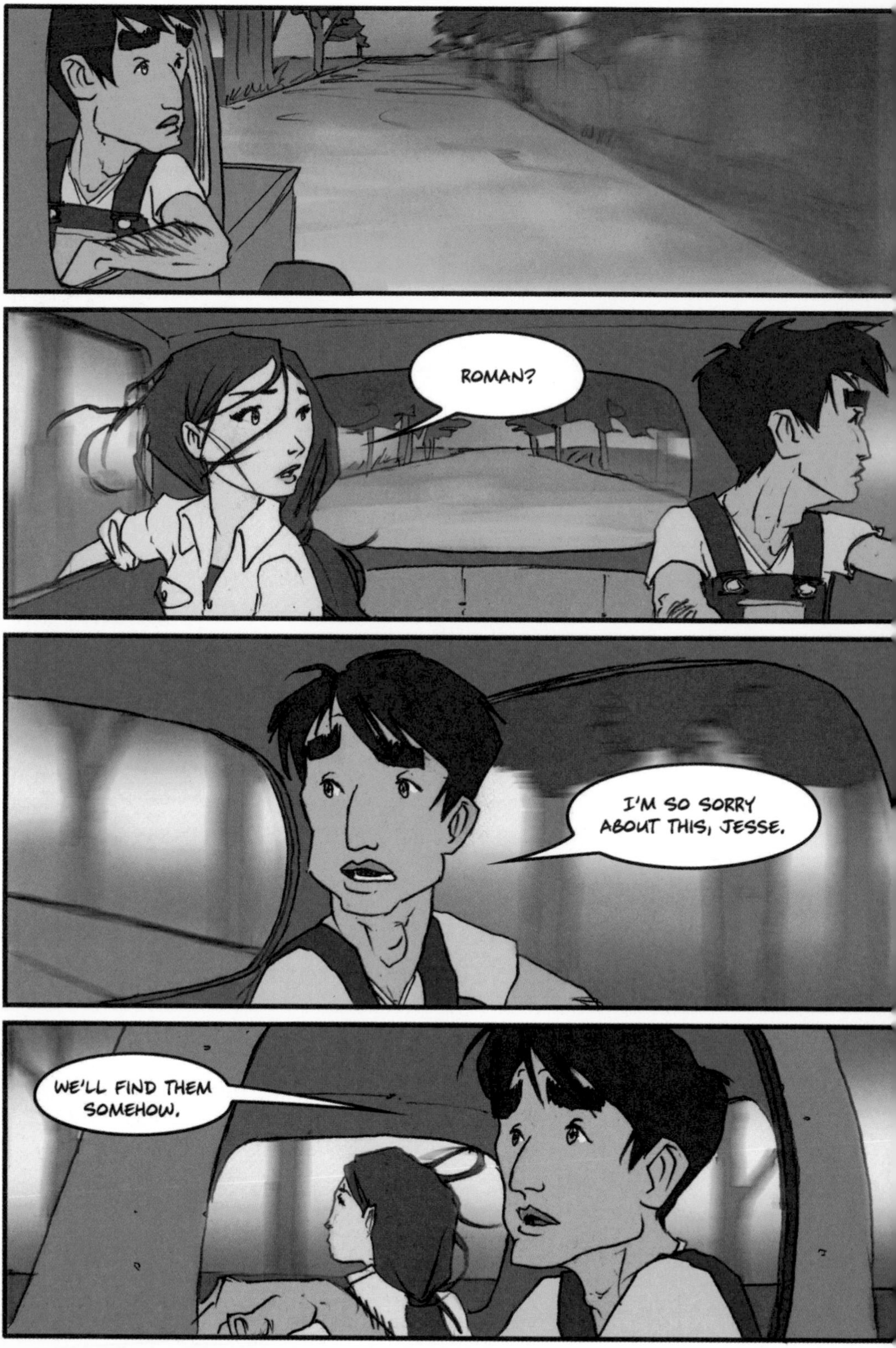
ROMAN?
I'M SO SORRY ABOUT THIS, JESSE.
WE'LL FIND THEM SOMEHOW.

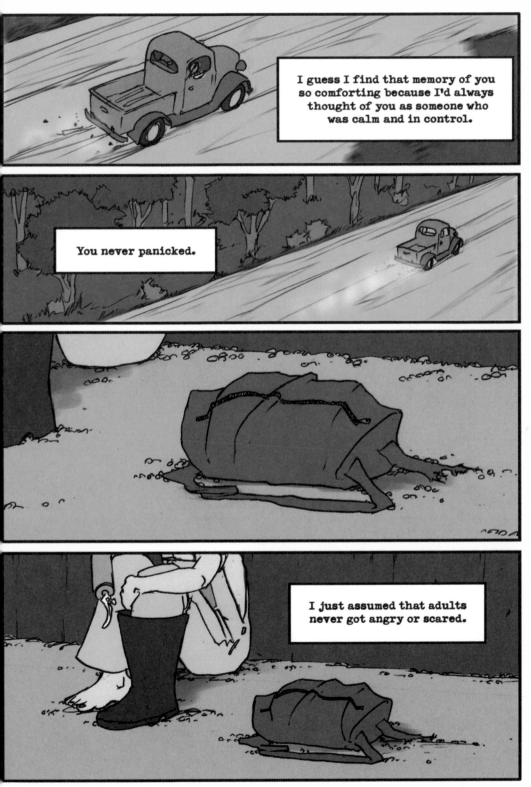

I guess I find that memory of you so comforting because I'd always thought of you as someone who was calm and in control.

You never panicked.

I just assumed that adults never got angry or scared.

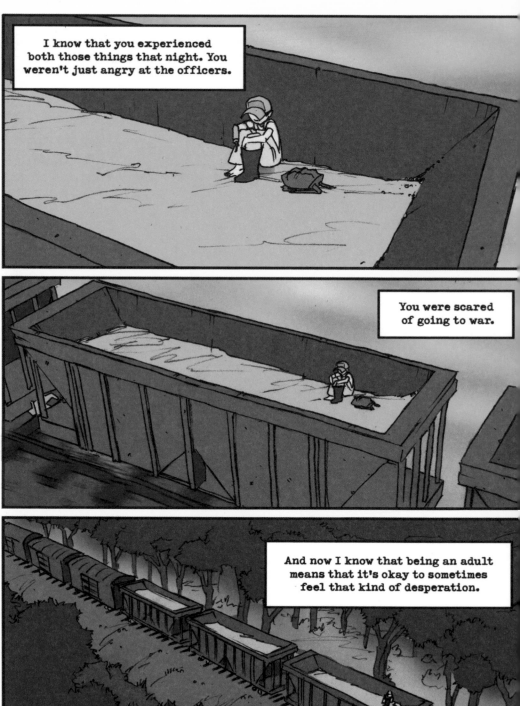

I know that you experienced both those things that night. You weren't just angry at the officers.

You were scared of going to war.

And now I know that being an adult means that it's okay to sometimes feel that kind of desperation.

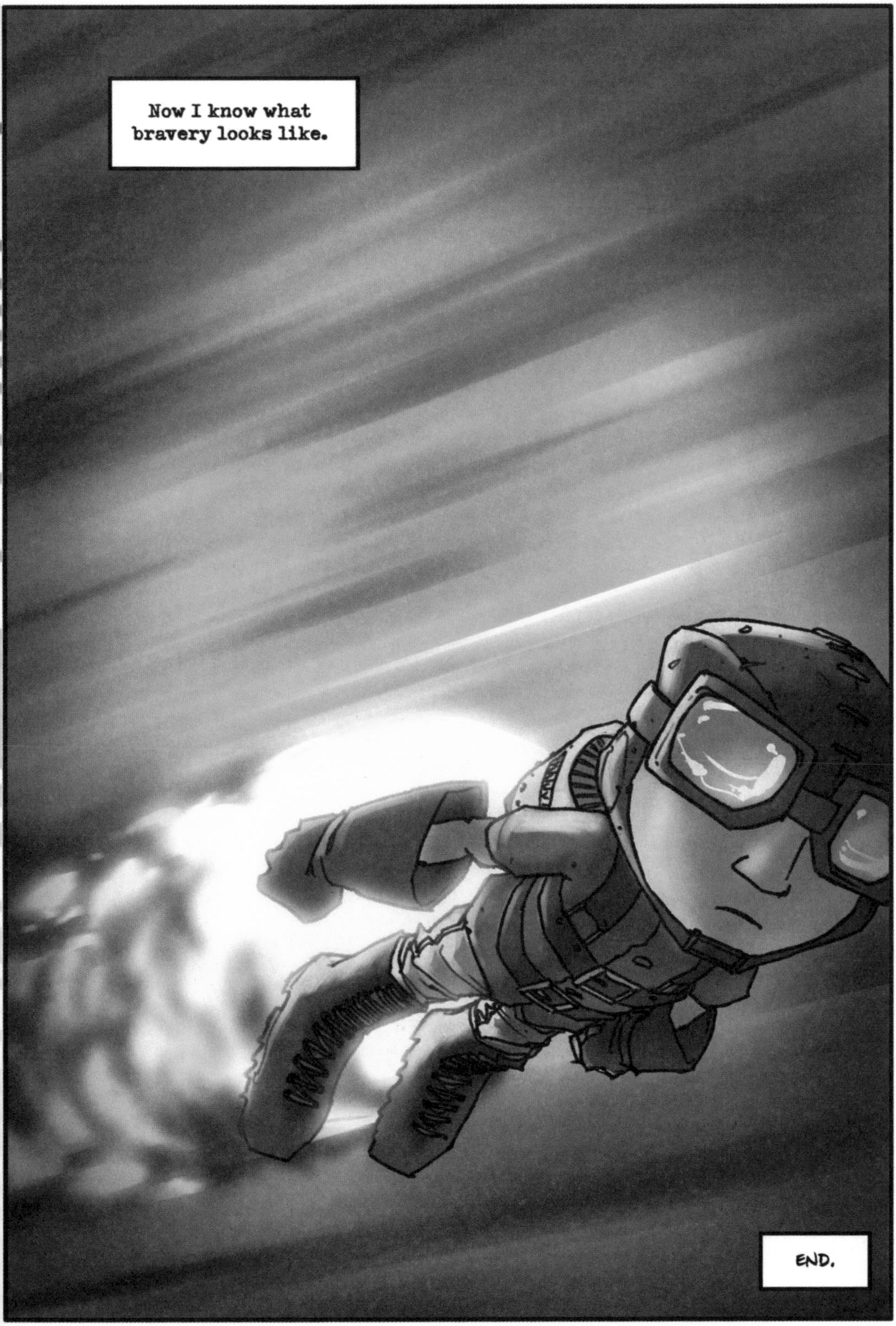
Now I know what bravery looks like.
END.

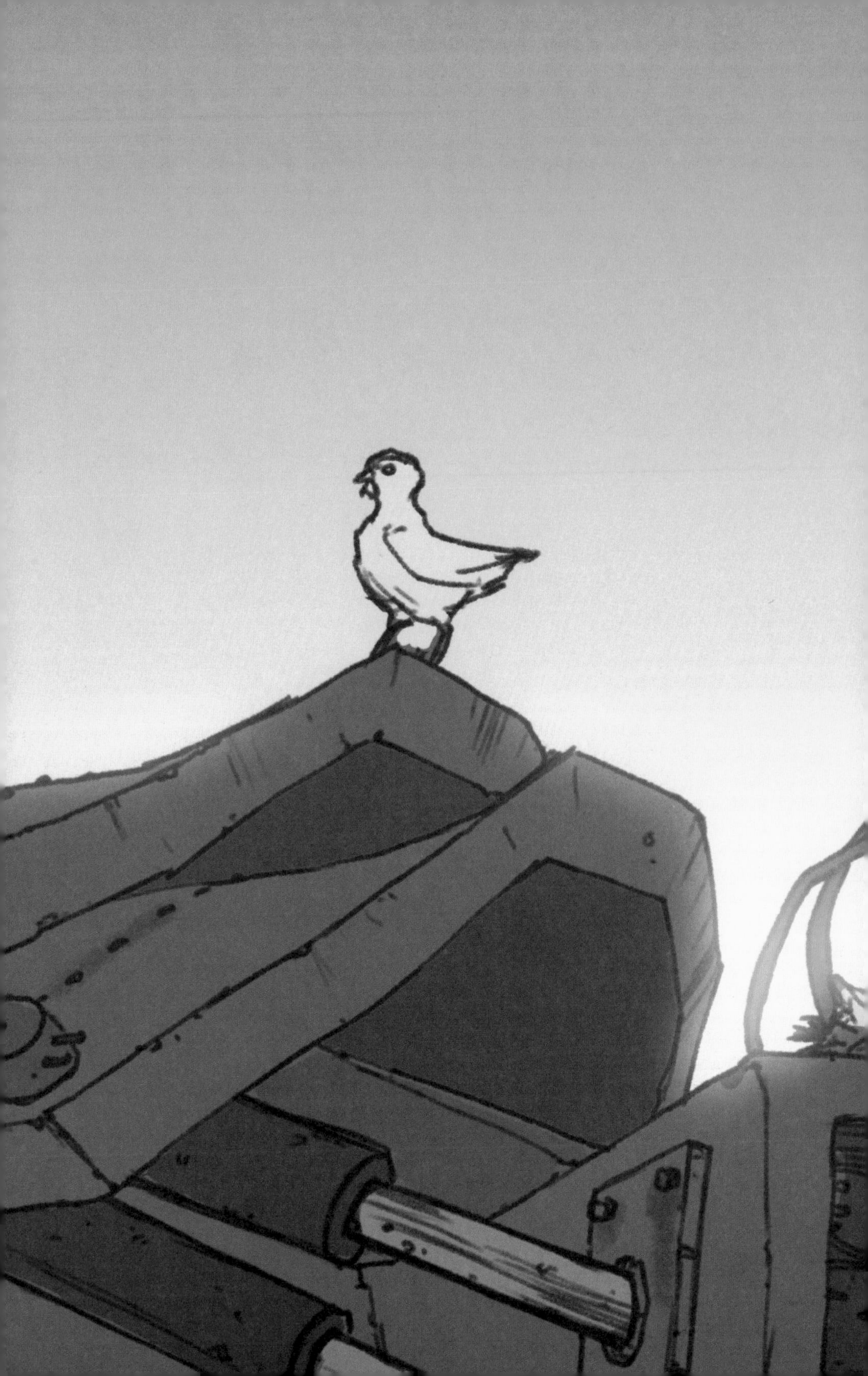

# Oswald's Letter

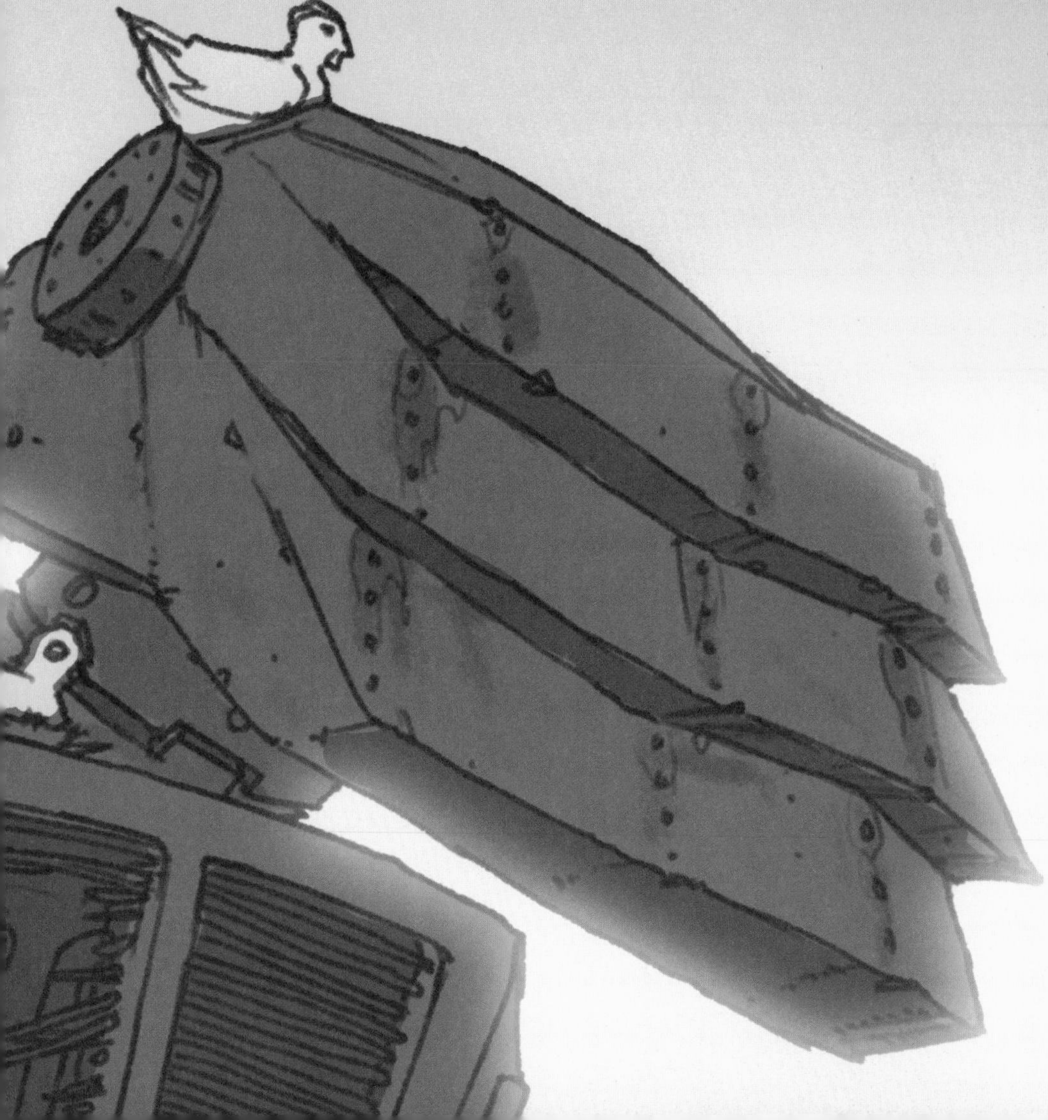

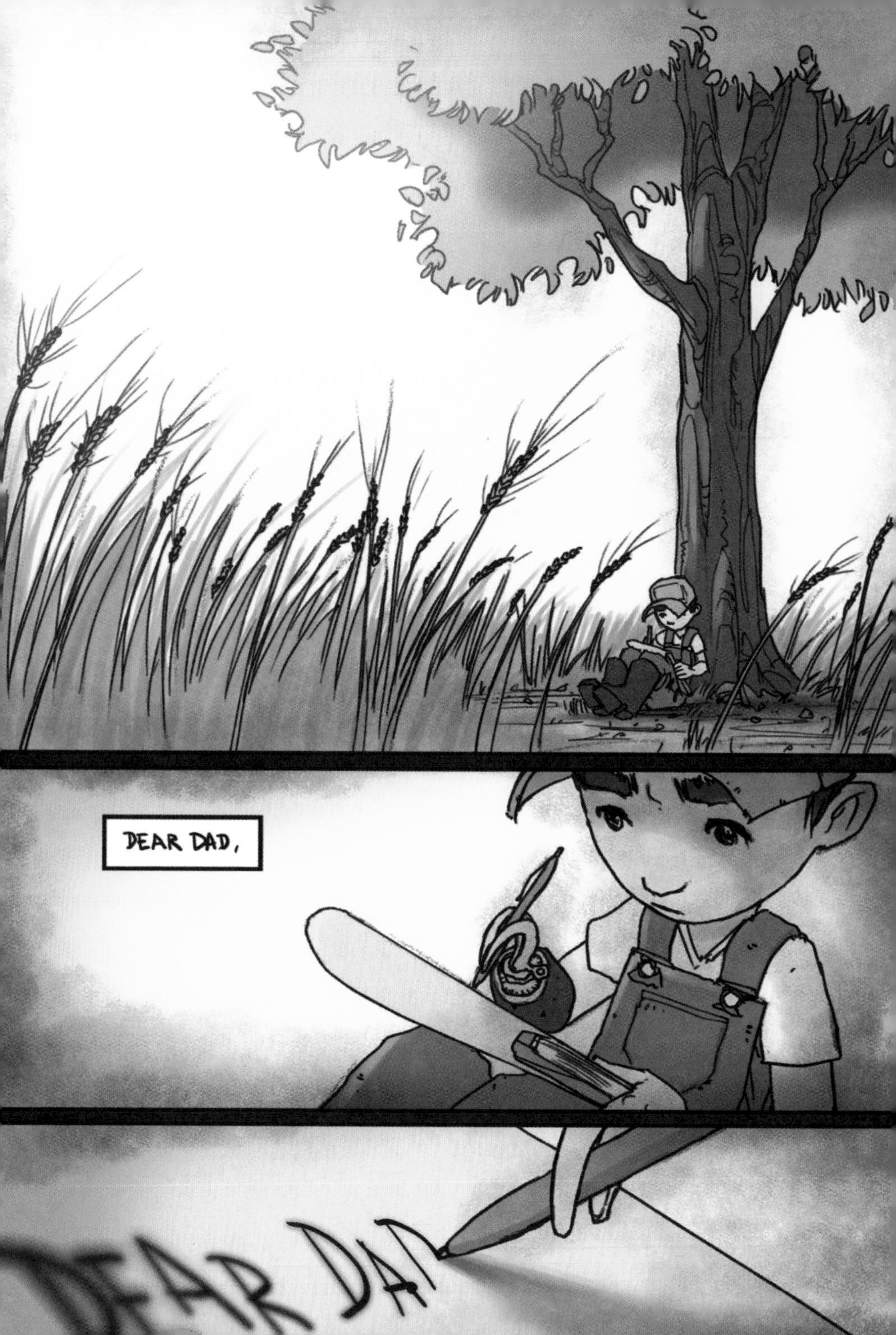
DEAR DAD,
DEAR DAD

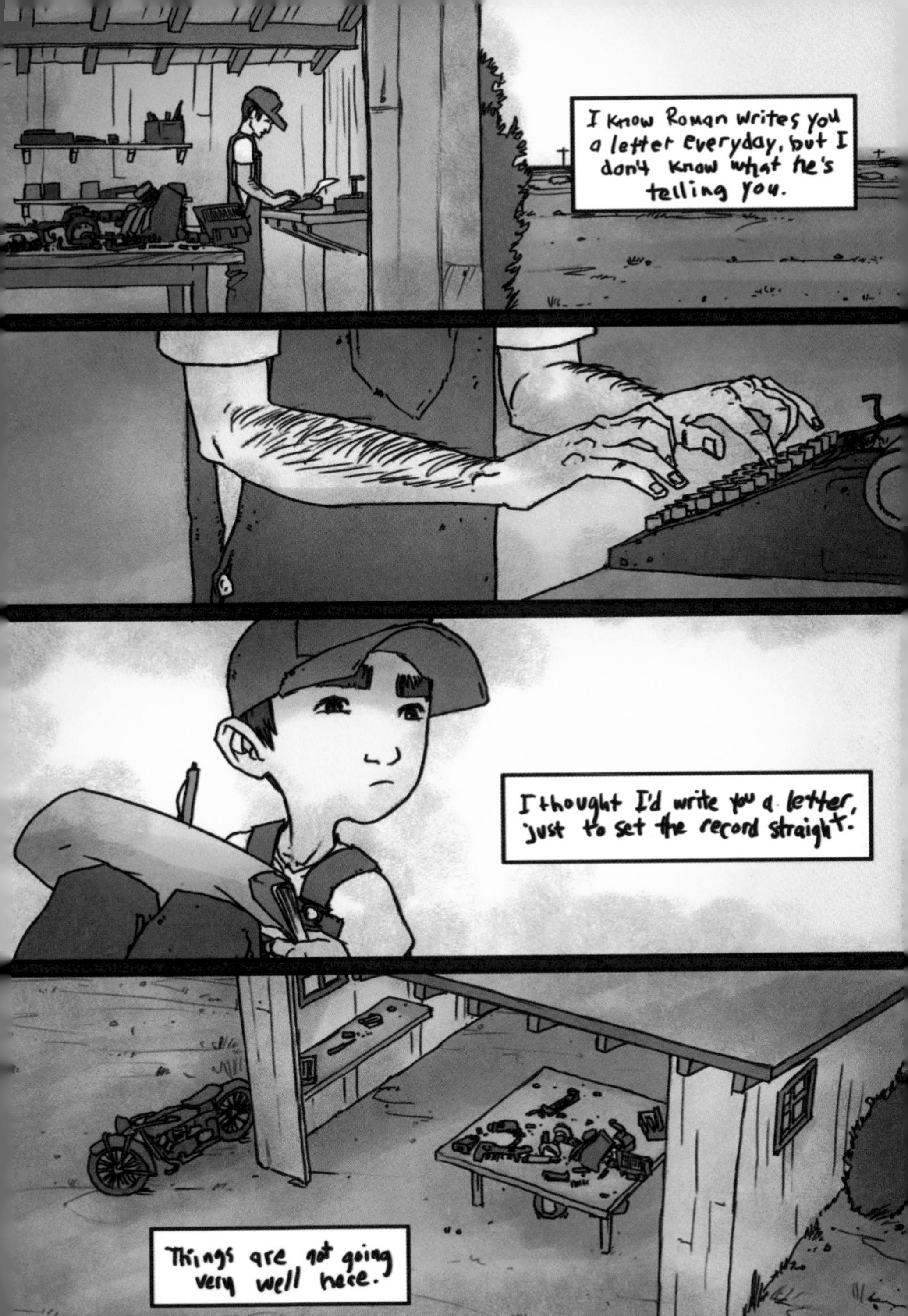
I know Roman writes you a letter everyday, but I don't know what he's telling you.
I thought I'd write you a letter, just to set the record straight.
Things are not going very well here.

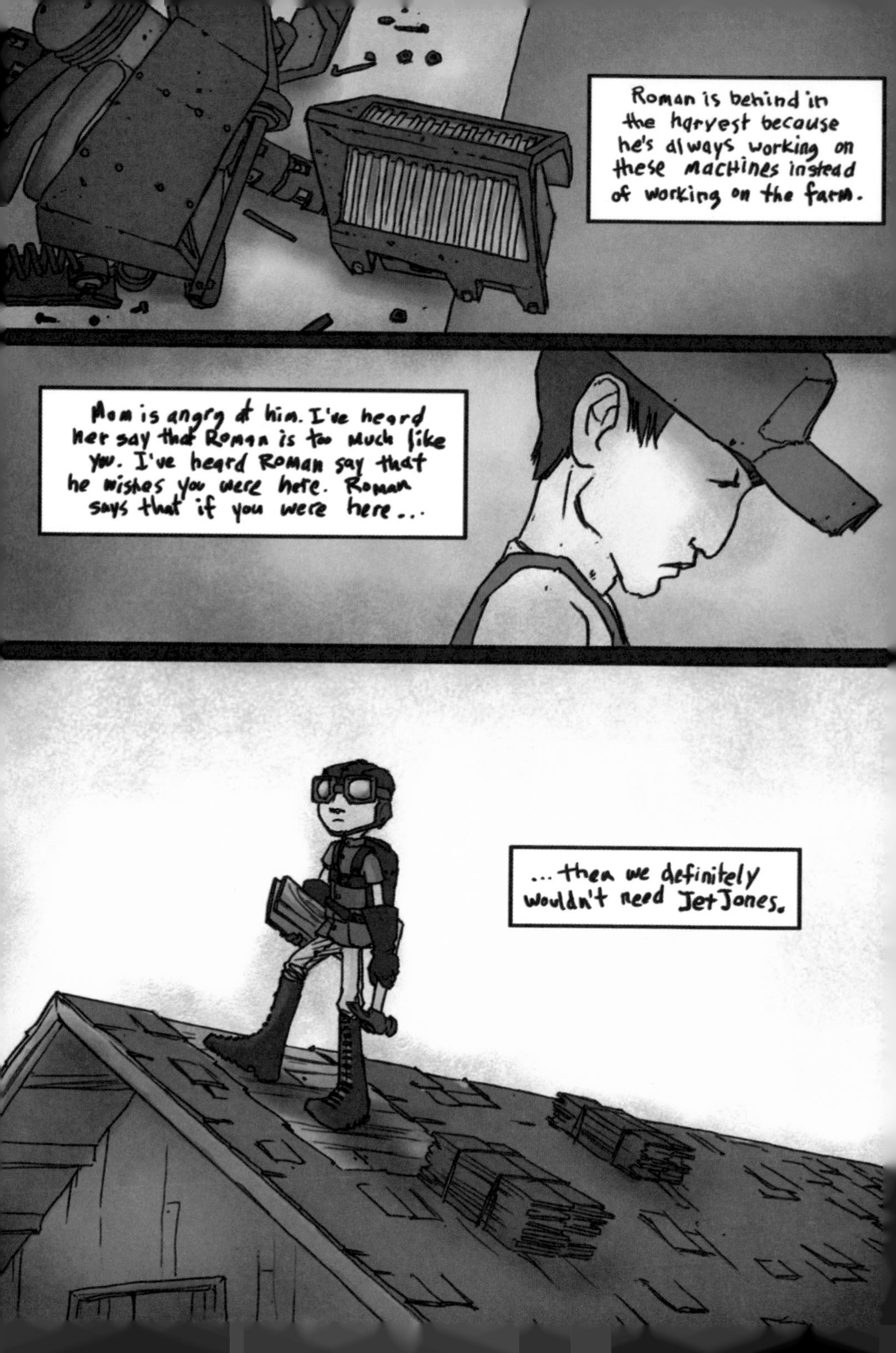
Roman is behind in the harvest because he's always working on these machines instead of working on the farm.
Mom is angry at him. I've heard her say that Roman is too much like you. I've heard Roman say that he wishes you were here. Roman says that if you were here...
...then we definitely wouldn't need Jet Jones.

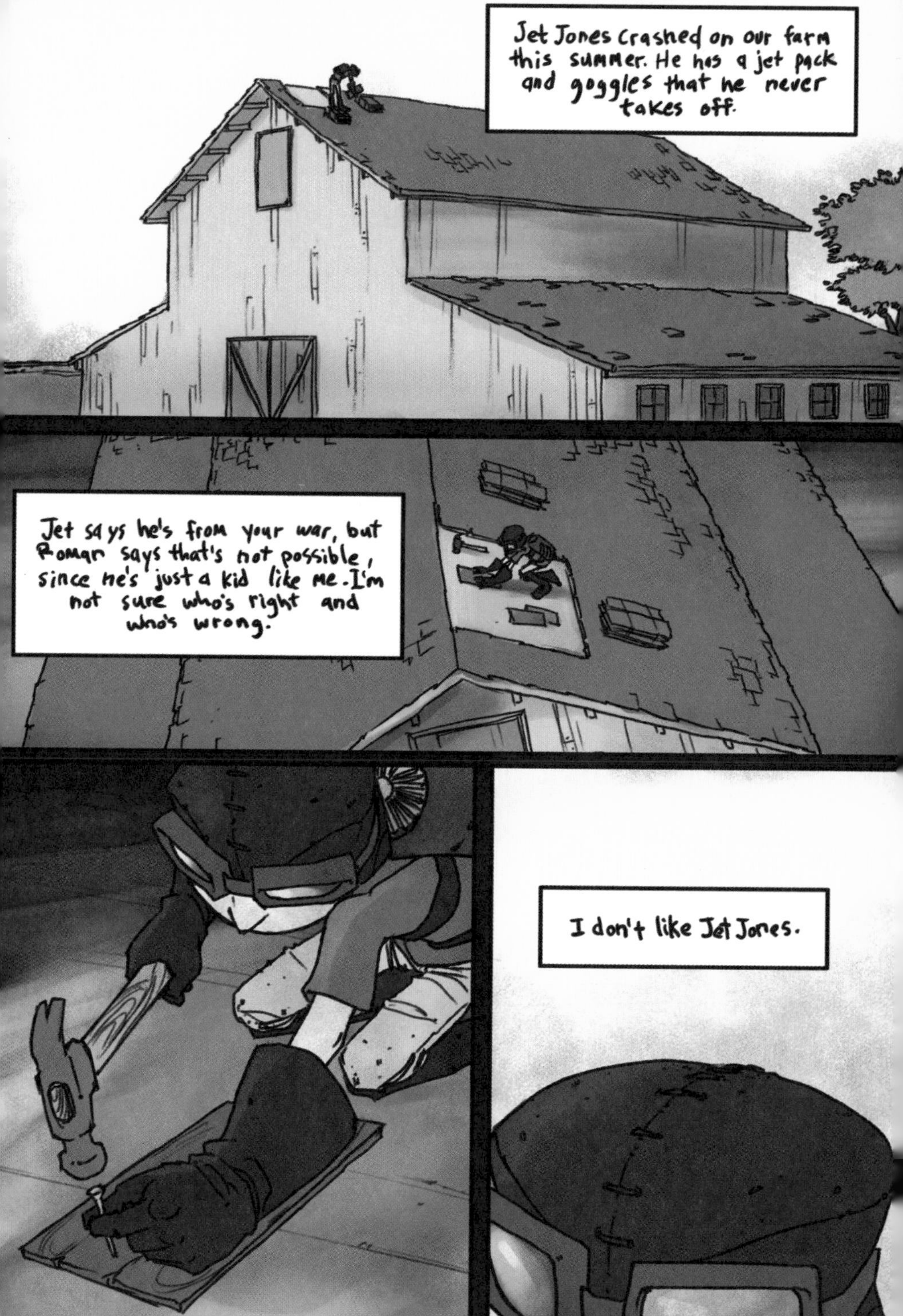
Jet Jones crashed on our farm this summer. He has a jet pack and goggles that he never takes off.
Jet says he's from your war, but Roman says that's not possible, since he's just a kid like me. I'm not sure who's right and who's wrong.
I don't like Jet Jones.

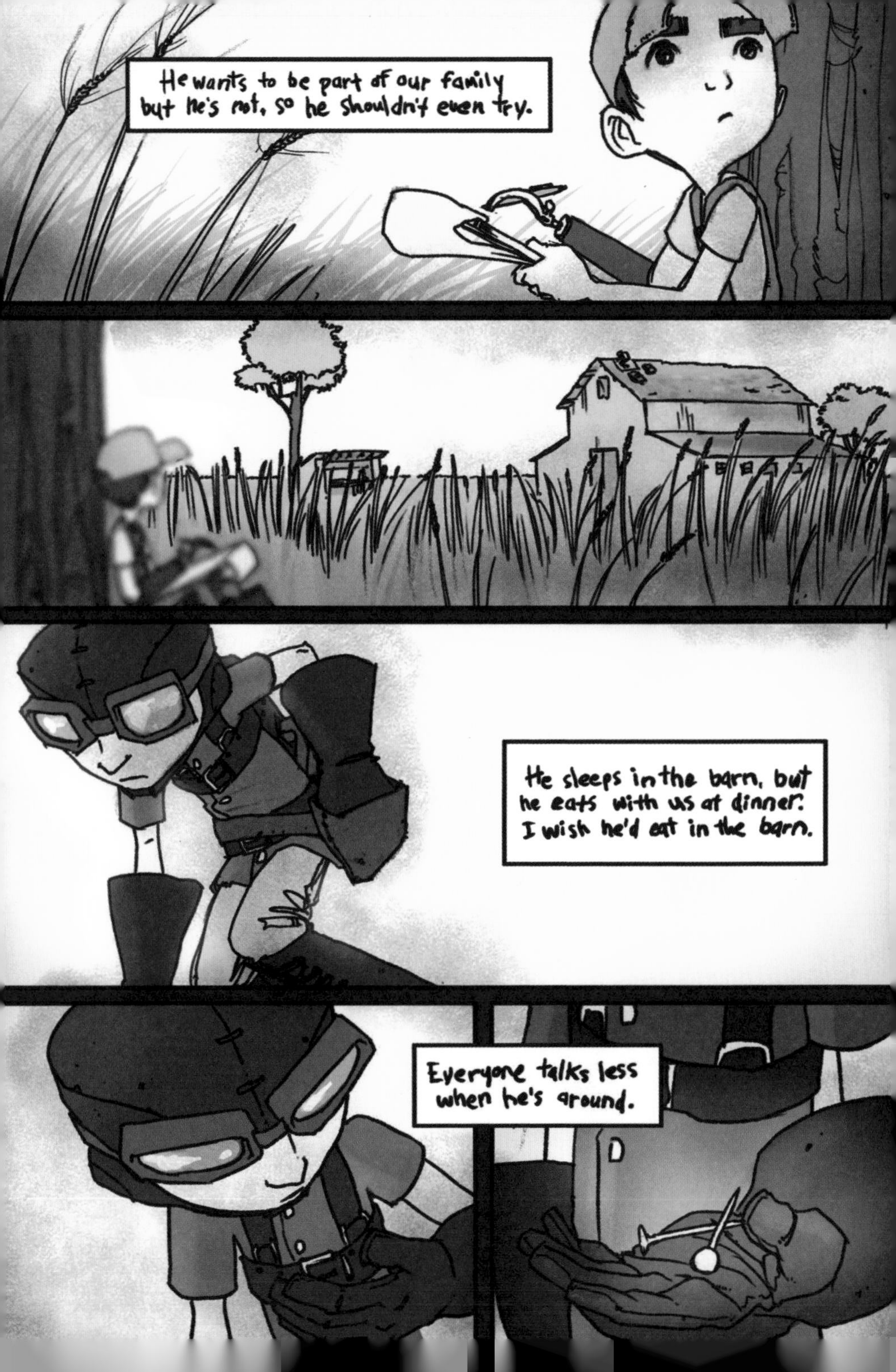
He wants to be part of our family but he's not, so he shouldn't even try.
He sleeps in the barn, but he eats with us at dinner. I wish he'd eat in the barn.
Everyone talks less when he's around.

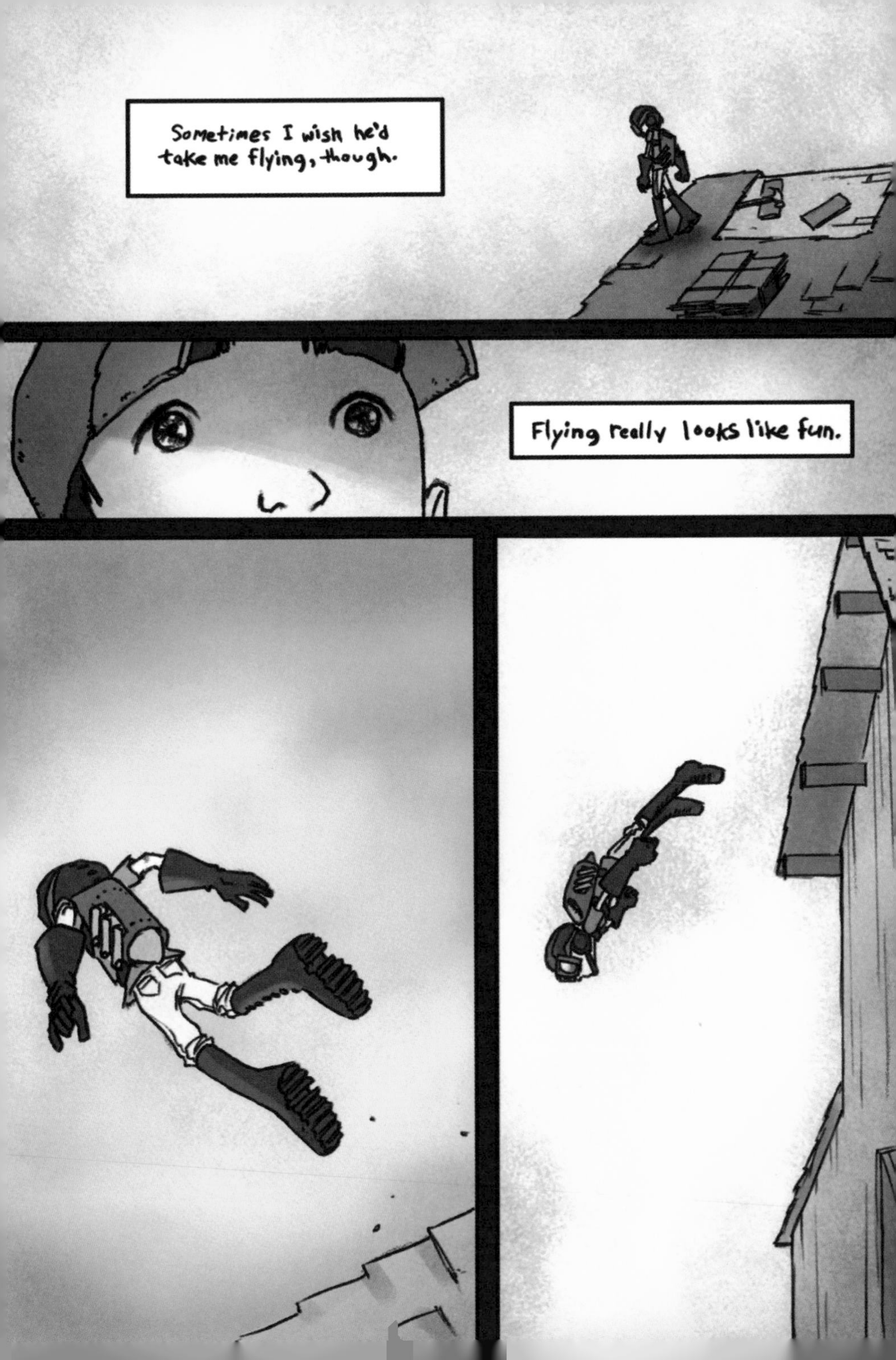
Sometimes I wish he'd take me flying, though.
Flying really looks like fun.

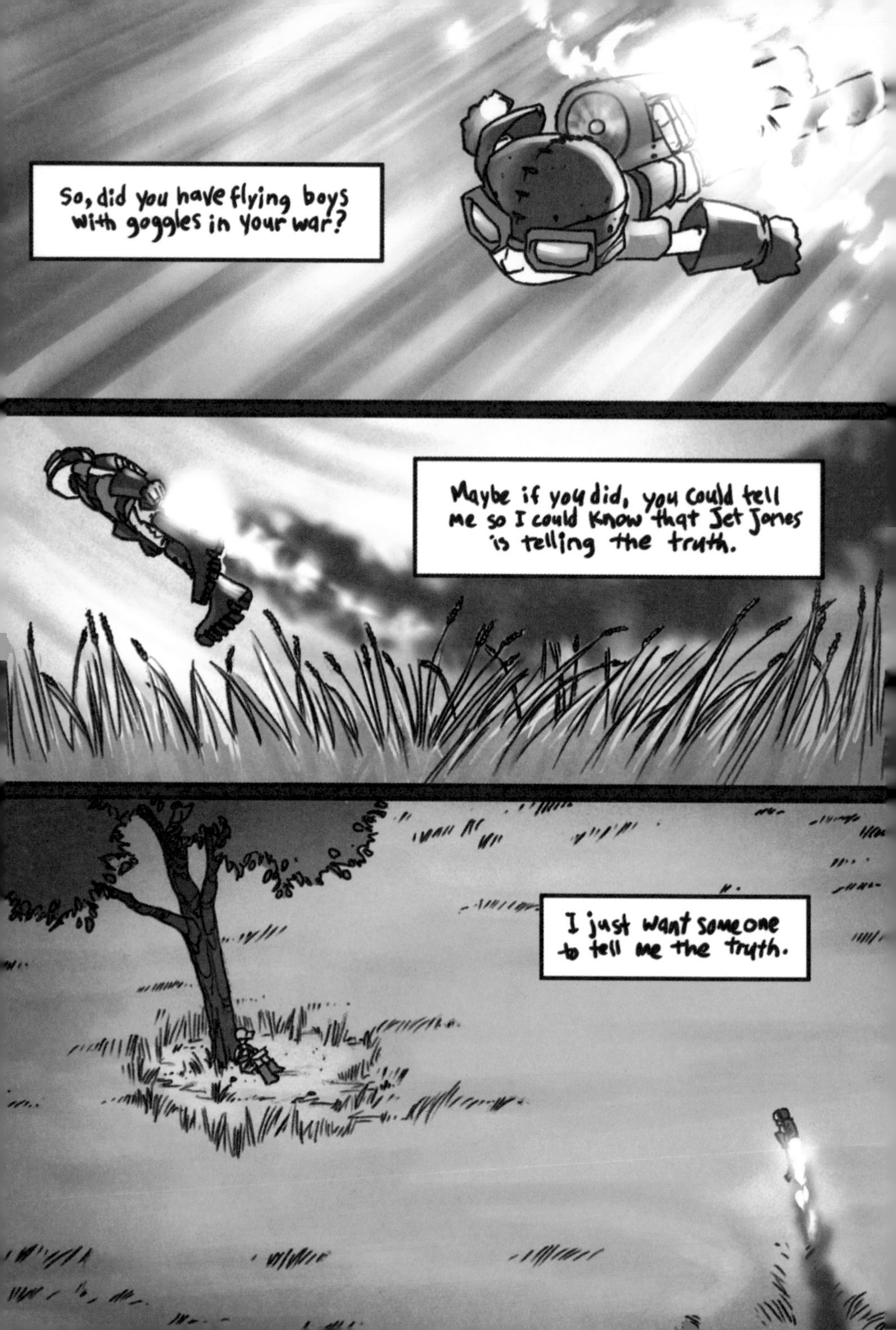
So, did you have flying boys with goggles in your war?
Maybe if you did, you could tell me so I could know that Jet Jones is telling the truth.
I just want someone to tell me the truth.

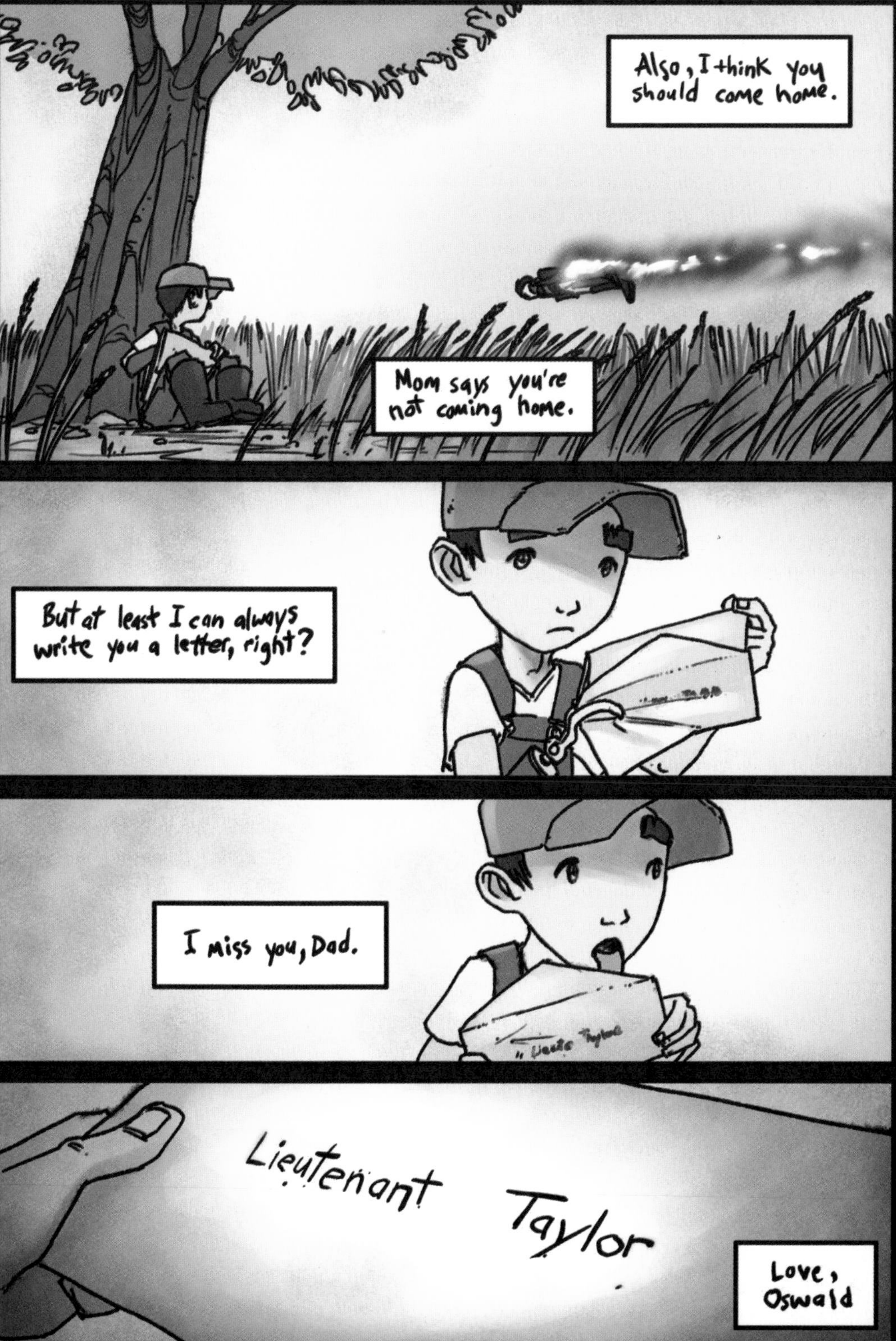
Also, I think you should come home.
Mom says you're not coming home.
But at least I can always write you a letter, right?
I miss you, Dad.
Lieutenant Taylor
Love, Oswald